Flirting with Fate

Flirting with Fate

J.C. CERVANTES

RAZORBILL

RAZORBILL

An imprint of Penguin Random House LLC, New York

First published in the United States of America by Razorbill,
an imprint of Penguin Random House LLC, 2022

Visit us online at penguinrandomhouse.com.

LIBRARY OF CONGRESS CATALOGING-IN-PUBLICATION DATA
Names: Cervantes, Jennifer, author.
Title: Flirting with fate / J.C. Cervantes.
Description: New York : Razorbill, 2022. | Audience: Ages 12 and up |
Summary: Ava Granados arrives too late to for her grandmother's deathbed
blessing, then Nana appears as a ghost asking for help so Ava, with the help
of her two older sisters and bumbling spiritual guide, Medardus, must
befriend the mysterious boy who received the blessing the night of the storm.
Identifiers: LCCN 2021049696 | ISBN 9780593404454 (hardcover) | ISBN
9780593404478 (trade paperback) | ISBN 9780593404461 (ebook)
Subjects: LCGFT: Paranormal fiction. | Romance fiction. | Novels.
Classification: LCC PZ7.C3198 Fli 2022 | DDC [Fic]—dc23
LC record available at https://lccn.loc.gov/2021049696

ISBN 9780593404454 (HARDCOVER)
1   3   5   7   9   10   8   6   4   2

ISBN 9780593524114 (INTERNATIONAL EDITION)
1   3   5   7   9   10   8   6   4   2

Book manufactured in Canada

FRI

Design by Tony Sahara
Text set in PT Serif

For Bella

This one was always *meant* to be yours

Fate's Prologue

On July 7 at precisely 9:01 p.m., a boundless, unforeseen storm claimed one life, two hearts, and six destinies.

The Southern California skies had been a brilliant blue dappled with wispy threads of white. A warm, easy, splendid kind of day where you'd think nothing could go wrong. Ah, but one's fate is not always built on solid ground. And *wrong* is always a question of perspective. Take, for example, the girl at the center of this tale, Ava Granados. She is stubborn, quick-witted, was born into a mystical family, and, well, she thinks very little of me. Perhaps things would have been different for her if she had afforded me an ounce of respect.

On this summer day, like most days prior, Ava woke early and suffered through SoulCycle with her older sister Carmen. Boring, routine, sweaty. She spent the afternoon making a Pinterest board with monochromatic bedroom ideas and ended up spiraling down a rabbit hole of DIY crafts for the tactically deficient, like tiny shoe pom-poms and rag wreaths.

In two months' time, she plans to begin her senior year and get a jump-start on college applications. Until then, she is committed to one thing: joyous boredom, much to her father's consternation. He desperately wants her to go to college nearby and work for the family's design firm. Raul Granados is always ranting and raving with some version of "Mija, why write about the people doing great things when *you* can be the great one? Look at our firm, right there in *Architectural Digest*. Eh? Someone wrote about *us*." He would poke his chest with his thumb as his face lit up brighter than the Virgen's altar.

Little does Ava know that in precisely five minutes and sixteen seconds, I will launch a lightning rod into her life. Death. Death always gets humans' attention.

Ava has always hated thinking about death in any capacity. When she was a child, she would pray for all the dead animals' souls to go to heaven. Then she began to include all the dead insects, because their ends always felt so untimely and unfair. She thought that the only thing those poor creatures had to look forward to was being squished under a shoe or flattened on a windshield.

I almost pity her—hunched over a dim desk, reading the black-and-white memories of strangers. With no idea that her life is about to be derailed in a way she'll never see coming.

It is 8:16 p.m. now, and Ava is at the *LA Times*, organizing digital archives. It is her ideal summer internship: words, spines, photographs, paper. An introvert's paradise.

Fifty-nine seconds to go.

Ava leans over her messy worktable and scans a 1959 photo of some young guy carrying a banner that says MARRY ME. No name, no other descriptors. A seemingly innocuous object. Or is it? She, of course, does not yet realize its significance. She merely looks at the date and thinks it is ironic that it is the same as today. Oh, humans.

She wonders, *Did she say yes or no?*

And this is all I need to strike the match.

One

Ava's cell phone buzzed, and a clap of thunder vibrated her bones. She reached for her phone, turned it over to see her sister's name on the screen.

"Hey, Carm."

Lightning lit up the night sky in great unpredictable flashes. The wind howled violently.

Carmen's garbled voice was swallowed by static and unceasing gales. Then, in a voice heavy with urgency, "Ava!"

The call was lost.

There was a moment of silence, stillness, nothingness. It was as if the universe had paused to take a breath and ask, *What are you going to do now, Ava Granados?*

A long shiver crawled up Ava's legs, and in the space of a single thought, *Something is wrong*, her phone lit up again. The single buzz prompted the sky to split open and unleash a torrent like Ava had never seen or heard.

"Carmen?" Ava couldn't control the tremble in her voice. "Is everything okay?"

"Where are you?" Carmen demanded.

A peal of thunder.

"My internship."

"This late?"

"Trying to impress the boss. Where are you?"

"That doesn't matter."

"Then why'd you ask me?"

"Why do you always have to be so immature?"

Carmen was twenty, three years older than Ava, but she acted like she was everyone's mother. She had an opinion about everything under the sun—an opinion no one could count on because it was likely to change by the next moon.

Rain pounded the roof. Lights flickered. The very air seemed to sizzle with an ominous energy that set Ava on edge.

"It's Nana," Carmen said. "Dad says this is it . . . as in . . . the end."

"Is he sure this time?" Ava's heart crawled up her throat. "I mean, Nana's been on her deathbed five times this month alone."

"Yes, pendeja! But I'm in the middle of a gel fill, and I don't know if I should leave or not."

Lightning flashed. Then again. The rain came faster, harder. More determined than before.

"Seriously?" Ava chided. "If this really is the end, who cares about your nails!"

"I do! And remember the last time I was at the salon? I was still processing my highlights, ran out, and ended up looking like a fried version of J. Lo? But you're right . . ." She took a breath. "This is Nana. How could she leave us like this? Hang on," Carmen was gone for a moment, and when she returned, their oldest sister, Vivienne, had been looped into the call.

"Are you on your way, Ava?" Vivienne asked.

"Carmen *just* called a minute ago," Ava grumbled as she began to make piles of the photographs and notes on her desk. "How can I be on my way?"

She lowered her voice, remembering the cubicles around her were filled with nosy people probably looking for a welcome distraction.

"That's a minute you've wasted on the phone because you don't move fast enough, and that's why you're late everywhere!" Vivienne nearly shouted.

"Hey!" Ava argued, accidentally knocking a few photos and documents onto the floor. She quickly retrieved them and tossed them back onto her desk as she headed toward the exit, past the roving eyes of her coworkers. "I was at the last seven deathbeds. You were only at three."

"What does it matter?" Carmen groaned. "Nana didn't die all those times, so no one missed the *blessing*!" She hollered the last word, as if any of them could forget what Nana's death *really* meant.

"And I need my blessing," Vivienne reminded her. "Like, bad." Twenty-two-year-old Vivienne worried she would never find Prince Charming. Ava worried, too, but not because her sister wasn't beautiful or smart or a newly minted architect who was also the most talented designer at the family's firm. Viv was . . . Viv. Hard-hitting, stubborn, picky. She'd probably demand a résumé before a first date.

"Same," Carmen chimed in. "I just hope I get something really good."

"Is that all you guys care about?" Ava said, her heart sinking.

"As if you haven't thought about it," Carmen accused. "And *she's* the one leaving us!"

It was so Carmen to make this about her. It was also so Carmen to deflect to ease the pain.

The lights flashed once, then croaked, plunging Ava and the entire office into total darkness. Groans rose up. Quickly, Ava turned on her phone flashlight. "I have to go," she said.

"*No!*" Vivienne shouted. "You can't drive in this storm. Are you crazy?"

"You just said—"

"Forget what I said," Vivienne argued. "It's getting worse. Dad just came in. He told me to tell you to stay where you are or he'll take your car away."

"She's right," Carmen agreed half-heartedly.

Ava asked Carmen, "Well, how come *you* can drive home?"

"I'm at the salon, point five miles away," she countered. "You're all the way downtown. This thing came out of nowhere, and it's too dangerous. No blessing is worth your life, Ava." Then, "Hey, you think Nana will give me yours too?"

She was joking of course, because Nana had made the fine print clear— only one blessing per person. All the women in the Granados family had this keen, odd, otherworldly ability to pass along *blessings* to their female descendants. But here was the catch: they could only do so from their deathbeds.

And if they died suddenly? Tough luck.

Ava's great-grandmother had graced Nana with an angel's voice. Before that, Nana couldn't even sing off-key. Ava's dad always said Nana used to sound like a dying cat in a Tijuana alley. And after the deathbed blessing? It was like listening to a Mexican Pavarotti when she opened her mouth to sing.

Ava rolled her eyes. "You joke at the worst times, Carm."

"Who's joking?"

"I don't care what you say. I'm coming," Ava insisted. In her mind's eye, Ava saw Nana lying in her linen-draped bed, wearing the gold bracelet she wore every day, saying only that it came from Fate. She remembered the long walks down the shore—always in the evening, because Nana loved the nighttime best. Ava set her jaw. Blessing or no, she wasn't letting Nana take her last breath without her. Yes, she was curious about the blessing her grandmother had chosen for her. She had begged her to tell her about it, but Nana had only said, "I won't know until the moment is upon us."

Pushing through the double doors, Ava's heart rate began to rise. *What if Carmen is right? What if this really is it and not a death rehearsal?*

The lights flicked back on as Ava came to her boss's office at the end of the hall. Drawing nearer, she saw him stacking another World War II book on the bookcase. *The guy is obsessed with warfare*, Ava thought.

Grant was twenty-five-ish and looked like one of those guys who sold overpriced T-shirts at a rock concert, except that he was a super-smart features editor who had made it clear that he had lost the coin toss when they were handing out the intern supervisor title this summer. He had two burner phones, so Ava thought he either worked undercover for the CIA; had a lot of girlfriends, boyfriends, or both; was a drug dealer; or was just paranoid. Ava asked him about the phones once, and all he said was, "I like my privacy." Ava wasn't sure if he was telling her to buzz off or if that really was the reason.

Even though Ava had only been interning at the newspaper for three and a half weeks, she and Grant had already arrived at this exact moment several times. The call. Ava's quick exit. The deathbed. The miracle recovery. Ava making up hours, and then some. Grant definitely knew the drill.

"Should I wait to say sorry?" Grant asked after she told him why she was leaving.

Ava shrugged, searching for the *yes*, but all she felt was *no, no, no* rattling around her chest.

He opened his mouth, hesitated. Then he turned his expressive hazel eyes on Ava in a protective, *geez, sorry, kid* kind of way. "You really going to drive in this wicked storm?"

Ava felt a mother of a headache coming on. "I have to."

"Came out of nowhere," Grant said, stroking his chin and looking at the blank wall as if there were a window there. "You want an umbrella?" he asked.

"I'm parked close."

"That's good," he said. "I don't think I even own an umbrella. Want me to drive you?"

"It's only a few miles," Ava lied. "I'll be fine."

With a full shrug and half nod, Grant threw his gaze back to World War II. "All right, but text when you're safe."

Outside, the turbulent rain came down not in drops but in sheets. Lightning flared, forcing Ava to shield her eyes. Unearthly shadows bent and writhed, leaped and thrashed. If she didn't know better, she would think this damned storm was *trying* to keep her away from Nana.

One, two, three breaths, and Ava sprinted into the squall, hoping she wouldn't be struck down by the fearsome bolts intent on killing the dark.

She ran, awkward and half-bent, splashing through ankle-deep puddles, using her thin arms for pathetic and useless cover while simultaneously soaking her brand-new Golden Gooses.

Finally, she found her Jeep, unlocked it with the remote, and hopped inside. She craned her head to look out the windshield at the storm-shredded sky. "Perfect timing," she groaned.

Another thunderclap shook the earth, making her jump in her seat.

For the first time, Ava was afraid. Afraid she wouldn't make it in time to say goodbye.

Ava squeezed back tears and started the car. *Fifteen miles*, she thought. *Hold on for fifteen miles, Nana.*

I-10 was nearly empty. It didn't surprise Ava. People in LA only knew how to drive in two types of weather: sunny and cloudy.

"She's okay," Ava said to herself, leaning forward, bent over the steering wheel as she struggled to see beyond the torrential rain. The windshield wipers were on the fastest setting, and barely helping.

"Listen, God," Ava said. "If you get me home with enough time, I'll go to confession for . . ." She hesitated. She hated confession, but these were dire circumstances, and she didn't think God was going to be impressed with anything other than something monumental. "I'll go for a whole week." She swallowed the promise like it was poison. And then realizing she hadn't been specific enough, she clarified, "Home in time to say goodbye."

Fifteen miraculous minutes and ten stiff knuckles later, she pulled off the highway and into the seaside city of Santa Monica. Her phone, sitting in the cupholder, buzzed. Ava cursed herself for forgetting to turn on Bluetooth.

Glancing down, she saw that it was Loretta, her not-stepmom, but she was afraid to take even one hand off the wheel to answer. Maybe it was better. She wasn't in the mood to get sucked into a drama-mama moment.

Buzz. Buzz.

Ava came to a red light. Looked at the phone's blinking screen. *What if it's about Nana?* Swiftly, she pressed the speaker button.

"Hello?"

The only response was an earful of static.

"Loretta, can you hear me? I'm only a couple of miles away."

There was silence, and for a second Ava thought the phone had disconnected, until she heard Loretta say, "She's fading fast."

Fading? No! Jeans fade. Memories fade. Not people. Not Nana.

Ava hung up and accelerated, trying to balance speed with safety.

A terrible combination under the best of circumstances.

"Please hold on, Nana," she whispered, so low she couldn't hear her own voice over the battering storm.

Ava had always known she was her grandmother's favorite, although Vivienne had worked really hard to dethrone Ava. The oldest Granados sister had even considered becoming a nun once. And poor Carmen was third in line for Nana's favor. Carmen had once been in second place, until she got a fake ID at fifteen just so she could get a heart tattoo on her hip.

The rain pounded unrelentingly.

And then, one mile from the house, the one thing Ava didn't want to think about, the one stupid word that plagued everything in existence popped into her head: *Destiny*. If Nana were in the front seat (refusing to wear a seat belt) she would tell Ava to quit fighting, that Fate had played her hand. And won. But Ava refused to believe she wasn't in control of her own life.

Wiping a tear with the back of her hand, she pressed her foot against the gas with more force. It was exactly 8:51 p.m.

The Jeep hydroplaned.

Ava braked, skidded, fishtailed before she righted the vehicle.

Too late to see the brake lights in front of her.

There are moments that define people's lives, moments that are wedged in between before and after, then and now, here and there. And some of those moments are balanced precariously on the steep precipice of *what if.*

Suddenly and without expectation, the storm ceased as if the collision had consumed the echoes of thunder, had swallowed the wind, had cast out the lightning and rain.

It took several breaths for Ava to realize that the impact sounded worse than it was. She was okay—the airbag hadn't even deployed.

In the headlights, she saw a white guy hopping out of the truck she had hit. He looked around Ava's age. Tall, loose-fitting jeans, unkempt hair, angular nose, defined jaw, and big feet. He wore a fierce glare, the kind that seemed capable of scaring a happy-go-lucky puppy.

Ava jumped out of her car. "What's wrong with you?" she cried, indignant. "Why were you just . . . sitting there?"

The guy scowled. "See the big red octagonal sign? It means stop."

Ava wanted to choke him. Twice. Hadn't he ever heard of a California stop? Roll and go? "I don't have time for this!" Her voice escalated as she realized she was wasting time arguing with a sarcastic someone she already didn't like.

The guy started in on how Ava should watch where she was going, and then his dark eyes caught hers, locking her in place. She felt a drop in her stomach just as his thick eyebrows lifted in surprise. "Oh, um . . . you're crying. I . . . uh . . . look, you didn't even dent my truck. It's all good."

"It's the rain," she said, wiping the tears away. No way was she going to snivel in front of some stranger who didn't know how to drive. Correction: who didn't know how to *stop*.

But then he said, "Hey, are you okay?"

The dam shattered. Ava broke down sobbing, telling him her nana was dying at that very minute, and the harder she tried to shut up, the more her mouth kept churning out words. "And now I'm late all because of you, and if I miss saying goodbye . . ."

He looked terrified, and was urging Ava into her car before she could blubber another word. "You need to go," he said. "Are you sure you can drive?"

Still sniveling, Ava nodded her head, closed the door, and took off. When she looked in the rearview, the guy was standing in the middle of the road, his truck headlights shining behind him, hands in pockets, watching her drive away.

Forty-five seconds later, she turned down a secluded cul-de-sac and pulled through the long driveway's wrought iron gates. By the time she made it to the backyard casita, everyone was gathered around Nana's bed: Dad, Carmen, and Vivienne, who strangely looked away when Ava entered.

Nana was sitting up, wide-eyed, gripping a pillow, rocking back and forth as she repeated Ava's name over and over and over.

"I'm here," Ava cried, rushing to her grandmother's bed.

As if no one else was in the room, Nana's eyes alighted on Ava, and with great effort, she rasped, "No . . . can't be." Then she grimaced, squeezed her eyes closed, and said, "Meteors, stars, 8:51. Collision. And the humming-bird. ¿Me escuchas?"

Ava's throat tightened. She wanted to tell her nana that yes, she heard her but that she wasn't making any sense, but what did it matter now? Ava merely nodded.

The old woman broke into a coughing fit.

Ava's dad reached for the glass of water on the nightstand, but Nana waved him away, gesturing for Ava to sit on the edge of the bed.

A rumble of thunder shook the house. The sky unleashed a greater fury than before.

Nana grasped Ava's hand, gripping it with surprising strength, tugging her closer.

"Ava . . . you are . . . you are . . ." Her voice was broken by another, more violent bout of coughing.

"It's okay," Ava told her, stroking her forehead. "Don't try to talk."

Urgently, Nana tightened her grasp. She held her granddaughter's gaze, silent and unwavering. The lights flickered. A window blew open. "You are . . ." Suddenly she seized. Gasped. Fell back with a heavy *thud*. And the last words to fall from her lips were "too late."

Two

After the shock of losing Nana, after the shock of being *too late*, Ava dragged herself to her room, fatigued and puffy-faced. Falling into bed, she felt an unexpected upsurge of emotion in the center of her chest: Grief? Frustration? Anger? Resentment?

Yes, definitely resentment. It was the same feeling she'd had when her mom walked out ten years ago. Ava was only seven. Caroline Granados had said she was going to the grocery store for some eggs, but as she drove away that night, Ava saw stacks of luggage through the car's backseat window.

She had left on a Tuesday. She took her clothes and her shoes and her handbags, but she didn't take her girls. And she didn't take her fairy tale. She left that in the center of Ava's memory and heart. But Ava didn't want to think about ridiculous fairy tales or her mother's soft, soothing voice whenever she told Ava the story she had created just for her.

Ava stared up at the ceiling's carved beams, shoving the tears and resentment back down into that place between her ribs where nothing could hurt her. It didn't stop the ugly truth from gurgling back up, though.

Ava had been too late.

Stupid storm. Stupid truck. Stupid boy! If she hadn't rear-ended that guy, she could have had more time with Nana. *But did it even matter?* she wondered. Short goodbyes were better. Like ripping off a Band-Aid.

She pondered briefly whether she had to keep her promise to go to confession. *Technically,* she had made it in time to say goodbye. But that's the thing about goodbyes: there is *never* enough time. And besides, Ava never said *when* she would go. Only that she would.

Just then, Carmen and Viv popped their heads into her room, turned on the light, and tiptoed in like toddlers scared to wake their sleeping parents.

"We need to tell you something," Viv said, contorting her face into that revealing expression that usually meant *You aren't going to like it.*

"I'm tired," Ava said, throwing an arm over her eyes to block out the light. "Can you ... tell me your blessings tomorrow?" She knew that's why they were here, and she didn't begrudge her sisters ... or at least she didn't think she did, but she just wanted to collapse into a world of sleep and darkness and forgetfulness.

Carmen crawled under the covers and put her head gently on Ava's shoulder. "It's not about that. It's ... it's something Nana said."

"To be fair," Viv reassured, planting herself on the edge of the bed, "*I* didn't hear it, but I told Carmen we had to tell you. That no way could we keep it a secret."

Because the number one Granados sister truth was that secrets rip families apart, and after their mom walked out, the trio had pinkie- *and* blood-sworn that they would always tell each other the truth; they would never ever lie, no matter how bad it was or how much it hurt.

"What is it?" Ava inched out from under Carmen's small frame so she could sit up.

"Go ahead, Carmen," Vivienne said.

Carmen sat up, folding her legs beneath her. She picked at her unfinished gel manicure. "I didn't think we should tell you what happened ... I mean before you got to the house tonight. I thought it would make things worse, but Viv is making me."

"Mm-hmm," Ava uttered, "since when can anyone make *you* do anything?"

"Since *she* got the blessing of persuasion!" Carmen's eyes popped wide, and she threw her hands over her mouth. "Shit! I wasn't supposed to say that."

Viv groaned. "Way to go, idiota."

Ava's eyes darted to her oldest sister. "Persuasion?"

Tugging on the strings of her silk hoodie, Viv said, "It's not like Carmen thinks. It's not like I can go around making people do anything I want them to. Nana said I would just be able to help others see my side of things."

"Like a vampire," Carmen put in.

Viv threw eye-daggers at Carmen. "Stop putting wild ideas into her head!" Then to Ava, "She's being dramatic as usual. I can't compel people, but we didn't come here to talk about our blessings, I swear."

Ava's spirits sank lower as the memory of *you are too late* hovered like a thundercloud. "Well, now I want to know what you got," she said to Carmen.

Carmen twisted her full lips into a pout, turned her gaze upward to the ceiling. "It's totally . . ." She hesitated before the certain complaint left her mouth. Then, as if she couldn't control herself, she blurted, "It's so pitiful! I got the blessing of memory, which I guess means that I can recall details, read or hear or see something once and remember it verbatim. I already tested the reading part, and it's weird—like having a camera in my head. I don't even like to read, and half the things I already remember I want to forget, so it's not exactly a blessing! What was Nana thinking?"

"I could seriously smother you with that pillow," Viv said as she shoved Carmen's hips out of the way to make more room on the bed.

"And I'd remember every awful detail of it," Carmen cried.

"At least you guys got blessings," Ava said, trying to swallow over the fat lump in her throat. She wondered what motivated Nana to give her sisters persuasion and memory.

I'll know the right blessing when the time is upon me, Nana had said.

Except when it comes to me, Ava thought. It wasn't necessarily the gift itself that mattered so much, it was the promise that Ava had held on to her entire life, a promise to have a piece of Nana forever: *The benedición is a single thread that connects us all.*

"Well, for once," Vivienne said, rolling her eyes, "we can trust Carmen's memory. Tell Ava the rest."

Carmen frowned. Opened her mouth to say something like she might argue, and under normal circumstances Ava was sure she would, and she would win by sheer determination and fiery temperament alone. Neither Ava nor Vivienne liked going head-to-head with the hurricane that thrashed inside of Carmen. It was too dangerous and too unpredictable.

"Right after my blessing," Carmen began with dramatic flair, "Nana sat straight up." She stiffened her own body to demonstrate. "I was still sitting next to her, and she said it in such a low voice, I swear it was like she only wanted me to hear, but she whispered, 'I can't wait. Ava. Ava, where are you?' And then her eyes got all creepy and faraway and she stretched out her hands kind of Frankensteinish, and . . ."

"And what?" Ava said.

Leaning closer, Carmen uttered, "And she said, 'I give you the blessing of . . .'"

Ava jumped to her knees. Her stomach twisted in agonizing knots. "Blessing of what?"

"I didn't hear the rest," Carmen admitted with a wince.

"What! Why?"

"I . . . I . . . sneezed."

"Carmen!" Ava grumbled. "How could you?"

"How could I sneeze?" she asked incredulously.

"It's not her fault," Viv said.

With a defeated breath, Ava sank back down. "It doesn't even matter because, guess what? I wasn't there to get the blessing anyways, so joke's on me."

"But aren't you curious?" Carmen said. "To, like, know what could have been?"

Ava hated those words, *what could have been.* They were better left in the made-up worlds of stories.

Viv sighed. "Don't listen to Carm. It's fate. If you were meant to—"

"Don't even start." Ava felt sick. "You know I don't believe in fate and destiny and meant-to-be." They were excuses for people to do bad things, to break people's hearts, to leave their families.

Carmen tugged a diamond hoop out of her ear and rubbed the lobe. "Well, I *do* believe, and you'll see—there's going to be a lesson in all of this."

"You sound like Nana," Ava whispered. She couldn't believe her grandmother was actually gone. She would never travel Mexico's back roads with her again. She would never take walks down to the ocean just because Nana loved the feeling of sand between her toes. She would never listen to Nana's velvet voice belt out Spanish ballads again. Never. Again.

As if by intuition, Viv rubbed Ava's shoulder gently and said, "And if Nana were here, she would agree with Carmen. She would tell you to trust that everything happened exactly as it should."

"Whatever," Ava said, hardening her heart. "All I know is Nana *isn't* here, and obviously I wasn't *meant* to know what blessing she wanted to give me, so what kind of cruel fate is that?" *And now I'll be forever* dis*connected,* she thought.

Vivienne and Carmen exchanged a knowing glance, then Viv said, "Wait . . . you're not getting it. We think she *did* give the blessing."

The walls seemed to be closing in on all sides, and Ava suddenly felt like a bird flying toward a window it doesn't see until *slam.*

"Maybe you were close enough to the house," Viv said with an uptick in her voice that sounded more hopeful than Ava dared to feel. "We can try and figure this out, Ava . . . but only if you want."

Ava chewed her bottom lip, thinking about the words no one had heard. Did she really want to know what she had missed, or was it better to *not* know? It wasn't like knowing would deliver the blessing. It was too late. Nana had said so.

Viv and Carmen each placed a hand on top of Ava's. The Granados sisters were exceptional at reading each other's minds, anticipating words, and reading expressions like letters on the page. Viv and Carmen stared at Ava expectantly, their breathing big enough to fill up the room. They probably knew what Ava was going to do before she did.

Ava had the choice of two words: *yes* or *no.* She was better built for the *no,* better built to forget and to move on. But that tiny space between her ribs quivered. "I'm not sure it matters now."

Carmen was doing that openmouthed breathing thing she always did when she was excited. "Well, I am sure, and Nana spoke your blessing at exactly 8:51. I remember because I looked at the digital clock right when I reached for a tissue."

"Do you remember where you were at that exact moment, Ava?" Viv asked.

"Driving home." Ava's memory tugged a crumb loose. "Wait. Nana said 8:51. And something about meteors and a hummingbird or . . . Carmen," Ava said. "What exactly did Nana tell me when I got here? Word for word."

Carmen blew out a long breath. "I can already see you guys are going to take advantage of my memory."

"Just tell me!"

"Fine. Nana said, and I quote, 'Meteors, stars, 8:51. Collision. And the hummingbird. ¿Me escuchas?'"

"Collision. That's it!" Ava cried. "I was in an accident. She must have known, right? That was about the time I hit the guy's car."

"You hit someone's car?" Viv said, switching into mama bear mode. "Was anyone hurt?"

Shaking her head, Ava explained, "It's why I was late. It was totally his fault. He was just sitting at the stop sign like he had nowhere else to be."

"A crash *isn't* a blessing," Carmen said.

Viv nodded. "What do you think Nana meant by the hummingbird and meteors, Carm?"

Pulling an exasperated face, Carmen adjusted her pink hair scrunchie. "How should I know? I have super memory, not super-spy skills. Maybe Ava is going to space on a rocket named *Hummingbird* or something." She yawned, fell back onto the pillow, and closed her eyes. Carmen could fall asleep anywhere, and once exhaustion settled into her bones, she was lights out.

Viv threw a woeful look to Ava. "Listen, Greeyo . . ."

Ever since Ava could remember, Viv had called her Grillo, Spanish for *cricket*, and ever since she could remember, Ava would ask her sister why she chose that nickname. It wasn't because Ava was quiet. She wasn't. And it wasn't because she was small; Carmen was a lot more petite. "It's because I annoy you," seven-year-old Ava had guessed.

Viv only smirked and offered, "Someday I will tell you."

"But why not now?"

"Because surprises make life so much better."

Except that Ava hated surprises.

Now, Viv said, "I know we can figure this out."

Ava wasn't betting on it. Most good things came in bite sizes. Not enough to fill anyone up. "I don't want to think about it anymore," Ava sighed. "Nana already said I was too late, so let's just forget it, okay?"

Forget, forget, forget.

A few minutes later, Ava killed the lights, and they fell asleep, curled on the bed like three snuggled bears.

Sometime after midnight, Ava blinked against the silent dark. She wasn't sure what had woken her. A sound? A dream she couldn't remember? A pain under her ribs? And just as she was about to steal her pillow back from Carmen, she heard it. Nana's voice: *Mija, are you there?*

Caroline and seven-year-old Ava sat on the beach, scooping up cool, wet sand for a castle. The waves were gentle that day, sweeping to shore with a soothing rhythm while seagulls floated across the silvery sky.

"First you have to dig the moat," Caroline said. "Like this."

Ava watched her mother's capable hands digging a chasm deeper and deeper. "Why?"

"To protect the princess."

"And the castle too?"

Caroline smiled softly.

"Someday," Ava said, "I'm going to live in a castle."

"Well," her mother said, brushing a stray hair back with her arm. "Castles are very pretty, but they are dangerous too. Some princesses get locked in them and they become prisons."

Ava tried to shape a pile of sand into something that resembled a tower. "But not this one, right?"

Caroline laughed. "Would you like to hear a story about a special princess?"

"Why is she special?" Ava said, more interested in the tale than the sandcastle now. "What happened?"

"She threw away her destiny," Caroline said slowly. "And she never wore the crown."

Three

It had been four days since Ava had heard her dead grandmother's whispering voice. But when Ava spoke into the dark that night, "Nana?", all she got was Viv's elbow to her spine. Ava was, of course, glad her sisters had been asleep. They would have thought she had officially lost it. She could hear them now. Carmen: *I always knew you got the weird genes.* Vivienne: *Your mind is on overdrive.*

Ava decided she had been dreaming, and, thankfully, she didn't hear Nana's voice the rest of the week. The Granados family spent the following days planning the funeral, meeting with Father Conrad, ordering Nana's favorite white roses, hiring caterers, and edging through the world half-dazed in a fog of disbelief.

Ava's dad insisted on having a grande celebration. The man did nothing small-scale. He had worked his way up from "nadaville" as a contractor to build his company, and swore he would never reduce himself or his family to *nothing* status again. Which meant that their eight-thousand-square-foot Spanish-style home—replete with seven bedrooms, nine bathrooms, and a kitchen any chef would die for—was now filled with at least two hundred people who let their hands touch things that didn't belong to them as they swept through the casa: silver frames, hand-carved santos, tin retablos, fine crystal vases . . . even the crucifix hanging in the entry, or more specifically Jesus's worn feet.

Two hundred people who didn't even know Nana, Ava thought resentfully as she stood on the exterior balcony, staring down across the multi-terraced backyard, a palm-lined sanctuary that had been photographed for magazines, style blogs, and even a few design books. The carefully cultivated garden of lemon, carob, and pomegranate trees was often described as "a step back in time," or a "stroll through Tuscany." But to Ava it was, and always would be, Nana's oasis.

Wishing she were anywhere but here, and in a less itchy skirt, Ava observed the strangers flow in and out of the house, mingling like rats eager to dig their next path to some influential somebody. Ava observed the strangers' eyes light up with forced amusement. Their voices carried mind-numbing small talk regarding kids (growing, Ivy-bound, married, promoted), trips to Europe (delightful, enchanting, magical), house projects (exhausting, delayed, expensive), and endless gossip (divorce, facelift, bankruptcy).

And in the center of it all, Ava's dad and Loretta, the woman he married three years ago. Loretta was nice enough—a petite woman with pale eyes and bright white teeth. She lived in yoga pants and turtlenecks because she "hated her jowls." She used no makeup except for mascara, and spent most of her time saving the whales or the elephants or the coral reef. But the número uno thing Ava liked about her? Loretta never tried to fill Caroline's shoes. And número dos? She made Raul happy. Not in a forever *Titanic* kind of way, but in a Timon and Pumbaa kind of way. Friends. Companions. *I've got your back* buddies.

Loretta and Raul floated effortlessly. Loretta with a pleasant smile that looked real to the untrained eye, but Ava knew it was painted on with careful precision. And Raul? His silver hair was perfectly combed. His Brioni suit impeccably tailored for his broad frame and average height. His smile was small, sprinkled with grief, but honest and open. He loved people, loved the grab-handling, the politicking of it all. "How do you think I built this business?" he always said.

Nana would hate all this, Ava thought. Of course, Nana's heart could always be swayed. For example, she really didn't care for Caroline because she was only *half* Mexican and acted like more of a gringa than a Fox News anchor. But then Caroline birthed Vivienne, and Nana melted an inch, and an inch and an inch.

Vivienne stepped onto the balcony. "If you're going to hide, the balcony probs isn't the best spot."

"Why are there so *many* of them?" Ava asked, wrinkling her nose.

"Moscas at a matanza," Viv said, tugging her exceedingly long dark ponytail over her shoulder to examine it for split ends. "But it's business," she said, frowning at her hair.

"You think sucking up to Dad really works?" Ava asked. "Like, does the firm actually take on projects—"

"Don't be naive," Viv huffed. "That's how the world works. Scratch my back; I'll scratch yours."

"That's depressing."

"Only if you're not getting any back scratches."

All the LA elites wanted the eminent Granados firm to design their homes, summer cottages, and sprawling villas. But really? Ava thought they just wanted someone to redesign their lives. Fill in the edges of their hearts. Raul understood the value of supply and demand, and when he hit it big fifteen years ago, he made himself desirable, appealing, and above all, selective. That was the bait. Then he wrote a few coffee-table books, started an online store, built the company to one hundred strong, and made strategic decisions as to who to take on as clients—aka, recognized names who were style leaders with big pockets and bigger mouths.

Carmen sauntered out just then. She was wearing the body-con dress Raul had called "unbefitting" a funeral and had made her take off before they left the house that morning.

"Dad's going to kill you for putting that back on," Ava said, raising a single brow.

"He said I couldn't wear it to a funeral, and technically this isn't the funeral. It's the after-gathering thing." Carmen pushed a honey-blonde strand of hair behind her ear. "Besides," she added. "This is Balmain, and I spent a fortune on it, and I figure to get a return on my investment I have to wear it twelve and a half times before it's not the *it* dress anymore."

"Balmain isn't going out of style anytime soon," Viv said. She knew all about lasting style, since she favored a classic, timeless look herself.

Ava adjusted the gray pencil skirt she had borrowed from Viv because her own closet was filled with joggers, jeans, and more joggers. "How do you wear a dress half a time?" she asked.

"Today is the half," Carmen said matter-of-factly.

Viv slung her arm around Ava's shoulders and pulled her in, planting a kiss on the side of her head. "Dad sent me up here to get you."

"Please don't make me," Ava groaned. "I already did my penance and said hi to at least, like, thirty people."

"He wants to make an announcement and wants us all there."

"What kind of announcement?"

"Probably for a photo op," Carmen said as she swept her gaze back to the crowd. Then her eyes lit up. "Who's *that* hottie?"

Ava followed her sister's gawk to Grant. He was gliding through the crowd like a well-fed shark. Ava had never seen him in anything other than jeans and stretched-out tees, and wondered where he had gotten the threads. "My boss?" Ava said, wondering why he'd come. *Not that anyone needs an invite to a funeral,* Ava thought, but he didn't seem like the kind of guy who liked hanging around with this type of crowd. Scratch that. He didn't seem like he would hang out with *any* crowd.

"Can *I* get an internship at the paper?" Carmen batted her eyelashes shamelessly.

Viv sighed. "Seriously, Carmen. Don't you have enough boyfriends?"

"Look," Carmen said, "there are a lot of boys to kiss in this world."

"He's not your type," Ava said. Not that she knew anything about Grant other than that he liked war, was really good at his job, and worked tons of hours. When Ava had first started the internship, she thought it was important to get her boss to like her, because when the summer was over, he would write her college recommendation letters to some competitive far-away schools like Columbia. So she always worked extra hours, did things outside of her copyediting internship, like archiving photos when no one else wanted to. And for insurance she would bring him coffee or muffins. Grant always said thank you, but then he'd add something like, "Is there anything else?" or "Can you close the door on the way out?"

"Hot is always my type," Carmen teased as she looked down at her buzzing cell.

Ava caught the name that flashed there. "Honey Badger?"

"It's code."

"For what?"

Carmen sighed. "Right now, I'm talking to Damian and Daniel. It's hard to keep those names straight, and worse, what if I called them some ex's name?" She visibly shuddered to make her point. "So, I only call them honey or some variation of it. Like Honey Bear, Honey Bunches of Oats, or Honey Badger."

"I don't get it," Ava said. "Won't Badger get mad if you call him Honey Bunches of Oats?" She was genuinely interested. She knew zilch about boyfriends, and didn't really see the point of having one. Relationships always ended badly, with a goodbye and a broken, unmendable heart . . . at least for someone. But last year she did kiss Bryce Wellington on the Haunted Mansion ride at Disneyland just to get it over with. Because she really hadn't wanted to go into senior year without knowing what that felt like. Sadly, it felt unimpressive.

Carmen smiled. As the family serial dater, she adored explaining love dynamics. "*They* will never know as long as I call them *some* version of honey. And they think the nicknames are cute. Win-win."

"But then how do you know who's calling?"

Carmen deadpanned, "Does it matter?"

Viv shook her head, then laughed. "Let's go."

The sisters made their way downstairs and into the backyard. Just as they found Raul on the raised deck by the pool, a group of twelve mariachis paraded out of the house singing "Cielito Lindo." Nana's favorite song.

"Girls." Raul smiled, extending his arms to welcome the sisters while the crowd seemed distracted by the live music. "As soon as the song is over, I want to make an announcement."

"Like what?" Ava said, terrified it would be humiliating, like the time he announced Vivienne's engagement at a party before Vivienne had *thought* about marrying her college sweetheart. The relationship fell apart after that, and the doomed couple never made it to the altar. Ava was secretly happy, because Doug was a douche with a capital *D*.

"You'll see," Raul said, his deep brown eyes twinkling. "Stand here next to me."

"Are we going to hate it?" Carmen was already scowling.

Raul studied her dress with narrowed eyes, then pulled a face that said, *How could you ask me such a foolish question?*

Easy, Dad, Ava thought. *We hate most of your announcements.* Their dad had a lot of excellent qualities, but modesty wasn't one of them.

The song ended, and the lead singer bowed and then told the crowd that Señor Granados had a few words. A hush fell over the scene. Dramatic and overdone like a *Bachelor* rose ceremony. *Cue the suspenseful strings.*

Ava's cheeks warmed. She tried not to fidget, but she couldn't stand all those eyes on her. Her strappy heels started to dig into her ankles.

"Good afternoon," Raul was saying. "I would like to thank you all for being here to honor the life of an incredible woman."

Ava's blouse suddenly felt tighter. Her dad's voice sounded far away.

"And in her honor," he said with a small tremble in his voice, "I am gifting . . ."

The afternoon sun beat down on Ava, making her feel woozy. She kept her gaze down, staring into the pool, wishing she were under the water, swimming deeper and deeper away from here.

". . . one hundred thousand dollars to Saint Bernadette's food kitchen."

Everyone erupted in applause, *oohs*, and *ahhs*.

Nana might not have liked this whole affair, but she would definitely love Dad's generosity, especially to the place where she spent every Saturday, feeding the needy and offering prayers like candy.

Ava squinted against the setting sun. Shadows dipped beneath the pomegranate trees. A figure emerged from the orchard a mere thirty feet away. Wide-eyed, dimple-cheeked, perfect auburn coif. Nana?

Ava blinked. Gasped. Blinked again. Nana was still there.

I'm so freaking tired, I'm seeing things, Ava thought as her heart thundered.

Raul continued spouting his mother's praises. His mother who was *still* standing there, smiling at Ava. For a second, Ava stupidly wondered if this was part of her dad's announcement. *Surprise! My mother is back from the dead.*

Instead, Raul said, "And now I thought this would be a nice time for the girls to say a word about their grandmother. Ava, would you like to go first?"

"Huh?" Ava forced herself back to the moment. *But I'm the baby. Why do I have to go first?* She threw a pleading look to Viv, who gave her a hard *you can do this* stare.

Clearing her throat, Ava wiped her sweaty palms on her blouse. "Um ... hi ... okay. So, my nana was ..." She inched forward on those stupid skinny heels, looking up toward Nana, who was now weaving between the people, heading in Ava's direction.

"She ... is ..." Ava's tongue twisted as dizziness swept through her.

"Ava?" Raul said quietly, gently placing his hand on the small of her back.

Twenty feet.

Who's that old man in the orange robe trailing Nana?

The crowd waited.

The world slanted.

Why is she walking so fast?

Fifteen feet.

Nana's lips were moving.

Ten.

Her hands were flying.

"Nana?" Ava barely got the word out before she fainted. Right into the pool.

Four

First came the throbbing pain.

Then the voices, worried and rising. Carmen: "Wake her the hell up!"

Dad: "Ava?"

Viv: "We're here, Gree."

Slowly, Ava opened her eyes. Three Granados faces hovered like the fruit their name derived from.

"Pomegranates, ghosts," Ava whispered dazedly from the sofa in Nana's casita. The leather stuck to her still-damp skin. Her wet hair clung to her neck. And more than ever she regretted the itchy, now clingy skirt.

"Don't try to sit up," Ava's dad said in his usual take-charge way as he laid a hand on her shoulder.

A woman appeared then. Thick bobbed hair, painted eyebrows. "I'm Dr. Vermouth," she said. Ava remembered her from the gathering. Or more specifically, she remembered the very regrettable taffeta pantsuit.

Ava could tell the doc was trying to reveal a small smile of reassurance, but too much Botox painted a frozen expression on her face like those creepy clown dolls that gave kids nightmares.

Ava sat up slowly.

"Just take some deep breaths." Dr. Vermouth held a glass of water to

Ava's lips, which Ava gulped greedily as her head began to clear. Who knew fainting into a pool could make you so thirsty?

The doc ticked off several demands as she held Ava's wrist, checking her pulse. "Breathe deeply. Follow my finger." Then came the questions, all of which Ava answered in the negative: "Dizzy? Have you ever fainted before?"

Once the doc finished checking Ava out, she gave Raul the thumbs-up and left.

"What happened to you, mija?" Raul asked.

As soon as the words were out of his mouth, the fully painted memory of Nana gliding through the pomegranate shadows came back to her. Ava's eyes darted around the room as if she might see her grandmother pacing there, wearing down the wood floors with her three-inch wedge slippers.

"You passed out," Viv said softly, her face a full moon of concern. That's when Ava noticed her sister's hair and dress were both wet. Leave it to Viv to jump in while Carm probably screamed from the sidelines that she would be forever scarred if Ava drowned.

Loretta's clickety-clack heels carried her closer. She wedged between the trio and peered down at Ava, blonde waves falling around her thin face. "I have some arnica for you," she said, holding out a small plastic bottle. "It helps with trauma."

"I don't have trauma." *Not exactly. Not unless you count hallucinations.*

"It will make me feel better," Loretta said. The woman had a remedy for everything. Headaches, sleeplessness, allergies, upset stomach. The list of ailments went on and on. And even though Ava had never known homeopathy to work, she didn't want to argue, so she took a few tiny pellets under the tongue as Carmen shooed everyone back, took Ava's hand, and climbed into the tiny sliver between Ava and the back of the sofa, sticking her bare feet beneath her sister's legs. Then she whispered, "Good thing you have on nice calzones."

Heat flushed Ava's cheeks. Did everyone really see her underwear?

"It's okay," Carm said, patting Ava's leg. "I don't think anyone saw, but why the fainting? Did you forget to eat, jita?"

"I . . . I saw Nana," she blurted. "She was here. Under the pomegranate trees."

Viv said, "You definitely need some carbs."

"It's very normal," Loretta said, nodding to Ava over Raul's shoulder. "Grief does surprising things to people's minds."

"Let's get you something to eat," Raul said. To Dad, food fixed everything. Got a bad grade? Cookie dough ice cream. Fighting with a friend? Chicken enchiladas. All-around bad day? Spicy tuna rolls from Sakura. There was only one time that Ava could remember this not being the case: the night her mom left. That night was just air and tears and bad dreams. And memories of her last words, of that dark, sad, fairy tale she always told her.

Viv's golden-brown eyes soaked Ava up. If eyes could hug you, tuck you into bed, tell you a bedtime story, they were Viv's. And right now, they were telling Ava everything would be okay. The only problem was—for the first time in her life, Ava didn't believe her sister's eyes.

After considerable convincing, Ava persuaded her family to let her take a shower, get changed, and just be alone. But even alone in her room, Ava could hear the sounds of the house and everyone in it. At least until the house was emptied of guests, and the cleaning crew swept in. Ava changed into a pair of black sweats, Birks, and a white long-sleeved tee before sneaking out the side door.

She needed air and distance and perspective. She needed to look at the bigness of the ocean and she *desperately* needed a Venti hot black tea with almond milk, steamed, and two Splenda. The stronger, the better. Not in the mood to drive, she struck out on foot. Maybe a nice long walk would clear her head and any hallucinations that still lingered there.

The night air carried the salty, crisp scent of the sea only a few blocks away. Santa Monica came alive at night with tourists in search of bougie restaurants and bars, high-end boutiques, and coffee shops that could be found on every corner. And some people just wanted a thrill ride on the pier's roller coaster or a turn on the Ferris wheel. Ava very much preferred to keep her feet on the ground.

Like now, except that each step brought her closer to a dreadful fear: *I'm losing my mind.* But each heartbeat brought her closer to a reality she could accept: *Stress made me see and hear things that weren't there. There are no such things as ghosts.* And then terror struck her to her core. *What if Carmen and Viv are right? What if Nana's blessing somehow reached me, and it's seeing ghosts? No, that wouldn't be a blessing. That would be like* Sixth Sense *hell. Definitely a curse.*

Pretending that last thought had never occurred to her, Ava hooked a right onto Montana Ave., where she stopped at Starbucks for the tea, then headed west toward Ocean Ave. Just as she was coming up on an Italian restaurant with sidewalk eating, she froze.

Blinked, then did a double take.

It was him.

Truck guy.

He was sitting at a table not fifteen feet away with two glammed-up girls who looked like they just stepped out of a blow-dry bar. He was laughing at something the skinny blonde was saying, like she was the most entertaining human in the world. *She must be the girlfriend.* But wait. Why then was he slinging his arm around the brunette while the blonde leaned on his free shoulder? Ava didn't know why, but the entire scene annoyed her.

She was about to cross the street to avoid the love fest when he glanced up. His eyes locked with hers. Dammit! Ava searched for something to hide behind, but there was nothing other than a small woman tipping the valet.

In the span of three seconds, three thoughts occurred to her.

Should I wave? Ignore him? Pretend I don't know him?

Before she could decide, her mutinous hand was flapping. The guy glanced over his shoulder, then back at her, pulling a face that said, *You're a stalking weirdo.* He whispered in blondie's ear, and before Ava knew it, the trio was staring at her, snickering.

The painful heat of humiliation swept through Ava, making her feel sick. And all she could think was *Flee, flee, flee.*

She spun into the street. Her phone flew from her hand.

The sound of screeching brakes. The black SUV missed her by mere inches. But the honk and curses landed with force.

Ava reached down for her smashed, very dead phone and stumbled to the other side of the road.

Heart racing, pride shrinking, she ran all the way to Ocean Ave. a few blocks away. By the time she got there she had spilled half of her tea on her white shirt and had banked mountains of hate thinking about that jerk. Seriously? Did he really despise her so much that he couldn't even wave? *I didn't even dent his stupid truck,* she thought angrily, *so what's his deal?*

He had been rude the other night too, but then he had softened and told her to go without making a big deal about hitting his car. Why? Maybe he was terrified of hysterical females.

Then, remembering her summer goal, she thought, *This is so not joyous boredom!*

Ocean Ave. was brimming with lights, cars, and animated pedestrians. Across the way was Palisades Park, a long lingering band of green that sat atop the sandstone bluffs. From here, the ocean view was breathtaking. And this, *this* view was the reason Ava and her sisters had organized a hunger strike when Raul had suggested they move to dreadful Beverly Hills. It took three days of convincing, several hidden packages of popcorn, gummy worms, graham crackers, Cocoa Puffs, and numerous stomachaches until Raul threw in the towel.

Ava leaned against the wood railing, peering at the dark rippling sea as she sipped her lukewarm brew. She wondered for the first time if she was making the right decision applying to colleges on the opposite coast. It seemed too soon, too sudden, too far. She still had her entire senior year in front of her, but Ava was built for worry. And then there was Elijah, her closest friend, who had been in every single one of her honors classes since middle school, was her right hand at the school paper, and had always been there, for every cut, scrape, bruise—the invisible and the visible, including Ava's all-night cry fest after her mom left. *That* Elijah had up and decided to spend his summer studying Spanish in Peru with a host family just so he could get college credits and improve his chances at the foreign service, his ultimate dream.

"Do you really have to go?" Ava had pleaded. "I can teach you Spanish, and what about our plan to do nothing?" Because they had busted their butts all year long at school, and this was their reward.

"Aves, we can still do nothing, just from different places."

Except that doing nothing with someone is a whole lot better than doing nothing with no one. And besides, nada really meant lazing around the beach, eating their way through every flavor of ice cream at Sloan's, having a John Hughes marathon, and plotting to be the lords over yearbook. Mostly Ava just wanted to enjoy and stretch out what felt like her last summer at home. Next year she'd be dorm shopping, moving, and big-time panicking.

Worst of all was that Elijah was in the countryside somewhere and the cell service was lousier than a distant planet's. But at least Ava had her sisters, who were her truest best friends, because sisters are loyal, and sisters can always be trusted. But mostly, sisters have to stick by you and love you even when you suck.

Ava laughed to herself at the image of her fainting into the pool and what Elijah would have done if he were there. He would have snapped a pic for "posterity" and found a way to plant it in the yearbook somewhere. She had thought about calling him to tell him about Nana, because he loved her too, but she knew he would fly home, and she didn't want to ruin his summer. He was like the grandson Nana never had. Stupid boys. They didn't have to worry about blessings and broken threads and . . . ugh!

Then another thought occurred to her.

What if Dad needs me to fill in for Nana? But Ava pushed the thought away. Viv was already at the firm full time, working with the architectural design team. Carm was half interning there this summer, bouncing from the catalog and online marketing to human resources and accounting before she went back to her *I have no idea what I want to do* independent studies program at USC in the fall. Besides, Ava could never fill her grandmother's slippers.

Nana had been instrumental in building the business. She had an exceptional nose for artistic talent and was the one who had taken Raul to tiny towns all over Mexico to source unique products. Within two years she became known as Reina of Discovery. To Ava, Margarita Alana Cortez Granados was also the queen of hearts, believing in things like soul mates and love at first sight. But what good had it done her? She had left her husband right after Raul had been born, incurring her father's wrath and causing him to then cut her off from the family both emotionally and financially. And as far as Ava knew, Nana had never found the love she so fiercely believed in. Seemed like a big fat waste of heart space.

Ava looked down at her phone's shattered screen. There was a dim green flicker, and if she peered close enough, she could see three small faint digits: 8:51. Her heart did a little dip. Just last week she was driving in a freak storm, slamming into a truck she hadn't seen. Minutes away from saying goodbye to Nana. To hearing her last words:

Meteors, stars, 8:51. Collision. And the hummingbird.

Tears stung Ava's eyes. The world went blurry just as a voice swept past her ear.

"Hello, mijita."

Ava whirled.

And there she was. Bright, healthy, not-at-all-dead-looking Nana. And she was smiling, as if it were entirely natural to sneak up on someone when you're supposed to be six feet under.

Two seconds passed. Five, maybe. Until Nana's snapping fingers shook Ava out of her trance.

Ava jerked back, dropped her drink, and shouted, "Jesus Christ!"

"No, just me," Nana said as she climbed onto the fence and planted herself there. She looked ten years younger. Her auburn hair was swept into a loose bun. Her dark eyes brimmed with both longing and delight.

"I'm seeing things," Ava said, squeezing her eyes closed, then peeling one open slowly as if Nana might disappear. She didn't. Ava backed up.

"Please don't scream again," Nana said, glancing around. "Someone might think you're drunk or a loca and you might get arrested."

"You're . . . you're dead."

"Don't remind me." Nana folded her arms over her purple cashmere sweater. The one Raul had bought her two Christmases ago. "Now," she said, "you need to cálmate, Ava. I must talk to you, and I can't do that if you're screaming all over the place like La Llorona."

Trembling, Ava inched close enough to poke her index finger into Nana's arm. It came up against not flesh and bone, but something softer, squishier, like a down pillow. "Holy shit!" Ava cried. "Why isn't my finger going through you?" *God, the movies are such a lie*, she thought.

Nana scowled. "If I were still alive, would you use such terrible, unbecoming language?"

"But . . . you're *not* alive," Ava reminded her.

"That doesn't mean I'm not here." Nana looked around at the people milling about. The cars cruising past. "Should we go someplace private?"

Nana or not, no way was Ava going to follow a dead person anywhere private. She found herself shaking her head incredulously as she poked Nana's arm again and then her cheek.

"Please stop jabbing me," Nana said, flopping her gold slipper against her heel.

"You feel like a pillow or firm flan or . . ."

"People are starting to stare."

Ava glanced to her right. A couple sitting on a nearby bench was gawking at her with raised eyebrows, but the moment she caught their gaze, they got up and headed in the other direction.

"They can't see you, can they?" Ava said, her voice quivering.

"Of course not. Now, we need to talk about why I'm here."

Ava heard the words, but her brain was trying to process the impossibility of it all. "How . . . how do I know I'm not imagining this?"

"I told you she wasn't going to believe me," Nana said over her shoulder.

Ava's eyes flicked about suspiciously. "Who are you talking to?"

"You'll find out soon enough," Nana said with a sigh. "Entonces, about the blessing."

A tiny thrill rolled down Ava's spine. "You're here to tell me what it is?" Her speech was unnaturally fast. Maybe it was the shock, or maybe it was the elation that Nana hadn't abandoned her, that at the end of everything Ava was going to get her blessing after all.

But then Nana said, "I don't know what the blessing is."

"What?"

"No recuerdo."

"How can you not remember?" Ava said. "It was just last week."

"Time is different for me. It's taken me quite a while to accept all of this," Nana whispered.

"You mean being . . . dead?"

"Among other things."

Ava's heart began to bend, to make room for the possibility that her grandmother really was a ghost visiting her here on this breezy cliff. The possibility made room for reality, and it was like a blow to the gut. Without another thought, Ava threw her arms around Nana. Tears stung her eyes. It was a strange, impossible thing, holding a ghost.

The moment Ava gripped tighter, Nana vanished, making her granddaughter stumble into the fence.

"Abrazos are for later," Nana said, reappearing next to Ava. "There is strict universe business to attend to. And if I don't follow the rules," she whispered, leaning closer, "I could get in serious trouble."

"What . . . kind of trouble? You don't mean like . . ." Ava winced and pointed to the ground before lowering her voice and adding, "being sent down there?"

Shaking her head, Nana sighed, "Are you ready to get down to business?"

"Right. Okay," Ava said. "But if you can't tell me the blessing, then what are you talking about?"

Nana's jaw twitched. Her eyes narrowed. Her lips parted enough for a small breath to escape.

"I've made a terrible mistake."

Five

Mistake, Ava could live with. But *terrible* mistake? That sounded like a recipe for catastrophe in ALL CAPS.

Ava felt like she was barely holding on. To reality. To her sanity. But Nana, *she* was the dead one, and she seemed to be doing pretty bueno. If the matriarch of the Granados family could kick the bucket and come back as a ghost, surely Ava could mute her logical brain under the half-moon in her tea-stained shirt and listen patiently without totally flipping out.

Surely.

A group of hooting kids on scooters zipped past, and one cruised right through Nana before she could get out of the way. The not-collision made a sucking sound like *shhlurrrpp.*

"What the holy hell," Ava gasped. "He . . . he went right through you, but you're a . . . pillow."

Nana glared as if the insult was too much even for a ghost.

"I mean . . . you *feel* like a pillow," Ava corrected.

"Apparently only for you." Nana's whole face tightened. "I truly despise being a ghost, mija, and do not recommend it."

I'm definitely keeping my promise and going to confession, Ava thought as she led her grandmother to a bench under a wide, drooping tree, where the two sat. "About the mistake," Ava said, eager for the truth.

Nana hesitated, then stuck her hands into her cashmere jogger pockets. "My second recommendation," she said, eyeing Ava, "is to avoid tea if you're wearing white. Have I taught you nada?"

"Nana."

"Sí. Sí." She stood and began to pace in front of the bench. "Apparently the afterlife has rules. One is that no soul is allowed to remember their deathbed scenes or their moments of death. Too traumática apparently."

"Okay . . ."

"The last thing I remember is that violent storm. The wind howling my name."

"The *wind* called your name?" Ava asked, even though she wasn't prepared to believe Nana if she said yes.

"That isn't what matters," Nana said. "My memory of dying is so muddled, which is why I can't tell you your blessing. Not that it would matter at this point, but it seems I somehow . . ." Nana fidgeted, twisting her fingers uncharacteristically. Ava had never known Nana, Reina of Discovery, to be a nervous woman. Which made Ava doubly nervous. Were afterlife mistakes exponentially worse than ones made on Earth?

"It's okay, Nana. Just say it."

"This is muy difficult." Looking down, Nana paced lightly in her heeled slippers as if one misplaced step would split open the earth. She threw her gaze back at Ava and said, "I gave your blessing to someone else."

"What?!" Ava's voice flew across the park. She felt like she was swinging between two poles: anger and shock. *Someone else. Someone else.*

Nana twisted her face into a pathetic expression. "I know. It's a tragedy, corazón."

"Is that even possible?" Ava said shakily, taking it down a notch. "But . . . wait! How do you know if you can't remember?"

"Mira," Nana said, regaining her self-possession as she planted herself next to Ava again. "I am going to introduce you to someone, but you cannot scream or faint. Do you promise?"

"I don't really want to see another ghost," Ava said.

"Ava, promise me."

"Fine. I promise."

Nana clasped her hands in front of her like she did in mass right before the communion ceremony began. "You can come out, Medardus."

Ava had a split second to think, *What kind of a name is Medardus?* when the man in the orange robe, the same one who had been trailing Nana earlier, materialized. He was shorter than Ava, maybe five foot five, with gray hair and a long thick beard. Under his robe was a white gown and on top of his head a gold pointy hat like the one the bishop sometimes wore for special occasions.

Ava kept her promise. She didn't scream, and she didn't faint. Although she definitely felt woozy.

"Ciao," the man said, flashing an enormous smile and leaning forward with a sort of mini bow. "I am quite pleased to meet you, Ava Granados. Although I do certainly wish it was under better circumstances."

"Who are you?"

"Oh, my manners," he said, touching his chest like he was going to break into the Pledge of Allegiance. "I am Saint Medardus, but you can call me Meda. I am the patron saint of weather, vineyards, brewers, captives, prisoners, and teeth. Mostly people call on me for toothaches. You wouldn't believe how many people have teeth problems. It's astounding," he said, still smiling. "I hail from the fifth century and am Margarita's guide, here to help her with this blunder."

Ava looked at Nana, dumbfounded. Nana stood, threw her hands on her hips, and shook her head. "I spent at least half of my life calling on Cecilia, the patron saint of music. Lighting candles, speaking novenas, singing songs for her, and can you believe she was too busy to be my guide?"

"We've been over this," Meda said. "Just because I am not as popular as Cecilia does not mean I am not stellar at my job." The guy looked genuinely hurt. "I'll have you know that teeth and prisoners are just as important as music."

Nana looked away. "Hmph."

"Teeth *are* pretty important, Nana," Ava said, worried that maybe Nana wasn't supposed to talk to a saint like that. Seemed kind of sacrilegious.

"Now for the second part of the news," Meda said. "We must find out who got your blessing."

"And get it back," Nana put in sharply.

Ava had spent three years in a magnet journalism program at her high school. She knew how to dig, how to ask the hard-hitting *logical* questions that led to real answers, not the fake ones that people usually gave to twist the truth.

"I've got two questions," Ava said, putting on her journalist hat. "First, *how* did someone else get my blessing, and second, how can you be sure that I didn't?"

Meda cleared his throat like he was about to make an important speech. "If the blessing had landed on you, then I would see a faint aura of light around your head. Margarita should have known better than to just let one fly. A very dangerous deed. Very dangerous."

Nana pushed her shoulders back and lifted her chin. "I thought I could only give a blessing to my female descendants!"

"Yes, well, that is obviously not the case," Meda said. "Although it is quite curious that anyone else *could* receive the blessing," he added. "Very curious."

Or maybe the other someone just needed it more than me.

"You cannot persecute me for something I don't even remember," Nana argued.

"You wouldn't believe how many prisoners have spoken those exact words," Meda said.

Ava took a deep, steady breath. "How do you know Carm or Viv didn't get my blessing?"

"Your sisters cannot receive two blessings, which means it went to someone not in the room that night."

"Wait," Ava blurted, realizing that something wasn't adding up. "Let me get this straight. When you spoke my blessing, because I wasn't there, it went to someone else. But how did the other person get it if *they* weren't there either?"

Nana shifted awkwardly and glanced at her watch. Ava followed her grandmother's gaze to the tiny black hands, frozen at 9:01—the moment of Nana's last breath, and her heart sort of buckled.

"I can only guess," Nana said, frowning, "that perhaps I thought I could throw the blessing far enough. A blessing is energy after all, and energy travels quite fast. And knowing myself like I do, I believe I would have thought that if all the stars were aligned, and the fates were kind, the blessing would have sailed right to you. But that's the problema with fate, Ava. Sometimes there is interference that no one is expecting."

"Interference?"

"Like someone out for a walk with their dog," Nana said.

Ava tried to imagine a world where you could be out walking your dog and a blessing just falls out of the sky, and you don't even know you've hijacked someone's whole future. "But it was raining," Ava argued. "No one was out that night, Nana."

With another bright smile, Meda added, "I am anticipating your next question, Ava, and to save you the trouble, no, you cannot leave your intended blessing with someone else. The universe is about balance and truth and really does not approve of such abandonment."

That was *not* Ava's next question, but she wasn't about to argue with the saint of teeth.

"I'm not abandoning anything," Ava insisted. "I didn't even know about any of this until like thirty seconds ago." Her voice rose, calling the attention of an elderly lady out on a stroll with her exceptionally groomed poodle. The dog started barking in the trio's direction, but its eyes were pinned to the exact location of a certain saint and ghost.

Ava waved at the woman, who scowled and jerked her pup away. Once she was out of earshot, Ava turned to Nana and Meda. "How are we ever going to find the person who has my blessing? Do you have any idea how many people live in LA?"

Glancing around, Meda said, "Yes, I do have an idea, and I also have the idea that I am dressed entirely wrong for this place." He removed his hat and smoothed back his white hair before tossing the hat into the sky. Ava watched it vanish into the darkness. "If I'm going to be here, I should look the part."

"Oh, so people can see you?" Ava said.

"Only you." Medardus straightened. "But it is the opinion of self that matters most."

"That is of little importance, Medardus," Nana growled. "What matters is fixing this."

"And if we can't?" Ava said. "What happens then?"

Meda looked up at the tree, stroking his beard distractedly as he began to whistle, while Nana shot him a glare, cleared her throat, and said, "I will remain a ghost . . . until this is made right."

"You'll be stuck like this?" Ava's stomach twisted into knots, scared and tense. "That's the worst rule I've ever heard!" Then a more pleasant, albeit selfish, thought occurred to her. "But . . . I mean . . . at least you could stay with me. With the family." *That would be better than any blessing*, Ava thought.

Nana placed a hand on Ava's arm. Her voice lowered to a hush. "You won't be able to see me or talk to me, and I will lose all memory of who I was here on Earth. I won't be able to move on."

Ava thought being a ghost would be terrible, but being a lingering ghost with no memory sounded worse than every twisted catechism story of hell.

Meda nodded sympathetically before breaking into another vaguely proud smile. "Would you like some good news? I have hundreds of years of guide experience, and in all that time, all my souls have gone on to mostly better places. Therefore, our chances of success are quite good."

Mostly?

"Why were *they* stuck here?" Ava asked.

Meda wasn't smiling anymore. "Unresolved business. Punishment. They didn't know they were dead." He shook his head sadly. "Those are the foulest."

They all went silent, watching the traffic buzz back and forth, and all Ava could think was, *Those poor drivers who have no idea about ghosts and rules and screwed-up blessings.*

"Okay," Ava finally said, "but how hard were those situations? Would you say they were worse or better than our situation?"

Meda's salt-and-pepper brows pinched together. "Certainly not as difficult as this whoops," he admitted. "But I am up for the challenge."

"Whoops?" Had Ava actually heard him right? "A whoops is spilling tea on your shirt because you almost get run over by a car," she spat. "A whoops is sending the wrong message to a group text!"

"Yes, excellent examples," Meda said, unfazed. "Now, we must work quickly. The clock began ticking days ago."

"Clock? What clock?" Ava said, feeling queasier by the moment.

"Ava." Nana spoke gently. "You must remain calm if we are to succeed. Do you hear me?"

"Yes, but about the clock—"

"We must find your blessing by August sixteenth."

"That's . . ." Ava did a quick calculation in her head. "That's four weeks from now!"

"That's the deadline," Medardus said. "On that evening there will be a glorious meteor shower. Energetic forces will be powerful and—"

"Did you say meteor?" Ava clenched her fists at her sides.

"Meteor *shower*," Medardus corrected.

Nana said, "What is it, Ava?"

Ava hit rewind, taking herself back to the moment she ran into Nana's room, a sopping, blubbering mess. Then she hit play and watched it all unfold just like it had that night, but this time with a different perspective. On this go-round, she noticed the way Nana's face had looked so worn and pale, the way the room smelled like roses and Chanel No. 5, the scratching of a branch against the window. The way Ava knew, the second she had arrived, that this was no death rehearsal. And then Nana's last words bubbled up from her memory. She didn't want to see the truth of it. But there they were, those words, staring at her with knowing eyes. They meant something. They weren't the incoherent ramblings of a dying woman.

"Oh my God!" Ava collapsed onto the bench.

"What is it?" Nana said.

"When you were dying . . . you told me something," Ava recalled. "You said, 'Meteors,' which must have something to do with this deadline, and then you said, 'Stars, 8:51. Collision. And the hummingbird.'"

"Ay, how cryptic of me," Nana groaned.

Meda said, "What does it mean?"

Ava looked from the saint to the ghost and took a long and deep breath before she uttered, "It means I know *exactly* who got my blessing."

Caroline sat at the edge of Ava's bed, her fine features lost in the shadows from the nightlight.

"Tell me my fairy tale again," Ava said.

Tucking her daughter in tighter, Caroline said, "It's such a sad tale."

"But we can change the ending."

"If only that were true," she whispered.

And so her mother began, and as always, her words, the soothing tone of her voice, carried Ava away to a place where magic and witches and dragons were real.

"The princess was beautiful," Caroline said. "Smart and talented. But she lived in a world that didn't know her true worth and power. Still, to possess the crown, to become queen, she had to marry.

"Many princes journeyed far and wide to try and win her heart. But, like everyone else, they didn't know her worth.

"Only one knew that: the dark bruja from the poison forest. And she *knew something else: The princess's terrible future."*

Ava had heard the tale so many times, and yet she still breathed in small, shallow, terrified breaths, feeling as if each were the very first. "What future?"

Caroline combed Ava's hair slowly. Were her fingers trembling? She took a small breath, then whispered, "The princess's kiss would kill the first prince she let into her heart."

Six

"Hurry! I know where he is!" Ava took off running, at least as well as she could in her sandals.

If Fate really exists, she's twisted, Ava thought, *to give* my *blessing to that player!*

She had no idea if Nana and Meda could keep up, or maybe spirits could just appear places? Ava only had one tiny window of opportunity to get back to that restaurant where she had last seen that *rude, self-absorbed* . . .

"Where are we going?" Nana's voice was loud and clear, coming from Ava's right, although she was nowhere to be seen. The invisibility implications were way too disturbing to think about right now.

"I'll show you," Ava wheezed.

And then, halfway up Montana Ave., her brain tripped on the question she should have asked fifteen minutes ago: *How do you take a blessing back?*

She had three more blocks to imagine half a dozen scenarios of her trying to reclaim what belonged to her. And in every one, the guy refused. He definitely didn't seem like someone who was going to give anything away for free. *But there was that one moment, the moment after the crash, when he softened, when he told me to go.* So much for first impressions—or in this case second, because when he got out of the car that night, pointing to the stop sign with an arrogant, snide expression, Ava definitely didn't register him as Mr. Nice Guy.

I'll just cry. It worked before. It'll work again, Ava convinced herself. Except that unlike Carmen, she wasn't a good actor and couldn't just turn on the waterworks whenever she felt like it.

A few minutes later, she reached the restaurant. Nana and Meda materialized right next to her, making her jump. "We have to come up with a better system than you guys popping out of thin air," she groaned as her eyes swept over the scene. The guy's table was empty. Ava's gut bottomed out. "He's gone!"

"Who is this *he* you keep talking about?" Nana asked the moment Ava spied the guest check holder still on the table. But she couldn't reach it from the roped-off street. "I hit his car," Ava explained, "the night you died. *He's* the collision." She bolted into the restaurant, telling the hostess she was meeting someone as she passed a waiting area filled with people.

One of the benefits of having Raul Granados as your dad? He taught all his girls how to walk into a room and make it their own. "Confidence is worn like skin, mijitas." He had said it was the first thing that attracted him to their mother the day he saw her walk into a local Hallmark looking for a valentine she would never deliver.

Ava thought she heard her nana whisper, "Collision?" but she couldn't be sure because Meda was talking so loudly.

"This place reminds me of a little café in Florence," he was saying jovially as Ava swept through the establishment. "Or was it Seville? What is that strange hat that man is wearing?"

"Pero, how do you know this person is aquí?" Nana asked.

"I saw him earlier," Ava said as she reached the table and snatched up the check holder. Maybe she could find a name or some kind of identifier on the receipt. "May I help you?" a tall waitress asked Ava, startling her.

"Oh," Ava said, "I . . . uh . . . I forgot to leave a tip." And before the server could argue, Ava peeked inside the holder, only to be met with defeat. There was no name, no identifier other than the miserable fact that the jerk had only left a five-dollar tip on a seventy-dollar meal. *Of course he did*, Ava thought as she picked up the pen and added a two before the five and handed it to the waitress. Whatever benefit of the doubt she might have given him for seeming like a decent human the other night was gone. Long gone.

The girl smiled at the tip and said, "Sure wish I had been waiting on this table."

"One of the downfalls of being a saint," Meda said, "is giving up food. Smell that divine garlic! And merlot . . . so full-bodied. So rich!"

"That reminds me," Ava said to the waitress. "Can you tell the server I need to speak to her?"

The waitress quirked her small mouth. "Sure. I'll tell *him*."

After the girl left, Ava stood there trying to look casual and do her best to ignore Meda, who was still going on about the smell of garlic as he poked his face into someone's bowl of carbonara and took a long whiff. Nana was leaning on the edge of the table, inspecting the patrons with those expressive raised eyebrows—she was definitely judging everyone's table manners. Nana was big on etiquette and even made the Granados girls sit through twelve Saturdays of professional lessons that never really stuck, because Vivienne could still shove half a burrito into her mouth and Carmen never could remember what fork to use. Ava nearly laughed, realizing Nana's gift of memory to Carmen might come in handy.

Nana said to Ava, "Did you find something on the check?"

"Only that he's a terrible tipper," Ava said under her breath so it wouldn't look like she was talking to herself, "but I could have guessed that."

Ava must not have been hush-hush enough, because a nearby old man threw her an awkward stare before returning to the giant bowl of bolognese that Meda was now sticking his fingers in. Just then a skinny college-aged guy walked over and said, "Yeah? You looking for me?" His gaze fell to the tea stains on her shirt. She instantly threw her arms up to hide them. "My boyfriend was just here and . . ." She leaned closer, lowering her voice. "He was with two girls."

The guy shook his head. "I don't get involved with personal stuff like that."

"Right," Ava said. "Of course you don't, but I was wondering . . ."

"Yeah?"

Ever since Ava was ten, she had wanted to be an investigative journalist. She had learned how to do "real" research beyond Google, how to be covert under pressure, and how to keep a straight face when you know you've drawn the worst card in the deck. She had point five seconds to stretch the lie or come clean. She decided to come clean.

"Look," Ava said, "I'm not his girlfriend."

"I didn't think so," the guy admitted. "You seem too normal for someone like that. The dude was pretty offensive."

"I'm not surprised," Ava said.

A satisfied expression passed over his face. "What do you want to know?"

"I need to find him, so anything you've got to help me do that?"

"All I've got is a name. It should help, because I've never heard anything like it."

"What is it?"

"Get this," the guy said, bending closer, "his name is Achilles North. I saw it on the credit card. Can you believe that? Like, who names their kid something like that? Or maybe it's a stage name. Who knows?"

"Right," Ava muttered. "That's definitely a name anyone would re-member."

"Hey, I gotta get back to work," the waiter said. "Good luck."

Back on the street, Ava walked slowly, turning the name over in her head, inspecting it for its flaws and intentions. She knew Achilles was a Greek hero with a heel problem and wondered why anyone would saddle their son with that name. The guy probably had some big god or hero com-plex, and that's why he was so infuriating. Or maybe when he was a kid, he'd been pulverized in the sandbox and scarred for life.

Whatever or whoever you are, Achilles North, I don't care. I'm going to find you and take back what belongs to me.

Ava explained everything she knew about Achilles as the trio walked back to her house a few blocks away. She would have immediately done a social media search, except for the fact that her phone was shattered to bits.

"That must be what I meant by collision," Nana said, "And 8:51. I bet that was the exact time it happened."

"And this collision is likely what interfered with the blessing! Like a channel of power." Meda practically cheered. "Indeed. That makes a bit more sense now."

"But I wonder what *stars* and *hummingbird* mean," Nana said, more to herself than anyone else.

The three walked up the long winding driveway. Ava stopped midway and said, "Once we find Achilles, how do I get the blessing back?" Ava didn't know if it was like a set of keys he could just hand over, or if there was some kind of ritual that needed to be performed. She really hoped it wasn't the latter.

Meda sighed. "We'll work on it. I shall ascertain the answers tomorrow."

"You mean you don't know?!" Ava's voice echoed into the night. "You came all this way, and you don't—"

"Not in this precise moment," Meda replied. "But tomorrow I will obtain the knowledge we need to ensure success."

"Please control your emotions, Ava," Nana said. "Getting upset won't help anyone."

Ava couldn't believe what she was hearing. "But, Meda . . . you're a saint," she pointed out, turning her voice down several decibels. "Shouldn't you know this kind of stuff?"

Meda shook his head. "If I knew the answers to difficult questions, how would I ever evolve?"

"Except that this isn't about you evolving," Ava groaned. Rubbing her forehead, she said, "Fine. So how is this supposed to work? I mean, you guys can't follow me around twenty-four seven."

"Why not?" Meda asked. "We have nowhere else to be."

"Because that would be weird," Ava argued. She was creeped out thinking she would have to pee or shower with them in the same room. "And you do have somewhere else to be. Finding answers!"

Nana sighed, staring up at their home longingly. Ava felt a sharp twist of sadness. Nana was dead. And ghost or no ghost, she wasn't ever coming back. *Things are never going to be the same*, Ava thought. *How easily that happens. What's here today isn't always here tomorrow.*

Nana said, "I understand, jita. Privacy for a young woman is important. We will only come if you call us. Agreed, Meda?"

Meda nodded cheerfully, then snapped his fingers. "That reminds me,

Ava. What is *vegan*? I saw many signs with this word."

"Oh, i'm pretty sure it's for people who don't eat animals or any animal byproducts."

With a snort, Meda said, "And this is popular? Oh my. I think this City of Angels is a bit strange. A bit strange indeed."

"Ándele," Nana said. "It's time to get on the computer and find Achilles." Then she walked right through the closed front door.

Ava turned to Meda. "That was weird."

"Much of the afterlife is weird," he said before following Nana through the closed door.

There was no way to get to Ava's bedroom without passing by the living room, which was where Ava found Vivienne and Carm. They were sprawled out on the sofa with a bowl of popcorn sprinkled with pretzel M&M's between them, watching *The Notebook* on the big screen. Ava didn't want to be seen or grilled or needled in any way. And she definitely didn't want to explain Nana or Meda—not that her sisters could see them, but Carm and Viv would see the lies on her face before she opened her mouth, which meant she had to steer clear of them, at least for a bit.

Ava inched down the hall behind her sisters while the scene where Noah and Allie were standing in the rain on the dock played. Like, seriously? Why not talk under a tree? And didn't they see the lightning flashing? Weren't they worried about getting fried?

For the first time, Ava cursed the size of this house with its long halls, particularly this one that was taking an eternity to walk. Silently, Ava crept along. But then...but then...her sisters went into cringeworthy role-play, halting Ava in her tracks.

Viv as Allie: "Why didn't you write me? Why? It wasn't over for me. I waited for you for seven years. And now it's too late."

Carm as Noah, in a deep Southern voice: "I wrote you three hundred and sixty-five letters. I wrote you every day for a year."

Blah, blah, blah.

"It still isn't over," Viv practically sang.

And then the grande kiss. In the rain. To some melodramatic music. *How stupidly predictable can you get?*

Meda stared into the living room with wide eyes. "Is this a common practice here in Los Angeles?"

Nana's mouth was turned up in the tiniest of grins, but the moment she caught Ava's eyes she straightened and said, "Vámonos. We have a job to do."

"Ava!" Viv shrieked, crawling over the back of the sofa before she threw an arm around Ava's neck. "Where have you been? Why didn't you answer my texts?"

Carm followed, carrying the bowl of popcorn. "Yeah, tonta."

Nana tsked. "Tell Carmen not to be so crass."

Ava held up her phone. "I just went out for some tea, and I dropped my phone."

"How did you drop it?" Viv said, already suspicious.

Clothes were now flying off Noah and Allie, and the last thing Ava wanted to do was stand there with her grandmother's ghost and a fifth-century saint while a monster sex scene played out ten feet away.

"It just fell, okay?" Ava slipped out from Viv's neck hold. "Where's Dad and Loretta?"

"Out for a walk," Viv said, her eyes piercing Ava in an *I don't believe you* dance.

Carm frowned. "You went to Starbucks and didn't ask me for my order?"

Ava started for her room so she could get on her laptop when Viv

FLIRTING WITH FATE

grabbed her arm and tugged her back. "What's up, Gree?"

"The sky?"

"I hate that joke," Carmen was saying while Viv told Ava, "Hey, we swore never to keep secrets, and I know you're not telling us something, so spill."

"It's nothing." Ava could feel the lie burning in her throat. Logic said otherwise, but she was certain the sisters' blood promise had spun some kind of magic making it impossible to lie to Carm and Viv.

Frowning, Carmen said, "Use your vampire skills, Viv, and make her tell us."

"Would you stop with the damn vampires?" Viv turned to Ava. "You know I can persuade you, or you could just tell us where you've been, why you're wearing tea, and why you have that deer-in-the-headlights look."

"You would force me to tell you something I don't want to?" Ava said indignantly.

"Ah," Nana said. "I gave her persuasion. Interesante."

"What do you mean interesting?" Ava said to Nana.

Viv and Carm shared a knowing look. "No one said anything about interesting," Carmen insisted, narrowing her eyes.

"I . . ." Ava could feel herself backpedaling toward the cliff that she was about to plummet off.

Viv said, "We made a promise."

"It's our code," Carmen added in a small voice.

There was a pause. Noah and Allie were living their best lives. Meda was sniffing the popcorn. Nana just stood there, head held high with excellent posture that gave the illusion that *she* had spent Saturdays at finishing school.

Ava's heart twisted. This way and that. If she could have stepped outside of herself, she would have shed her skin right there just to get away

61

from it all. She turned, began to walk away, and the action immediately conjured the image of her mother walking out the door, slipping into the car, checking her red lipstick in the rearview mirror. Why did this moment feel like it had consequences? Like whatever Ava decided would change things forever.

They'll never believe me.

Her heart squeezed tighter.

Ava spun back around, grabbed the bowl of popcorn from Carm, and said, "You better sit down."

Seven

Caroline had once told Ava that the greatest truths are always found in the stars, out of reach and so far away.

That's how this felt. Like some existential heavy truth, one that needed to be told under the wide-open sky.

Ava led everyone to the pool deck. The pool's light glowed pale blue, casting stark shadows across Viv's and Carm's expectant faces.

"Well?" Carmen said, gliding a bare, perfectly pedicured foot into the water.

Viv lay back on the chaise longue and tilted her head up to the clear night sky, her eyes searching. Ava briefly wondered if her mom had told Viv the same thing. Never taking her gaze from the stars, Vivienne tugged an oversized towel up to her chin. "I might need a glass of wine."

Nana stood right beside Ava, in the same spot Ava had stood this afternoon before she passed out.

Before. Before. Before.

"Just remember," Nana said with a warning tone, "to be careful if you choose to tell them."

Ava turned away from her sisters and whispered, "Will it mess something up?"

"Inviting them into this is like pulling a thread, one that will likely affect their destinies. Ay, who knows how complicated Fate has woven this tale?"

That sounded ominous and immense and totally ridiculous. Ava had never believed in fate. Her phone getting smashed? That had been an *accident*. Running into Cheap Ass again? Chance. Telling her sisters? Choice. And this was *her* choice to make. Fate didn't control her decisions.

Meda sat at the edge of the pool with his skinny white feet dipped into the water. "Mind if I take a swim?"

"Yes," Ava said. Her mind was too filled up to have to worry about some robed saint floating around her pool.

"Yes what?" Viv said.

"We should go." Nana nudged Meda with her slipper.

"But we just got here," he said.

"They need privacy." Nana turned back to Ava. "Just call when you need us."

And before Ava could blink, the two vanished, which left her feeling both deserted and relieved.

"What the hell are you staring at?" Carm asked.

"You're freaking me out," Viv added, glancing around the yard.

Ava turned to her sisters. "Are you one hundred percent sure you *really* want to know?"

"Well, when you put it like that . . ." Viv feigned indifference, then, "Of course we want to know!"

"Jesus," Carmen groaned, "why do you always have to be so dramática. Just spill."

Ava was about to argue with the irony of that statement but let it go in light of the real drama she was about to share. She steadied her breath.

"Okay. Just remember *you* asked. But first you have to promise me you won't think I'm loca."

"I already think that," Carm said.

"Same," Viv teased with a smile.

Ava took a deep breath, knowing the moment she began talking there would be no going back. "Nana is still with us . . ."

Carm and Viv stared, unflinching, unblinking. Viv spoke first. "Like in spirit."

"Well, yeah, but more than that," Ava said. "She was just here, standing beside me."

Carm sniffed. "I told you you're loca."

Ava twisted her fingers and began to pace by the pool. "This isn't coming out right."

"How about you start at the beginning?" Viv suggested gently.

Ava looked at her sisters. A soft breeze wafted through the trees, carrying the scent of citrus and something else she couldn't name. With a deep breath, she began . . . at the beginning. It was hard to get the words out when her sisters kept interrupting with:

"Whaaat . . ."

"Howww . . ."

"Whennn . . ."

But when Ava finally spilled the whole story, Viv looked crestfallen. "Poor Nana."

Carm said, "Fifth-century saint? Shit! That sucks." Then she threw a hand over her mouth and cried, "Did Nana just hear me say that?"

Viv was sitting straight up now, her eyes dancing around wildly. "We miss you, Nana."

"And we love you," Carmen added.

"She isn't here right now," Ava said.

"Can she come back?" Viv said, getting to her feet. "Not that I don't trust you or anything, but, like, you did fall today, hit your head . . . and, um . . ."

"Yeah, I mean, we believe you, but . . . can we see her?" Carmen chimed in.

Ava hated when they ganged up on her. That was the problem with three. Someone was always the outsider.

"I guess only I can see her, since it's my blessing," Ava admitted.

"Okay," Viv said, drawing the word out slowly.

"You don't believe me," Ava said, insulted until she realized she would feel the exact same way if the roles were reversed.

Carmen raised her hand. "I believe Nana is a ghost. Sounds like something she would do. She can never let go of anything. But a saint of teeth named Medardus? Totally sounds made-up."

There was a massive ripple in the pool just then. A wave of water swept over Carmen, leaving her soaked and shrieking.

"Holy Mary, Mother of God!" Viv cried.

Ava glanced over to the other side of the pool where Meda did a little bow. "She should be careful if she's going to use my name. Want me to do it again? It's all in the flick of the wrist."

"No!" Ava shouted.

"Is it Nana?" Viv asked, sidling up to Ava now. Carmen quickly followed. "Or is it the tooth guy?"

"I am the saint of prisoners and weather and many other things," Meda said. "Tell her. Tell her I am more than teeth. She may think teeth aren't a big deal, until *hers* start falling out."

The air sizzled with electricity, and Ava half expected a bolt of lightning to split one of the trees in half. Was he allowed to be such a nuisance? Weren't saints supposed to just carry prayers around in their pockets?

"He wants me to tell you that he's more than teeth," Ava said.

Meda vanished, but his chuckle lingered for a second longer, drifting away on the breeze.

Viv and Carmen were clinging to Ava, who peeled her sisters off her and said, "He's gone. You can calm down. And just so you know, if you say his name, he thinks it's some kind of invite to hang out."

Carm shivered, widening her gaze.

"Listen," Ava said, "I know it's wilder than wild, but—"

"We believe you," Viv said as she tossed Carmen the towel.

"But we're talking ghosts and saints," Ava replied, suddenly realizing it was as if she was trying to talk herself out of believing *any* of this.

"And we were raised in a house with saints on the walls," Viv countered, "and ghost stories in our hearts, and hello . . . Nana is . . . was . . . is all mystical with her blessings."

Carmen was open-mouth breathing again. "Maybe our brains were built for this sort of . . ." She paused, biting back the cuss word that Ava knew was on the tip of her tongue. "For this stuff," she went on, "but I'm not sleeping alone tonight or tomorrow. Or maybe ever."

A minute later the three sisters were huddled around the firepit, and Ava answered all their questions patiently until Vivienne and Carmen knew every detail that she knew. But as she recounted every fact, careful not to leave a single morsel out, she noticed something unusual: A strange kind of pulsing light in Carmen's eyes, and for a second she thought it was the fire's reflection. But the light twinkled like tiny fireworks exploding behind Carm's irises. Ava stopped midsentence—somewhere between the meteor shower and the bad tipper. She must have had a stupefied expression as she got up in her sister's face, because Carmen placed her hand over her eyes. "You're making me uncomfortable looking at me like that."

And that was when Ava realized that her sister was committing all this to memory—every last word, pause, and exclamation.

"Your eyes sparkle when—"

"Almost supernatural looking, right? Like, *Twilight* vibes." Carmen pulled her hand free. "But it only happens when I'm really focusing."

"That's so amazing!" Ava nearly shouted. Then she turned to Viv. "Do you . . ."

"No." Viv shook her head. "It kind of makes sense," she said with a small grin. "That way no one knows when I'm persuading them."

"It's rude," Carm groaned as she typed something on her phone.

"It does seem unfair," Ava put in.

"I didn't make the rules," Viv said with a shrug.

"There *are* no rules." Carmen stood and held up her cell, twisting it back and forth toyingly as she pranced around the pit. Ava hated when she got that look on her face. It usually meant trouble was coming.

"Just tell us," Viv groaned.

"I just found the a-hole, Achilles North."

Ava nearly tripped over her own feet racing to Carmen's side. She stared at the Instagram feed of bikinis, boats, beer, and basketball.

"What a terrible name," Carmen said, pulling a disgusted face. "And he's not even hot."

"What does that have to do with anything?" Viv was now peering over her shoulder too.

"Only hot guys get to be cocky," Carmen reasoned.

"Or *no one* should be cocky." Ava rolled her eyes.

"Well," Viv said, "I think if he wasn't as awful as Ava said he is, he'd be cute in an *I could play Spider-Man* kind of way."

Carmen pulled another face. "No one wants sticky, skinny Spider-Boy. Batman is where it's at."

Ava said, "Okay, so we have his Instagram account, but how do we find him?"

"I already messaged him," Carmen replied with a sly smile.

"What!" Ava was going to throw her sister in the pool and hold her under until she turned blue. Nah—the fire was closer.

"Sometimes you have to take control, and you already said you only have a few weeks," Carmen argued.

Ava propped herself onto a barstool while they waited for Achilles North to message Carmen back, and he would, because once he saw her profile pic with her Gucci shades, golden hair swept across her full lips in an effortless manner that said, *I can even control the wind*, his ego would definitely grow exponentially.

Viv, staring down at her cell, twisted her mouth into a satisfied grin and said, "You can wait for him to message Carm, or you can find him this Saturday just down the road."

"How do you know?"

Viv handed over her phone. On the screen was a business article from last year highlighting an orange grove called Maggie's Orchard located just outside the city. Ava and Carmen hunched together on the stool to read the article. The exposé featured the family farming business run by someone named Charles Bennington. Ava scrolled slowly until she reached a photo of an old guy, Charles, standing next to his grandson, Achilles North. Straight-faced Achilles had his arms folded over his chest.

Carmen read the last part aloud. "You can now get a taste of the delicious organic oranges at Santa Monica Farmers Market, run by grand-son Achilles North." With a huff, she added, "I already wish I could forget his serial killer face."

"He does *not* look like a serial killer," Ava argued, and then realized she was sticking up for Mr. Rude himself. "I can't believe all the times I've gone to the market in the last year that I didn't run into him."

Ava scrolled the article again, wondering why there was no mention of Achilles's parents. Maybe they weren't into oranges. "I hate that we're los-ing three more days!"

"Then you better hustle that blessing back as soon as you meet Prince Charming," Carm said, snapping her fingers.

"You guys are coming with me, right?" Ava felt like someone was wring-ing out her insides. She was going to have to see him again. And if history was any indicator, it would be another humiliating encounter. Saturday. It was too soon, too late, too . . . everything.

"Of course," Viv said. "You're going to need me."

Carm snorted, clearly catching on to something Ava wasn't.

"What am I missing?" Ava asked.

"Once we find Achilles at his orange booth," Viv spoke slowly, deliber-ately, eyebrows raised.

Ava smiled. "You're going to persuade him to give me back my blessing."

"Exactamente."

Viv reached behind the bar and handed out three bottles of Topo Chico soda water. The sisters toasted.

"We have to say what we're toasting, *and* we have to make eye contact. Otherwise it's bad luck," Carm suggested mischievously.

With a smirk, Viv said, "To the guy who has no idea what's coming for him."

Eight

The morning was a flurry of music, muffins, and the typical summer-morning madness. Plus, the glorious, shiny truth that they had found Achilles.

And by 9:00 a.m. Ava was still basking in the glow of their success. *Thank the saints for social media*, she thought as she moved about the sweet-smelling kitchen putting the finishing touches on breakfast—orange-cranberry muffins, egg biscuits, and fresh fruit—while singing (badly) to some throwback Spears: "Lucky."

Carm and Viv had already poked around, looking spooked, asking if Nana and the saint were there. When Ava assured them that they were alone, the sisters made a pact: Ava would warn them if the spirits were nearby.

Now her sisters lounged at the bar: Viv reading the news on her iPad, Carmen scrolling through her phone. Both acted like they were allergic to the kitchen. Carm burned everything she touched, even boiled eggs. And Viv was happy to live on things that came out of the ground and required no cooking, but Ava? She loved trying new recipes, mixing unusual flavors, but most of all she loved creating something from scratch.

Carm yawned, still staring down at her phone groggily. "Can you make me waffles, Ava?"

"Ooh," Viv said, still engrossed in whatever she was reading. "Waffles sound so good. Buttermilk with those candied pecans you make."

"I'm not a short-order cook," Ava said as she set the warm biscuits in a French linen–draped basket.

Carm's eyes widened, and a smile spread across her sleepy face as she held up her phone triumphantly. "Well, well, well . . . Guess who messaged me at midnight? I totally missed it."

Ava dropped a biscuit and practically launched herself into Carm's lap to see the phone. "What did he say?"

"'Hey. What's up?'" Carm put on a deep Joey-from-*Friends* kind of voice.

"That's it?" Viv huffed.

Carm's fingers danced across the screen.

"What are you telling him?" Ava asked, trying to read over her sister's shoulder.

"That he's boring and rude and doesn't he *wish*."

"Don't send that!" Ava shouted.

"But it's true."

"We need him, Carm," Viv argued. "Just say *hey* back or something."

Carmen's eyes nearly rolled to the back of her head as she muttered unrepeatable things under her breath. "I am not saying *hey* back. I'm not five." She typed out the message while simultaneously grumbling, "God, this is killing me." Then she showed the message to Ava and Viv before sending. Want to hang out sometime?

Achilles must have had the fastest fingers in the world, because in less than a second he had already said, Sure. And then in a separate message: Sometime.

Carmen gasped. Her mouth stayed open as she stared at the screen. "Sometime? Is he joking?" She wore a murderous expression as her fingers began to tap furiously.

Viv yanked the phone away and used her height advantage to hold it out of Carmen's reach.

"Give it back!" Carmen shouted, climbing to stand on the stool with doubtful balance. Ava stood behind her in case (or when) she fell.

"This isn't about your ego, Carm," Viv said. "Just think for a second. Pissing him off isn't going to get us anywhere."

Carmen's frown deepened as she plunked back down. "This is totally about my ego. Like, who sends a separate message, *sometime*? What an asshole. Fine. I won't send anything. Just give me back my phone."

Viv's eyes cut to Ava's before she took a deep breath, handed over the cell, and said to Carmen, "Just ignore him for now."

With a suspicious glare, she said, "Are you persuading me right now?"

"Is it working?"

"Kind of." Carmen's face reddened. "I already hate this guy. And to think he has *your* blessing, Ava! That *he* is the reason poor Nana isn't at rest."

Ava grabbed the bowl of sliced papaya and topped it with pecans and honey before setting it on the table with the muffins and biscuits. "Do you think he *knows* he has the blessing? Like, that something is different?" she asked.

"Only one way to find out," Viv said as she sat down at the farm table, knees pulled into her chest.

Carm wrinkled her nose at the food and complained, "I really wanted waffles."

Ignoring her, Ava said to Viv, "But even if he does know he has some new ability or whatever . . ." Ava's wheels were turning, spinning her thoughts out of control. "I mean, even with your mad persuasion skills, Viv, he might not have the power to give it back. And that would put us back at square one. Even Meda said he doesn't know how any of this works."

"Don't say his name!" Viv warned.

"Fine," Ava sighed, "Mr. M said he doesn't know how any of this works."

"Can't we just beat the blessing out of him?" Carm suggested.

"Listen," Viv said to Ava, "Mr. M told you that he'll have answers today, right?"

Ava nodded.

"Gotta trust the saint," Carmen said as she ripped off a piece of muffin and stuffed it into her mouth. She stopped chewing and looked around in terror. "He isn't here, is he?"

Ava shook her head.

"It can't be that hard," Viv added. "If Nana can speak a blessing, then I bet Achilles just has to speak it back or something."

"Or we could go with my plan and beat it out of him . . ." Carm said again through a mouthful of muffin. "Or maybe if we accidentally murder him, it will just magically come back to you."

"Who are we murdering?" Raul said as he strolled in, poured himself a cup of coffee, and sat down at the table with the newspaper in hand.

Viv smiled. "Oh, it's some new video game all the kids are playing."

Ava was always astonished at how quickly Viv could pluck a lie out of the air and breathe credible life into it.

Carm stuffed half a biscuit into her mouth and wiped a hand on her T-shirt. "You could squeeze butter outta these things," she said, crumbs falling from her lips.

"Por favor, Carmenita," Raul said. "Use a plate."

"It's already gone," she said, polishing off the last bit, which only made Raul sigh louder.

"How are you, Dad?" Viv asked, and those four small words reminded everyone at the table that Nana's funeral was only yesterday—which was the only reason they were all together at the breakfast table on a work day. Viv was always the first to say the right thing. Always the first to apologize. Always the first to make peace. Ava wished she could be more like her oldest sister, but words didn't come easy to her. Her very nature was willful and stubborn. She could hold on to a grievance for eternity, and not because she was petty, but because she found stability and control and power in it.

"Nana lived a good long life," Raul said with a small smile before sipping his coffee. "She wouldn't want us to be sad."

"Do you believe in ghosts, Dad?" Carm asked so abruptly everyone's heads snapped in her direction.

Ava kicked her under the table as Raul raised an eyebrow but thankfully didn't take the bait. "I'm glad you're all here," he said, scooping some papaya onto his plate. "Loretta and I are going on a buying trip."

Carmen threw her napkin at Ava as a warning. "Do it again."

Ignoring her sister, Ava folded the napkin and sat back. "Where are you going, Dad?"

"San Miguel," he said. "And I wanted to check with you all first."

"Why?" Viv rested her elbows on the table. "You always go on buying trips."

His dark eyes scanned each of his daughters' faces. It was the first time since Nana died that Ava saw how tired he looked, how drawn his face was. "We'd like to take an extended vacation afterward," he added slowly, as if he were asking permission. "To Costa Rica."

Extended? Ava thought. As a family they had traveled the world, but Raul's idea of a vacation was five days tops. Nana always went along so the girls could "see and experience" the world for longer periods of time. Plus, she loved scouting out unusual stores and shopping until everyone's feet were going to fall off, and there was no way she could do that kind of damage in just five days.

"Why?" Carmen asked, picking a piece of fruit out of the bowl with her fingers.

Raul sighed. "For rest."

"You never rest," Ava said matter-of-factly.

"Maybe it's time."

That was the moment when Ava wanted to tell her dad that Nana wasn't gone entirely. That her ghost, her essence, lingered, and all Ava had to do was call Nana's name, and she would appear right there at the breakfast table. It wouldn't matter that no one else could see Nana—they could talk to her through Ava, and surely that would bring her dad some kind of peace.

Picking at her napkin, Ava said, "Dad, I have something to tell you."

Viv dropped her fork onto the stone floor. Carm leaned closer like a cat ready to pounce.

"What is it?" Raul said.

"Yeah," Carmen added with a twisted grin, "what is it, Ava?"

The words sat on the tip of Ava's tongue, but then she realized that if she told her dad, he would never go on vacation. He would never get the rest he so badly needed. But bigger than that, if Ava told her dad that Nana was a ghost, she would also have to tell him that her grandmother was in danger of losing her memory, her name, herself. No. Ava couldn't throw down the truth. Because in the end, if she failed, if she didn't get back the blessing, Raul would suffer with the terrible knowledge that his mom was a lost soul. And it would be like losing her all over again.

"I . . . I decided to change my bedding to cream and gray," Ava offered, "not just gray and white."

Raul titled his head in that way that said, *I will never understand the female species.*

And before he could say anything, Ava rushed on to an easier topic. "So . . . how long will you be gone?"

"A month," he said.

"A *month*!" Carmen shouted. "How could you leave me so long?"

"This isn't about you, Carm," Ava said. Then, to drive her point home, she served her dad a biscuit and said, "You should go."

"Don't tell Loretta I ate this," he said conspiratorially. Then with a nod, he added, "Carmenita, I am not leaving you. This is a hard time for all of us, and I want us all to be together. We are all going!"

"No!" Ava shouted, then quickly reeled her outburst back in with, "I mean . . . you should go without us." No way could Ava go anywhere right now. Not until everything was settled with her bendición and Nana.

"I won't take no for an answer," Raul said. "I've already bought the tickets and you will love the—"

"Dad," Viv said, wrapping her hand around his as her gaze lifted to meet his eyes. "Ava is right. It's important for you and Loretta to take a vacation without us. We can manage things here. We can use the tickets another time."

Raul narrowed his eyes. "Are you playing me, Viviana?"

Viv wore an expression of utter innocence. "Of course not. Just stating the facts."

And just when Raul looked like he was going to argue, he sat back in his chair and sighed. His expression went from intense and worried to relaxed, maybe even resigned. So *that's* what Viv's blessing looked like in real time. Ava was awestruck.

"Well, maybe *I* want to go," Carmen said.

"Then you should," Viv retorted, calling her bluff.

Carmen shrugged. "Nah. I'll make the sacrifice, because I know you and Loretta need a vacation alone, Dad."

Raul was nodding his agreement as if each second that passed, he was more convinced that this was a brilliant idea. "We have the right people and managers in place," he said. "Plus, we already have next season's catalog finalized, and Viv, you're good with the Hoffman project?"

"We're making awesome progress. And don't worry, Dad. We can keep an eye on things too." But the tone in Viv's voice betrayed the lie. Ava knew Viv didn't want her dad to go, because she worried about him. She always had. *Dad, did you swim your laps today? Did you drink enough water? Lettuce on tacos is not a vegetable, Dad.*

"Yeah," Carm put in. "We'll totally be your spies."

"When do you leave?" Ava asked, curling her toes tightly.

"Sunday morning."

Sunday, Ava thought, *the day after I get my blessing back.*

Nine

After breakfast, Ava replaced her phone and hurried home, where she went into her room, shut the door, and whispered, "Nana? Are you there?"

Ava's mind was doing laps across what felt like a forever ocean, picking up speed and a whole lot of worry that maybe this whole blessing transfer business wasn't going to be as easy as it sounded. And more than ever, Ava just wanted Nana to speak the one line she always did when things got rough: *Todo va a estar bien.* But was it? Was everything going to be okay?

When Nana didn't appear, Ava tried Meda, but all she got was radio silence. At first, she thought she was doing something wrong. Maybe she wasn't talking loud enough. Or maybe she needed to close her eyes and visualize them. Hadn't Nana said, *Just call when you need us*? Seemed simple enough, but it didn't matter what Ava did or how many times she spoke their names, they were MIA, which twisted Ava's stomach into thick knots. *Where are they? What if something bad happened to them? Can bad things happen to saints and spirits? Maybe they didn't have as much time as Nana originally thought?*

All the *what if*s quickly turned into *oh God*s. *Oh God, something bad happened. Oh God, they're not coming back.* Ava knew when the ridiculous illogical part of her brain kicked into high gear, that was coping mechanism número uno, and it was worthless. Yet she couldn't help herself. The ache the words *they're not coming back* created gutted Ava because her brain processed them to sound and feel like: *they've left you.*

But Ava refused to give in to her panic. Nana *had* to come back if she didn't want to turn into an amnesiac ghost. And Nana would never abandon her. Not if she could help it.

On to coping mechanism two: Ava didn't want to be alone. Typically, she would have been at the paper, but Grant had given her the week off for "grieving purposes." She couldn't exactly call him and tell him, "Psych! Don't need it yet."

And the *yet* carried her to the brink of another thought she wasn't ready to embrace. The inevitable goodbye.

So, that left her sisters. When Carmen took off to hang out with boo number two, Ava sought out Viv. Except that her older sister was heading to the office to "pick something up."

"I'll go with you," Ava suggested, thinking it would be good to get out of the house.

"It's okay," Viv said all too quickly. "I won't be long."

"Why are you acting weird?" Ava blurted, spurred by a sudden tension in the air. "Are you hiding something from me?"

"Gree, why would I hide anything from you?" The knot in Ava's gut loosened an inch until Viv punctuated her sentence with a light laugh. A nervous laugh. A laugh that spelled *lie.*

"You tell me."

Viv planted a kiss on the side of Ava's head. "You think too much," she said before she took off.

Ava didn't want to believe that her sister wasn't keeping their blood oath of no secrets and no lies. Nonetheless, she had a weird feeling that Viv was hiding *something*.

And then she remembered her desperate and thoughtless promise to go to confession. Except she hadn't been since she made her first confirmation last year, and it had been terrifying sitting in that dark confessional with only a voice on the other side of the screen, urging her to tell all her secrets like God was hard of hearing or something. Ava thought the church really needed to start online confession. But after a quick, hopeful Google search, she realized she had to make good on her promise and go to confession in person. Eventually.

After mindlessly scrolling through Pinterest for new recipes, ordering new running shoes, baking three dozen oatmeal cookies, and doing everything she could to *not* look at Achilles's Instagram feed, she googled his name, but only came up with the article Viv had already found.

One look, she told herself as she opened Instagram and typed in his name. And there he was: The poster boy for annoying rude behavior. Smiling like he didn't have a care in the world. Water skiing. Snow skiing. Surfing. Sailing. And always giving a thumbs-up. It was infuriating. And then there were the girls. So many of them. Each clinging to him like some kind of life raft. All they had to do was check out his feed to know the guy had a dating shelf life of what? Five days? Ava didn't see the connection. Achilles was only moderately cute, and he had a terrible personality, so how was he getting so many girls?

Ava imagined Achilles's headline. Everyone had one, and they could change daily. Sometimes to pass the time, Ava would write them in her head. "Vivienne Granados: Mind Games." "Achilles North: Fake Hero."

I'm obsessing, she thought, reminding herself of the things she hated about Achilles North: Bad tipper. Bad boyfriend. Bad driver.

Her phone rang, alerting her to a FaceTime call.

Elijah!

Ava's heart raced with jubilant giddiness.

"Where have you been?" were the first words she had spoken to her best friend in twenty-three days. Well, unless you counted that one time they connected for thirteen seconds of half-garbled words that amounted to nothing.

Elijah. Perfect, full-cheeked, thick-browed, bighearted Elijah. "Hey, Aves. Missing me that much?"

If Ava could throw something through the screen, she would have. "No! Yes! Absolutely not. How is it? Tell me everything." She sat up on her bed, propping herself on her elbows. "How long do we have?"

Elijah was in some kind of café that was buzzing with chatter, jazzlike music, and clanking dishes. His face went rigid. "I'm so sorry about . . ." His voice cracked. "Why didn't you tell me about Nana?"

A lump began to throb in Ava's throat. "You're in Peru, and how did you know?"

"Your dad sent me a text," he said. "He knew you wouldn't."

"I didn't want to ruin—"

"Aves—she was my family too."

"I know. I'm sorry," she whispered. "Wait! How did you get the text?"

"A few come through every once in a while, or at least the ones not swallowed by the wastelands of internet service." Then with a sigh, "I guess I was just meant to know."

The noisy café seemed to slip away, and all that was left was a gulf of silence as Ava and Elijah stared at each other through phone screens. Finally, he said, "You doing okay?"

Other than the fact that my grandmother is a ghost and I am on a hunt for a blessing that she accidentally gave away to a jerk?

Ava nodded. "But I don't want to talk about sad stuff when we probably don't have a lot of time. Tell me something happy."

"I don't think—"

"Elijah! Make me feel better."

"You really are bossy."

"And you love me."

"Fine, but before I forget, promise you'll text me. Like, all the time. About anything. It's awesome getting a stray message every once in a while."

"Isn't that like talking to a black hole?"

Elijah pulled a face, then said, "Okay, you want to hear something happy?"

The way his right brow raised and the left corner of his mouth lifted was Ava's first clue. "You met someone!" she nearly shouted.

Elijah blushed and leaned closer. "Can you keep it down? Jesus. You want all of Peru to hear you?"

Ava dropped her voice to a whisper. "You met someone, didn't you?"

Elijah broke into a goofy smile and nodded. "Pierre. He's from London, and you'd like him. He reads biographies and boring shit like that, but I won't hold that against him. I mean he's amazing and, dude, he even got me to climb Machu Picchu."

An enormous feat, Ava thought, given that Elijah was terrified of heights. In the sixth grade, he got stuck on the school roof trying to save a cat and nearly fell off himself. There he was dangling from the railing for fifteen minutes before the fire department showed up, saving both

Elijah and the cat—who he kept and named Death Wish. The whole ordeal scarred him, and ever since he had kept his feet firmly on the ground.

Ava felt the heaviness inside dissipate like a fine mist as she imagined Elijah, her Elijah, finding someone who made him smile like that. Or at least until she remembered the inevitability of love: goodbye. "Do you have a pic?" she asked brightly.

"Didn't you get my letter? I sent you a photo of us at the top of Machu Picchu. Took me a shit ton of time to print it out, never mind the three stores I had to go to for stamps, so you better damn well appreciate it."

A dish smashed somewhere in the café, making Elijah jump.

"No letter. Are you sure you put enough postage?"

Elijah's shoulders collapsed and his mouth fell open. "See? This is why we're friends. So you can save me from myself."

Ava laughed. "So, are you, like, in love with this guy?"

"According to you, love doesn't exist," he said. "It's just a chemical reaction of dopamine. Remember?"

"Well, it is, but I know you don't believe that, so . . ."

Elijah shook his head and snorted. "If you really want to know, it was like this mini explosion in my chest, like my heart dipped and fluttered and seized all at once."

Dipped. Fluttered. Seized. Sounded more like a heart attack. "That sounds painful."

Elijah smirked before his face broke into a wide smile. "And that was only the—"

The café background noise disappeared and, in a flash, Elijah's lovesick face was replaced with his frozen face and half-closed eyes.

Ava jumped onto her knees and waited. "Call back," she said as if she could will the internet gods to smile down on her. She waited another five minutes before realizing Elijah wasn't calling back.

She quickly texted. Only the what?! If you get this, how could a heart do all three at the same time? EXPLAIN. Like I said, chemical reaction! K. Bye.

That brought her to coping mechanism number three: when panic and denial didn't work, there was always the water. Ava threw on a swimsuit, climbed onto her dolphin raft, and floated to the middle of the pool as the sun dipped and the air cooled.

"Nana?" she whispered for the hundredth time. "Meda?"

The only response was the light sea breeze and some rustling leaves. With a deep breath she closed her eyes. But all she saw was *him*.

"Get a grip," she told herself before rolling off the raft and beneath the water. When she was little, Caroline would throw shiny objects into the pool for Ava and her sisters to retrieve. Pennies. Gold bangles. A bottle of glitter nail polish. "You're like mermaids," their mom had said.

But now there were no shiny objects to reach for. Just a warm, watery cocoon that wrapped around Ava in blissful silence.

Until a wink of light flashed across the silver drain. Ava whirled and swam to the surface to see what caused it.

Nana stood at the pool's edge, turning her bracelet around her wrist. Its gold flashed in the sun's rays.

"Where have you been?" Ava cried, swimming to the stairs and filled with so much relief she thought she might cry.

"I'm sorry, mijita. But Meda and I were a bit detained."

"I . . . I've been calling you. Wait, detained?"

Just then Meda appeared, wearing a pair of navy sweats and an ill-fitting LA Chargers T-shirt. "Do you like my new look, Ava?"

Ava didn't have the heart to tell him he had picked a losing team.

Scowling, Nana threw her hands onto her hips. "Tell her why we've been gone so long and why I couldn't answer. Tell her."

"Oh," Meda said brightly, "Well, I wanted to complete research on the blessing, and that took us away so I could talk to some other saints, which is very difficult considering that they are some of the busiest souls in the universe. You should see their lists of prayers. Alas, it took some time and some travel. I truly didn't realize that we would be out of earshot, so to say," he said. "Rules always seem to be changing." He let out a light laugh.

"And what did you find out?" Ava climbed out of the pool and wrapped a towel around herself.

"Well, it appears there are competing points of view, but that is typical of the saints, depending on what century they come from," Meda twisted his beard. "Everyone always wants to be right."

Ava pinched her eyebrows together. "Meda."

Nana said, "It appears that there is consensus on one thing. The blessing cannot be transferred between strangers."

Ava didn't speak for a moment. She was processing the absurdity of it all.

"But we aren't strangers," Ava argued. "I ran into his truck, and he humiliated me. Definitely not strangers."

"Ava, you do not have to do this," Nana said flatly. "I would never force you into anything."

Ava looked from Meda to Nana, realizing the meaning of Nana's words. "You're telling me I have to . . . be his friend?"

Nana took her granddaughter's hands in her own. "It makes sense that emotions would be involved in something this important."

Meda said, "But finding him is the first part of the equation."

Ava rubbed her forehead, staring down at an ant scurrying by, gripping a cracker crumb that looked like it weighed more than the sky. "I found him," Ava said. "He sells oranges at the local farmer's market."

Nana's mouth formed a small O, which quickly morphed into a tenuous smile as Ava explained the market to Meda. She felt nauseous. So, it wasn't just going to be a matter of siphoning off the blessing at the orange stand. This was going to take time, time they might not have. And it was going to take resolve Ava wasn't sure *she* had.

"More challenging duties have been met in the course of history," Meda said confidently, bushy brows furrowed. "Surely you can befriend this boy."

More challenging duties? Yeah, well Meda didn't live in the twenty-first century. What could be worse than faking a friendship with Achilles North?

"And, Ava," Nana said gently, as if she could read her mind.

"Yeah?"

"You cannot fake this. The emotions must be genuine for it to work."

And just like that, Nana answered Ava's *what could be worse* question. Attempting a real friendship with Achilles North. That.

That would be way worse.

Ten

*H*e *probably doesn't even like puppies.*

Or children. Or chocolate chip cookies. Or movies that make you cry, Ava thought as she threw on a pair of workout shorts and a hoodie Saturday morning. She had already changed six times, replaying her sisters' words from last night after she told them about the whole friendship, *real* emotion thing: *Your life sucks,* Carm had said. And Viv went silent, which meant she totally agreed with Carm.

"You do know it's after eight o'clock, right?" Viv said, popping into Ava's room. "Get a move on."

Sullenly, Ava looked around at the piles of black and white clothing on her floor. "What the hell does someone wear to make friends with a tight-wad villain?"

"Armor," Viv said with a smile as she swept into the room like a fairy godmother and plucked clothes off the bed. Ava was glad Viv had canceled a client meeting to go with her on this agonizing quest.

Viv said, "Go with these boyfriend jeans, this cropped tank." She pointed to the floor. "Your AF1s, and you can borrow my new mini Prada bag. It'll say, *I'm simple yet chic, and I didn't try too hard.*"

Ava would never understand the way Viv thought clothes talked to her, the way any and all design had a *story to tell.* To Ava, they were all just things with the single purpose of looking good or bad or invisible.

"I thought you said armor, not summer *Cosmo*," Ava said. "And since when do you approve of boyfriend jeans? You said they're grunge and over-rated."

"They aren't *my* style, but you're not me."

Wanting a second opinion, she said, "Nana? Are you there? What do you think?"

Within two blinks, Nana appeared so close to Ava, Ava tripped over a discarded pile of cashmere, catching herself on the edge of the dresser. Nana shook her head as her eyes swept from one side of the room to the other. "I've been gone one week and mira, your room looks like a cyclone hit it."

"I'll pick it up," Ava promised, "but Viv says I should wear that." She pointed at her sister still holding the jeans and tank.

Viv's eyes darted around the room. "She's here?"

Ava nodded.

"Viviana is right," Nana offered as she gestured to the clothing.

"Styled by Vivienne Granados it is," Ava said with a hint of resignation. Something as easy as getting dressed shouldn't take this much work or thought or strategy.

"Hi, Nana," Viv said cheerfully, looking in the wrong direction. Then, in a low whisper to Ava, "This is so awkward. How do you talk to a ghost?"

"The same as you would if you could see her."

"Mira," Nana said, motioning to Viv. "See how well her classic, tailored clothes drape across her body? Look at those cropped linen pants and the fitted tank top that shows off her lithe arms. And the—"

"Okay. I get it," Ava groaned. "Viv is a fabulous dresser." *If you're forty!*

Smiling smugly, Viv plunked onto the bed, tossing a bra out of the way. "Nana always did have impeccable taste."

"Gracias, mija." Nana said to Viv, which Ava quickly relayed as Nana gave her a once-over and added, "Meda and I will meet you at the market. Ándele." And then she was gone.

Ava quickly changed into Viv's recommended outfit sans the bag, because who carries a tiny Prada bag to a farmer's market? Try-hards who don't need both hands, that's who. Instead, she opted to stuff some cash and gloss into her pockets, then put on one more light coat of mascara before throwing her hair into a messy low bun. Ordinarily, she'd wear a baseball cap, but Viv always said hats spoke volumes. And ratty caps? They told the world, *Hey, don't talk to me.* Not exactly the right message when you're trying to make friends with Mr. Rude himself.

The sisters had decided Carmen shouldn't come, given that Achilles might recognize her from Instagram and that could blow this whole thing up. Of course, Carmen played up her sacrifice, saying things like, "I'd rather set myself on fire than miss this." She stood in the driveway barefoot, waving with a pouty face as Viv and Ava pulled away in Viv's Range Rover.

Ava hung her head out the window. "We love you, Carm."

"Don't come back to this house until you have him wrapped around your finger," Carm said, tightening the belt of her fuzzy robe.

A minute later Viv and Ava were cruising down Fourth Ave. with the sunroof back. The cool gray sky would burn off soon enough, but for now, Ava enjoyed the calm quiet of a non-blue, nondemanding sky.

"So, you know what to say?" Viv said.

"We've been over it a million times," Ava groaned. "I'm going to act surprised to run into him and then I'll tell him I'm really sorry for running into his car. Next, I thank him for telling me to go so quickly, because I got to say goodbye to Nana." Surely knowing her grandmother died would melt even the coldest of player hearts. "And then maybe I'll buy an orange or two. Or should I buy the oranges first?"

"Play it by ear," Viv said, nodding her approval as she glanced over. "And smile, for God's sake. You look like someone being led to their death."

"I feel like it. I mean, come on. Real emotion? How is that ever going to happen?" Ava closed her eyes, feeling neurotic just thinking about it. "And I don't know if I'm going to get *almost nice guy* from that first night or *mega-jerk*, which makes this even worse."

"Be prepared for jerk. But, hey . . . you can always find something to like in someone," Viv said. "Want some pump-up music? Hip-hop? Rap? *Rocky*?"

Ava shook her head, feeling like she was going to throw up as she went through the music on her new phone, trying to find the perfect battle song.

"Just remember why you're doing this," Viv said.

For Nana, Ava reminded herself. Ava could make friends with the devil if it meant freeing her grandmother from an afterlife of wandering and forgetting.

Stopped at a light, Viv scrolled through her phone, and a second later "Greased Lightning" boomed out of the speakers. Ava laughed, and the two sang and did their best movie-night choreography for the next few miles until they arrived.

The market was already bustling with morning customers. Wisps of lemon, peach, lavender, and honey wafted through the air as Viv and Ava strolled down Second Ave. in search of Achilles.

Ava stopped near a flower stall. "I think I should look like a real shopper," she said, hurrying over to another booth to buy a couple of tomatoes and avocados.

"You're stalling," Viv said, taking the sack of produce from her. "Call Nana."

"I'm not stalling," Ava argued. "Believe me, I want to get this over with as fast as possible. But I do really like avocados."

"Friendship is never as fast as possible," Viv said. "Now come on . . . adjust the attitude. You might be in this for the long haul, and the sooner you accept that, the easier this will be."

"Let's see if you're saying that once you really see who he is."

Viv always had really good zingers, one-liners, and pep talks . . . except for today. Or maybe Ava just didn't want to hear it, because she knew her own heart wasn't in it. And adjusting an attitude was one thing, adjusting a heart was entirely something else.

But for Nana, I have to be all in.

Ava glanced around at the crowd, then under her breath said, "Nana? Meda?"

The saint and the ghost appeared at her side. Meda was still sporting his Chargers gear, except now he wore a matching cap too. He looked around at the market, threw his head back, and took in a deep inhalation. "Glorious. Magnificent. Superb. Do you smell that fresh sourdough bread?"

Nana stepped closer. Her eyes slid down Ava's face, then back up. "Are you ready, corazón?"

Ava fought the sinking feeling in her stomach. "Ready as I'll ever be."

They made their way down the row, searching for the orange booth. As they walked, Meda went on and on about how beautiful all the produce was, reminding him of a serene summer he spent in Provence before he was a saint.

A minute later, Ava spotted Achilles. In the morning light, his skin glowed with a perfect tan. He was wearing a bright yellow apron with green lettering: MAGGIE'S ORCHARD. His light brown hair was combed back neatly, and he wore an earnest expression so unlike the guy who almost got her run over the other night. He was flashing a genuine smile at a customer as he handed over some change.

"There he is," Ava said, stopping in her tracks.

"He looks quite presentable," Nana said with a tone of approval that made Ava want to gag.

"That's him?" Viv said. "He looks so . . . so . . . nice."

"Yeah, well, looks can be deceiving," Ava suggested, but she was deeply clinging to the hope that Viv and Nana were right. Maybe deep down he *was* presentable. And nice. After all, he did let her rush off to her grandmother's deathbed, but then, what kind of a monster wouldn't?

"You are quite right," Meda put in, "he does look pleasant."

"Okay, guys," Ava groaned. "I don't need everyone going all Team Achilles so soon." And then it hit her. "Meda, you said you would see a faint aura of light around my head if I had the blessing, so does that mean you can see it around his head? I mean, we might as well make sure before I have to go over there and . . ."

But Meda was already shaking his head. "I'm not sure. Maybe?"

That was not reassuring.

"But," he quickly added, "if you touch him, I might see the blessing trying to connect to you, if that makes sense. I might also see nothing."

The ghost, the saint, and Viv all stared at Ava expectantly as if to say, *Go and get 'em.*

I'm going to be a damn journalist. I can do this. I can totally do this. She pushed her shoulders back, smacked her glossy lips together, and said, "I totally got this." It was a facade, of course. She didn't have anything but a million butterflies in her stomach. And not because she was scared of

Achilles, but because she couldn't afford to mess this up.

"Want me to go with you?" Viv asked, as if sensing her sister's reluctance.

Ava shook her head. "He might get weird or feel ganged up on if there are two of us."

"Too bad I can't just *persuade* him to be your friend," Viv lamented. "Save you all this trouble."

"This must be natural," Nana reminded them.

"And above all, it must be genuine," Meda said as he went over to the booth and poked at the oranges while sticking his face into the bins.

"I'll stay close by," Viv promised. "Over there by the herb booth. Throw a wave if you get into trouble."

"I'm not going into war."

"Always expect the unexpected," Viv said.

Ava looked to her grandmother, whose warm brown eyes were filled with sympathy and love. "I'll be right by your side, mijita."

Together, they walked toward the booth.

Eleven

Ava was moving toward Achilles North, one foot in front of the other. She felt like she was on some kind of forced autopilot, repeating the script she had been playing in her head for the last hour. Before she knew it, she was standing in front of the bins as Achilles finished with another customer.

"These look delicious," Nana said just as Achilles ventured over.

"What can I help you with?" he said with an easygoing flair that immediately put Ava on greater guard.

Acting nonchalant, Ava kept her gaze averted and on the fruit. "Uh . . . can I try one?"

From the corner of her eye she could see Achilles slicing open an orange and cutting it into smaller pieces before handing her a wedge. "Best anywhere," he said.

"If only I could taste one," Meda said, as Ava took the sample and sucked the pulp out. Achilles's taste in fruit was definitely on point. The orange was sweet, delicious, and totally divine.

Look up. Look up. Just. Look. Up.

Slowly, Ava lifted her gaze. Achilles stared. She stared back, waiting for that sign in his eyes that he recognized her. "Did you want some?" he asked, both eyebrows darting up.

Ava felt off-kilter. She had been so sure he would remember her. How could he not? Unless this was just some game he had in his arsenal to torment her further. "Two pounds, please," she said, suddenly unable to remember her script.

As Achilles reached for a paper sack, Ava lowered her head and whispered to Nana, "He doesn't recognize me." The plan was based on him recognizing her! Ava sucked at pivoting. At improvisation. It was the one area of journalism she was still trying to pin down.

"Well, make him remember," Nana said in a low tone, as if anyone else could hear her.

Ava gave her grandmother a sidelong glance edging on a glare. Then, turning her attention back to the task at hand, she said to Achilles. "You look really familiar."

"I get that a lot."

Ava's stomach turned. *Look for something to like. Anything.*

"What's your name?" she asked. Alarm bells were screaming in her head, *This is not the script.*

"What's *your* name?"

Putting her ego in check, she managed, "Ava."

Another customer came up just then, asking Achilles a million questions about the farm's organic certification. He answered them all cool and calm and collected, but with a hint of boredom, like he had spoken the same words a million and one times before. Ava reached for the oranges in front of her, not bothering to squeeze or sniff them as she stuffed them into the paper sack.

Meda was eavesdropping on Achilles's conversation, nodding diligently like he had never heard a more scintillating topic than organic orange farming. Achilles was still chatting it up with the inquisitor a couple minutes later, and before Ava knew it, she had filled the entire bag. "Um, excuse me," she said, interrupting his convo. "How much do I owe you?"

"Be calm," Nana urged. "You look like an overexcited Chihuahua."

Ava took a deep breath, realizing that of course Nana was right. But she couldn't stop the process of quiver, shake, bounce. Repeat.

Ava was sure Achilles could see her trembling. He nodded at her, held up an annoying finger, finished his discussion with the customer who bought nada, then quickly weighed the bag before setting it back in front of Ava. "You said two pounds. This is five and a half."

"Sure. Okay. I'll take all of them."

"That'll be thirty dollars."

Ava reached into her pocket and tugged out the money. Meda stood right next to her, clearing his throat. Okay, this was it. One touch. That's all. She handed over the bills and as he took them, she gripped his hand.

Surprise registered in his eyes. He tried to release her hand, but she tightened her grasp, desperately searching for an excuse as to why she was practically accosting the guy.

"Don't let go," Meda said. "Just one second more."

But Achilles had already broken free. He wiped his hand on his apron like she was some kind of pariah. "What's your deal?"

"Deal?" She feigned ignorance, quickly changing the subject, "So . . . how long have you been growing oranges?"

"Forever." He set her change on the table.

Ava pointed to the sign. "Who's Maggie?"

"That's a secret."

Ava thought he might smile, laugh, smirk to tell her he was kidding, but he stayed straight-faced. "Like your name," she said, channeling Carmen, including the playful smile. "You never told me."

"I know."

Did this guy go to whatever the opposite of etiquette school was? Rude school? How-to-be-a-jerk school? How-to-repel-fellow-humans school?

He pointed to the badge planted right above his heart. "That's because it's right here."

Ava faked a laugh. How in the hell had she missed *that*? She was an investigative journalist, for God's sake. She was all about detail, nuances, and hidden meanings. "Achilles," she managed. Then choked out, "Like the hero."

"Or the god."

"Half god," Ava muttered before realizing she had actually said the words.

Achilles snorted.

Nana sighed. "I take back the pleasant comment."

Meda groaned. "Ava, perhaps you should just get to the point."

"Meda's right," Nana said softly.

Ava wanted desperately to show her grandmother and the saint that she could do this, that maybe she wasn't built for fancy footwork, but she was definitely built to succeed. So maybe she wasn't going to get to cling to him long enough for Meda to get an accurate blessing read, but that could come later. After she befriended him. Clenching her fists, she forced out, "Hey, you're that guy . . . oh my gosh, I *thought* you looked familiar."

"I have no idea what you mean," he said.

Was she going to have to spell it out for him? "The other night," she said. "I ran into your car. At the stop sign. During the storm."

His dark eyes swept across her face, then down her neck and back up. A small smile played on his very mediocre lips. For a moment Ava thought she saw recognition there.

"This is the part where you tell him 'thank you,'" Nana urged. "¿Recuerdas? Offer him a coffee or flan or something."

"I . . . I got to say goodbye," Ava rushed on, "and I just want to thank you. Maybe buy you a coffee or something."

He was still wearing that stupid smirk disguised as a smile. "You crashed into my car." It wasn't a question.

"Exactly."

"Right," he said, nodding as his annoying hand moved back and forth across his clean-shaven chin like a principal deciding how to dole out punishment. Clearing his throat, he said, "Except you've got the wrong guy. I wasn't rear-ended the other night. Or any night actually."

Ava was about to argue vehemently that it might have been dark but no way could she forget his suddenly dull face. He snapped his fingers and pointed at her. "Wait a sec."

Finally!

"You're the stalker chick," he said with something that sounded like a chuckle. "The one from the restaurant waving at me."

Ava imagined herself as a ridiculous cartoon melting into a puddle.

Nana made a sound halfway between a sigh and a groan. Meda rubbed his chin. "He is quite disagreeable."

"Ya think?" Ava said, which only drew a curious stare from Achilles, who must have thought she was answering his question.

"Uh, actually I know you're her," Achilles said, hiking a thick brow so high it nearly touched his hairline.

Ava dug deep. Deeper than she ever had. "So, do you want the coffee or not?" Yikes. She hadn't meant to sound so . . . so forceful.

"You're trying to ask me out now?" He visibly cringed.

"No, not out like *that*," Ava tried again, even though her ego was dying a slow and painful death inside her.

He frowned, folded his arms across his chest, and narrowed his eyes. "Are you *following* me?"

A diminutive blonde came up to the booth then. Oh God, she was the same one from the other night. Achilles's eyes lit up as she swept behind the table and threw herself into his arms with a squeal so high-pitched she could have called dolphins to shore.

"Hey, baby," Achilles said, smiling down at her. "Do you remember this girl? Ava, was it?" he said, sweeping his eyes back to Ava. "She was the one staring at me from the street the other night and waving all weirdlike." Then, in a mock-low voice, "I think she's stalking me."

Ava felt the heat of a thousand suns burning her cheeks, neck, and chest. Under normal circumstances, she would have thrown an orange into his smug face and stalked off, but these circumstances, were desperate. How was she ever going to get him to like her, to be her friend when he was so clearly repulsed by her?

"Ha!" Ava attempted a good-humored response but ended up sounding like a small animal choking on a cracker. "I'm not following you. I shop here all the time. The market. Not *here* at the booth here."

"Baby" scowled at Ava while Achilles went on as if Ava wasn't even standing there. "She wants to take me out for coffee, but . . ." He slung his arm over the perky blonde's shoulders. "I told her I had a girlfriend."

But that didn't stop you from messaging my sister, Ava wanted to scream. Her blood was boiling. She imagined shoving an orange down his throat until he drew his last deceitful, arrogant breath.

Ava planned to say, *You have it all wrong. I just want to be friends*, but what came out was, "I could totally make you go out with me!" She instantly regretted the words. "I mean my sister could make you ... I mean ..."

Baby's scowl melted into an expression of total pity, as if to say, *You should stop talking now.* But Achilles showed minus-zero pity. Actually, he wore an expression of pure entertainment.

"We should go," Nana suggested, and there was no mistaking the disappointment in her voice.

"You must feel so deflated, Ava," Meda said, shaking his head. "And dispirited. Maybe defunct. But it's all right. We can try again another time. We still have several weeks."

"Keep the change," Ava said awkwardly, as she grabbed the sack of oranges and spun away. She ran down the row, nearly tripping over a woman pushing a stroller. Nana was calling her name. Meda was shouting, "He's merely a scoundrel."

Viv shouted, "Wait up!"

Ava kept running, holding tight to the ridiculous bag. Her eyes blurred with angry tears.

I hate Achilles North. We will never be friends. Ever.

And the reality of the pathetic truth was like a dagger to the heart.

The edges of the world pulsed, receded, advanced.

And then ... as if things couldn't get any worse, someone stumbled right into her path. She lost her footing, tripped. The oranges flew out into the air, tumbling down on Ava, who was now on her butt.

Quickly, she rolled to her knees. The asphalt bit into them as she tried to desperately collect the fruit. That's when she heard a guy's voice. "Crap. I didn't see you. I'm really sorry. Are you okay?"

Ava looked up, ready to give this guy a piece of her mind. She froze. Those eyes. The nose. That sun-kissed face.

His not-so-mediocre mouth moved slowly. "It's *you*."

Ava sat on her mother's lap while Caroline's hands danced airily through her hair, weaving a French braid. "The princess," she said, "didn't know how to choose a prince. How could she, when she knew her kiss would kill him? But the night of the selection ball came anyway. She danced with every suitor until her feet throbbed and her heart ached. She found them all so boring, so similar, she couldn't even tell them apart.

"'It's time to choose,' her mother told her.

"'I can't.'

"'If you want to be queen, you must.'

"The princess ran. She ran from the ball and into the gardens, deep into the snowy labyrinth, where she fell onto a bench and began to cry.

"The full moon stared. The night sky sighed. The stars waited."

Ava turned her small face to her mother's and asked the same question she always asked. "That's so sad, Mommy. Why does she have to be queen?"

"It was her fate." *Caroline kissed the tip of Ava's nose and went on.*

"And then a boy, the gardener's son, appeared and said, 'Why are you crying?'

"The princess looked up into his warm brown eyes and told him, 'I don't want to be a murderer.'"

Twelve

I t was him.

Storm guy. Identical in every way to Achilles, except *not* Achilles. In point five seconds Ava's brain made this deduction based on two facts: First, Achilles couldn't be in two places at once. Second, this guy had stubble on his jaw, unlike Achilles.

"Are you okay?" the guy repeated. He helped Ava to her feet. His hands were calloused and rough. Solid and cool to the touch.

She gave a quick nod. "I'm fine."

Meda appeared next to her, standing taller than usual. "Ava." But Ava was too busy going after the runaway oranges that people were already stooping to retrieve for her. She thanked them as Not Achilles swept up the rolling fruit, lugging them back to the bag.

Nana appeared right next to the guy, so close that he nearly ran right through her. She studied him suspiciously and then let out a long breath as the recognition became apparent in her pinched brows. "Twins! Ay Dios— qué suerte."

Meda said, "Ava—"

"You think it's lucky?" Ava cried.

"Er . . . I didn't say anything about luck?" the guy said.

Meda drew up right next to Ava, placing his face mere inches from hers.

"Ava," he tried again, this time more forcefully. "He . . ." The saint pointed like a well-trained crossing guard. "*He* is the one. The blessing is all over him. I saw it when he helped you to your feet. We have found it! What success. What good fortune." He tugged on his NFL shirt proudly. "What saintly skill!"

Ava's heart skipped one, two, three beats before she could even out her breathing. She fought the urge to smile and revel in the fact that she had found the right guy, and even better? He wasn't jerk-face Achilles.

Nana looked pleased, but she withheld a full celebratory smile. Probably because she knew as well as Ava that there was still a long road to travel.

"Remember to make friends with him," Meda reminded Ava, as if she could forget. "But do it better than you did with his twin."

Plucking one of the oranges from the asphalt, Ava said, "Thanks for your help."

"They're everywhere," the guy said, sweeping past Ava to retrieve another orange like a kid on a scavenger hunt.

"Can you guys just let me handle this . . . alone?" she whispered to Nana and Meda.

"But what if you get into trouble?" Nana asked.

"You will need our wisdom," Meda put in.

"I'll call if I need you."

Nana sighed, taking Meda by the hand as the two vanished.

At the same moment, Ava saw Viv rushing toward her. Ava gave her the nonverbal bug-eyed, clenched jaw cue of *not now*, which halted her sister in her tracks. Viv's gaze settled on Not Achilles. Confusion washed across her face as she glanced down the row at Maggie's booth then back again before mouthing, *Oh my God!*

"I'm Rion, by the way," the guy said. "And this is the last one." He set the orange in the bag victoriously and pushed his hair back. "But one got away."

Ava clung to the sack, holding it in front of her chest like armor. "I'm Ava . . . and . . ." Maybe it was the shock of the moment, but her mouth accidentally spit out, "You have a twin." Then, seeing how he stiffened like someone bracing himself to get punched in the gut, she gestured to the oranges awkwardly. "I just bought these from him."

"You should have waited for me," he said casually, letting his words hang for an instant. His expression was unreadable. One eyebrow raised, the left side of his mouth pulled back to reveal a tiny almost-dimple. A cross between confused and . . . playful? "I would have given you a discount."

Think nice. Think pleasant.

Ava smiled, then, trying to match his demeanor and tone, she relaxed her shoulders and said, "Can I still have the discount?"

"All sales are final."

There was a long and uncomfortable pause like he was waiting for Ava to say something, but her mind was drawing a blank. God, the pressure of trying to make someone you don't know your friend was draining.

"Oh. Okay," Ava finally said, trying to keep the conversation going. *Go by the script.* Except that the script didn't account for everything going off the rails with Achilles, or twins. Or slamming into Rion for the second time. She needed to leave here today with his phone number. With an excuse to call him. To see him again. "What if the oranges are bruised?" she said. "Do I get a refund?"

"Oranges don't really bruise, or not very easily," he said, keeping his gaze on the fruit. "Their skin protects them."

What was Ava supposed to say to that? She could play the doe-eyed girl: *I had no idea. Tell me more about this amazing citrus.* Or she could channel Carmen and just dive in: *Well, you should give me your number just in case.*

"So . . ." he began just as Ava blurted, "So, your brother gets stuck with a name like Achilles and you—"

"It's Orion," he said, cutting his eyes back to Ava as if he was expecting some kind of reaction. When she didn't give him one, he added, "My family has a thing for constellations."

Constellations. Stars! Was that what Nana meant? Ava wondered, when Rion said, "Lucky for me, my name can be shortened, but Achilles?" Rion nearly grinned. "He couldn't exactly go by Kill, or Ache."

Couldn't he?

A bubble of laughter rose in Ava's chest, but she bit the side of her cheek, forcing it back down just in case Rion wasn't kidding. Laughing at a non-joke would be a really lousy way to start a friendship.

Ava tried to think of something witty or engaging or interesting to say next. Viv always told her that people just want to talk about themselves, and when in doubt give them a compliment. But what could she say? *Nice jeans? Nice smile? You're taller than I remember?* She decided on "You definitely got the better name."

Rion didn't skip a beat. Actually, he didn't even seem like he had heard the compliment. "I'm glad I ran into you."

Ava shifted the bag into one arm. "You are?"

"I've been wondering if you . . ." He glanced around, leading her out of the flow of the crowd to the sidewalk near an ATM. "I was wondering if you made it . . . to say goodbye."

Ava studied Rion, searching for even the smallest of physical differences between him and his brother, but she came up short. They looked identical in every single way except for the scruff. As a matter of fact, she had never seen twins so perfectly identical in her life.

"I did," Ava said, then rushed ahead to the next part of her script. "And I . . . I want to thank you. I made it just in time."

"So . . . your grandmother . . ."

"Nana's gone," Ava confirmed, instantly wincing because Nana and Meda materialized just then, beaming like eager beavers that they were invited back so soon. Ava wanted so badly to tell them she didn't call them and that she had this under control, but how could she when Rion was standing right there?

"Oh, hey, I'm sorry," Rion said, and he looked like he genuinely meant it. Not like so many of the people from the funeral who seemed to just say words without *feeling* them.

Nana sized Rion up and down like she was inspecting a racehorse. "I think you're right, Meda. I can almost sense my blessing inside him. Is there any chance you can see what it is?"

"I don't have X-ray vision like that one character. What's his name? Captain America?"

"Who is Captain America?" Nana said.

"It's Superman," Ava groaned, regretting her lack of control that probably made her look like an instant weirdo.

Rion tilted his head to one side. "Huh?"

"Oh, um . . ." Ava could feel her cheeks warming. Why couldn't Nana have sent her to ad-libbing school instead of etiquette school? "It's a thing I say . . . my Nana taught me . . ." This was coming out all wrong.

"Like an inside family thing," Rion said.

"Exactly!"

Nana said, "Just invite him out."

"Yes," Meda put in, "before you say or do something that makes him change his mind about you."

"Well," Rion said, squinting against the day's first bit of sun peering out from a passing cloud. "That's good that you got to say goodbye."

"And to thank you," Ava plowed ahead, "can I buy you a coffee or . . ." She had meant to say a bagel, but at the same moment Nana said, "You could go for flan," and somehow it flew right into Ava's brain and out her mouth as if the idea were her own. "Or flan."

Nana palmed her forehead.

"Flan," Rion said without changing his absolutely unreadable expression.

Ava could feel the heat rush to her cheeks. "I mean—"

"I love flan. When?"

"Now," Meda urged, nudging Ava's elbow.

"Good idea," Nana said. "The sooner the better."

"Tonight," Ava suggested, regaining her footing. She needed to go home, gather herself, lick her wounds, and most of all, she needed to confer with her sisters.

Rion gazed up at the sky like he was thinking of all the other things he could be doing or would rather be doing on a Saturday night. Then, looking back at Ava, he said, "Yeah. Okay." And for a second he sounded surprised by his own agreement. "Do you know a good flan place?"

Ava unloaded the bag of oranges clunkily onto Rion so she could fish her cell out of her pocket. "What's your number? I'll text you the time and place."

With his free hand, Rion took her phone and entered his number. "But you can't text me."

Ava shot him a confused look. "Why?"

"My phone's got problems, like missing letters, apostrophes in the middle of words." He gave a single shoulder shrug. "So, if you don't want me to end up at the wrong place, you should probably just call me."

"Seriously? You don't text?"

"My *phone* doesn't text," he corrected.

"Why don't you get it fixed?"

"If it's not important enough to call, it's probably not that important."

"Okay," she said, feeling triumphant. "I'll call you."

Rion released the bag back into her arms. "You should give me your number too. I'm really bad at answering numbers I don't know."

Ava hesitated. *Friends share numbers. Lighten up.* She dialed his number. When his phone vibrated, he answered, "Hello?"

Ava laughed.

"Okay, then," Rion said, pocketing his phone. "See you tonight."

"See you tonight," she echoed.

As he turned to walk away, a sudden panic coursed through Ava. *I found the guy . . . who has my blessing.* It was what she wanted, what she *needed*, but now she realized that the hard part hadn't even begun. She still had to create a *genuine* friendship before she could take the blessing back.

But how do you build something genuine when the premise is a big fat lie?

Thirteen

Ava headed to the corner, lugging her five and a half pounds of over-priced, organic, unbruisable oranges. Her mind was on hyperdrive, bouncing her thoughts around like a Whac-A-Mole with each step.

I found him.

Step.

It's going to be okay. Nana is going to be okay.

Step. Step.

He's nice. Step. Step. Step.

And then cartoon Ava walked into a brick wall. *Did I really suggest flan?*

Ava halted. Shook her head. She needed to get a grip on herself and her runaway mind. It was time to invite logic back to the party. So, she made a quick list of factual observations:

1. He's chill enough to say yes to flan with a stranger. Could also mean he's a killer waiting to pounce.

2. He was thoughtful to ask about Nana. But he could also just be nosy.

3. His calloused hands could mean manual labor, or weight lifter? But he was skinny, so probs no to pumping iron.

4. He must not have a lot of friends if he has no texting. And if he has no friends, he could also be a killer.

A horn startled Ava out of her trance. Her gaze followed the sound down the side street. Carmen was poking half her body out of the Rover's sunroof, still wearing her fuzzy robe, smiling, waving, and shouting, "Did you wrap him around your little finger?"

Ava hurried over and hopped into the car, feeling like a criminal fleeing a bank robbery. "Do you really have to shout it to the whole neighborhood? And why are you here?"

"Viv texted me and told me about the plot twist, and I *died*, so she picked me up. Tell me, did you or did you not?" Carmen asked, settling back into the front seat.

"No . . ." Ava said, putting the sack of oranges next to her in the back seat. The scent of fresh citrus filled the car. "But he agreed to meet me for flan tonight."

"Flan?" Viv wrinkled her nose playfully, pulling away from the curb.

"Don't ask."

Carmen buckled her seat belt and huffed. "I can't believe I missed all the fun. And that I messaged the wrong guy! Ugh! I feel like telling Achilles off." With her fingers hovering over her phone, she asked, "What's Mr. Blessing's name?"

"Orion," Ava said, "but he goes by Rion for short."

A second later, Carmen stretched her legs onto the dashboard. "Looks like he doesn't have Instagram. How are we going to stalk him if he doesn't have social media?"

Ava felt herself smiling. *Of course he doesn't have social media. He doesn't even have a smartphone.* She loved the fact that Rion didn't post his life on Instagram, that he didn't have a need to, unlike his brother, who posted the most obnoxious highlight reel that screamed, *Look how great I am. No, really. Look!*

"Oh my God!" Viv nearly shouted. "What if that's what Nana meant by *stars*? He's named after a constellation!"

Meteors, stars, 8:51. Collision. And the hummingbird.

"Right," Ava said, "So we know meteors have to do with the deadline, and 8:51 is the time of the collision. But what the heck does *hummingbird* mean?"

"We'll figure it out," Carm said, tapping her toes happily on the dashboard to the beat of some sad country love song. "But you can't deny that this is all playing out to Fate's tune."

Ava found herself rolling her eyes as she watched the world pass by outside the window. It wasn't fate. The future wasn't set in stone. Ava had choices. She *chose* to look for Rion. She chose to go to the market today. It was hard work and good old-fashioned digging that had brought her to this point. Not some elusive idea that people cling to so they can make sense of their world.

And yet.

The whisper rose up inside her. And as much as she wanted to shove it back down, she knew the next words before they emerged: *And yet what would have happened if I hadn't run into Rion? I would still think Achilles had my blessing, and I might be gouging out my eyes by now. Coincidence*, she told herself, doubling down on her belief that fate *did not exist*.

Viv adjusted her sunglasses. "Flan will have to happen after dinner with Dad. Reservations at Nobu, six o'clock, since he's leaving at the crack of dawn."

"I swear he has a thing for dramatic goodbyes," Carmen said.

"You spot it, you got it," Viv said.

"Nobu?" Ava cried, "That could take two hours!"

Viv smiled into the rearview mirror. "Dude, you're not going to turn into a pumpkin at midnight."

That wasn't the problem. The problem was sitting on her nerves for the eternity of Saturday.

Ava spent the next two hours retelling all the details to her sisters, and with each pass, and each sister, the story grew bigger and bigger until Achilles was Diablo in the flesh and the market was overrun with demon oranges on legs. The sisters howled with laughter, gripping their sides, begging each other to stop. The laughter, the ease, the unbounded joy reminded Ava of their childhood, of simpler times. Before their mom had up and left them.

Before she told Ava the words that Ava had still never repeated.

Tonight's script came next. Only to be scrapped. Then came another. And another. And another. But no matter what, it was wrong. All wrong.

"I just want to be myself," Ava finally said as she swam to the edge of the pool.

"No!" Carmen screeched from a lounger. "You cannot be yourself."

"Rude," Ava said, insulted. "Why not?"

"Everything is a negotiation," Carm reasoned. "Everything is a give and take, an act, a way to manage your image. You have to know what your brand is before you even sit down with him. And just remember, being yourself got you flan."

"Being myself got me a yes," Ava retorted. "And Nana said it has to be genuine."

Viv cleared her throat, already nodding her agreement. "I think you should be as natural as possible, but with a bit more . . ." She hesitated, looking up at the underside of the navy umbrella above her. "With more, you know . . . niceness."

"I am nice!"

"But you don't let a lot of people see it, Gree," Viv said, tossing her sister an oversized towel. "All I'm saying is be open. Try to relax. This is about trust."

What Viv meant was, *You don't let a lot of people see you.*

Carm sprang upright. "Trust? Seriously? She doesn't even know him, and trust makes you . . ." She hesitated and gave that *what?* look she always gave when she knew she had stepped in it. Ava could guess the words that didn't leave Carmen's mouth: *weak, vulnerable, pathetic.* All of the above.

Ava lifted herself out of the pool, dried off, and sat in a wicker chair staring at her phone. "Should I call him now or wait?" She had already selected her favorite Mexican restaurant near the Third Street Promenade. It had two things going for it: The place was open until midnight. And she had been eating there since she was a toddler, which made it feel like home.

"Friends don't play games," Viv said resolutely. "Just call him."

Carm tugged off her shades. "Don't listen to her. Everything is a game. I mean, no offense, Viv, but it's not like you've had a lot of boyfriends, or, you know . . . had my extensive experience in romance."

"Mm-hmm . . . poor me," Viv mumbled sarcastically.

Boyfriend? Ava was definitely fired up now. "Who said anything about a boyfriend?"

"You know what I mean," Carm said nonchalantly.

Viv gave Carmen a long hard stare and looked like she was going to take her down a few notches with a brilliant retort but must have thought the better of it, because she looked back to Ava. "It's up to you. But it's already three o'clock, and he *is* expecting your call, *and* he's already said yes. Just pretend like you're calling Elijah."

"Friends," Ava insisted with a scowl as she dialed his number. *Nana said friends!* Her sisters' dark eyes were pinned to her like hawks surveying their prey. One ring. Two. Five. "He's not answering," Ava said. Then Rion's voice echoed in her ear. "You know what to do." The long, hard beep sent her heart plummeting as her mind raced toward the worst-case scenario. *He's changed his mind.* She was about to hang up when her mouth betrayed her. "It's me . . . Ava," she stuttered. "Um . . . I guess call me back. Okay. Bye."

Carm's face fell. "You *guess*?"

And then, as if Viv knew what everyone was thinking—*why didn't he answer?*—she said, "He might be in the shower, or maybe his phone is on mute. I'm sure he'll call back."

"Or maybe he got in an accident on the way home," Carmen suggested, clearly annoyed that Ava didn't know how to play her *image negotiation whatever* game.

Ava grabbed the beach ball at her feet and hauled it back like she was going to torpedo Carmen when her sister recoiled. "It was a joke, Ava. Geez. Cálmate. I'm sure he's not in the hospital in a coma. But can you imagine?" Her voice trailed off on a note of intrigue.

Just then Ava's phone rang. Rion's name flashed across the screen. "It's him!" she said, nearly dropping the cell.

"Let it ring three times before answering," Carmen instructed.

Just to show Carmen she wasn't her puppet, Ava let it ring only twice. "Hello?"

"Hey," Rion said, sounding a little out of breath. "I left my phone on the ground."

Ground? Ava was trying to put the image together when Rion added, "I was in a tree. Checking on some oranges."

The mental image expanded to him rushing down the tree like a monkey. "Oh, okay," she said. "Well, are we still—"

"I've been thinking about flan all day," he said, and there was a smile in his voice. She turned away from her sisters, liberating her own smile that had been building as she quickly relayed the name of the restaurant. "Eight thirty work?"

"Yeah. I've been there," he said. "Okay. See you then."

After Ava hung up, Viv smirked. "See how easy that was?"

Everything was going according to plan. Or at least until Ava had to pick an outfit appropriate for Malibu's trendiest restaurant *and* one of Santa Monica's most casual. She finally settled on a black tank dress. Not too tight, not too short, and with a leather jacket she could put on before she met Rion. She stood in front of the full-length mirror in her closet and tried her best to ignore the thought creeping into the edge of her awareness.

Easy. According to plan.

That's what worried Ava. Whenever things were easy, it usually meant the other shoe was going to drop.

"It's going to be fine," she said, thinking she had covered all her bases. She had already talked to Nana and Meda earlier in the day, and they had promised to stay away tonight so she wouldn't be too self-conscious. Or look like she was talking to someone who wasn't there.

"But you call if you need me," Nana said, as if Ava needed reminding. "And no olvides," Nana added. "Be natural. Genuine."

After two hours of the beautiful Malibu coastline, a sashimi salad, yellow-tail, black cod, and vegetable tempura, Ava patted her dad's arm. "Gotta go now."

"So soon?"

"She's meeting a boy," Carmen teased, just as she popped a piece of spicy tuna into her traitorous mouth.

Raul's eyes flicked to Ava's. And he had that concerned dad look he always got when it came to his youngest. "You said you were meeting a friend. You didn't say anything about a boy."

"He *is* just a friend, Dad," Ava said, wishing that she were not only sitting next to Carmen but that she were wearing stiletto heels instead of her flat sandals, so she could impale her sister's toes one at a time.

"Do I know this boy?" Raul asked. His eyebrows were lifted and his chin was tense. His dad radar was about to go off.

"You've never met him," Ava said, fumbling for the right balance between casual and respectful. "Maybe when you come back." *Stop talking.* "He's really nice." *Stop. Talking.*

Then Carm redeemed herself with, "His family owns an orchard in San Fernando Valley."

And just like that, Raul Granados's face melted into the familiar open expression that said, *Oh, business owners? Go ahead, mija.* Ava could recite her dad's words verbatim. *Business ownership takes hard work, and hard work takes discipline, character, and accountability.* And above all, he respected those traits.

Ava stood ready to escape just as a man came up to the table.

"Raul!" Emmanuel Escalante. Avant-garde producer and star-maker. His smile was effusive, and his voice projected some of the highest, most genuine enthusiasm Ava had ever heard from one person. It was what made her like him immediately the first time she had met him.

The Granados firm had renovated his Malibu estate eight years ago, and he and Raul became quick friends. Mostly because they were two boys from the barrio, but also because they shared a love for "exquisite" tequila.

Raul was on his feet, hugging Emmanuel before inviting the over-six-foot-tall, broad-framed man to join them.

No. No. Say no.

And before Ava knew it, Emmanuel pulled up an empty chair and sat down. "Only for a minute," he said, flashing his smile around the table as everyone greeted him with "So good to see you" and "It's been too long." It hadn't. Emmanuel had been at the house for a tequila tasting just last month. And the only reason he wasn't at Nana's funeral was because he was wrapping up some espionage film in Finland. But he had sent a boat-sized bouquet of white roses that took up the entire church altar. Like Raul, Emmanuel never did anything small.

Ava stood there. Hovering. And when Raul gave her the side-eye, she plopped back down, defeated.

"How was Finland?" Viv asked, leaning forward. Most everyone leaned forward whenever Emmanuel was going to tell a story, because it always promised to be a good one.

"No, no, no," he said, waving a hand. "Tell me about you young people. What adventures have you been up to?"

"Just ghosts and saints," Carm said with a smile that Ava wanted to stab with her chopsticks.

"Ooh," Emmanuel said, looking intrigued. "Sounds like a book title. *Just ghosts and saints*," he echoed to himself as he patted his chest like he was looking for a pen. "I like it. And you, Ava?"

"Uh . . . just doing an internship at the *Times* and thinking about colleges and stuff," Ava said, more tensely than she had meant to. She glanced down at Emmanuel's gold watch. It was already 8:10 p.m. Even if she didn't run into any traffic on the PCH, she was going to be late. But she knew if she excused herself now, her dad would be furious. In the Granados clan, if a friend stopped by the house, you gave them food and drink. If a friend stopped by your table in a restaurant, you invited them to sit with you. If a "friend" was waiting for you across town, you left them there waiting.

"Dad," Viv said, "Ava should go."

Raul only nodded and gave the hand signal for *just another minute.* But another minute to Raul Granados could be infinity.

Ava sat there miserable, wishing and hoping and praying that Emmanuel would leave. And just when she thought he looked as though he might stand, he waved down a server and ordered some sake.

Every second, every word of chitchat, felt like another brick laid on Ava's chest, until finally the sake arrived and Emmanuel raised his glass. "I want us to toast to my mamita. A lovely, inventive, muy fuerte woman who will always be with us in spirit. Salud!"

If you only knew, Ava thought as she clinked her water glass with the others. Raul's eyes were moist, but his smile was strong, and Ava had to look away to hide her own tears. She had always been a sympathetic crier and hated how vulnerable it made her feel.

Emmanuel downed his drink, and as he finally stood, he announced a fiesta he was having next week. "I just put the final touches on it today." He rubbed his hands together gleefully.

"I'll be out of the country," Raul said regrettably.

"But the girls can come," Emmanuel replied with an edge of hope in his question that made it sound like more of a statement.

Ava hated parties. Any and all. Because 1. They felt like some kind of exam of her social skills. 2. Ava hated the pressure (and exhaustion) of circulating. And 3. They always involved too much noise, too many try-hards, and too many tiny finger foods sufficient only for those riding the latest LA diet train.

"I'm always down for a party," Carm said, folding her arms on the table. "Unless it's stuffy. Who's going to be there?"

Emmanuel's eyebrows danced. "You'll have to come to find out." Then, tilting closer, he said quietly, "Pero I promise you will love it."

I'm going to hate it.

Viv's face set into a determined expression, and Ava knew instantly what was going to come next.

"We are excellent secret keepers," Viv began. "You can tell us—"

"Viviana," Raul said, cutting her short before he threw in a scowl to make his point. No way was he about to let her persuade Emmanuel of anything. Viv sighed dramatically before sitting back in her chair as Emmanuel said his long-winded goodbye.

Five thank-the-saints minutes later, Ava was standing outside the restaurant waiting for the valet to bring around her Jeep. It was already 8:25, so she quickly dialed Rion to tell him she wasn't going to make it on time. *Because that's what friends do. They communicate.*

He answered on the first ring with, "You're going to be late, and I should definitely not eat two bowls of salsa and chips before you get here."

"You're already there?"

"And I have a surprise for you."

Fourteen

Ava sat in her car in the parking garage, the engine idling. She had already checked her face twice: no smudges, no seaweed between her teeth; nothing was out of place. And yet she couldn't bring herself to get out of the car. And all because Rion had spoken the dreaded words that always made Ava's stomach bottom out: *I have a surprise for you.*

Ava hated surprises, loathed them like meatloaf or flare jeans. She cut the engine and sat in silence, listening to the distant hum of traffic. She was about to call Nana but then breathed the whisper back in before it left her lips.

I can do this.

She didn't need to call for backup every time she got nervous or scared. Was that what she was? Scared? Of Rion? It *had* crossed her mind that the blessing could be something to be used against her, like Viv's persuasion ability. Except something told her Nana wouldn't bless her with something like that.

Besides, Rion seemed like a really nice guy. The kind of guy who would be easy to be friends with. Even *genuine* friends with.

Ava sent a quick text to Elijah. You probs won't get this, but I'm going to hang out with this guy. I crashed into him the other night. Why aren't you here? How's Pierre?

Taking a deep breath, Ava opened the door and stepped out. She was not afraid of Rion, she decided as she walked to the elevator. She was afraid of failing, of being the reason Nana would wander the afterlife like some tormented soul from Dante's *Inferno*.

Memoryless.

Ava couldn't imagine a worse end to her grandmother's story. And she couldn't, *wouldn't* let it happen. There was too much at stake. No matter what, she was going to get her blessing back.

The Promenade was brimming with lights and music and life. Street artists danced, painted the sidewalk, and sang bluesy songs. It would be easy to get distracted, to stop and watch or listen. To get lost in someone else's life. But Ava had already reached her destination. Just as she was about to open the restaurant's glass door, she caught sight of Rion. He was sitting at a table for two, head bent down as he scribbled in some kind of pocket-sized notebook. A flop of brown locks fell over his forehead, and his tongue was pressed into the corner of his mouth like he was in deep concentration.

She briefly wondered what he was so focused on, then her eyes drifted to a small paper sack on the floor by his feet. The surprise.

Ugh.

With a deep breath, she stepped into the colorful, bustling restaurant and headed over. Rion looked up as if he could sense her approach, and he smiled. A wide, warm, welcoming grin that nearly countered how quickly he disappeared the notebook into his jacket pocket.

"Hey," he said, standing so abruptly he knocked over his glass of water on the table, splashing Ava's legs as the plastic cup tumbled to the floor.

"Crap!" Rion said, offering her a napkin and mopping up the mess. "Sorry about that."

Ava wiped her legs off and reached for another napkin to help him. "I thought you almost had it," she said good-humoredly. "I bet one more second and—"

"And I definitely would have made the save," Rion threw in as they sat down. He tapped his fingers on the table and leaned back in his chair, tipping it back on two legs.

He's going to fall.

But then he righted the seat and said, "See that couple over there?" He gestured with a tilt of the head, trying to look covert but doing a really terrible job. "They ordered a flan and then another. It was torture watching them eat it."

Ava laughed. Her nerves melted away. "So, we should get some right away," she said, popping a tortilla chip into her mouth.

After the waiter took their order, a woman burst onto the scene. The scent of gardenias reached the table before she did with her lively voice, "Qué linda. ¿Cómo estás, mi amor?"

"Hi, Maria," Ava said, giving the owner a big strong hug, because anything less would result in ten more abrazos to make up for it. "This is Rion," she offered, feeling suddenly awkward that she was introducing someone she barely knew. "Rion, this is Maria. She owns the restaurant."

"Hi," he said, getting to his feet to shake Maria's hand. "Your salsa is awesome."

"Yes, nice to meet you," Maria said, casting her gaze to Ava. "¿Finalmente tienes novio?"

Ava could feel her cheeks flush. "Somos amigos," Ava said as Rion ran a hand over the back of his neck and looked away. Maria eyed him warily and told Ava in Spanish that she really needed to get out more often, find a nice boy, quit being so picky.

"You guys are busy tonight," Ava said in English, hoping to change the subject.

Maria's grin spread across her entire face, nearly making her eyes vanish. "Always busy. Say hello to your papa." Another hug, and then she was gone.

After they sat back down, Rion looked like he was fighting back a smile.

"What?" Ava asked.

"Nothing, just glad you set her straight."

Ava stiffened. "Huh?"

And then the smile split Rion's face. "About us being friends."

Heat spread across Ava's cheeks and down her neck. In five seconds, she'd have humiliating red splotches flashing across her chest like neon signs. She instantly regretted her choice of dresses. Why couldn't she have worn a damn turtleneck? "You . . . speak Spanish," she managed, trying to decide which part of the convo was more embarrassing. The fact that Ava was too picky, or that Maria made her sound like she had zero social life.

"Fluently," Rion said. He was still smiling. But Ava saw absolutely nothing amusing about any of this. *See?* Ava could imagine Nana saying. *This is what happens when you assume.*

"Are you Hispanic?" Ava asked. Even though she wanted to say, *But you look like such a gringo, like, not even a white-passing Latinx,* and in her experience most white people didn't speak Spanish.

Rion shook his head. "My grandfather taught me."

"Is *he* Hispanic?"

"German, Irish, some Scottish," Rion said as the two orders of flan arrived. "He spent some time in Mexico when he was younger. Almost moved there."

"Why didn't he?"

"Something about a girl," Rion said as he managed to balance nearly half of his flan on his fork before shoving it in his mouth. Nana would definitely *not* approve. And then Rion was nodding his endorsement as he swallowed the baked custard. "Wow! That's delicious." He gave a thumbs-up. "Good call."

Ava didn't know why, but she was holding her breath, and in one full swoosh she let it out. "Glad you like it."

"Like it? I can see why *they* ordered three!" Rion set his fork down. "I almost forgot." He reached down, picked up the paper sack, and set it on the table between them. "Your surprise."

And just like that, all the ease of the moment went up in smoke, and Ava cringed. "Oh" was all she managed to say as she took the now soggy sack and peered inside. "It's ... an orange," she said, removing the fruit and setting it on the table. "It's ... red."

"To replace the one that got away."

It took a minute for Ava to remember the one orange that had rolled under a stand this morning. Was this why he was in the tree earlier? Looking for a replacement? "Thanks." She was grateful the surprise wasn't some Granados-worthy outlandish thing that would set her cheeks on fire.

"It's a new variety we're working on," Rion said, still fixated on the fruit. "A cross between a Cara Cara and a blood orange. It's super sweet, but check out the peel. Super tough."

Cara. Blood. Tough. Right. This is not the conversation she thought they would be having. Actually, she didn't know what they would talk about, and as far as a subject went, maybe oranges wasn't a bad one.

"Should we eat it?"

Rion's expression tightened. Ava thought maybe she had said something wrong until he pinched his brows together and through a small laugh said, "Uh, I don't think this will go with flan."

Ava laughed too, tilting back as Rion leaned forward on his elbows, revealing that single half dimple. That was the instant that Ava thought he was nothing like what she had imagined. He was so far from that grumpy, sarcastic guy who had hopped out of his truck last week. And she couldn't help but wonder if it had something to do with the blessing.

Pushing her plate away, Ava spoke first. "So, have you always worked on your family's farm?"

"I grew up there," Rion said. "It's really my gramps's orchard. That's my mom's dad. Anyhow, I helped in the summers and stuff, but that was really it until . . ."

He cleared his throat, and when he didn't finish the sentence, Ava rushed in with, "Until what?"

"I thought we came here so you could say thanks," he said. "Not hear my life story."

"Thanks," she said, thinking how much more comfortable she was with being the interviewer. "Now that that's out of the way, I like life stories. So, tell me everything."

"It's really not that interesting." He crossed his arms over his chest and sat back, making a show of his stubbornness. "Are you always like this?"

Ava flinched, then decided to make a joke of it. "Ha. Annoying?"

"Curious."

"Pretty much. So—"

"So . . . yes, I grew up here; no, I don't like country music; and yes, I'm older than you."

Ava wasn't about to admit defeat. "I wasn't going to ask those questions."

She tried not to squirm in her seat. "And how do you know you're older?"

His eyebrows lifted playfully and expectantly. "I'm eighteen this September."

Ava took a slow sip of water, trying to figure out if she was entertained or annoyed by this guy's easy confidence. "Fine, you win," she said a moment later. "So you're still in high school too. I'm eighteen next May."

Rion balled up the straw wrapper and rolled it back and forth across the table. "Yeah, but I try not to be."

"What does that mean?"

"It means I don't spend a lot of time on campus, since I already have so many credits. I wanted to graduate early in December, but . . ."

"But what?"

His mouth lifted into a half grin. His dark eyes met hers. "You ask a lot of questions."

"That's the word on the street."

"It is?"

"If you're graduating early," Ava said, "I guess you're applying to schools already, right?"

A pause. Ava could feel some kind of push and pull. As if Rion was struggling with how much he was going to tell her, which only made her more curious.

"Nah, I'll still head out in the fall. I just plan to take the spring to chill."

"But you'll miss out on prom and senior trip and your graduation ceremony. All the fun senior stuff."

"Are you trying to talk me out of it?" He threw her a playful smile.

"I just think the best part of being a senior is the spring."

"Then you'll be glad to know that my school will still let me do all that stuff even if I finish classes in December. So, what about you?" he said. "Are you a senior too?"

Folding her arms, she rested them on the table and nodded. It was time to come at the truth from a different angle. Ms. Barnaby, her journalism teacher last year, taught her that to be a good investigative journalist, you need to ask the right questions and get into someone's mind. To be a great investigative journalist, you have to get into their heart. "Can I ask you something?"

"More?" he teased.

"That night at the stop sign. Why were you just sitting there?"

"If I tell you, I'll have to kill you."

"Really."

His expression changed from lighthearted to full of dread. Ava could feel the familiar butterfly wings beating under her ribs. She had hit on something. But she couldn't rush him, or pounce too soon. This was the moment where she had to be patient, tread cautiously, allow him to open up to her.

Rion opened his mouth.

Ava leaned closer, holding her breath.

"I was . . ."

"Yeah?"

"On eBay."

"eBay?"

"I was just about to win the auction when you slammed into me."

"Auction?"

"Are you going to keep repeating everything I say?"

"Yes, I mean no . . . I mean . . . I'm afraid to ask." She hadn't meant to say the last part, but there it was.

Rion broke into a wide smile. "Finally. No more questions."

Ava threw one of the wadded straw wrappers at him. "Seriously. What were you trying to win?"

"My gramps collects coins. His birthday is in a few weeks, and—"

"Now you have no gift."

"I found something better." Rion shrugged and scrubbed a hand through his hair. "I just wanted it to be awesome, since . . ." There was a moment's hesitation. Rion gave a light shrug, then said, "He's getting up there in years, you know. So, every birthday counts."

Why did this conversation suddenly feel heavier than it should?

"And Achilles?" she asked. "He helps out too?" Ava didn't really care about Achilles, but she wanted to switch to something that might feel like a lighter topic. Elijah always told her if he needed a therapist, she would be the last person he would go to. She used to get offended until she realized he was right. She was no good at the touchy-feely stuff. Unlike Viv, she never had the right words.

Rion quirked an eyebrow. "Hold on. I'm doing all the talking. How about you tell me about you?"

"There's nothing to tell, really. I grew up here. I have two sisters. And . . ." There was a short hesitation before, "I want to go to Columbia after graduation and become an investigative journalist."

Rion threw her a blank stare.

"What?" she finally said when the silence grew too thick.

"You don't sound very excited about it."

"Which part? My sisters?" she teased.

"Your future."

"What?! I am! I mean, it's just . . . a lot of planning. I have to think about second and third schools beyond the reach one, so I started an Excel spreadsheet listing all the pros and cons and stuff."

Excel? Really?

"Mmm . . . okay," Rion replied, stuffing another piece of flan into his mouth.

Feeling suddenly defensive, Ava said, "Okay, what?" It probably wasn't the fastest or best way to become *friends*, but her annoyance got the better of her, and besides, the words were already floating in the air between them.

"Okay, cool. Okay, I am not as organized as you are. Okay, are you going to eat that last piece of flan?" He pointed to her plate, flashing a smile. He had really nice teeth.

Ava relaxed, and as she pushed her flan toward Rion, he turned his ear to the front door. "Hey. You hear that?"

Ava shook her head. Was this some clever way of trying to get out of answering her question? That was the thing about getting to know someone. It felt like an endless torturous game of guessing: what they meant, what they were thinking, why they did *X*, *Y*, *Z*.

"Come on," Rion said.

Rion tried to pay at the register on the way out, but Ava insisted. "It's *my* thank-you," she reminded him as she quickly scanned the bill. The total was eight dollars and fifty-one cents.

$8.51

Ava stared at the three numbers as a jolt of nerves passed through her. *A coincidence*, she thought, handing her card over.

She and Rion made their way toward the Promenade, where the crowds had thinned to a few stragglers. All the shops were now closed, and yet there was a single musician on the corner, playing the saxophone. The musician's eyes were closed, his lips pressed tightly over the mouthpiece. His whole body swayed to the longing, sad notes. It was clear he wasn't playing for anyone but himself.

Ava stared at Rion as he watched the man with a strange gaze. She was trying to see what couldn't be seen. Maybe the blessing was some kind of heightened hearing for music? But that didn't make sense. Why would Nana give something like that to Ava? Blessings weren't superpowers. They were enhancements, keys to dreams, and "destinies."

Rion looked suddenly lost. Was this *his* dream? Music?

"Is this what you want to do?" Ava spoke quietly but with the confidence of someone who knew she was right.

Rion snapped his attention back to Ava. "Do?"

"Like for a job."

"Ha. No. I don't even play."

Had Ava read him wrong? Wait. This was all wrong. She was excellent at reading people. She could tell if someone was real, fake, a liar, a bragger, a hater, a wannabe in less than a minute. "But you seem like you really love it," she said.

"Just because you love something doesn't mean you should own it or do it for a living."

Rion went over and put a ten in the musician's case. He said something to the man, who was still playing, but Ava didn't catch what it was. All she knew was that it made the man smile.

When Rion returned, they sat on the curb. "We should eat this together," Ava said, opening the paper sack.

"Next time," Rion said, patting his stomach. "I'm stuffed."

Next time. Ava breathed a sigh of relief. She hadn't blown it. There was going to be a next time. Maybe it was corny, but she felt a swell of pride.

She hadn't run Rion off. She was doing the thing, completing the quest, saving Nana from a terrible afterlife.

Rion lay back on the sidewalk where a million feet had trampled. He didn't seem to care that he was mingling with all those germs as he stared up at the sky. "At the orchard, you can see the stars perfectly." He patted the sidewalk next to him.

The man played a new tune, sadder, bluesier, fuller than the one before. There was a silence between some of the notes, a silence that spoke volumes.

"I'm good," Ava said. "I can see the sky from here."

"Not the same view. Come on. The dirt won't kill you," Rion promised.

Reaching for her inner adventurer, Ava tugged her dress toward her knees and lay back.

She stared up at the pale night, muted by the city lights. The sky felt bigger. She felt smaller. Her mother's voice floated into her mind out of nowhere: *The greatest truths are always found in the stars, out of reach and so far away.*

Ava pushed the words out of her mind, refusing to let her mom into this moment. Rion was talking about the orchard, and Ava, who had gotten distracted, drew herself back to the conversation. "Maggie's Orchard," she said, remembering the name. "Is that your grandma?"

"No. My gram was Naomi."

"Oh, I just thought the orchard was named for ..."

Rion shook his head, keeping his gaze locked on the night sky. "It's a long, sad story," he said with a wistful sigh.

Ava wasn't built for sad stories, but now she had to know who Maggie was and why Mr. North would name a place after someone who wasn't his wife. "Is it *something about a girl*?" she guessed, remembering what Rion had told her earlier.

Rion sat up on one elbow and turned to Ava. "Do you believe in fate?"

And by the way he was asking, Ava knew *he* did. Would she kill their beginning, the night, this moment if she told him the truth? That there was no fate?

Rion laughed. "It's not a hard question."

Be genuine.

"I think fate is a way for people to give up control," Ava said, sitting up. "Like, they think, *What's going to happen is going to happen*, but I don't believe that." Ava's inner voice was telling her to stop talking, but the words just kept coming. "I think we make our own decisions. That destiny isn't real, and there is no *meant to be*."

For a long second, Rion didn't say anything. He gave Ava the kind of look that made her want to hit the delete button with a sledgehammer. Why couldn't she have just answered the question with a simple yes or no?

Rion said, "Oh, too bad."

A defensive chord struck Ava in the chest. "Why?"

With a shrug, Rion turned his gaze back to the sky and said, "Because if you don't believe in fate, then you won't understand the story of Maggie."

Fifteen

The story of Maggie.

The story of Maggie.

Those four words were an incessant whisper pecking away at Ava's mind as she drove home. Rion had spoken the magic word that every journalist wants to hear: *story*. And now Ava *had* to know more.

Lost in her thoughts, Ava cruised up to a stop sign. A slow, sleepy song played. The night beyond her windows was calm and peaceful with no signs of traffic in the residential neighborhood.

And then Nana appeared in the passenger seat.

"Jesus!" Ava screamed, gripping the wheel.

"Ay, qué dramática," Nana said, shaking her head as Meda materialized in the back.

"You said you wouldn't come unless I called you!" Ava reminded her grandmother.

"Well, this is an emergency," Nana said resolutely.

Ava peered at Meda in the rearview mirror. His expression was grim, which made her chest tighten. "You should bring this contraption to a stop," he said.

Ava drove through the four-way stop and pulled alongside the curb across from a small park. "You guys are freaking me out. What's up?"

"Let's get some fresh air," Nana suggested.

Ava got out of the car and leaned against the hood. A distant street lamp cast lingering shadows across the road.

Nana's eyes tilted toward the pale night sky. "You aren't going to like this."

Ava felt her whole body go rigid as she braced herself for the worst. "Just tell me."

"If you do not retrieve the blessing . . ." She turned her ghostly eyes back to Ava. For a flickering instant, Ava thought she saw a trail of mist pass across their darkness.

Ava raced to fill in the blanks. "Then you're going to be a memoryless ghost. We already know that."

"It's worse than that," Meda said, rubbing his chin.

"Worse?"

Nana said, "If you do not get the blessing back, then our ability, you and your sisters' ability to pass on blessings to your descendants, will end."

The world felt as if it was imploding. Ava had been so consumed with losing Nana, with losing the blessing, that she had never considered whether she could pass on her own when the time came. "Wait." With a deep frown she bit the inside of her cheek. "How do you know?!" Ava's voice rose. "Are you sure? Who told you?" Like, was there some kind of all-knowing afterlife council?

"We have our methods, and they cannot be shared with you," Meda said resolutely, but Ava could tell he relished the secret-keeping part of his job. "It's just not allowed. But you can be assured that our information is accurate."

Ava threw her gaze to Nana. "So, you mean that Viv and Carm and I won't . . ."

Nana jutted her chin forward and stood taller. Ava knew that look. It was her General stance, the one that said, *Onward!* And Ava hated it.

"We will be investigating further," Meda said pitifully. Not exactly giving off the confident vibe Ava so desperately needed. He clapped his hands together gleefully. "And soon we will know *how* to transfer this blessing. Isn't that good news?"

"Which means that we have to be away for a few days," Nana said. "Is that okay?"

Meaning, *Will* you *be okay?*

Ava nodded, but really, she wanted to melt into her grandmother's arms and cry, "Make it all go away!"

But *onward* was nipping at her heels, and now she had to go home and tell her sisters the ugly truth. For half a second Ava considered not revealing this new morsel of information, but there was the Granados sister blood vow. No secrets. No lies. Ever.

"And don't forget," Nana said, "be genuine and natural with Orion."

"Or this won't work," Meda added, patting Ava on the shoulder.

Viv and Carmen were waiting in the foyer, bouncing on the balls of their feet like five-year-olds on Christmas morning. They were both wearing slimy sheet masks, making them look like horror-movie villains.

"Well?" Viv began.

"Tell us everything," Carm said.

"I can't talk to you with those things on," Ava said, trying to shake her frustrations, her endless worry that too many futures counted on her when all she wanted to do was head upstairs, take a hot shower, crawl under the covers, and watch a good action movie on Netflix.

"'Kay," Viv said, "we only have one more minute."

"To hydrate and brighten," Carm chimed in as she hooked her arm in Ava's and dragged her into the living room, where she plopped the two of them onto the linen sofa. "And don't leave anything out," she insisted.

Ava set her bag down and righted her dress. She knew she had to tell them the worst part, the dreaded dragon part of the tale. Her mother's words circled back to her in an infuriating echo: *Every fairy tale has a monster.*

Ava began with, "I found something out tonight."

Carm and Viv tilted their heads at the exact same angle, as if puppet strings were controlling their movements.

"He's got a girlfriend," Carm guessed.

"Umm . . . no. I mean, not that I know of."

Viv rolled her eyes, "Not everything is about boys, Carmen." Turning to Ava, she said quietly, "What is it?"

"If I don't get back the blessing, then . . . then it dies," Ava said. "*It* meaning our ability to pass along blessings; it's all gone."

There was a breeze of a moment, like the last whisper before the storm erupts.

Carm screamed, then she exploded into a tornado of cussing and threats that basically equaled *You better sure as hell get that damned blessing back.*

"We don't need you coming undone right now," Viv warned Carmen, but her voice trembled, and Ava could tell she was getting frustrated too. But being the firstborn meant holding it together at all costs, which in Ava's book sucked big-time.

"Undone?" Carmen's eyes were fire. "Seriously? What am I supposed to tell my daughters? 'Oh, sorry your tia Ava ruined your life?'"

"*You're* the one who sneezed!" As soon as Ava said the words, she realized they carried no weight. Sneeze or no sneeze, the blessing was already gone.

"Guys!" Viv was shouting and standing between the two sisters now. "This isn't helping. Can you please just cálmate! Let me think. Let's regroup. Okay, Gree, how do you know?"

Carm's shoulders sagged like the weight of the truth had broken her. "My poor jitas," she cried. Ava fought the nearly uncontrollable urge to roll her eyes.

"How do you even know you're going to have daughters?"

Carm peeled off her mask and wrinkled her nose. "Because I just do, and if I have sons, they're going to Viv."

Viv sighed. "Fine by me. Loud football Sundays and more pedis for me."

"Oh, I hadn't thought of that," Carmen said with a pout as she collapsed onto the ottoman. "But still, my tiny darlings are going to live a life of suffering."

"No one's tiny darlings are going to suffer," Viv assured.

"Guys, I'm going to get the blessing back," Ava said. "I swear it."

Carmen curled her legs underneath her and turned to Ava. Her eyes were all-consuming, like a hungry cat's. "Tell us. Is he wrapped around your finger? Are we closer to success?"

Ava sighed, reached into the sack, and held up the orange. "He gave me this."

"It's an orange," Viv said flatly as she peeled off her mask for a better look.

"Gross," Carm added. "What kind of a surprise is that?"

"You're so rude, Carm," Viv chided.

"It's for the one that got away," Ava echoed. "And he said. . . ." She paused for effect, or maybe just to drive her sisters to the brink of losing it. It wasn't often that she was the center of the story. Most of the time she felt like a bee buzzing around the blooms that were Vivienne and Carmen. "He said that we should eat it together next time."

There was a moment of silence and then, "Next time!" Viv was nodding and smiling.

"Boom!" Carmen threw her arms up like she'd just won a gold medal, flinging her mask into the air. It landed on the TV screen, where it stuck before flopping onto the stone floor in a gooey heap.

Viv moved onto the sofa and pulled a pillow to her chest. "He actually brought you an orange?"

"It's a really bad gift." Carm wrinkled her nose. "But don't feel bad, Ava. I've gotten my share of pathetic gifts. Remember that busted gumball machine Terrance gave me in ninth grade? And he didn't even include the gum!"

"He also just got recruited to play for the NBA," Ava said.

Carmen released a pathetic sigh. "True."

"Anyway, it's a special variety I guess they're growing," Ava said, as if that answered her sister's question, which was really: *Why would anyone bring a piece of fruit as a gift?*

Because it's unexpected, Ava thought, *and sweet.*

After the details had been spilled, parsed through, examined, and consumed, Carmen scowled at her fuzzy slippers. "So," she said, "he didn't mention any weird shit, like special abilities?"

"I would have led with that, Carm."

"Whatever." Carmen tossed her hair over her shoulder. "We need to build a solid plan. What are the next steps?" she mumbled, and Ava could tell she was asking no one but herself.

"Should I wait for him to call me?" Ava said, knowing *that* probably wasn't the next step Carm was looking for. It was hard getting into her sister's devious brain, especially when it came to guys. Ava could never tell what half-concocted ideas were going to sprout in her sister's imagination.

Carm let out a disapproving groan.

"Earlier you told me not to call him, to let the phone ring three times," Ava cried. "You're such a hypocrite."

"That was then, and this is now," Carmen said. "You have to be strategic based on the information in front of you. The guy gave you a gift." Her face fell. "I mean, a lousy gift, but still he tried, so that means you have to make the next move. We have to think long game. Which is three weeks. Don't you know anything?"

Viv squeezed her pillow tighter. And just when Ava thought Viv was going to toss it at Carmen and come to Ava's defense, she said, "Carm's right."

"What?!"

"I am?" Carm blinked.

Ignoring Carmen, Viv said to Ava, "Well, she's right about being strategic but wrong about the long game. We don't have oodles of time, and he might not call for days."

"Especially if you were yourself," Carmen put in with a smirk.

Nodding her head toward her smirking middle sister, Ava said to Viv, "Can't you persuade her into being a nice person?"

Viv brightened. "Ooh . . . great idea!"

"You better not have tried to touch my mind," Carmen protested, pressing her hands over her head as if that could protect her from Viv's blessing. "And I am a nice person. You just don't like to hear the truth."

Ava looked down at the orange, ignoring her sister's outburst. "He said we'd eat this together, so he has to call soon. Right? I mean, how long do oranges last?"

"He told you it's a new breed," Carm offered. "Maybe it's a super fruit that lasts forever or something."

"He didn't say anything about a super fruit," Ava groaned. "And I can't believe we're talking about fruit expirations as an estimate for when he wants to hang out next."

"Well, his grandpa did name an entire orchard of them after someone," Viv said.

"I bet she was his first kiss or first unrequited love or something extra like that," Carmen suggested.

"No one names a whole orchard after a kiss," Ava argued.

Carm gave Ava a coy smile. "Depends on the kiss."

As if on cue, Viv and Ava threw pillows at Carmen, who rolled off the ottoman with an exaggerated shriek.

When Viv and Carmen headed up to bed, Viv glanced over her shoulder at Ava. "You coming?"

"In a little," Ava said.

But a little turned out to be a lot. Ava had only meant to put the orange in the fridge and get some water. She had planned to send another text into the black hole of Elijah's life and then call it a night. But when she opened the refrigerator door, the crème fraîche she had special ordered called to her. So did the eggs and butter and all things pastry.

Before she knew it, she had gathered the ingredients, thrown on her favorite striped apron, pulled her hair into a messy bun, and was making a St. Honoré cake named for the French patron saint of bakers and pastry chefs. The cake was a beast. Time consuming. Complex. The perfect project to get lost in, with its layers, puff pastry base, pate a choux pastry, crème patissiere, and decadent crème chiboust.

The kitchen was Ava's confessional, her therapy, her refuge from the world. It was the perfect place to not think. Not about Nana's plight or the power of blessings or Rion or fate or Maggie's story.

Except she did think. About Rion.

Objectively, of course. About the fact that he was awkward but easy to talk to. About how she might even naturally be friends with him. But mostly she thought about how he seemed to be holding something back, while at the same time trying to push something to the surface, which only confused her more.

By 3:00 a.m., Ava finished the cake and set the final choux pastry puff on top. She planted herself on a barstool and stared at the orange like it might grow a face and give her all the answers she was still searching for. Rion's voice replayed in her mind: *A cross between a Cara Cara and a blood orange. It's super sweet, but check out the peel. Super tough.*

Resting her chin on her folded arms, Ava blew a stray hair out of her face.

Who are you, Rion North?

The next thing she knew, her dad was nudging her awake. A predawn gray light filtered into the kitchen. Ava wiped the drool from her mouth and looked up, disoriented at first. Then she saw the luggage near the back door and remembered her dad and Loretta were leaving on their vacation this morning.

"Princesa, did you sleep here?"

"I . . . I must have dozed off."

"Go to bed," he said, popping a puff into his mouth with a mischievous grin. "¡Qué deliciosa!"

Sleepily, Ava stood to hug him goodbye. "Have fun."

He held her at arm's length and smiled, his eyes crinkling around the edges. "Keep an eye on Carmenita."

"Dad, no one can even keep up with her."

"And, por favor," he said, "go to Emmanuel's party."

Ava started to protest, but her dad added, "For me."

With a grunt, Ava agreed. As she carried herself to bed, she stopped at the back window and watched her dad and Loretta pull out of the driveway just as a glint of rising sunlight reflected off a piece of luggage in the SUV's cargo window. The old familiar pain wrapped itself around Ava, the memory of her mom sinking its teeth and claws into her heart.

Sixteen

It was time for confession.

To keep the highly regrettable promise Ava had made the night Nana died. Secretly, she wanted to pretend the promise had never been spoken, but at the end of the day, she figured she couldn't afford the guy upstairs's wrath, not when so much was riding on her success.

I'll go for a whole week.

Ugh!

She cursed her past self for being so generous. And then she wondered, with equal parts hope and dread, if God considered a week as a typical business week of five days, or seven?

It was awful when she went last year. And it was going to be awful now.

After a morning snooze and a shower, Ava found Viv gone and Carm still sacked out. So she threw on a pair of leggings and a long-sleeved T-shirt and headed to Saint Mary's church on foot, since it was only a few blocks from the house. The sky was an endless gray. A gloomy backdrop to the small stone church nestled between fragrant eucalyptus trees that swayed in the distant ocean breeze. Ava walked up the blue Spanish tile steps, through the archway, and across the rose-filled courtyard to the side entrance where the confessionals were located. She wished for the millionth time that there was an express lane for two sins or less.

Inside, the church smelled like burned wax and Band-Aids.

Ava's heart thudded dramatically. And then came the catastrophic thinking. *What if I see someone I know? What if the priest laughs at me? What if I get it all wrong?* She re-rehearsed the usual opening line in her mind: *Forgive me, Father, for I have sinned.*

Then I kneel and make the sign of the cross. No, I do that first. Right? And then what? She drew a blank just as she lifted her gaze to see a line of four silver-haired people standing behind a sign with creepy Gothic lettering that might as well have spelled GET OUT. The sign read NEXT IN LINE FOR CONFESSION.

Thankfully, no one turned to scope her out, but she dropped her gaze anyway and kept her fingers busy texting Elijah a message just so she could pretend she was anywhere else.

> Elijah!
> If you only knew where I am right now.
> And how I got here . . . and the world sucks.
> You suck.
> Why did you leave me!
> Talking to you is like talking to God.
> Never get an answer.
> And no, you are not God.

By the time Ava sent off five more pitiable messages and googled *how to confess your sins to a priest*, she had moved up in line to número dos.

She quickly scanned the how-to article on her phone. "Come on," she groaned. *Just get to the point.* Only to cringe when the willowy woman in front of her tsked and scowled.

"Sorry," Ava whispered as the woman took her place in the now empty confessional.

And then the absolute worst. Ava could *hear* the woman talking to the priest. Or at least the pitches and drops in her voice and a few words here and there: *Awful. Lies. Poison. Chicken.* Ava's imagination fired on all cylinders, and the woman's headline popped into her mind: *"Woman Murders Husband by Poisoning His Chicken Pot Pie."*

There were more mutterings, and finally the black wooden door opened, and the woman stepped out before a totally distracted Ava could finish the article.

With a deep breath, Ava made her way into the dark box. Through a screen she saw the silhouette of a bearded man's face. *Thank you, baby Jesus, that it's not Father Conrad.* It was much easier to confess to a stranger than to the guy who baptized and confirmed you and regularly came to dinner at your house.

Ava took a seat on the red velour cushion. *Damn. Where's the kneeler?* "Um . . ." she began. "Forgive my sins. No. I mean, forgive . . ."

A chuckle.

"We are less formal here," a thick, scratchy voice said. "Why don't you tell me what you'd like to get off your chest?"

"Like my sins?"

"Whatever you think you need to repent for."

Dropping her voice when she heard footsteps outside, Ava spoke in a library whisper. "Oh, well, I gave up ice cream for Lent and ate it anyway."

"Go on."

"And I . . . I lied to my dad about my credit card bill." *But in my defense, I really needed those sunglasses.*

"And?"

Ava paused, hesitated. "Isn't that enough?" Was there a quota?

"You tell me."

Ava racked her brain. "Well . . . I sort of cussed out a slow driver the other day. Only in my own car of course."

"I see," the priest said.

"That's it." Ava sat back, thinking that she had to pace herself if she had six more visits to the black box.

"We all fall into those patterns and behaviors."

"You mean everyone but priests . . . and nuns."

Another chuckle. "Your penance is to say five—"

Ava's phone rang. She flinched, and without looking to see who was calling, she quickly silenced the phone. "Sorry."

"Say *six* Our Fathers and three Hail Marys."

What happened to five? "Okay. So, is that all?" Ava asked.

"Would you like more?"

"No, I mean . . ." Ava picked at her tragic nails. She really needed a gel fill. "Before I go, can I ask you a question?"

"Of course."

"Do you think the saints are smart? Like, do you think they're good at their jobs?"

A pause and then, "They are excellent interceders."

"So, you would trust one to help you out."

"I always do."

As Ava got up to leave, she swung back. "Are you the priest who hears all the confessions?"

"There is a schedule online. I'm Father Gustavo."

"Okay, I just wanted you to know I'll be back six more times."

The sun had slipped through the blue-gray clouds, forcing Ava to shield her eyes when she stepped outside. *One down, six to go*, Ava told herself as she nearly skipped down the steps into the courtyard. And then she remembered the call she had silenced. She glanced down at her phone.

Rion.

He hadn't left a message, so she quickly dialed him back.

He answered with, "Hey."

"Hey."

"What are you doing?"

"You won't believe me."

"Try me."

"I just finished confession."

"Really?" His tone was light and easy. "Was hanging out with me so bad that you had to confess about it?"

Ava laughed. "You were *not* part of my confession."

"Oh, good. So I called to see . . ."

A loud engine roared in the background, cutting him off.

Grinding gears. A barking dog. "Hang on," he nearly shouted. He must have muted his phone because everything went silent and when Rion came back, Ava heard a door close before he said, "I called to see if you're busy Thursday night."

Ava felt a small jolt of surprise. Or was it triumph? She reminded herself that for this to work she had to be genuine and natural. No airs. No falsehoods. No pretending to be someone or something she wasn't.

"Why?"

"Can you meet me at Travel Town at six?"

"That little outdoor museum with the old trains?" *Why would he want to go there?*

"That's the one," Rion said.

Ava was scheduled to work, but since her schedule changed each week according to what Grant and others needed, she had to check her phone calendar to be sure. "Hang on." Quickly, she scanned the week. She breathed a sigh of relief. She'd be off in plenty of time to meet Rion. "Yeah, I can do that."

"Good," Rion said. "You won't want to miss this."

"Miss what?"

"It's a surprise. Oh, and don't forget the orange."

"I forgot to tell you I really hate surprises."

"Tell me that after you see this."

Seventeen

Taking care of an orange like it's a damn baby was fatiguing.

Ava named the thing Bloody Cara, and for the next three days, she left BC in the fridge with a sticky note that said *poisonous*. She couldn't trust that her sisters wouldn't screw everything up and accidentally eat the prized fruit. And then there was the dreaded surprise. Rion seemed to be full of them, like a walking, talking surprise factory. So, when Thursday finally came, Ava found herself at the *Times* counting down the hours instead of focusing on her work, which happened to be copyediting a story on how to grow succulents.

The two other interns, Anmol and Corbin, were gabbing in their nearby cubicles, but their voices were low enough that Ava couldn't hear the details. And then there was Harold, a squatty grad student in need of a shave and haircut who also worked in archives, except that he got paid. He and Ava shared a cubicle wall, and if she didn't wear earbuds, she could hear his breathing and woeful sniffling. The guy's nose was a faucet.

Anmol rounded the corner, twisting her shiny dark ponytail over her shoulder. "Hey, Ava, do you think I should make up a life challenge for my Duke essay? Corbin says to lie, but I feel like—"

"I said to stretch the truth." Corbin stood behind her, wearing a devilish grin. "I mean, what gives with the *tell us about a challenge you've overcome*? How should I know?"

Anmol sighed. "I just think it's so invasive. How is it their business?"

"Totally agree," Ava said.

"With the lie or the invasive?" Anmol asked.

"Um, I don't think you should lie."

Corbin groaned. "So, what do we say, our challenge is this horrible essay prompt?"

Ava hadn't even started thinking about her college application essays yet. Mostly because she knew this was a popular question, and she didn't see how it made her a better candidate to bare her heart and soul to a committee of strangers.

"Or maybe," Anmol said, "we could talk about this boring internship. I file more than I read or write. Like, where's the journalism part? Totally free labor."

"Yeah," Corbin said. "Ava got the good gig, copyediting real stories. I copyedit social media posts."

"At least you *edit*," Anmol argued.

Ava really wished they would keep their voices down. The last thing she wanted was for Grant to hear them and throw their ungrateful butts to the curb. But lucky for her, the office was buzzing with enough activity to keep their convo private.

Rerouting the subject, Ava leaned back in her chair and said, "Anmol, didn't you tell us last week that you had to try out for the gymnastics team three times before you made it?"

"Are you trying to make me feel worse?"

"No," Ava said. "But there has to be a story there about how hard you trained, and I think it shows your determination."

Anmol's sullen expression brightened. "And I did break my ankle!"

"Do me," Corbin said, muscling his way in front of Anmol. "What's my challenge?"

Ava laughed. "I've only known you three weeks."

Corbin twisted his face into an anguished expression. "I got into a fender bender once."

"Don't think that counts," Ava said, while Anmol nodded her agreement.

He sighed. In the next instant his eyes went wide with an idea that Ava could see was blooming. "I got lost on a camping trip. Totally survivor mode, man."

Ava sat up. "Really? For how long?"

"Days."

Anmol crossed her arms tightly. "You don't seem like someone who would survive for days, Corbin."

He feigned shock. "Look, the point is I was out in the wilderness alone. No water. No food. Fighting off wild animals. I still have nightmares."

"Really?" Ava asked.

Corbin smiled. "No, but it sounds better, right?"

"What are *you* going to write about?" Anmol asked Ava.

Ava blew out a long breath. "No idea." And then she thought of the other question she was bound to have to answer: *Why do you want to be a journalist?* On the surface, it made sense. She was always good at English. But if she really thought about it, her goal had nothing to do with writing and everything to do with the field's foundation of cold hard facts. Ava liked facts, not a world of make-believe. And what journalist ever fell apart reporting a story? None. Emotions were kept in check. Ava liked that too.

At 5:00 p.m. Grant stood in front of her desk. He wore a blazer, but underneath Ava spied a faded yellow Aerosmith T-shirt that looked like it had seen better days. The screenprinted letters were peeling off except for *eros*, which made Ava laugh inside, and she briefly wondered, *Is he trying to be ironic?*

She tugged out an earbud. "Hey."

"You doing okay, kid?"

She nodded. "Thanks for coming to the funeral," she said. "You didn't have to do that."

"It was a nice gathering."

Oh. Ava was low-key impressed at how often Grant could surprise her with his words or attitude or sometimes even his expressions. If she had had an older brother, she thought maybe she would want him to be like Grant—except for the sloppy, stretched-out tees. Those were just tragic.

"And your speech was . . ." His mouth turned up into a half smile before he added, "Unforgettable."

Ava wanted to bury her head under the files. An embarrassed bubble of laughter spilled out. "Grace under fire. That's me."

Grant frowned, suddenly serious. Was the chill moment over? "So, do you want to talk about anything?" he asked.

Ava felt her insides go sideways. And just like that the convo had turned super awkward. Grant who never ventured over to her desk, Grant who clearly didn't want to be the intern supervisor, Grant who always sent the vibe he'd rather be alone than talk to a seventeen-year-old girl, *that* Grant was suddenly playing big bro?

Talk? Like a therapy session? Is he joking?

"I've got a lot to catch up on," Ava said. "And, um . . . is my time off last week going to hurt my letter of rec?" She had to ask, to know where she stood. This prestigious high school internship was a first for the *Times*, sort of like a test run, and she felt grateful to have gotten the gig. But at the end of the day, it was Grant's letter of recommendation that would be the difference between Columbia and, well, some other school.

"You already work more hours than you're supposed to, and you deserved the time off." Grant reached behind her and pulled a pink, sparkly folder from her shelf. The one with the word *Dreams* written on the cover. Viv had bought a stack of them for her when Ava landed the internship and now, in Grant's hand, the thing looked flimsy and painfully immature. "I forgot to thank you for working on those photos that night."

Ava could already imagine how his letter would read: *strong work ethic, goes above and beyond.* Her cartoon head was swelling at the thought of it.

"I found some photos on the floor when you took off," he continued, handing the folder over. Someone called for Grant across the room. He merely held up a hand, signaling to wait.

"I wasn't sure what you had already organized," he went on, "so I didn't want to put them back on the desk."

"Oh, thanks," Ava said.

"If you need anything, you know where I'll be."

After he left, Ava peeked inside the folder to find five photos. But only one was seared in her memory. *Marry Me* guy.

She turned it over, knowing she was going to find only the date, July 7, 1959. And the invisible message: *I'm a mystery man.* But here was the thing. Most photos around here had once appeared in the *Times*, which meant there had to be some information on this guy somewhere.

Under the harsh fluorescent lights, Ava pushed aside the succulent article she had already marked up and pulled a magnifying glass from her desk drawer to peer closer. The white guy looked to be in his early twenties.

He was handsome in a young Ben Affleck kind of way, but it was the hope and promise in his eyes that drew her to the photo. And then she saw the detail she had missed the other night—there in the background was a clock tower, faded and fuzzy with the exception of the conspicuous black hands pointing to 8:51.

Ava felt the ground tilt beneath her. *No way. It's a coincidence. Just like the bill the other night.*

Coincidence.

The word pecked away at her resolve until she shoved the picture back in the folder and into the drawer, chastising herself for letting her brain jump down an absurd rabbit hole.

Get ahold of yourself. It's just three harmless numbers.

Ava was very good at convincing herself of whatever reality suited her. One where destiny and fate and meant-to-bes didn't exist. One where she was in control, like of being on time to see Rion.

More than ever, she felt the need to assert that control over her own life, starting now.

That's when she caught a whiff of citrus. Her stomach plummeted.

Rushing around to Harold's cubicle, she gasped. His thumbnail was jammed into Bloody Cara!

"Stop!" Ava screamed. Did he seriously swipe it off the desk when she went to the bathroom? She inspected the orange's peel. Thankfully, there was only the one small puncture wound.

Harold jumped, dropping BC onto his desk with a miserable *thud.* "What's your problem?"

"My problem?" Ava glowered, snatching the orange away. "This is my orange! It was on my desk!"

Anmol's eyes floated over the cubicle wall. "Dude, that's not cool."

Harold pushed his glasses up his nose. "Well, it must have rolled off. Jesus, Ava. It's just an orange." He glanced around at the others in the office, who were too busy to look up from their computers or conversations or phones.

"Just like my pen and stapler and . . ." She scanned his jumbled space. One of her pink folders with the word *Magic* written across the front sat on his dented minifridge. "And this!" She grabbed the folder and stuffed it under her arm.

"I bet that's where my bagels have been going!" Anmol accused.

"I'm gluten intolerant, Anmol!" Then, turning back to Ava, Harold threw his hands up in surrender, but he was wearing a stupid, painfully forced expression of mock innocence. "*That folder* was in the trash."

"And it's not just an orange," Ava said, recalibrating, imagining her cartoon self growing devil horns with each word she spoke, improvising as she went. "It's part of a story I'm working on, and this *orange* is a new variety that . . . that . . ."

"Repels all sorts of insects," Anmol threw in with a convincing nod.

"And it isn't safe to eat, Harold." Then, with a straight face, Ava said with more conviction than a criminal defense lawyer, "You could have poisoned yourself."

Anmol played the part with a gasp. Harold's face went white. Quickly followed by a smirk. "You expect me to believe that bullshit?"

Ava shrugged, feeling the satisfaction expand in her chest like a balloon. "You should be thanking me for saving your life." And then, with Bloody Cara in tow, she smiled at Anmol, grabbed her purse, and strolled off.

When she got to the Jeep, her phone vibrated. Once. Twice. Six times.

She had five texts from her sisters in their group chat named *Brujasteria*.

Carmen: Ava, did you take my new leather jacket? The tan one?

Viv: Are you there yet? Don't be late.

Carmen: if you wore it I'm going to KILL you!

Viv: Text when you're there.

Carmen: slowly. I'll kill you slowly.

Ava texted back: no to jacket and yes I'm on my way. Stop texting me!

Then she turned her phone to silent.

Ava found parking in the lot adjacent to the locomotive museum, just like Rion had instructed. The evening air was cool and fresh and uncharacteristically clear.

A few stragglers milled about, coming and going as Ava made her way across the lot, her eyes scanning the area until she found him.

Rion stood at the edge of the road, wearing loose-fitting jeans and a backpack. He was holding a huge E.T. balloon. And he had shaved.

Ava stopped in her tracks.

Oh. My. God. Is that the surprise? A half-deflated alien balloon? Is he a total weirdo?

If it was possible to die and still breathe, Ava did it. Right there on the spot. Thankfully, she was still twenty feet away, and Rion hadn't seen her yet. *Should I leave? Pretend I got sick? Tell him I'm lost? That I'm going to be lost forever?*

It would be honest. And genuine.

"Ava!"

Too late.

Rion stood there waving eagerly as if Ava could miss him and E.T. She forced a tight-lipped smile and practically dragged herself over. *It's just a balloon*, she told herself as Viv's words echoed back to her. *Be nice. Be nice. BE NICE.*

When she reached Rion, he looked as if he might go in for a hug but then changed his mind last second. "You made it," he said, like he was surprised she showed up.

Just as Ava began to respond, a little boy of maybe seven raced over, sweaty and panting. Rion high-fived him and handed him the balloon. "I took good care of your friend here."

"'Kay, thanks," the boy said before spinning away to return to his mom.

Ava felt a rush of relief, so much so that her chest nearly caved and her shoulders nearly sagged. Was it possible she wanted a better surprise than a balloon? That she didn't want Rion to be so ... typical? *No*, she reasoned. *Why would I care if Rion is typical? And I hate surprises because they take away my control. But if E.T. wasn't the surprise, then what is?*

Wanting to keep the mood light, Ava said, "You're ... a balloon watcher."

"He wanted to climb a tree with his mom," Rion said with a shrug. "So, I offered."

"You could have run away with it," Ava teased.

Tilting his chin up, Rion said, "Look at this trustworthy face."

Ava laughed. So did Rion. And for a moment they stood there like that, feeling the leftover effects of a good joke. Rion's eyes darted to her mouth, then back up. A strange sense of gravity registered there, making Ava feel off-kilter. "You thought it was for you, didn't you?" Rion said.

"The balloon?"

"Yeah, the balloon."

"Um ... no."

"You totally did." His honey eyes danced with amusement. "Admit it."

"I've got nothing against E.T."

"How could anyone? He's amazing."

"Exactly. But why are they selling E.T. balloons at a train museum?"

"He got it at the store yesterday. His mom said he's been carrying it ever since," Rion said. "Did you bring the orange?"

Ava patted her tote bag. "Yup."

"Okay," Rion said, clapping his hands together, "you ready for your surprise?"

"Please quit using that word. You're making me nervous."

"Okay, drama queen." Rion laughed. "Don't be nervous; I probably oversold it. You might not even like it." A slow smile spread across his face. "Actually, I think you might be amazed."

Caroline relaxed on a raft next to Ava's as they floated across the pool. The limitless night sky embraced Ava like a warm hug. She loved these moments alone with her mom when she didn't have to share her with her sisters, with the world.

"The gardener's son was not boring. He told the princess stories." Caroline spoke with a smooth, calming voice. "Stories to make her laugh. Stories that filled up her heart. Stories she had never heard before."

"Like what?" Ava asked, keeping her gaze on a single distant star.

"Oh, stories of love and heartbreak and chance and hope. Stories with dragons and magical places."

Ava liked the idea of dragons and magical places.

Caroline said, "Minutes, hours, days, and weeks went by. The princess's mother grew tired of waiting. She told her daughter that she had selected the prince for her.

"'No,' the princess told her mother. 'I have already decided.'

"By choosing the gardener's son, the non-prince, the princess thought she could get around her own destiny to kill with a kiss the first prince she let into her heart. She thought she could trick Fate.

"She thought she was such a clever girl."

Eighteen

Ava didn't know which was more panic inducing: to be surprised or to be amazed. She supposed amazement was the better choice and didn't carry the same weight of expectation. But what could be so amazing about steam engines?

When Rion headed in the opposite direction of Travel Town, Ava said, "Aren't you going the wrong way?"

Rion gave her a quizzical glance. "Oh . . . you thought we were going to Travel Town? Trains aren't as cool as what I'm going to show you. Come on."

Ava felt a small tug of unexpected excitement. She had just promised herself that she would be in control from here on out, and already Rion was twisting the plan.

They crossed Griffith Park Drive and turned onto a wide equestrian trail. Pretty soon they entered a deep shade under oak and sycamore trees. Bits of sunlight filtered through the twisted branches.

"Where are we going?" Ava said, glad she'd worn comfy tennis shoes.

"Has anyone ever taught you the concept of a surprise? It's not much farther."

There was a prickling sensation that started in Ava's feet and wound up her legs. Was it really a good idea to follow a stranger into the woods? *You've watched too many horror movies,* she told herself. *Besides, he's not a*

total stranger. We've had flan together, and he has my blessing! And my sisters
know where I am and would totally raise hell to find me.

As they hiked a small rise near a gurgling creek, Ava could feel the stress of the city melting away. Her breaths became deeper, easier, more relaxed.

"This is really pretty," she said. "I've never been here before."

"It's one of my favorite places."

Ava could see why. There was an unexpected beauty in the ancient-looking trees, the way the leftover sun sifted through their twisted branches. It was hard to imagine the hustle and bustle of the city just miles away, or that Los Angeles was once this wild terrain.

For the next few minutes they made small talk. Ava pounded him with questions, trying to get at a nugget of truth that might lead her to figuring out what the blessing was. Surely, Rion could feel that something was different. Right?

But the only things she learned were that Rion's favorite food was pizza topped with jalapeños dipped in ranch dressing. His favorite music was any and all except country, because the songs always seemed to have sad endings. His favorite person was his grandfather. He read over thirty books last year, mostly graphic novels, outdoors was his favorite place to be, and he volunteered with Paper Bridges, an organization that brought orphans and individuals together around the globe through letters.

"So, you're like a pen pal?" Ava said, intrigued, as they continued up the shadowed path.

"I write to a ten-year-old in Greece; his name is Basil," Rion said. "Awesome kid."

"That's so cool. How did you get involved with them?" But what she really meant was, *Why did you choose to write letters to an orphan? That isn't some random thing.*

Rion was silent for a few more steps. He readjusted his backpack and said, "My parents died when I was ten. Car accident. And I don't ... I guess I really relate to kids who don't have their mom and dad, you know?"

"I'm so sorry," Ava said lightly. She felt like she should say something else but couldn't find the words. Then she wondered if Maggie was Rion's mom. Didn't he say that his grandfather was his mom's dad? She wanted to know if that's who the orchard was named for but didn't have the guts to ask. Because maybe, like her, Rion didn't want to talk about parents who weren't coming back.

Rion's shoulder bumped her gently. "It's all good. I mean, Bruce Wayne turned out okay." He laughed, relaxing the moment. "Some things are just meant to be," he went on, "and I'm lucky really. My gramps is the best."

There is no meant to be, Rion.

"What about you?" he asked. "What are your parents like?"

Ava swallowed. She wasn't ready to tell him about her mom, if she *ever* told him. It was the secret she carried, the lie always on the tip of her tongue, ready to be told at a moment's notice. Like when she was in the third grade and a kid asked why her mom wasn't at parent night, she told them her mom had died. But she knew if she acted weird about it with Rion, he would only get more curious, so she gave him a morsel. "They're fine. Dad's cool. Mom ..."

She hesitated, reaching for a truth that wouldn't invite more questions. "She's in her own world."

"What do they do?"

God, Ava hated getting-to-know-you chats. They were the worst, but if she was going to do this, if she was going to be genuine and build a real friendship with Rion, she had to share *something*. So she steered Rion in the direction of the people she *was* willing to talk about. "My dad owns a design company. My oldest sister, Viv, is an architect and works for him. Carmen, my other sister, interns in the summers. She goes to USC and has no idea what she wants to do or be."

"I get it." Rion was nodding thoughtfully as the two continued down the shaded path. "And you? Are you going to work for your dad?"

Ava was already shaking her head before the words made their way into the open air. "Doubt it. So you don't know what you want to study either?"

"Not a clue. Isn't that what college is for? Figuring it out?"

Ava would break out in hives if she stepped foot on campus with no idea what she was going to study. "Where do you want to go?"

"Somewhere close." Stopping in his tracks, Rion surveyed the area before announcing, "This is the spot. Come on." He hiked off the path, up a small mound, and into the trees. Ava followed.

Thirty feet in, Rion stopped under a wide oak that looked older than the rest. He shrugged off his backpack and patted the thick, rough trunk. "To see the amazement, you have to climb the tree."

"Seriously?" Ava had climbed plenty of trees in her own backyard, but not since she was like ten.

"If you're too scared, we don't have to."

"I'm not scared."

"Or if you don't think you can . . ."

"I know how to climb a tree, Rion." Ava retied her joggers and adjusted her T-shirt.

Rion leaned against the thick trunk, his full mouth turned up into a half smile. "But can you do it with your eyes closed?"

"What! You're joking, right?"

"Do I look like a kidder?"

"Actually . . ."

"You have to trust me."

Trust. Right. Of all the things for Rion to ask her for, he had to request the one she was allergic to.

Seeing her obvious hesitation, he said, "I promise it will be worth it."

Ava set down her bag, pushed back her shoulders, and said, "Okay, but if it's not worth it, I'm going to murder you."

"That's pretty violent." Rion laughed. "Get yourself into the tree first," he said as he easily gripped the lowest branch with one hand, wrapped the other around the trunk, and hoisted himself into a wide foothold. His triceps were surprisingly toned, and Ava realized she had mistaken thin for weak.

He turned and extended his hand to help Ava.

"I can do it," she said, waving him away. She was gloriously grateful that she was athletic. Maybe she never took tree-climbing lessons, but she played tennis and volleyball and could swim a mile.

Without overthinking it, she mimicked Rion's ascent, nearly knocking him out of the tree when she overextended and swung herself into the foothold.

Rion pivoted, replanted his feet, and grabbed ahold of a higher branch to stabilize himself. "Okay," he said, "now you have to close your eyes."

"You were actually serious."

"It's an easy climb. I'm going to guide you," he said. "And it isn't that far."

Ava glanced up into the thick crisscrossing branches, wondering what could be so special about this tree. Some unexpected spectacular view? Made better by closing your eyes? From where she stood, the only view was more trees. And Rion, who she suddenly realized was mere inches from her. He smelled of citrus and earth and leather. His skin was even more golden up close.

"Fine," she muttered, trying to create some distance. "But if I fall and break my neck and can't be the one to murder you, I guarantee you Viv and Carmen will find you quickly."

Rion smiled. "Deal."

With a deep, very untrusting breath, Ava closed her eyes.

"Okay," Rion said, "place your foot about eight inches to the right." He grabbed hold of her hand to guide her. She felt a sudden surge of what could only be described as a warm jolt of energy. Did he feel it too? If he did, he said nothing. He stayed close as she found the toehold. "There's another branch about a foot above you to the right. Grab it and pull yourself up."

Ava did as he instructed, hand over hand, foot over foot, using knots and holes along the way to help her. She didn't know what surprise Rion had in store for her at the top, but the surprise that was growing in her chest at how easy it was to follow his voice and not be terrified of falling was totally unexpected. And that kind of trust felt like something tightening in her stomach, ready to explode. "Are we there yet?"

"Close."

Another hoist and grip. "Now?"

"You might be the most impatient person I've ever met."

Half a minute later, Ava hauled herself up another foot and leaned against the massive trunk. Rion said, "You can look now."

Ava opened her eyes. They were only twenty feet above the ground, not nearly as high as she had expected. Rion swung himself past her and onto a higher branch with the ease of a monkey. "Okay, so where's this amazement?" she said.

"You told me you like life stories."

"Mm-hmm."

He pointed to a branch to her right. There were words carved into the bark:

Ellie and Edwin April 4, 1963. 12 years old. Friends forever.

It was sweet to think of two kids climbing this tree and carving their names, but had Rion really brought her all the way up here to see this? And before she could ask, he said, "You can follow the story down now."

Ava's gaze followed his to the branch beneath her. She climbed down to get a better view of another etching.

A crooked heart. *1964. Kiss.*

Inch by inch, Ava lowered herself, finding more words. A strange vibration began in her chest.

Dec. 1964 I love E. And then right next to it in a different hand, *Me too.*

Ava found herself smiling as she imagined these two kids growing up together, climbing this tree so they could mark the moments that mattered most to them. She could almost hear their laughter and whispers, their arguing over whether the kiss was good or bad.

A cool breeze drifted through the tree, rustling its leaves.

Feb. 1965 xoxo

Ava wasn't sure what was significant about it, but whatever it was, it was their secret.

May 1968. Come home safe.

1968. That was during the Vietnam War. Was that what this meant? Had Edwin gone off to war? Ava's heart closed in on itself as she pictured a girl her own age sitting on this very branch worried about the person she loved.

Ava felt an unexplainable frantic energy bubbling up in her as she searched for the next engraving. *Please let there be another one.* But there was nothing more. Until she found a toehold and looked up beneath a small branch.

In smaller letters than the rest was this:

Dec. 1969, thank you

And right next to it, *Jan. 1970, she said yes!*

Ava traced her fingers over the dates, the words, the moments. A part of her felt voyeuristic, like she was reading someone's diary, but she had to know what happened next.

August 1972 Warren.

November 1974 William.

January 1976 Sarah.

Inch by inch Ava's heart made room for the possibility that this couple had found their happy ending. He had survived war. They got married, had three kids.

10 years E&E

And then the trail went dead as Ava stepped back into the original foothold. *Is that it? Is that how their story ended?* She dropped out of the tree and circled the base, hunting. And then she saw it. She squatted to read the last inscription.

Goodbye, Edwin, April 22, 1984

Friends forever.

"Oh my God, he died? That's a terrible ending!" Ava blurted. A huge knot grew in her throat. *Love always ends in goodbye*, she thought bitterly. Her eyes burned with stubborn, unwanted tears. An unexplainable anger surged.

Rion hopped down from the tree, swiping his hands on his jeans. "I'm sorry—I thought you would like it." He patted his pocket like he might have a handkerchief there. "Don't cry."

"I'm not crying." Ava stood and wiped the lone tear away, frustrated she didn't have better control over her ridiculous tear ducts. "It's just so sad. He was so young." She didn't even know Ellie and Edwin, so why did she feel so totally devastated?

"But they had three kids and all those years together."

"It wasn't enough." Ava's words surprised her.

"I just thought you would . . ." Rion ran a hand through his hair. "You said you liked life stories."

Ones with impossibly happy endings. Tilting her gaze to the top of the oak, Ava said, "I do . . . I just wasn't expecting . . ."

This. You.

Ava felt a sudden drop in her stomach. She had the strangest sensation that she knew Rion, that she had met him before that night at the stop sign. But it was impossible.

"So, how did you find it?" she asked, shaking the last thought away.

"I was hiking here last year and saw the carving on the trunk," Rion said. "I followed the trail to the top. So, I guess I read the story backward."

"That's a better ending." Two kids with the world at their feet.

Rion's mouth lifted into a hesitant grin. "Was this a bad idea?"

Ava shook her head and stared hard at Rion, whose gaze was now averted. She squinted, trying to see the blessing. *Maybe it has something to do with story.* It made total sense given Ava's desire to be a journalist.

"Why are you scowling at me like you want to hit me?" Rion said, hoisting his pack over his shoulder.

Ava's hand flew to her brows. "Oh, I frown a lot." *Lie.* Ava did her best to not frown ever since Carm freaked her out by telling her that every frown equals a future wrinkle. Although, Ava could find nothing to support her sister's preposterous claim.

"So, how about that orange?" While Rion rifled inside his pack, Ava caught a glimpse of the same book he'd had with him the other night. Closer now, Ava could make out the details. It was a plain black leather book with white pages. But what was inside?

Rion's voice pulled her back to the moment.

"So I brought napkins, since oranges can be kinda messy," he was saying, "and some water and soda. I didn't know what you liked."

"About the orange."

Rion froze. "You ate it."

"Um . . . Harold, this guy I work with, he almost ate it."

"Tell me that you saved it just in time."

Ava laughed, glad to relieve the pressure in her chest. "Something like that."

A few minutes later they had found a bench along the trail. The sky had faded to a pale blue with traces of the day's last light. Rion quickly peeled the orange, shaking his head and snorting his disbelief (and maybe approval) as Ava told him the full Harold story.

He held out half for Ava. "Okay, if you don't like it, if I oversold it, just lie to me. No, scratch that. Tell me the truth. It's not like we've been working on this variety for a million years or anything."

"You really love the orchard, don't you?"

Rion's eyes met hers and held her gaze for longer than was humanly comfortable. It was like some thread was connecting them in a silence that threatened to swallow them both. Ava blinked first, breaking the connection.

"How do you do that?" he said.

"What?"

"Get me to tell you things; it's kinda creepy. Like I've known you forever."

So, he felt it too.

"All those journalism classes?"

But what Ava really wanted to say was, *I know the feeling.* And then an idea struck her. Maybe this bizarre familiarity had something to do with the fact that he had her blessing.

"I've never heard of journalism classes that taught that."

"Well, psychology too, but I go to a magnet school with a really big journalism program. It's pretty intense. But we were talking about the orchard."

Not me.

Rion threw his gaze back to the sky. "*Love* isn't the right word. It's more . . . I don't know, like destiny. You know"—his tone shifted to light and easy—"that thing you don't believe in."

What was Ava supposed to say to that? *You're right. But will you still tell me the story of Maggie?*

Rion handed her a napkin, staring at her expectantly. "Don't laugh. They were the only ones I could find." His light brown hair ran in so many directions it was hard to know which was the natural path.

"Ninja Turtles?"

"I was obsessed with them when I was a kid," he said. "These must be left over from some birthday party."

Ava tried to imagine the orchard. In her mind's eye the farm was a sprawling green shady place with tire swings, an old barn, a rickety tractor. She could see the ramshackle house where three guys lived with a wraparound porch and drawers filled with Ninja Turtle napkins. She tugged a wedge free and plopped it into her mouth. Sweet juices exploded across her tongue. No, sour. Wait. It was both sour and sweet, but how was that even possible?

"It's . . ." Ava made a show of dragging it out. "It's both . . . let me see. It's . . ."

"Say it!"

Her face broke into a smile. "It's amazing!" She tossed the rest into her mouth, blotting the juices that slid down her chin with her napkin.

"See? What did I tell you? You can have my half too." He extended his hand, and Ava was already refusing when his phone rang.

He unpocketed his cell and flipped the ancient thing open. Ava's eyes veered to the name on the screen: *Shelby*.

"Do you need to get it?" she asked, feeling a flash of irritation that confused her.

"It'll just take a second." Rion headed down the path to take the call.

Ava straightened, feeling like she was doing something she shouldn't be doing, which was utterly ridiculous. But she couldn't keep the sharp-edged questions at bay: *Is Shelby his girlfriend? Is he one of those guys? Maybe she's just a friend. Has he ever taken her to the story tree? Oh my God, Ava, get ahold of yourself.*

She was still getting ahold of herself when Rion came back a few minutes later. Meda materialized right behind him, startling Ava so badly she nearly tumbled off the bench.

"What's wrong?" Rion said, glancing behind him.

"I . . . nothing. I thought I saw a bug." She cringed. *A bug? Really?*

Meda was inches from Rion, inspecting him so closely, Ava was sure Rion would sense the saint.

Ava stood abruptly. "Hey, I need to call my sister. I'll be right back."

She distanced herself down the trail enough that Rion couldn't hear her. She held her phone to her ear, pretending to be on the call. "You aren't supposed to come unless I call you!" she whisper-shouted at Meda.

Meda said, "This an emergency."

"It's always an emergency."

"I expected a much more pleasant response. Perhaps that your ungrateful soul would want to know that we have found a piece of the puzzle. A very large piece."

"Is this going to be more bad news?" Ava was pacing, gripping the phone tighter. "Where's Nana?"

Nana appeared next to Meda, but her gaze was on Rion. "I see things are progressing. Qué bueno."

"What did you find out?" Ava asked impatiently.

The trees swayed in the cool breeze as if in response.

Nana deadpanned, "We know how to transfer the blessing."

Nineteen

Ava was seeing red.

Miles and miles of red brake lights as she sat idle in freeway traffic, continuing the conversation they couldn't have until they were safely in the car and away from Rion. Now Ava felt overwhelmed, listening to Nana and Meda yammer in her ear at the same time with such ferocity that Ava couldn't make out a single cohesive sentence.

"Stop!" she finally shouted, bringing both Nana and Meda to a stunned silence. "Please," she said, then, remembering who she was talking to, quickly added, "Sorry, but I only need one of you to talk. Nana . . ."

"Truly?" Meda scoffed. "You would choose a ghost over a saint?" He crossed his arms and threw himself against the back seat like a kid who didn't get his Happy Meal treat.

Eager to make him feel better, Ava tilted her head. "You can both tell me, but maybe let Nana start."

Nana tapped her ghostly fingers on the armrest, nodding with authority. "To get the blessing back—"

"We have to re-create the collision!" Meda threw in.

Nana rolled her eyes and exhaled loudly.

"What?" Ava cried. "Wait. You want me to crash into Rion's car?"

"Of course not," Meda said, like it was the stupidest question he had ever heard.

"That would be muy peligroso." Nana patted Ava's hand. "We must re-create the night the blessing went missing. Specifically, impact, storm, and high emotion." She ticked off the three elements on her fingers like they were items on a grocery list.

"How am I supposed to do that?" Ava said, making all sorts of dramatic arm gestures, because the moment called for them. It was a Granados thing. Whenever they got excessively worked up, the arm gesticulations always came next. Unless you were Carmen, in which case head bobbing and exaggerated gasps were included. "I can't just make it rain!"

"I can," Meda said brightly, looking pretty pleased with himself.

Ava felt like she was slipping off a steep cliff, desperately trying to cling to any scrap of earth she could. She knew she sounded like a whiner, but she was exhausted by each turn in the road, facing a new hurdle, wishing they could just find an easier path. One that didn't require lying to Rion. At least by omission. At first it hadn't bothered Ava, because she didn't know him. But after just two outings she decided they really could be friends. She liked him. How he was so honest and unguarded and easy to talk to. So unlike Ava.

"You said you didn't hit his car that hard, right?" Meda's voice pulled her out of her reverie. He was leaning into her space now. "So perhaps a little bump will do."

"Oh, I get it," Ava said sarcastically, grateful the cars were finally moving again. "You make an insta-storm, I run into him like a linebacker, and boom, the blessing is mine?"

"Don't forget high emotion," Nana reminded her.

Ava groaned. "I was joking about the linebacker."

"I know," Nana said, and Ava could tell she meant it. It wasn't often the Granados matriarch looked sullen or sorry, but in this moment, in the dimming evening light, she momentarily appeared both. Then, with a tight clasp of her fingers, she lifted her chin and said, "Mira. We do not always get the circumstances we wish, Ava, and life is not always a bowl of roses, but this is the situation in front of you, and you must face it. Con grit and—"

"Grace," Ava finished. *And it's "bed of roses."* "Yeah, I know." It was the narrative of Ava's upbringing. She had grown up with stories of the previous generation who had made so many sacrifices, who had endured much greater hardships and heartbreaks than she would ever know. Ava was certain that there were stories her grandmother had never told her, and even guessed that one of the heartbreaks Nana was talking about was personal. Ava couldn't imagine what kind of person could ever break Nana's iron heart. But whoever they were, they had to have been exceptional.

By the time Ava got home it was 9:00 p.m. Her sisters were nowhere to be found, and strangely, they hadn't bombarded her with a million text messages while she was with Rion.

She fired off a text to Viv. Where are you? When she got no response, she went to Carmen next. Are you coming home? Then to both in the Brujasteria chat, I have so much to tell you guys!

Carmen was the first to ping her. Is it big news? w/ some friends. Do I need to interrupt?

Next was Viv. Eating sushi. Do I need to call you?

With who? Ava asked her oldest sister, her Spidey senses sounding alarm bells.

But she didn't get an answer, only, Is everything okay? Viv was deflecting, but why? So much for telling each other everything. Ava was a bundle of twisted emotions. It had been an exhausting day, and she was still feeling the effects of Ellie and Edwin. *Strangers*, she reminded herself. But it had made her think, *What would my own story tree look like? What would it say?* Then there were Rion's parents. All reminders that goodbyes were inevitable and sucked. And now she was sure Viv was keeping something from her, which meant she didn't trust Ava, and that was probably the deepest cut of them all.

I'm fine, Ava texted them back. She wasn't sure why she didn't just tell them she knew how to get the blessing back. Maybe because she didn't want to ruin their plans by interrupting them, or maybe she just wanted a moment's peace before the storm hit.

Ava heard the friends Carmen had texted about the minute she walked into the kitchen. Music blared out back, and the sound of splashes and laughter spilled into the open windows, which Ava quickly closed. Meda was sitting on the kitchen counter, staring at the cake on display in the glass dome with an intense gaze. "Saint Honoré? You baked his cake?"

"I'd offer you a piece, but . . ."

"I wouldn't eat it!" He folded his arms over his chest. "Pish. Bakers. No one ever named a cake after moi!"

"Do you know him?" Ava asked.

"Of course I do, and guess what?" Meda said, "You can't eat cake without teeth, especially if there are nuts or dried fruit. And in this case, those little puff pastries would be quite difficult!"

"Valid," Ava admitted. "You should definitely get your own cake."

"I don't care for pastry," Meda said with a sneer.

Nana dragged her gaze from the kitchen window and peered at the pastry like it was an ancient relic at the Getty Museum. "You did not get your culinary talents from me."

Nana had never spent her time or energy in the kitchen. She was a sharp-eyed, tough-nut businesswoman who could make grown men go weak in the knees with just one glare. Ava imagined how hard it must have been for her to leave her family's security and raise Raul alone. How desperate she must have been to get out. Although she never said why.

Meda swung his legs, his head tilted back. He was clearly in deep thought.

"Ava, do you have any clue what the blessing might be?" Nana asked. A series of whoops and whistles penetrated the kitchen walls. "Maybe I should check on them."

Ava bit back the laugh as she imagined the ghost trying to break up a pool party.

"What if it has to do with the story?" Ava said, pulling her grandmother's attention back to the matter at hand before telling her and Meda about Edwin and Ellie's tree. "Rion seems kind of big on them. And he even mentioned some other story about a woman his family's orchard is named after. I mean, maybe it's connected?" Her voice trailed off on a question she wished she had the answer for. "It's a long shot, I know."

"Hmm," Nana hummed. "Story—is that a blessing I would give to you? You don't care for them, or at least not the made-up kind, so why would I? Bah! Why isn't my memory better?" She turned to Meda. "Someone really needs to change the rule book."

"Rules don't get changed in the afterlife," Meda said solemnly.

Nana didn't look convinced. It was as if the memory of the blessing was tucked deep inside her, in a place she just didn't have access to. But Ava wouldn't let that deflate her confidence. It was the most logical idea anyone had presented. Journalists are storytellers. Nana must have blessed her with something that would help her career. It made perfect sense.

Except that there was a slow simmer beginning inside her that made her question her choices. What if being a journalist was her way of deflecting, of hiding from the world by shining a light on other people's lives?

Ava felt like she was drifting in a fog. She was so worn out, she couldn't remember taking a long hot shower, or slipping into her comfiest pj's, or sliding under the cool sheets, welcoming the dark and the beginnings of a dream in which . . .

A *ping* ripped her from precious sleep. She tugged off her silk eye mask and peered down at her phone. It was only 11:00 p.m., and yet it felt like she had been asleep for hours. She had a text from Raul. Your old dad went horseback riding today.

Ava sent a thumbs-up. Did you break a hip?

I'm not that old. And no olvides la fiesta.

"Except I did forget," Ava groaned. Emmanuel's party was this Saturday! She really wanted to bail, but she knew that if she did, it would be a one-way ticket to guilt city, and she already had more guilt than her heart had room for.

How are your sisters?

Everyone is good, Ava texted back. "Carmen's throwing a pool bash, and I'm pretty sure Viv is keeping a secret," she uttered aloud.

She rolled over and sent a text to Elijah: If you had to create an excuse to collide with someone, how would you do it? Give me a list.

She knew the list would never arrive, but texting Elijah made her feel connected to him. Sitting up, she thought about Rion. She hadn't even thanked him before she rushed their goodbye earlier.

Is it too late to call him? It'll go to voicemail if he's asleep.

One ring. Two.

"Hey," Rion said. There was a *thump*, and then, "Ow!"

"Are you okay?"

A dog barked in the distance. "I just walked into a trailer. Tres, come on, girl," Rion said. "The raccoon is long gone."

Ava's mouth turned up into a faint smile. For the second time she tried to imagine the orchard. Tonight, it was an expanse of dark with millions of stars hanging overhead and a golden retriever or maybe a black lab tearing after some vermin with a barefooted Rion chasing after her.

"You named your dog Three?"

"Yeah, she's got three spots on her back, and it's my lucky number."

Ava chuckled. "Okay, well, I just wanted to say thanks for the tree and everything."

"Tres!" Rion shouted. "I'm freezing huevos out here." Then to Ava, "Sorry about that. Tres thinks the world is her oyster. But you're welcome. What are you doing?"

Tres barked three more times, followed by the sound of Rion chasing after her, breathless. "You better go catch Tres," Ava said. "I'll talk to you later."

"Okay, but don't forget, next one is on you."

"Huh?"

"It's your turn."

Ava felt dense asking, but she had zero idea what Rion was talking about.

"Turn?"

"Yeah, you took me for flan, I took you for a hike. Now it's your turn. Tres!"

"Is that how this works?"

Another series of barking. "Tres says yes."

Ava's smile went from faint to full as she rolled onto her stomach. "Deal."

"You have to *what*?" Carmen had shouted on the drive over to Venice Beach Monday morning. Ava relayed everything Nana and Meda had told her, and by the time the sisters were seated at the Butcher's Daughter, the ridiculousness of the situation had worn down to *maybe this is manageable*. But even more than *how* to get back the blessing, Viv and Carmen were fixated on Ellie and Edwin's tree.

"That's seriously so sad," Viv said.

"Kind of sappy, if you ask me," Carm put in. But there was affection in her voice that told Ava she thought it was sweet too, but admitting it would likely put a chink in her armor. She stared into a compact mirror. "God, look at these bags. I look thirty!"

Checking her phone, Viv said, "I have to hustle, guys. I have a meeting in an hour." Then, to Carm, "That's what happens when you're up all night."

"Hardly all night."

"No more parties while Dad's gone."

Carm fixed her gaze on Viv, unblinking. "You're not my mother."

There. The words were out, darting around them like the poison they were. Carm quickly corrected course. "I meant . . . just forget I said that. Bad choice of words."

Viv and Ava shared a side glance and nodded simultaneously. They were all more than happy to forget it.

The three sat in the bustling café staring at the menu, even though they each already knew what they wanted to eat. Viv would order a matcha and an acai bowl. Carmen always vacillated between the avocado toast and waffles, depending on how much she had worked out in the last forty-eight hours. But her drink was always the same: the Mexican Cacao Elixir. Ava was the only one who tried something new each time. Today she ordered a cardamom chai and a breakfast burrito loaded with green chile.

Gary the server, a lanky, red-cheeked guy, pulled an apologetic face when Viv surprised everyone and ordered a kale salad. "Uh, sorry," he said, "but the salad is only served in the evenings."

Viv smiled, arranging her utensils neatly. "Right. Okay." She glanced up, making eye contact with Gary.

There were three beats of awkward nonconversation. Then Gary glanced around and said, "I can totally check if you want."

"I don't want to be any trouble."

Gary leaned in conspiratorially, like he was planning a heist. "We've got the kale in the fridge. It's no big deal."

Ava sat back, watching the interaction, wondering if this was her sister's blessing in full force or . . .

Gary was already nodding before Viv got out, "You're the best."

"That is seriously twisted," Ava said, watching Gary head back to the kitchen. "You made him think it was his idea."

"Am I a horrible person?" Viv scrunched up her face like she was in pain. "I just really want kale."

"Who *really* wants kale?" Carmen muttered, not quite under her breath.

"But you didn't even try," Ava said, still in awe over Viv's gift to persuade without even talking. "You just looked at him."

"I've been testing things out, trying to figure out limitations," Viv said.

Tightening her messy bun, Carmen said, "Does it work every time?"

"Depends on the person's frame of mind and how stubborn they are," Viv said with a one-shoulder shrug. "But no, it doesn't always work."

"Try it on me," Ava said.

Viv narrowed her gaze. "It won't be effective on you."

"Why?" Carm asked before Ava could.

"Okay, I'm only guessing, but I think when love is involved, my blessing doesn't quite work as well."

Carmen fidgeted with her cropped sweatshirt. "Who says I love you?" She let out a snarky laugh.

"But you talked Dad into vacation," Ava said.

"I said it doesn't work as well," Viv suggested. "Not that it doesn't work at all, and Dad just needed a little push."

"But for real," Carm said, "it's probably because it would make your relationships unbalanced and everything in the universe is about equilibrium."

Viv and Ava both stared wide-eyed at Carmen.

"Who told you that?" Ava wondered if Carm had made that up or if she was really onto something.

"I'm reading this book on Buddhism, and it just makes sense, right?"

"You hate to read."

"Well, maybe not anymore," Carm bit back. "I mean, I can remember all these cool facts, and it's like . . . who knew books were so interesting?" Her face lit up. "Imagine how easy school is going to be now!"

"If love is my kryptonite," Viv said with a frown, completely ignoring the fact that Carmen was reading Buddhism, or gaming her blessing to get good grades, "then what's yours, Miss Memory?"

Gary brought over the drinks and handed out napkins as Carm sipped her cacao. "Apparently, if whatever I read or hear is a 'secret'"—she made air quotes—"I can't repeat it. The universe is so mean." Her face collapsed into a miserable pout. "Karly got a nose job as if no one would notice, and she doesn't want anyone to know. But I wanted to tell Bree, because Karly is a terrible person and stole her boyfriend; remember *that* big scandal? I thought it might make Bree feel better. But when I tried, the words were, like, stuck in my throat. And no way am I writing anything down that would implicate me as a traitor. Isn't that a total joke? Like, what's the point of knowing gossip if you can't share it? And why wouldn't Nana tell us the blessings came with weaknesses?"

Ava shifted in her chair. "Except you just repeated it, so that means you can spill secrets to us, right?" She hated the idea that Carmen wouldn't be able to share confidences. It flew in the face of their blood oath. It was a slam to sisterhood!

Carmen glanced over, eyes flashing. "I guess I just told you, so maybe I can spill the beans if love is involved too?" Her eyes searched Ava's face. "Call Nana. Let's ask her."

"We can ask Nana later," Viv said, tugging off her fitted blazer and hanging it on the back of her chair. "More importantly, we have to figure out how to re-create the night of the blessing."

Ava sipped her spicy chai. "Hang on. First, tell me who you were with last night."

Viv looked taken aback, as if she hadn't been expecting a redirect in the convo. "A couple of people from work, why?"

"Sounds like a new boy toy," Carmen said in her singsong know-it-all voice.

"Hardly," Viv said. "Unless you count Gabriel and Marlene as new love interests. We're working on a big project in Malibu. God, the views are stunning, so I want to make sure to preserve—"

"It's too early to listen to you talk about architecture, Viv," Carmen moaned.

Ava studied Viv, looking for any crack in her demeanor. Was she just being overly sensitive? No way. Her sister radar was a finely honed instrument. Something was up with Viv, and whatever it was, Viv wasn't going to talk about it. But worse, Ava felt that twinge down between her ribs that told her Viv was lying. A memory bubbled to the surface. It was a month before their mom left. Their parents had been arguing again—about something Ava couldn't remember now. She sometimes thought her mom picked these fights to assuage her own guilt, because she figured Caroline always knew she was going to leave and needed a reason to point to. And when she finally did walk out the door, Ava asked her dad when she was coming back. He told her *soon*, but soon turned out to be never. Now Ava understood some lies are meant to protect. But she knew the only one being protected here was Viv.

Ava pulled herself out of the mental spiral, thinking she would deal with it later when she and Viv were alone. "Meda can make it rain," she said, trying to ignore the pain blooming in her chest. "So, we've got the storm covered. But then there's the collision and high emotion."

"I've got it!" Carm slammed her hand on the wooden table, making the old man next to them jump.

"What?!" Ava said in a whisper-shout.

"We can rent some of those inflatable sumo-wrestler suits, and you can run into him as much as you want."

Ava imagined herself suited up as a sumo wrestler and shoved the idea aside immediately. No way. Her pride had limits.

"I have a better idea," Viv said with that knowing smile that told Ava it really was a good idea. Carmen and Ava looked at her expectantly.

"Football!" Viv said brightly, as if the answer had been sitting with them at the table all this time. "We can get a game together on the beach, and you can tackle him."

The more Ava thought about it, the more she liked it. But then her acceptance hit a brick wall. "But who's going to want to play football in the rain?"

"Have you not seen *Invincible*?" Viv argued. "That scene where Mark Wahlberg and his friends are playing in the abandoned lot, and it's perfect in every single way?" Her face lit up with the memory of it. Viv was obsessed with football. When she was in middle school she had begged Raul to let her try out for the team, but he wouldn't. It was tragic, because she could throw a spiral better than any of the guys. Ava was pretty sure her sister had never gotten over it.

"Okay, so I tackle him on the beach in the rain," Ava said, going with the flow. "What about high emotion?"

"Pain is emotion," Carm said as Gary delivered their plates, flashing an extra smile as he set Viv's salad in front of her.

Ava tossed her napkin at her sister. "Really? You want me to get hurt?"

"I never said that. I just meant that—"

Viv cut her off with, "Maybe your desire to help Nana, to keep the blessings alive, will be enough emotion."

Ava tapped the side of her glass. "Okay, but what if he doesn't play football?"

"Then I guess you'll have to find other ways to collide into orange boy," Carmen said with a wink.

"Or I could persuade him," Viv said as she stabbed her fork into the salad.

At the same moment Carmen's gaze shifted to the door. She *ooh*'d appreciatively. A group of five guys came into the Butcher's Daughter. They all wore basketball shorts and sweaty tees; some were definitely Carmen's type. Tall. Dark. Chiseled. And then there was the one carrying a ball under his arm.

Rion.

Their eyes met.

Ava's heart took off at a breakneck gallop. Her chest tightened. She wasn't sure why, but seeing him out of context and so unexpectedly, when she and her sisters were just plotting to steal something from him without his knowledge, filled her with a sort of terror.

Oh God, he was coming over. And before Ava could warn her sisters, he stood at the edge of the table and smiled.

"Hey, Rion." Ava tried to sound chill.

A silent pause. A smirk. And that was the moment Ava knew: This wasn't Rion. It was Achilles.

Caroline sat at the edge of Ava's bed, stroking her hair.

"Fate was angry with the princess. Angry with her for making foolish plans."

"What did the princess do?" Ava asked, wondering if the answer would ever change.

"Well, against her mother's wishes, she planned a wedding to the gardener's son, to the boy filled with stories. But it was never to be. The night before, one of the princess's suitors who she had thwarted sent her a gift of pomegranate juice. The princess took one sip and fell to the ground. Poisoned."

Silence stretched between them while Ava tried to process her thoughts. Tried to think of a different ending for the princess. One in which she could be happy. "I would never drink the poison."

"Mmm."

"And it's so mean!"

"Yes, my love, but like I said, Fate was angry, and you should never anger Fate."

Twenty

Ava's stomach bottomed out.

"Rion?" Achilles's brows shot up. "My brother?" He held a chill stance, which was totally unmasked by his defensive tone. It was uncanny how Achilles and Rion not only looked exactly alike, but their voices were nearly identical too. The only difference wasn't in depth or tone, but in inflection. Rion tended to end his sentences with the smallest of singsong lilts, like he was always waiting for an answer or a pleasant surprise. Or both.

"Uh . . . yeah." Ava scrambled for the right words, searching frantically for equal footing. "Remember, the car crash? I thought *you* were the one I rear-ended." And then, for a morsel of satisfaction, she added, "I thought I was crazy when you didn't remember, but I had no idea you had a twin brother." Code for *You didn't bother to tell me!*

"Until she met him seconds later," Carm said with a biting smile.

"So, you're the . . ." Achilles stopped midsentence, and Ava suddenly and desperately wanted to know what he was going to say. But he was already scanning Viv's and Carm's faces like some kind of CIA operative getting ready for an interrogation. "Hang on." Achilles snapped his fingers and said to Carmen, "Do I know you?"

Ava imagined her cartoon self fighting against a torrential wind that was hell-bent on blowing her off the face of the earth.

"Definitely not," Carmen said with an air of superiority. But Ava could tell her sister's brain was in full panic mode, struggling for a solution. If Achilles remembered her from Instagram, no way would he chalk it up to coincidence.

"These are my sisters, Carmen and Vivienne," Ava said, trying to change the subject while Carm not-so-inconspicuously tugged a thick strand of hair over her face.

Ugh! If Carm had just minded her own business and not messaged him. Thank God she doesn't use her real name on Instagram.

Ignoring Ava entirely, Achilles rubbed his annoying chin and said to Carmen, "I'm pretty sure I've seen you before."

"Do you go to the Wilshire SoulCycle? Early morning class?"

He grunted. "Uh, that would be a big no."

And then Carm threw a hand up as if she might tighten her messy bun again, but instead knocked her coffee over. The dark, bitter liquid poured over the side of the table and onto Achilles's shoes. He jumped back. "Whoa, bro!" And then, as if even the rude, brooding, arrogant jerk realized how bad he must have looked to half the restaurant now gawking at them, he grabbed some napkins off a server stand nearby and handed a few to Carmen before wiping off his shoes.

"Oops," Carmen said, rolling her eyes with fake flirtation. "Sorry 'bout that." But Ava knew that deep down her sister wasn't remotely sorry and just wanted to cut him down to size with something Carmenesque like, *Do you want cream with that?*

Achilles fisted his soggy napkins. "It'll come to me," he said. There was something immensely threatening in those four words that made Ava want to throw up. She couldn't believe that Achilles might possibly hold Nana's *and* their futures in his hands, because if he ever remembered Carmen from Instagram, he'd tell Rion, and the whole mission would blow up in their faces.

Viv, who had been in observation mode this whole time, must have picked up on it too, because she stepped into big-sis role. She was always willing to take a hit for Ava, like jumping into the pool at Nana's funeral to save her while Carm watched. But Carm had her own method of protection. She would fight anyone who picked on Ava, like the time a Nordstrom sales clerk was rude to Ava when she tried to return a pair of shoes. Carm drove down to the store to give the woman a piece of her mind *and* get a full refund. To Ava, Vivienne was body armor. Carmen was emotional armor.

Viv sat taller and, speaking with a pleasant yet authoritative tone, said, "My sister has a really unremarkable face that looks like a lot of other faces. Kind of common. I'm sure you have never seen her before."

Ava could barely swallow the bold-faced lie. And then she saw Viv's angle.

Carmen scowled, and looked like she might defend her beauty, but then she must have realized Viv was turning her blessing on too, because she sat back with a satisfied sneer.

"Unremarkable," he echoed. "Right." There was a moment when he hesitated, when his eyelids relaxed and his whole expression softened. That was the look that told Ava Viv had triumphed.

And Ava felt like she could breathe again. For now.

"Well," Carmen said, "We're having a family meeting, so . . ."

Achilles clearly didn't get the message, because he inched closer and said to Ava, "So, do you like my little brother or what?"

Wait. How did this become about her so quickly?

"He's nice," she said, then, thinking she needed to provide absolute clarification, she added, "We're friends." *Good friends.*

"Nice?" Achilles grunt-chuckled. "You just haven't seen his other side."

The way Achilles emphasized *other side* made Ava tense up. Were they talking about the same Rion?

He babysat an E.T. balloon.

"I'll tell Rion I saw you," Achilles finally said. "What's your name again?"

Ava glared at him, wondering how the same face on Rion could be so pleasant and on Achilles it made her nauseous.

"It's Ava."

"See ya, Ava." He flashed a sideways grin as he backed away to his table, then nearly tipped into a bow and said, "And sisters."

Trying to look as natural as possible, Ava fixed her gaze on Viv so they wouldn't accidentally swing over to Achilles's table. She wouldn't give him the satisfaction. "Well, now you know Rion's evil twin."

"That was too freakin' close," Carmen growled through gritted teeth. "God, I wanted to wipe that stupid grin off his stupid face. Like, seriously? I wasted a whole drink on that asshole. Who has that kind of arrogance and obnoxiousness—"

"Guys," Viv said, looking calm and polished and totally self-possessed, "fine, he's a jerk, but don't get distracted. Gree, you need to call Rion and invite him to the beach Saturday. Carmen, you need to make sure your Instagram—"

"It's set to private, and I just changed my profile pic to some random mountain," she said.

"Definite improvement," Ava teased.

Viv raised her glass. "Here's to football and blessings."

For the rest of the week Ava felt like she was lying in wait to be found out. It was worse than awful, as if she had robbed a bank and knew the cops had evidence that they just hadn't noticed the significance of yet.

She had called Rion, and he immediately said yes to her football invite. Oddly, he never mentioned Achilles saying anything about seeing her. She tried to shake the comment about Rion's *other side* and was hoping it was just a guy/brother thing. And why hadn't he told Rion he had seen her? Was that a guy thing too? Because no way would she not tell her sisters.

By Friday she had made two more trips to see Father Gustavo.

"Forgive me, Father, for I have sinned," she began.

"You're back," he said good-naturedly.

Ava laughed lightly. Father Gustavo was easy to talk to. Maybe it was the screen or the darkness or the fact that she didn't know him, but talking to him felt like writing in a journal you're absolutely certain no one will ever read. It felt like whatever words she spoke in that confessional floated away like dandelion dust.

"So, can I talk to you about something bad I haven't done yet?" Ava asked. "I mean . . ." She took a deep breath. "Okay, so there's this guy . . ."

"Go on."

"And he thinks were friends. I mean, we are, but I lied to him to get him to be friends with me, and I keep lying to him—but just about becoming his friend. Not about being his friend."

I sound like a weirdo.

"Does that even make sense?" Ava said.

There was a moment of silence that hung on the question *Is he judging me*? before the priest said, "Why do you keep lying?"

"It's for a really good reason. I mean, it didn't bother me at first, but now

I know him, and he's really nice and I feel all this guilt, but I . . . can I just ask for future forgiveness?"

"For the lying?"

Ava stiffened. God, it was so much worse than the lying. "No, I'm . . . I'm going to take something from him. I mean, it belongs to me, but what if he needs it too?"

"As in steal?"

"I mean, not really. Not if it belongs to me, right?"

"You said you lied to him, that you are going to take something from him, but why not just tell him the truth? If he's your friend, he'll under-stand."

Would he?

Maybe it was the quiet or the false security of the dark, but Ava actually considered Father Gustavo's suggestion. Except for one small issue: Rion had to *want* to give the blessing back, and Ava was pretty sure once he knew she had tricked him, he wouldn't give her jack. Plus, there was no guarantee he wouldn't think she had lost her mind once she started talking blessings. No, it was better to follow the plan, re-create the night of the blessing, and then . . . Ava's mind stalled. And then what?

Ava had already completed her required fifteen hours but decided to head to the *Times* to do some extra work, see if anyone needed an extra hand, and to keep her mind off Rion and the blessing that was starting to feel a whole lot like a curse. On her way over, after her depressing confession in which the priest did not make her feel an ounce better (wasn't that kind of his job?), Rion called.

"Hey," he said, "so who's coming to this football game anyways? Is this like a one-on-one thing or . . . ?"

"Nope. We've got teams."

"So is it cool if I bring a friend?"

"Sure," Ava said, thinking it would be kind of fun to meet one of Rion's friends.

Unless it was Shelby, and in that case it would so not be fun. Which was ridiculous, because Ava had just met Rion, hung out with him all of two times, and didn't have a claim on the guy, weird connection or not. But surely the story tree counted for like ten hang sessions? Ava didn't know why, but she felt like she'd known Rion a lot longer. "Who is it?" she said, to be sure and to prepare herself just in case.

"Alfonso. He's chill. You'll like him."

Alfonso. *Alfonso,* Ava thought with a smile. *Yes, so much better than Shelby.*

The office was buzzing with energy and voices and the whir of computers. By the time Ava got to her desk, Harold the thief was gone for the day and the *Magic* folder she had tossed on her shelf was back on the center of her desk. Seriously? Had Harold gone through her things again? "What the . . ." she groaned as she began to toss the folder in her file cabinet. Except that she knew what was inside. *Marry Me* guy. And her question still hadn't been answered. *Did she say yes?*

Ava's investigative spirit wouldn't let it go, and she desperately needed a distraction.

"Hey, Anmol, Corbin?" she called as she rounded their cubicles. "You guys want to help me with a project?"

"Not if you keep coming in on your days off to make us look bad," Corbin half joked.

"Okay, next week I'll keep regular hours if you help me out."

"Is it filing?" Anmol asked sullenly.

"Or anything social media–related?" Corbin's voice matched Anmol's tone. "'Cause I am so not down for that."

"No to both," Ava said, her excitement growing by the second. She showed her colleagues the photo. "I need to find out who this guy is."

"Why?" Anmol asked.

"It's a long story and . . ." She hesitated. "I'm bored. So, can you guys dig up any records you can find from this date in 1959?"

An hour later, they had come up with nada on the date, so they pored over any and all records from 1959, and they still came up empty-handed.

Why would the *Times* have ever run this photo in the first place?

If Ava were writing the story for this picture, she would say that obviously the guy was on his way to propose. His stride looked wide and quick. His eyes, hopeful and intent.

Ava stared at the picture like it were some kind of lifeline, some kind of answer to questions she hadn't asked yet. Maybe Edwin and Ellie's story had affected her more than she thought, but Ava had to know how this one ended. She went into Grant's office. He was intensely focused on whatever he was reading on his computer screen.

Ava didn't want to interrupt him and was about to leave when Grant looked up and said, "What's up, kid?"

Ava set the photo on his desk. "Where can I find out who this is?"

"I thought you were going to start that museum article I just gave you."

"I am, I just . . . wanted to finish up with these photos too." But really,

Ava just wasn't into copyediting, or any of the articles she was supposed to be working on. In the three years of her magnet program, she had loved writing and editing articles, but now? The process felt empty and unimportant. Like there was a whole world beyond the page beckoning her.

Grant flipped the picture over. "Only a date?"

"Exactly," Ava said, "so I don't know how to file it. And I was wondering if you knew where I could find out more information. I've already searched by year."

"Why not just toss it in the unknown file?"

With a one-shoulder shrug, Ava blew out the half-shaped lie. "I've never had to do that and don't want to start now."

Scratching his chin, Grant hesitated, studied the photo, then lifted his gaze to Ava. "Maybe find out who the photojournalist was who took the pic? Who was on staff that year? That was a long time ago, so I wouldn't hold your breath."

Ava ignored his lack of optimism, feeling a sudden quiver of excitement. "Great idea."

Grant waved her off as his office phone rang. "That's why they pay me the big bucks."

With Anmol's and Corbin's help, she learned that there were three photojournalists on staff at the time. Two were now dead. That left Reed Barker. Turned out Reed was active in community service in Carmel, and was a woman. *Shows you can't assume*, Ava thought. She found Reed's number in an old nonprofit newsletter.

"Are you going to call?" Anmol said, her dark eyes bright and eager as she and Corbin stared at Ava expectantly.

Ava's heart raced as the phone rang. One. Two. Three.

Voicemail.

"It's Reed. Please speak slowly and loudly, and I'll call you back."

Ava left a quick message, explaining the reason for her call, and ended with, "So, please call me as soon as you can. Okay, thanks."

That night Ava sat out by the pool, staring up at the night sky, trying to see the stars she knew were there, just hidden. The water's blue light cast a decidedly calming hue over the yard.

"Nana?"

Two seconds later, her grandmother appeared at the pool's edge, and from this angle the backlight gave her an angelic glow. "Are you okay?" Nana asked softly.

"Do you think tomorrow will work?"

Nana came over and sat on the lounger by Ava. "Espero, but it does you no good to worry about what you cannot control in this moment. Why don't you get some rest?"

Ava sat up and swung her legs over the side of the chair. "Why didn't you tell us there were weaknesses?"

"Ah, you found out about those, did you?"

"I don't understand why you never told us."

"I didn't want to influence you," Nana said. "If I'd told you, you would be focused on that and not on the strength. ¿Verdad?"

Yes, it was true. If any of the Granados girls knew that each blessing came with a weakness, they would spend all their time trying to figure that out instead of honing the power of the blessing. It's how the sisters were built. Put the fires out. Put the problems away. Find a solution.

After Nana left, Ava called Rion.

"Hey," he answered.

"It's so quiet over there."

"Tres is in dog jail."

"Really?"

"No, but I gave her a bone, so now she's chillin'."

"So, what did you do today?" Ava was avoiding the question she really wanted to ask, which only made her stomach churn more.

"Oh, um, worked around the orchard. Raced dirt bikes with some buddies of mine. Thought about making an Excel spreadsheet for schools, but then decided nah. What about you?"

Ava smiled at his joke. "I was at my internship. Excel would make it easier. So, did you win the races?"

"I should tell you yes, so you'll think I'm cool, but nah. Not even close."

There was an awkward moment of silence. A voice was screaming in Ava's head, *Ask him!*

"Can I ask you a question?"

"Another one?"

"Seriously."

"Shoot."

"It might sound weird."

"Should I sit down?"

"Remember the night I hit your truck? Since then . . ." Ava swallowed. "Okay, here's the weird part—have you felt different? Like, has anything weird happened to you?"

"Uh, I found a five-dollar winning lottery ticket in a parking lot. Does that count?"

"I was thinking like something bigger."

Rion hesitated. Ava's stomach dropped.

"Can you hold on?" he asked.

Oh my God. He knows something. Why didn't I ask this simple question earlier?! Fail.

"Sure."

After a minute of muted silence, Rion came back on the line. A chorus of crickets sang in the background. "Are you outside?" she asked.

"Sitting in the bed of my truck."

Ava imagined him stretched out on his back, an arm behind his head, staring up at the sky. She imagined what it would be like to be there, lying next to him. Her heart fluttered faster than her logical brain could vanish the image. What had Elijah said? *It was like this mini explosion in my chest, like my heart dipped and fluttered and seized all at once.* Ava exhaled. Flutter does *not* equal dip and seize.

"I'm outside too," she said, "but I bet my view isn't half as good as yours."

"I guess you'll have to come here someday so I can show you."

An unexpected longing spread in Ava's chest, but she couldn't get distracted again. "So, about my question."

There was a brief pause before Rion said, "Damn. I gotta take this call. I'll see you tomorrow and tell you then, okay?"

Ava wanted to scream into the phone, *No! Tell me now!* But Rion had already hung up.

"The princess was laid to rest in a glass coffin," Caroline said as she tucked Ava into bed, *"deep in the poison forest. Hidden away from the world and the boy who loved her.*

"The gardener's son spent night and day searching for her. He didn't sleep. He didn't eat."

"Because he loved her?" Ava asked.

Caroline sighed. "Yes. And the bruja even warned him. But he didn't listen. He couldn't see past his love for her."

"Is that bad?"

"Yes, because he didn't know that the princess was more dangerous now than she had ever been."

Here is where the story sometimes changed, the answer different from the time before, so Ava asked, "Why was she dangerous?"

Caroline paused, sighed. "Love is always dangerous."

Twenty-One

It was a perfect day for football.

The air was crisp. The sky was overcast, which meant the beach wasn't packed with sun worshippers and tourists. Only a few joggers, dog walkers, and treasure seekers with their metal detectors.

"Okay, so here's the plan," Carmen said as the trio staked out their spot on the shore before the others arrived. "We have to make sure you and Rion are on opposite teams."

"Right," Viv said, tossing the ball up and down. "So that means I'll play QB, and pick other receivers. Ava, you have to be a blocker when we're on offense. On defense, we need to make sure he's QB, so you have reasons to sack him."

The idea of sacking Rion made Ava's insides twist into annoying little knots. He had at least five inches on her, and then there were those concealed muscles acting like some kind of secret weapons. "How am I supposed to do that when this is touch football?"

Carmen set a hand on Ava's shoulder and looked her directly in the eye. "You are going to have to be an outstanding actress, act like you're a football fanatic, or pretend to run into him. Who cares, as long as there is a collision? Oh, and we have to make sure I'm on Rion's team, so I can do some sleuthing in enemy camp."

"He isn't the enemy," Ava argued, tugging on her sweatshirt sleeves.

"Quit fidgeting," Carmen insisted.

"I'm not fidgeting."

"You are," Viv agreed. "Why are you so nervous?"

"I just feel kind of bad, you know. Like I'm a thief or something."

"It's not stealing if it belongs to you," Carm said with her usual nonchalant flair.

Ava looked out past the breakers all the way to the thin gray line that was the horizon. *When did everything get so twisted?* she wondered. Just three weeks ago, Nana was still alive. Ava didn't know Rion existed. Life was calm, normal, expected. She hated how quickly everything could change—this was the constant that always kept her on guard. "We need some pump-up music."

"We *need* the star of the show," Viv said, glancing around. "No rain, no gain." She snickered at her own joke, but Ava wasn't in the mood to laugh. She just wanted to get this over with. Last night when she couldn't sleep, an out-of-the-blue thought had occurred to her. What if it worked? What if she actually got the blessing back and Nana could move on, and future generations' blessings were safe? Wasn't that the endgame? Then why did she feel so lousy just thinking about it? *These feelings are pointless*, Ava told herself. There was only one way to move forward, and that was to collide with Rion North.

Nana's words resurfaced in her memory.

Meteors, stars, 8:51. Collision. And the hummingbird.

All of it now made sense, except for the hummingbird.

Once Nana and Meda appeared, it was near game time; the waves seemed bigger, the sky grayer, and Ava's chest heavier.

"Okay, Meda, when I give the signal," Ava said, "bring the downpour."

"What level would you like?" the saint asked. "One being mild, and ten being a hurricane. Not that I am limited to ten. I have been known to go beyond hurricane level. One time—"

"We won't be needing a hurricane," Nana interjected. She looked tired. Her eyes seemed further sunken into her skull, and her cheeks sagged like they carried the weight of the ocean. Ava's heart felt like it was shrinking. She didn't want to lose the woman who had raised her, who had taught her the meaning of *onward*, who had slept next to her and her sisters for a month after Caroline had abandoned them all.

"Hi, Nana," Viv said so lightly she seemed like a small child too shy to speak. Carm pressed her lips together and merely waved. Were they feeling the side effects of the inevitable outcome too? Except, in theory, they had already lost Nana entirely. Ava still had her ghost. And a ghost was better than nothing.

"Give my preciosas besos," Nana directed Ava, before straightening and adding, "And ay, tell Carmen her shorts are too short."

After Ava relayed the information to her sisters, minus the shorts comment, Meda placed a hand on Ava's shoulder, guiding her a few feet away from the others. Nana followed. The saint's head was dipped low near her ear like he had a secret to tell. Ava braced herself for some grand wisdom, but all he said was, "Hit like hell, kid."

"Are you allowed to say things like that?" Ava asked.

Meda only laughed.

"We don't want to distract you, Ava," Nana said. "So, you won't be able to see us, but know we are here."

Meda was already nodding. "I'll wait for the signal. What should it be? A tug of the ear? A shrug?"

"That'll be too easy to miss," Ava said. "How about I raise my hands over my head and pump my arms twice?"

"Twice," the saint echoed. "Got it."

With a raise of her head and a lift of her small shoulders, Nana regained her queenly stature. "I believe in you, Ava."

And then a depressing thought occurred to Ava. "Nana, if this works, what happens next? I mean, will we . . ." A lump formed in her throat. "Get to say—"

Nana pulled her into a warm embrace. "I promise to say goodbye."

A part of Ava wished she could prolong the blessing transfer, but she knew that in the end there was no way around the inescapable goodbye.

There never was.

A couple of Viv's and Carm's friends showed up next. Leo, a young guy from the office who had just moved here from Brazil. He was taller than a tree, and his legs looked like they were made of granite. Taryn, a friend from their high school days. She was a killer athlete and wore bruises like trophies. Then there was Donovan, Carm's friend from college. He was three years older than her and was Hollywood-chiseled from his chin to his abs, which were on full display, because he had already taken off his shirt. His brown skin glistened even in the gray light. He was also off the market, because he had just proposed to his lifelong girlfriend. Or, in the words of the oldest Granados sister, his *sandbox love*.

When Ava unglued her eyes from that should-be-illegal six-pack, she caught sight of Rion walking down the misty shore in a dark tee and a pair of board shorts. Ava didn't know if it was an overload of dopamine or some other chemical brain response, but she felt a swell of happiness just at the sight of him. And the fact that he looked good. Really good. But not because of his clothes or his hair or his not-so-mediocre mouth. It was in the confident expression he wore, matched only by his confident stride. Ava realized in that moment what she liked most about Rion. No airs. No trying too hard.

He was . . . effortless.

And then her heart did a little dip.

He was with another guy who had to be Alfonso. Ava jogged over to meet them. "Hey."

"You picked a good day for some ball," Rion said, sucking in a lungful of sea air. "This is Al. Al, this is Ava."

Alfonso. Tall, broad-shouldered—not too thin, not too thick—black hair begging for a trim, an inch of a red tattoo that poked out from his T-shirt sleeve, and a smile that looked like it could reach across a continent. "So, you're Ava," Alfonso said, shaking her hand. Ava's head swam with the endless possibilities those three words carried, depending on where the emphasis was placed.

What had Rion told him about her? *I met a girl who doesn't believe in fate?*

Al slapped Rion in the chest and laughed. "This guy told me—"

Rion shoved him. "You're here for some ball, dude."

Rubbing his chest, Al shook his head and smirked. "Right. Okay. Let's do it."

Under normal circumstances, Ava might have joined in the banter, but she was so much more interested in what Rion couldn't (or wouldn't) tell her last night. But everyone was waiting, and no way was it going to be a quick convo.

After introductions, teams were made. Ava, Viv, Alfonso, and Taryn named themselves the Ball Busters. Taryn's idea. Carmen, Rion, Leo, and Donovan were the Bone Crushers. Donovan's idea.

"All right," Viv said, clapping her hands together, "We've got a thirtyish-yard field. The end zone is marked by that red flag down there," she said, pointing.

"And there are no rules," Carmen put in, "except no one goes to the hospital. And no blood. I'm wearing white."

"What do the winners get?" Alfonso said, rolling up his sleeves, revealing his entire tattoo. A compass.

"Pizza from Jon and Vinny's," Viv suggested.

Alfonso stretched his hands over his head. "Stakes seem pretty low," he teased.

Rion socked him in the chest. "Chill, dude." Then, to everyone else, "They do seem kind of low."

Carm eyed Alfonso with an emotion Ava couldn't quite read. Disdain mixed with curiosity and a pinch of annoyance?

"I like this guy." Donovan nodded emphatically. "Let's make this worth something."

Oh, but it is, Ava thought.

"Like what?" Rion asked.

"Cash?" Ava guessed.

"Boring," Carmen said, keeping her eyes locked on Al. "You want stakes? If you win, we'll give your team fifty-yard-line tickets to the Chargers. Any home game you all want."

"Dad's going to kill you," Viv said in a near whisper.

"Dad isn't here."

Ava didn't think it was much of a prize for her and her sisters, since they were family tickets, but she didn't say anything, because the focus was the blessing, not some ridiculous football game.

There were some hoots and high fives. Except for Al. He just nodded and smiled like he never really cared what the prize was, he just wanted something to fight for.

Rion kicked off his shoes. "And if we win?" He swung his gaze to Ava. Why did she sense a challenge?

"An invite to Emmanuel Escalante's party next Saturday night," Ava blurted before she could stop herself. Viv jerked her attention to Ava in a nonthreatening but wholly *are you crazy?* way.

"He said we could bring plus-ones," Ava insisted. "What's a couple more?"

Anyone who knew Emmanuel knew he was supremely selective about who he allowed at his fiestas. Security was always high, and if your name wasn't on the list? No entrance, or as Emmanuel always liked to say, *Adios, Jack-o.* But it would only take a phone call from one of the Granados girls to get their friends into the fiesta.

"*The* Emmanuel Escalante who was nominated for an Oscar two years ago?" Alfonso did a backflip across the sand.

"The one and only," Ava said, leaning into her bravado. "Plus, whoever loses buys pizza after the game."

"Fine," Viv said, braiding her hair to the side. "Whoever gets to fourteen first wins."

After Ava's team lost the coin toss, she caught Rion's gaze as his team huddled up. He lifted a playful brow, threw her a crooked grin, then hunched beneath his teammates, breaking eye contact. Carm had done her job well, because when they came out of the huddle, Leo lined up as center with Rion as QB.

One goal, Ava thought. *Hit Rion. Hard enough to be considered a collision.* She glanced around, half expecting to see Nana and Meda with bullhorns, but the shore was an empty, dismal gray.

Ava played close to the line with Viv, while Alfonso and Taryn hung back to attack any receivers. Viv whispered in her ear. "He's going to throw."

"How do you know?"

"He looks like the kind of guy to test the defense on the first try," she said. "I bet he goes long, so loosen up, take this as a test shot, okay?"

Ava nodded, crouching low, digging her toes into the moist sand.

A second later the ball was in Rion's hands; he fell back, glanced from side to side, cocked his arm back. Viv had been right. He was going to launch it. And the only thing standing in Ava's way was the wall of muscle that was Donovan. Ava cut right, ducking out of his grasp. She raced toward Rion, but catching speed in the sand was nearly impossible.

Five more strides.

Rion scrambled like a pro, his eyes darting across the imaginary field, looking for his target.

Four.

He was motioning for someone to go long.

Three.

He's mine, Ava thought.

Two.

One.

She dove. The ball launched. Rion zoomed left, and Ava face-planted into the sand.

There were some cheers downshore where the action was playing out. And then there was Rion's voice. "Ava!" He was there before she could spit the sand out of her mouth.

"Are you okay?" He hauled her to her feet.

Brushing herself and her ego off, she said, "You're fast."

"I didn't know you were going to come at me that hard," he said, his voice filled with an edge of humor that made Ava laugh at herself.

"It's football, Rion."

He ran a hand through his already messy hair and smiled. "You must really not want me to come to that party."

She forced a frown through her smile. "Absolutely not."

He stared down the shore at his teammates chicken-dancing after their touchdown. "Looks like you're *absolutely* not going to get what you want, Nine."

"Nine?"

He laughed and took off to high-five his teammates.

"What the hell does *Nine* mean?" she whispered, brushing the sand off her bare legs with a scowl. As everyone came back to center, Ava lifted her arms and pumped them twice. No more testing the waters.

It was time for a storm.

She waited. Maybe the clouds needed time to gather?

Viv was barking instructions in the huddle, but all Ava heard was "fake."

"Are you listening, Ava?"

"Huh? Yeah. Fake play. Got it."

"So, when I toss a lateral to Alfonso, he's going to pitch it downfield to Taryn. You need to keep Rion off our asses."

Ava glanced up. Rion was watching their huddle with a knowing expression that made her think he knew the play Viv had just called.

Taryn rotated her neck and popped her knuckles.

As they lined up, Ava was surprised to see Rion fall back. She was hoping he would line up toe to toe with her. It would make the tackle a lot easier. Now she was going to have to chase him down.

Three things happened at the exact same moment. Ava pumped her arms again. The ball was snapped. And Meda appeared.

"Now!" Ava shouted as the ball whizzed through the air. The entire scene played out in slow motion. In a blink it was like the sky had been ripped open. Rain drenched the shore. Thunder boomed. And Ava ran toward Rion.

He was blocking Taryn, whose eyes were skyward. Ava turned on the heat. The muscles in her legs burned. The rain fell so hard and fast, her line of sight was diminished, but she didn't slow down. A second later she locked eyes on the target.

Rion never saw her coming.

She threw all her weight into a low hit, wrapping him up by the waist. He lost his footing, and the two went crashing to the ground.

They tumbled once, twice.

Ava found herself on top of Rion, chest to chest. Eye to eye. He was breathing hard. She was breathing harder. *Why would a heart ever have to beat this fast?* was her first thought. Rain streaked down Rion's face, a face that wore both an amused and a confused expression. *What would it feel like to kiss you?* was her second thought. Probably *not* unimpressive. Probably amazing and . . .

God, Ava. Get ahold of yourself!

Rion's arms twitched or tightened; Ava couldn't be sure. In that instant, Ava could feel a strange energy buzzing between them. It had to be the blessing—it was trying to make its way back to her!

The normal thing would have been to get off the poor guy, but she was afraid to move, afraid she might disrupt the blessing transfer. Rion smiled. "You have a habit of slamming into me, don't you? Are you obsessed with me or something?" he teased.

Were his eyes always this brown? With flecks of gold?

Meda materialized, crouching next to Rion, making it hard for Ava to concentrate.

And before she could stop herself, she asked the saint, "Did it work?"

"Did what work?" Rion said.

Meda shook his head sadly. "He's still wearing your blessing."

The rain ceased as Ava scrambled to her feet, feeling suddenly ridiculous and self-conscious and totally discouraged. There was a celebration going on downfield. Taryn must have scored.

"It's the emotion that's missing," Nana said, appearing by Meda's side. "We had everything else."

Emotion? I practically kissed the guy!

"Ava?" Rion was standing now, wiping his hands on his shorts. "Are you okay?"

She nodded. "Sorry," she deflected. "I guess I got a little too into the game."

"I wasn't talking about the game."

Ava met his gaze. If only she could see what Meda saw, the light radiating all around Rion.

Ava forced a laugh. "That storm came out of nowhere," she said. "That was wild."

"Yeah," Rion said, "just as wild as how fast it stopped."

Ava forced her attention to the end zone celebration. "Looks like we're tied."

"Guess I'm going to have to up my game." He jogged off to huddle with this team, leaving Ava feeling like no matter how hard she tried, she wasn't going to win.

"Do you want to try again?" Meda asked.

"Nana's right," she grumbled, making her way to the edge of the sea like she needed to wash off her feet, but what she really needed was distance from the others so she could talk to the saint and the ghost. "It doesn't make sense to keep running into him unless we have the other piece of the puzzle. He's going to think I'm obsessed with tackling or that I'm an aggressive weirdo." Ava paced a few feet into the ocean. The freezing water sent an icy chill through her. She retreated and turned to her grandmother. "How do I get the high emotion?"

Nana stroked her cheek, staring past the waves. "I thought your desire to help me and the family would be enough, but clearly I was wrong."

Viv and Carm were there in an instant, breathless, asking simultaneously, "Did it work?"

"Nope."

Meda was already shaking his head. "This is all wrong. How did I not see it before!"

"See what?" Ava asked with a hint of hope that the saint had the answer they so desperately needed.

"We need a bridge!" the saint cried delightedly.

"A what?"

"Tell us what Nana and Meda are saying!" Carm insisted.

"We apparently need a bridge," Ava said.

"There must be real emotion for *both* of you," Meda nearly squealed. "To create a bridge for the blessing to cross over."

Ava felt gutted. She thought maybe with the way Rion had looked at her, the way his arms might have tightened around her, that he had felt the connection too, that . . . *Oh my God.* Ava put an end to her endless dream chatter. *What if he doesn't feel the same way at all?*

She relayed the information to her sisters, hardening her heart. Then, to the saint, "Please do not tell me this is some dumb fairy tale thing where we have to have true love's kiss or something ridiculous like that."

"Jesus," Viv muttered.

"Heavens, no," Nana said, peering sidelong at Meda for confirmation.

"Nothing like that." Meda wore a deep frown. "Friendship is a bridge. Kindness is a bridge. Hope is a bridge. Just no hate. Or anger. Or anything that would send you to confession or . . ." He pointed to the ground.

"But we *are* friends!" She briefly wondered if her guilt for deceiving Rion was blocking the whole process. But if that were the case, she would never get the blessing back. Unless she could miraculously disappear her guilty conscience, which was highly unlikely.

"Apparently high emotion is what is called for," Meda said way too energetically.

Ava told her sisters what the saint had said. Viv scowled. Carmen sighed, then said, "Well, now we're in a worthless game, and we might as well win. Come on." She took off up the shore.

Ava started to follow before turning back to Nana and Meda. "We only have three weeks to figure it out." And more and more, Ava was staring to doubt the intel Meda and Nana had been collecting. Everything felt like a big, fat crapshoot.

Viv hooked an arm around her little sister, tugging her back to the game, all the while telling her, "It's going to be okay."

"Do *you* know how to build a bridge?"

Viv laughed. "I'm an architect, remember?"

Thirty minutes and many bruises later, the Ball Busters suffered a humiliating defeat when Taryn fumbled the ball and Donovan ran it in for the winning touchdown.

Apparently Rion would be at Emmanuel's party. And if Ava were lucky, maybe she could learn how to build a bridge by then.

Twenty-Two

"You did *what*?" Viv cried when Donovan told everyone he had booked the honeymoon without telling his fiancée.

"Oof." Carmen pulled a face.

"I just wanted to surprise her," Donovan said, wolfing down half a slice of pizza in a single bite.

"A surprise is Hawaii or Barbados or Cancún," Taryn practically hissed. "Not a dude ranch in Montana."

"A surprise is always a bad idea," Ava said, drawing a quizzical expression from Rion, who sat across from her. She knew he wanted to argue the point, and she was more than ready, but Carmen jumped in with, "Exactly." Ava felt a strange swell of satisfaction.

"Whatever," Viv said, brushing out the ends of her still-damp hair. "I think surprises are nice."

What's gotten into her? Ava wondered, but she wasn't about to ask in front of the group, which was already starting to disband anyway.

Ava collected a few empty plates and made her way to a trash can. After tossing the garbage, she spun to find Rion standing two feet in front of her.

She let out a small yelp, grabbing her chest. "You scared me."

He pitched a few empty water bottles and a pizza box into the recycling bin. "Sorry. I thought you might need help."

Ava gave herself a second for a deep, calming breath before she blurted, "Are you always like this?"

"Like what?"

Surprising. Thoughtful. Mysterious. "Nice."

All amusement drained from Rion's expression. "No," he said with the same push-pull vibe he'd given off the other night over flan.

Ava let out a small laugh, but when Rion didn't even smile, she felt suddenly self-conscious and like she had said the wrong thing.

"Well"—she swiped her hands together—"you seem pretty nice to me."

"It's new."

Ava's heart thudded. Worthless thing.

"I meant that . . ." Rion rubbed the back of his neck. "Never mind."

Ava was about to dismiss the strangeness of the convo when she realized this was a clue. She recognized it from her interview training. He was leading her to an answer without outright telling her. But where? If Nana were here, she'd tell her to dig deep. To focus and to set aside any doubts or reservations. To keep her eye on the prize, and the prize was that blessing standing two feet in front of her.

Ava pivoted. "Remember last night when I asked if you felt different since—"

"The night you hit my truck."

"Right."

"I thought it was a weird question."

"I know it sounds strange, but—"

"But then I saw where you were going with it."

"You did?"

"Like, your life flashing before your eyes or something, right?"

"Rion, I barely hit your car."

"Hey!" He crossed his arms over his chest. "It was pretty scary to be sitting there in a storm, and then out of nowhere you feel a sudden impact, and . . ."

"And what?"

"You're going to laugh."

"Ava!" Carmen called as she jogged over. "We're going to split."

Ava wasn't ready to go, not when Rion was possibly on the verge of telling her what she had been waiting to hear. "Oh," she said, throwing her sister the *I'm not ready* gaze.

One of the best things about sisters was that they got it: they got the looks; they understood the meaning of the sighs and gestures. And right now Ava was crossing her arms, tilting her head an inch to the left, and straining her eyeballs so hard she felt a headache coming on. Her stance was clear: *I'm not ready to go.*

Carm, reading Ava's silent language to glorious perfection, glanced down at her phone, pretended to read a message, then looked up and said, "Ack. I totally forgot. Viv and I have something to do real quick. Can you meet us at the pier in an hour?"

Rion's eyes danced with amusement, and for a heart-stopping second, Ava worried he could read the Granados language. No way. They weren't even close to obvious. Even Raul couldn't understand it.

After Ava agreed, and her sister left, she turned back to Rion. "You were saying?"

He stood there, rubbing his chin. "I forgot."

Biting back her exasperation, and wishing she knew him well enough to read *his* language, Ava said, "About me laughing."

He stared blankly.

"And I won't," she added, feeling like she was stumbling over her words. "I promise."

Rion's gaze fell to the sand briefly as he rubbed the back of his neck and glanced back up.

"I saw a bright light, like they say in the movies, and for two seconds I thought maybe I was dead." Then, with a decisive nod, he added, "It was pretty traumatic."

The blessing.

Ava definitely wasn't laughing. Not even close. She might not have been breathing either. "What happened after that?"

"Nothing. I got out of the truck, and there you were."

"And I had messed up your eBay bid." Ava was trying her best to keep it light, even though she felt the weight of a thousand moons pressing against her chest.

"It wasn't meant to be mine," Rion said with a shrug.

Everything stilled in that moment, as if the waves and the breeze and the clouds came to a halt. Ava could feel every muscle in her body shudder. Rion must have sensed it too.

He laughed, clarifying his comment. "The eBay thing? It wasn't meant to be."

Ava matched his laugh, but hers came out high and pitchy and overdone. God, she wanted to sink into the sea. She wanted to be anywhere but right in front of Rion's inviting gaze. So, she turned and began to walk down the shore. Rion fell into step beside her.

"But you don't believe in meant-to-be, do you?" Rion said as they circumvented a yoga class rolling out their mats.

"A lot of people don't," Ava shot back. "If everything was so controlled by fate and was meant to be, then why not just sit in your house and wait for things to happen?"

"Pretty sure that's not how it works," Rion offered with a raised brow. "But what do I know? I'm the guy seeing white lights."

Blessings. You're the guy seeing my *blessing.*

Rion said, "Did something happen to you too?"

God, his expression was so open, so earnest, that Ava wanted to punch her two-faced self. "What do you mean?"

"Well, you asked me last night if I felt any different or if anything had happened, so I figured something must have happened to you too. Did you see the light?"

"No, but . . ." She had to reach for something to create the bridge, a commonality. "A lot changed that night."

Rion waited a couple of beats before he said almost solemnly, "Because your nana died?"

Ava released a nervous breath. *How much do I have to tell him? How much does he need to know?* She ordered her feet to keep moving. "I'm not sure," she said softly. "Just the world and . . . everything felt different, it looked different . . ."

"I think I know what you mean," Rion finally said.

"You do?" Ava stole a side-glance to see him nodding.

They walked in silence a few more paces. Past two kids building a lopsided sandcastle. To the strangers on the beach that day they must have looked like two normal teens cruising the shore. But to Ava they were anything but normal.

"Ever since that night," he said, slowing to pick up a half-broken shell, "I've been sketching again."

"Sketching? Like art?"

"Yeah, I used to draw a lot when I was a kid. I was pretty obsessed with it." He let out a nervous laugh as he tossed the shell into the water. "And then I just kind of stopped after my parents, and . . . I think after seeing that light and stuff, I don't know, it sounds weird, but I felt like drawing again."

Ava's heart stopped. Could that be the blessing? Art? Creativity? It was definitely possible, especially since Nana was always telling Ava to embrace the creative part of herself, to get inspired. But Ava *was* inspired. Wasn't she?

"What do you draw?" Ava asked, eager to see where this led. And then it made sense. The notebook Rion carried.

He stopped and stretched, throwing his gaze out past the breakers. It was the same look he got that night when the guy played the saxophone, and then at Edwin and Ellie's tree. Like he could see things other people couldn't. Ava didn't know why she did it, but she held her phone at a side angle and snapped his picture before he noticed. Her phone vibrated at the same moment, startling her so badly, she dropped it into the sand.

Rion bent down to pick it up. He stared at the screen with a blank face, then held the phone out to her. "It's Elijah."

Ava's breath caught as she snatched the phone away and answered the FaceTime call. "Finally!" She wanted to crawl through the phone and hammer Elijah over the head for picking this summer of all summers to go and be a Good Samaritan or whatever.

"Hey, Aves. Where are you?"

"The beach." Ava spun away from Rion, gripping the phone like a lifeline. "I can't believe you're here!"

"Well, not technically."

"Tell me everything new, and be fast."

"Who's that behind you?" Elijah said, craning his neck.

Ava turned to see Rion hovering behind her shoulder. Her cheeks flushed. "Oh, that's Rion," she said with as much casual calm as she could muster, but no way was Elijah going to let it go. The guy had no filter and couldn't be trusted to ever say the right thing. As a matter of fact, if Ava were betting, she would wager her whole future on the fact that Elijah was most definitely going to say the wrong thing. Ugh. He had the worst timing. "Rion, this is Elijah, my best friend. He's in Peru, studying Spanish."

"Hey," Rion said. "I was there last year. That place is awesome. Have you tried cuy yet?"

Ew.

Was it just Ava, or had Rion's voice gotten deeper—and had he just hijacked her conversation?

Elijah laughed. "Nah, man. Maybe we'll give the guinea pig a try though."

We? So, things were still going strong with Pierre.

"Hello!" Ava waved her hand dramatically in front of the screen.

"Sorry, Aves," Elijah said through his signature snort-laugh. "So, who's this Rion dude?" he asked, as if Rion wasn't standing two feet from her. Ava imagined her cartoon self slamming a hammer over cartoon Elijah's ginormous head.

"She ran into my truck," Rion put in.

Elijah's eyes flew open wide. "You were in an accident?" So, he never got the text.

"No," Ava assured brusquely. "I mean, yes. But it was like a teensy fender bender."

"I saw white light," Rion said, leaning closer. "It wasn't that teensy." He smelled like orange Tic Tacs. Elijah opened his mouth to respond, then his entire face froze.

"Elijah?" Ava shook her phone as if that would bring him back. She tried dialing him back three times but couldn't connect again.

"Ugh!" Ava's frustration came out in one long stream of breath. "I hate how awful the connection always is." There was truth in those words, but the real meaning was hidden in the deepest recesses of Ava's lying heart: *I hate how awful lying to you is.*

Ava felt like a volcano of emotion getting ready to explode. Elijah was only the tipping point, but he was the perfect target at the moment, so Ava wouldn't have to explain her outburst. She inhaled sharply. "I just wanted to talk to him because—"

"You miss him."

Why was Rion staring at her like that? All soft brown eyes with golden flecks. *That's the physical difference between Achilles and Rion,* she unexpectedly realized with such force someone could have knocked her into the waves with a single breath. If she looked close enough, she could see so clearly that their eyes were worlds apart. Achilles's didn't have gold specks. She was sure of it.

Just the thought of Achilles invited his words into the moment. *You just haven't seen his other side.*

Ava wanted to dig to see if she could figure out what Achilles had meant, because the more she knew about Orion North, the better chance she had of building a bridge. "I ran into your brother in Venice," she announced suddenly.

"Really." There was no lilt in Rion's voice this time.

"He didn't tell you?" Ava said through a slow exhale she was hoping Rion didn't hear.

"He doesn't tell me a lot of things." Rion's expression turned dark. But in the next blink it was gone. Had Ava not been paying close attention, she might have missed it entirely. She wished she hadn't said a word.

"What's the deal with you two? You're brothers." She couldn't imagine being at odds like that with her sisters. Ever. What could be so bad that they clearly didn't like each other?

"A lot," Rion said. "It started a long time ago. And . . ." He sighed. "I think part of it is that when my grandpa got sick, he told me and Achilles that he wants me to run the orchard someday. Like, things are equal as far as assets, but I'd pretty much be Achilles's boss. I don't think he meant it. Maybe he was just trying to make a point because he was mad at Achilles. Let's just say my brother was pissed."

Ava knew her dad would never do something like that, create tension between her and her sisters. It seemed wrong and so cruel. "But why would he do that?"

"I think it's his way of controlling Achilles? My brother doesn't want to go to college. I do."

"So . . . what? He thinks this will make Achilles go to school?"

"It sounds worse than it is. I really think he believes he's just doing what's best for Achilles." Rion rubbed the back of his neck. "I mean, Gramps doesn't care what Achilles studies, as long as he gets an education."

"And Achilles is stubborn," Ava guessed.

Rion quirked a dark brow and sighed. "How about some ice cream?" And then there was that *I've got the world in my pocket* smile again. Ava added how quick he could turn it on to her growing list of all things Rion.

She so badly wanted to press for more information—it was her natural tendency, but she also knew that if she pushed too hard, too soon, too fast, Rion could shut down entirely, and she would never know why he and Achilles seemed to be at war.

"Sloan's?" she suggested.

"Perfect."

A few minutes later they had hiked the concrete steps up the cliff into Santa Monica, meandering through the Saturday crowds, talking about safe topics like movies and music. A few minutes later they arrived at the Willy Wonka–ish bright pink-and-green neon store with its to-die-for aroma of fresh-baked waffle cones. Ava ordered a scoop of vanilla with graham cracker crumbs and rainbow sprinkles while Rion stared at the list of more than fifty original flavors. Finally, he settled on a combo of coffee ice cream topped with chocolate glazed donuts.

They scouted an outdoor table just outside the shop.

"So, about your art. Can I see it?" Ava might have been curious, but she was so much more interested in assessing his talent, to see if it was good enough to be blessing status.

"It's not that great." Rion spooned some ice cream into his mouth. "But *this*? This is crazy good."

Build a bridge.

"I still want to see it."

The air between them shifted. A span of tension and amusement as a street performer began to belt some tunes down the way. Then, in the most disarming, maddening way, Rion said, "Okay."

Out of nowhere, a big, blond shaggy dog trotted over, jumping up to try to lick Rion's ice cream. A deep laugh floated from Rion's throat as he held his bowl above his head. "Sorry, buddy, but chocolate donuts and dogs don't mix."

The exuberant pup pressed his paws on Rion's chest, forcing him to lose his balance. It all happened so fast, Ava didn't have time to react to the ice cream crashing down onto Rion's lap.

She tossed him a wad of napkins, trying not to laugh, but the laughter bubbled out of her as the dog took off down the Promenade toward a voice calling for Benny.

Rion began to wipe away the mess good-naturedly. A smile hung at the corners of his mouth. "Something funny, Nine?"

She caught her breath. "What is the deal with *Nine*?"

A patch of sun broke through the clouds. Rion glanced up, shielding his eyes. Then he dropped his gaze back to Ava, squinting one eye closed. "Sorry. What was the question?"

"Rion."

He blinked. "It's the number of teeth that show when you smile."

Twenty-Three

"**I** still can't get over that he counted your teeth," Carmen said with an air of revulsion as the trio made their way through Neiman Marcus a few days later.

Carmen was insistent that she needed some retail therapy after all that "masculine-induced toxic energy" that was football.

"I think it's sweet," Viv said, holding a sleeveless silk blouse up to her athletic frame.

"What if the blessing is his art, guys?" Ava hated Neiman's. It had a certain vibe that said, *Welcome to the overpriced version of yourself.* The air was stuffy, the clothing stuffier.

"So what if it is his art?" Carmen chimed, glancing at her phone.

"I mean, he seemed really happy that he's sketching again, and if that's the blessing and I take it"—Ava lowered her voice when two older women walked by—"isn't that like robbing him of his joy or something?"

Just last week, Ava was ready to hate Orion North. She was ready to put him in a camp he probably didn't belong in. But then he went and disarmed her by saying something unexpected or doing something nice. *Or maybe that's part of his game*, Ava thought cautiously. *Maybe he's one of those guys with two faces.* His own brother said Rion had another side. This was the narrative Ava had begun to create for herself, but there was a hole in her story. There was that smile and the way Rion looked at her like he was trying to figure out a never-ending equation. And there was the way her heart fluttered and dipped. But it had to be the blessing.

It *had* to be.

And then there was that moment when they were chest to chest on the sand with only the rain between them. Why hadn't he jumped up? Rolled her off him? Why did he just lie there all stupefied, blinking up at her? Everything about him was surprising. And maybe for the first time, she didn't hate surprises.

"You can't think like that, Gree," Viv said, interrupting her thoughts before turning her attention to Carmen. "When Emmanuel said 'Winter of Spies' theme, do you think he meant winter-winter or California winter?"

"I think it's the *idea* of winter," Carmen said, "not like actual North Pole temps."

"Why are we even here?" Ava cried. "You both already have something to wear."

Carm slung an arm over Ava's shoulders. "The party is tomorrow night, and I'd bet my life that you have absolutely no idea what *you're* wearing."

As usual Carmen was right. Ava hadn't even thought about it. Her entire plan rested on one premise—*keep my promise to Dad and attend*. She had never said how long she would stay. But now that Rion was going, her premise had changed significantly. "A sweater and jeans?" Ava was totally serious, but by the looks on her sisters' faces, she knew *that* was out of the question.

"Told you," Carmen sang in Viv's direction. "Thank the baby Jesus that someone in this family is always thinking and planning."

"Listen, Ava," Viv said, ignoring Carmen's inflated ego. "If you're going to build a bridge, you gotta look good doing it, right?"

Ava stared pitifully at the sparse racks of designer clothing with a sinking feeling that she had been set up. "Except it's summer, and there aren't any winter clothes out yet," she argued with a triumphant smile.

Carm sighed. "Ye of so little faith."

Just then Blanca Ortiz appeared, looking like she had just stepped out of a Balenciaga ad. The thirtysomething was wearing a tight black dress; her auburn hair cascaded right above her shoulders in bouncy waves, her full lips were painted an understated nude, and her brown, flawless skin was illuminated to dewy perfection.

"Hermanitas!" she squealed, pulling them into a four-way hug.

Blanca had been their nanny extraordinaire for five years. She had even stayed on after she graduated college. But then she married some guy who owned auto parts stores from San Diego to Los Angeles, and she needed to start thinking about living her own vida.

"Mis hermanitas," she squealed again, going in for another round of squeezing. And bouncing. As if she hadn't just seen them at Nana's funeral. She never made it to the after-party on account of spraining her ankle in her six-inch Louboutins when she was leaving the church.

"How's your ankle?" Viv asked, glancing down at Blanca's more sensible wedges.

"Mejor. Mejor." Her eyes danced excitedly. "Now, Ava. You need something to wear. And soy your fairy madrina."

Ugh. Ava did not want or need a fairy godmother. It's not that she didn't want to look nice or be her best; it was just that *her* version of herself was different from what her sisters saw. She didn't feel the need to display her every single feature. She was much more comfortable behind the story, tucked into the corners of other people's lives. That way her back was always covered.

In the two minutes that followed, Ava learned that Blanca was now a lead buyer at Neiman's and had a room in the back filled with racks of past years' fall/winter collections that she had been meticulously collecting for a special fundraising fashion show coming up.

"And I know we can find something sensational for you." Blanca beamed so hard, there was no way Ava could tell her no.

The Granados sisters followed Blanca through a side door into a maze of pale, cold hallways until they reached a large stockroom filled with row upon row of shelved boxes pushed up against the walls. At the center of the room were a blue mid-century sofa and wide velvet chairs. Near the sitting area were a three-way mirror, several racks of clothing, and a curtained area that Ava guessed was a makeshift dressing room.

"I have already picked a few pieces for you, Ava," Blanca said, waving her arms animatedly. "Very throwback. Very you. I'm thinking no color— maybe gray? White?"

Ava felt herself sinking into a puddle of nerves. *Why did I have to open my big mouth and invite Rion? Because I'm building a bridge*, she reminded herself.

"Something super simple," Ava said, grazing her fingers over the racks of feathers, metallics, furs, and leathers. Everything *except* simple.

"Oh my God!" Carmen squealed. "Look at that ostrich ballet skirt. It's amazing!"

"For an ostrich," Ava groaned. That's when she saw Viv set down her phone on a small table, so she could use both hands to rifle through the clothes.

Slowly, carefully, like a well-trained spy, Ava inched toward the phone, taking full advantage of her sister's obsession with fashion. She would have five, six seconds tops to punch in her code and glance at her text list.

I'm a terrible sister.

I can't.

Ava glanced over her shoulder to make sure Viv was fully occupied, and then she made her move. Grabbing the phone and punching in the code with trembling fingers, she searched the text history. Her eyes landed on a number she didn't recognize with only the letter *H* as a descriptor.

> **H:** Oh yeah the bash is tonight.
>
> **V:** wish you could come. I hate secrets.
>
> **H:** Soon

And that's as far as Ava got, because Blanca called her name from across the room, forcing Ava to abandon Mission Viv.

I was right. Viv's seeing someone. And she's lying about it. But why? Is he married? Forty? Too awful to claim?

But Ava's thoughts were quickly cast to the side when Carm dragged her to the dressing room with an armful of outfits, practically shoving Ava into each one. Python jumpsuit. "Snakes hibernate in the winter," Ava said, tossing it back to her sister. Next came a silver miniskirt with a feather top that made Ava sneeze. "I look like an alien bird." Every outfit made her look ridiculous and feel even more ridiculous. Finally, she drew the line at the eggplant-colored fur dress.

While Viv, Carmen, and Blanca fell into an easy flow of conversation and chisme, Ava slipped out the back curtain and wandered between the racks, trying to find something suitable and not entirely humiliating. Her spirits sank lower as she eyed the garments. Yes, perfect for the runway, but for real life? Not even close. There was a fantasy element to fashion that Ava loathed, a make-believe world where princesses were saved from high towers and knights in shining armors existed. A place of monsters and curses and shadowed forests.

Ava's eyes fell on an iridescent white gown that shimmered in the light. *Fit for a snow queen*, she thought.

"Gree?" Ava hadn't even seen Viv turn down the narrow space between racks.

"Hey," Ava said as nonchalantly as she could, trying to ignore the firestorm burning in her gut.

"You okay?"

"Yeah, why?" Ava diverted her attention away from her sister's peering eyes to the dresses in front of her.

"I know that look."

There was no hiding anything from Viv, especially a firestorm. *But you're hiding something from me, aren't you?* Ava thought bitterly. She was about to call her sister out when she saw it. The simple, white cashmere one-shouldered dress that screamed simplicity. Viv followed her gaze, and before Ava could tug the dress free, her sister whispered, "It's perfect."

Ava had just stepped out of the shower when her phone rang. She threw on a robe and grabbed her cell. The number on the screen looked familiar, but Ava had made it a rule to never answer anyone who wasn't in her contacts. And then it dawned on her who was on the other end.

With a racing heart, she answered quickly. "Hello?"

"Hello, I'm calling for Ava from the *Times*?"

"Reed?"

"That's me," the woman said. "You called about a photo I took?"

"Yeah, I'm so glad you called. Thanks . . ." Ava was fumbling over her words when she needed to get to the point. Turning on her inner journalist, she matter-of-factly explained the details of the picture, hoping it would ignite a memory.

"Sounds awfully familiar," Reed said, followed by what sounded like the tapping of a pen against metal. *Tap. Tap. Tap.*

"Might be one of the photos I took as part of a project I was working on," Reed continued. "I did all sorts of things back then related to arts and culture. I was obsessed with the camera and capturing emotion, which is why so often I snapped strangers' photos." She released a nostalgic-sounding sigh. "Sometimes I forgot to get their permission, though, so the picture couldn't run in the paper."

Ava could see why *Marry Me* guy had piqued Reed's interest. Anyone with a pulse would want to know the answer to his question.

Reed said, "Can you text me the photo? Maybe if I see it, it'll jog my memory."

Ava was glad she'd had the forethought to take a picture of the image. A second later, Reed had the photo.

Tap. Tap. Tap.

Ava waited. Water trickled down her neck, chilling her skin. *Please remember. Please remember.*

"Of course," Reed exclaimed gleefully. "I was in Mexico City and saw this young man get out of a taxi. With this sign. I couldn't help myself. I had to ask him about it. But he was in a hurry, said he couldn't stop, had to get to the train station before the woman he was going to propose to arrived. So, I snapped this photo as he walked away."

"Do you know what happened to him?" Ava had no idea why it even mattered. She didn't know this guy, had never laid eyes on him. And yet she felt her heart stirring inexplicably, as if something about him did matter.

"No. I didn't follow him," Reed said. "I was late to an appointment, or I would have. Imagine that photo. A woman descending the train, seeing this sign. Running into her lover's arms." There was a pause, like Reed was leaning into the past. "But I'll never forget his last words to me as he hustled down the street."

Ava wrapped her robe tighter, hugging her waist. "What?"

"She's my destiny."

"When the gardener's son kissed the princess, she woke up, but he collapsed, dead," Caroline said as she cut out a wad of gum Ava had gotten stuck in her hair. "It was very sad, but I told you that love is very dangerous."

But you said so is hope and trust and destiny, *Ava thought.*

"The princess was so confused," Caroline went on, "because the prophecy had been clear. Only a prince would die from her kiss.

"But when the bruja appeared, she told the princess that her mistake was in believing the gardener's son's stories, for thinking he couldn't die because he wasn't a prince.

"The princess clutched her heart, terrified that her own heart was no longer beating."

"How was she awake with no heart?" Ava asked, knowing the answer but hoping for a different ending.

"She had a heart, but it was made of fire. And all it knew how to do was

burn, burn so brightly that it consumed anyone she cared about," Caroline said. "So, the princess spent each night hidden in the poison woods, trying to understand why her heart wasn't like anyone else's."

"And then what happened?"

"That's when she met the wolf."

Twenty-Four

Something cold washed over Ava's skin.

She had been hoping for something else, an ending to a story worthy of more than destiny.

The word sent a flicker of annoyance and anger through her like a hot rod of lightning. "What if she said no?" Ava muttered after ending the call with Reed. *Wouldn't that mean she wasn't his destiny?* she thought miserably. Ava may not have believed in destiny, but she believed in her instincts, and something was nagging at her, an unfinished answer. She replayed Reed's words, checking for any stone unturned.

I was obsessed with the camera and capturing emotion, which is why so often I snapped strangers' photos. Ava wanted that kind of obsession, and more and more it didn't feel like journalism would ever give her that kind of experience.

Thinking about Reed's photos reminded Ava of the pic she had taken of Rion at the beach. There he was—slanted because of her phone's odd angle, but to anyone else it might look like he was balancing on the edge of the world. His jaw was a solid piece of granite. His not-so-mediocre lips parted ever so slightly. And his gaze was locked on the horizon. Searching. *Seeing.*

Ava enlarged the photo, wishing she had a front angle of his eyes.

She quickly texted Anmol and Corbin to tell them Reed had called, giving them the shorthand version.

Anmol: Now I have to KNOW. Right, Corbin?

Corbin: No idea what we're talking about.

Ava glanced at the clock on her nightstand. *Crap!* She was way behind schedule, and if she didn't pull herself together for Winter of Spies, her sisters were going to kill her.

After blow-drying her hair in braids, Ava removed them and let her locks falls down her back in messy beach waves. She tugged on the dress in front of the full-length mirror in her closet and took a step back. Viv was right. It was perfect. The comfy cashmere was soft and warm against her skin. Like a blanket of protection.

"Oh my God, you look gorgeous!" Carmen bounced into the walk-in closet unannounced. "I officially hate you." She wore a silvery sage blouse, sheer enough to give Raul a heart attack, even though she had a nude bodysuit underneath. But it was the illusion of what was beneath that Carm always said made the biggest statement. Her matching fitted skirt and silk sash embroidered with diamond-like beading was the perfect Carmen Granados touch.

"You too," Ava said, and she meant it. Carmen could pull off a trash bag with a silk tie and make it look like high fashion.

Viv popped her head in next. She wore a long black tulle skirt, wide equestrian belt, and a fitted white turtleneck. She had straightened her dark hair, which fell behind her shoulders in perfect sheets of shine. "Ándele," she said, "It's already eight o'clock."

"What shoes are you wearing, Ava?" Carm said, eyeing the rows of sneakers and sandals. "God, this is dreadful."

"I like to be comfortable."

Viv smiled and held out a pair of nude Stuart Weitzman over-the-knee suede boots she'd had hidden behind her back. "These will go perfectly. Not too high, but not"—she wrinkled her nose—"running shoes either."

Ava shoved her feet into them, grateful her sensible sister hadn't tossed her five-inch heels.

Viv had already called Emmanuel to put their guests on the list. He'd asked why the sudden change, and Viv had to admit she lost a football game. Then he teased her mercilessly.

A minute later the sisters were in Carmen's BMW headed north up the 101.

Malibu was a world of its own. Ava always loved the easygoing, casual vibe, but she knew that was only its exterior. Underneath that skin was a whole system of wealth, affluence, and social capital that always felt like it was an untouchable inch away from make-believe.

As Carm pulled up to the imposing gated entry, Ava was stricken with a heavy dose of anxiety. She hadn't stopped long enough to consider what Rion would think of this world. He drove a truck, lived on a farm. Had a dog named Tres that chased racoons. How in the hell was she going to build a bridge between that and this?

Jorge, the longtime gate guard, waved the sisters through with a smile. But Viv, being Viv, leaned over from the passenger seat and asked him to confirm that their guests' names were on the list. Satisfied, she said thanks, and Carm made the ascent up the long, wooded drive that would lead them to the floor-to-ceiling glass house dubbed the Sea of Love.

Once they arrived at the motor court (which was more like a parking lot filled with exotic cars), a valet took the keys.

"So, where's the Winter of Spies vibe?" Carm mused with an air of irritation.

It wasn't until the trio stepped through the massive carved wooden gates that the world was transformed. They were met with dramatic crystal chandeliers that hung from the sweeping trees, illuminating a snowy landscape.

"Holy shit," Carmen breathed.

"He brought in fake snow?" Ava rubbed the evening's chill off her arms. *Or maybe he rented some arctic winds too*, she thought.

"So Emmanuel," Viv purred, her voice dripping with appreciation.

Ava fidgeted with her dress as they followed the snowy path toward the sound of music. Okay, more than music. It sounded like a one-hundred-piece symphony playing a score from a blockbuster action flick. As they turned the corner, Ava sucked in a sharp breath. At least a hundred people milled about, dressed in furs, feathers, and wings. Men and women wore suits, tuxedos, and gowns. Some wore long silk gloves; others wore shimmering scarves. And the most avant-garde wore lion, bird, or other animal masks.

It was incredible, and the beauty and charm of it stole Ava's breath. She had spent plenty of time here over the years, but tonight Emmanuel's home felt like a page out of a fairy tale.

The massive yard had been transformed into a movie set to look like a scene from Emmanuel's latest spy-slash-fantasy film he had just wrapped in Finland. Every deck, patio, and walkway looked like a winter version of itself, covered in snow, illuminated by pale green, pink, and gold lights that sparkled across the life-sized ice sculptures of the movie's main characters. The servers milled about, expressionless in their throwback 1950s slim black suits, carrying silver trays with delectable finger foods no one could name.

"He's outdone himself this time," Viv muttered just as Emmanuel spotted them and headed over. He wore a fitted white sport coat with a black shirt and no tie, a sharp contrast to so many of the guests.

"Mis princesas!" He smiled wide, passing out his usual abrazos. "Now tell me"—he leaned into their circle like he had a secret to share—"is it the surprise I promised?"

After a round of sufficient, deserved praise and *ooh*s and *ahh*s, Viv said, "Is this a promo party for your movie?"

"An early screening for my closest friends." He beamed.

You have a ton of close friends, then, Ava thought, stepping closer to the outdoor heater.

"This film feels closest to my corazón," Emmanuel said, "more than any of the other stories I've told." He arched a thick brow and raised his hands animatedly like he was painting images in the air. "Spies. Intrigue. Monsters. Magic. And, of course, amor! A blend of genres that will either win me another Oscar or kick me into the depths of hell. And I trust your opinions so much. I wanted you to be here. To tell me if I hit the mark."

"I'm just here for the monsters," Carm chimed.

"There are plenty," Emmanuel said in an ominous tone. "And you must see the ice-skating rink. It's on the north side of the tennis courts."

"You put in an ice rink?" Ava said, totally unable to contain her astonishment.

Emmanuel matched her excitement. "Claro! There is a key scene in the movie that takes place on ice, perhaps my favorite," he boasted with boyish charm. "I've even provided skates in every size if you want to try it."

"I am not ice-skating in this outfit," Carm announced.

Emmanuel smiled and dropped his exuberant voice to a near-whisper. "Pay close attention to your surroundings, chicas. You never know who's watching."

"What does that mean?" Viv asked.

"Es una sorpresa." He turned to leave before spinning back and snapping his fingers. "And por favor make sure you are here for the screening." And then he was gone to hobnob with a woman who was dressed like a swan.

Viv frowned. "I totally should have made him tell me."

"Except that you love Emmanuel," Ava said, thinking how convenient everything would be for Viv if love weren't a thing.

"Coming from Emmanuel," Carmen added, "it makes me super nervous."

"It's probably just some metaphor," Ava guessed, "or something to do with the whole Winter of Spies theme."

"Dude, this better not be one of those awful role-playing parties," Carm groaned.

Ava suddenly felt itchy. "Why does everything have to be a surprise?"

"Lighten up." Viv chuckled.

A few minutes later the sisters were helping themselves to sparkling waters while keeping an eye out for their football crew.

Viv said, "Do you think everyone got in okay?"

Carm stood on her tiptoes, as if that were necessary in her five-inch heels. "Oh, there's Taryn and Donovan," she said, heading over to collect them while Viv got looped into an adult conversation about the family firm and next season's designs.

Ava slipped free, trying to ignore Viv's angry *how could you abandon me?* scowl. She found a somewhat isolated spot under a sprawling tree not too far from the entrance and far enough away from the crowd to hopefully enjoy some nonhuman interaction. She imagined a circle of invisibility all around her, something she had learned in first grade after some kids at school had called her a beaner because she accidentally answered her teacher in Spanish. It was also Ava's first introduction to cruelty.

There are people who will try to make you feel small, Raul had told her. *People who will not like the color of your hair or skin or shoes. People who will decide they do not like you because of your name. There will be all sorts of razones ridículas.*

Ava couldn't remember what he said after that, but she would never forget what her mom had told her that same night: *Only you have the power to create a circle of invisibility. To lock the world out of your heart and mind. Because if you let them in, they will try to destroy you.*

And six-year-old Ava didn't want to be destroyed.

Tonight, though, she just didn't want to get locked into small talk with a stranger posing as her friend. *How's your father? Where is he? How is your summer? You've grown up too fast.* Blah, blah, blah.

For the umpteenth time she scanned the scene for Rion, thinking he for sure would have called if he were already there. Plus, they had agreed to meet by the entrance, and she had a perfect view of it only thirty feet or so away.

Ava started to fidget. With her dress, her hair, her nails. And then the worry crept in.

She imagined her cartoon self trapped under a cloud of words, each raining down in equal misery.

He's not coming.

He got into an accident.

He's with Shelby.

What if I never get close enough to get the blessing back?

Ava swept away the annoying cloud and told herself to get a grip. Rion didn't seem like the kind of guy to stand someone up. And then in a burst of frustration she remembered that she had set her phone to silent. She jerked it free from her clutch. There were three missed calls. All from Rion. Voicemail number one: "Hey, I'm running late."

Number two: "Hey, me again. I'm on my way. Okay. Bye."

Number three: "Okay, maybe I need to get texting. Or you should answer your phone. Do you even listen to voicemail?" There was no judgment in his voice, only curiosity.

Relief spread through Ava, and she wasn't sure if it was relief that he was coming or that her assessment of him had been accurate. Her mind floated back to Emmanuel's words: *You never know who's watching.*

So, what? she thought, scanning the shadows. *Are there spies planted everywhere?*

That's when it occurred to her that she had the greatest kind of spy anyone could hope for: A ghost. One that could look for traps or whoever the so-called watchers were. Ava called Nana.

When her grandmother appeared, she was all smiles. "Qué guapísima" were the first words out of her mouth. "I love that dress on you."

"Thanks, Nana."

Nana glanced around, her eyes drinking in the life pulsing all around. Ava thought her grandmother might comment on the elegance or the beauty or the ostentatiousness, but instead she said, "Why did you call me?"

"To spy," Ava said, thinking her answer came out too rushed to be accepted.

Nana's mouth quirked into a near smile. "On who?"

Meda materialized in the same instant. "Did someone say *spy*?"

Nana's enthusiasm waned. "Me, Medardus. I am the spy."

"Well, you know what they say," the saint retorted. "Two spies are better than one. It's in Ecclesiastes."

"I don't think the Bible says anything about spies," Ava said, instantly regretting her decision to argue the Word with a saint. She barely paid attention in catechism, and the only parts she could even remember were in the catastrophic book of Revelation when everything goes to hell. "How about both of you look around?"

"For what?" Nana said.

Meda scratched his chin. "Is that human dressed as a rabbit? Oh no. I am terribly underdressed." Ava was about to argue that no one could see him when he began to blur at the edges, then vanished entirely.

"Where did he go?"

Before Nana could answer, Meda returned. Gone was the casual California look. In its place? A long silver robe and a stag headdress complete with tawny fur and antlers. "Not bad, eh?" Meda spun in a circle to give Nana and Ava the full effect.

Ava nodded appreciatively. She had to admit, it was a pretty cool look.

Nana's eyes slid over the saint. "Ay, Meda. No importa."

"It does matter!" Meda argued, running a hand over the smooth fabric lovingly.

"Guys," Ava said, reining them back to her original purpose. "Emmanuel told me to pay close attention to the surroundings, because you never know who's watching, and knowing Emmanuel, it's something I'm for sure not going to like."

"And you want us to find out who is watching."

"Exactly!" Ava said. "And you know . . . just make sure I don't get stuck on their radar."

"We are on it!" Meda announced, adjusting his headdress. "Will report back soon."

Nana and the saint vanished an instant later, but not before Ava heard her grandmother sigh loudly.

Ava was smiling when she looked up. She saw him before he saw her.

Rion stood near the entrance, looking around. His hair was a heap of almost-waves that fell over his forehead. He wore a pair of dark slacks and a white button-up with the sleeves pushed up. Maybe it was a trick of the iridescent lights or the music or the button-up, but Rion looked like a guy she would notice.

She could have waved, called his name, headed over, but she did none of those things. She was too swept up in watching him watch the party.

He looked . . . Ava couldn't find the right word. It wasn't *perfect*, or *awesome*, or *handsome*, or even *nice*. Maybe there was no word for how he looked, because the word she was searching for was wrapped up in how she felt.

His dark eyes passed over her head more than once, and she wondered how long it would take him to realize she was in his direct line of sight.

Casually, he pocketed his hands, looked left then right. His eyes brushed past her, then immediately back, landing on her with an intensity that made Ava's skin feel like it was on fire. Quickly, she whirled to face the tree. *Oh my God. Did he see me staring? Seriously? I just turned my back on him! He's going to think . . .*

And then came the tap on the shoulder.

Doing her best to hide all traces of mortification, Ava spun around just as Rion said, "I found you. Sorry I'm late."

"Yeah, um . . . I just barely got your messages." Why did her face feel so hot?

Rion smiled, crossing his arms in a near defiant pose. "Were you watching me?"

"What . . . ?" Ava searched her empty brain for words, any words. Then, as if by a miracle, she found them. "Oh, just now? I wanted to see how long it would take you to notice me standing right in front of you."

Rion let out an easy laugh. "Was that what that was?"

Ava nodded, suddenly second-guessing what she was agreeing to.

Rion patted the top of her head like she was a puppy. "You're taller."

She felt an inexplicable sting that Rion made no mention of how she looked. *The guy has never seen me in anything but shorts and leggings, bare-faced, sporting messy buns; you'd think he would give me a single compliment.*

Standing straighter she said, "Or maybe you're shorter."

Rion positioned himself at Ava's side and took in the scene. "Well, you weren't lying."

"I should have warned you," Ava sighed. "But Emmanuel doesn't do anything small."

Rion's eyes flicked to the house. But there wasn't the usual flash of intimidation Ava had seen on so many faces over the years. He just observed with a sense of detachment. "So, are we supposed to mingle or something?"

"Definitely no mingling." The thought of walking around this party, of circulating with all these LA muckety-mucks sent a shiver of despair through Ava's chest. "Hey, do you know how to ice-skate?"

Rion quirked a single, distrustful brow. "Is this a real question?"

"Come on." Ava grabbed his arm and tugged him down the grassy slope toward the tennis courts she had played on dozens of times. "Don't make eye contact with anyone," she warned as they hurried along the edge of the crowd.

"Why?"

"It's always an invitation to talk," she said, finally releasing his arm.

"And you don't like to talk?" Rion said, quickening his stride. "But aren't you a journalist?"

"No, I mean, yes. I mean, I hate small talk. No one ever tells their stories at a party like this. It's all just make-believe and managing their images." Besides, she couldn't imagine how she might introduce Rion.

This is Rion, the guy who accidentally got my blessing.

This is Rion, the guy I'm totally setting up.

This is Rion, the guy who makes my heart flutter and dip.

Her mind went blank as they cut around the wooded bend and the ice rink came into full view. Ava stopped midstep.

And then she gasped.

Twenty-Five

The rink was small, maybe thirty by thirty feet, but it was the shimmering sky that floated just out of reach that stole her breath. The ribbons of pink, blue, and green light were like a mini aurora borealis. Majestic sycamore trees encircled the space, and for a moment Ava could believe she was in the middle of an enchanted forest.

"Whoa," Rion breathed, as if they had come upon some kind of sacred site.

"Exactly," Ava said, grateful they had the place to themselves. The moment reminded Ava of the first time she saw a shooting star. Or the first time she breathed underwater using a snorkel. The feeling was one of uncontained joy.

She rushed over to the rack of ice skates, pulling her size free before planting herself on a wooden bench. Rion followed her lead and was soon seated next to her with skates in hand. But just as quickly as he had sat down, he was on his feet again, going through some nearby baskets filled with scarves, gloves, and hats.

Rion held up a knitted fox hat complete with furry orange ears. "You want to be the fox?"

Ava went over in socked feet and rummaged for a second before she found a polar bear hat. "If you'll be a bear."

"Why does he have these kid-looking hats?" Rion asked.

"I think the movie's got some creatures in it?" Ava guessed. "Or maybe they're left over from something else. He's always throwing parties, and he lives for anything that involves costumes."

She thought Rion would immediately refuse, but he smiled and fixed the hat on his head with way too much pleasure. "If I fall and break a hip or something, will you make sure to take this off before the ambulance gets here?" He stuck the fox hat on her head.

"Deal," she said, pulling the cap down over her now-freezing ears before snatching a thick cable-knit scarf for added warmth.

Ava had only skated three times in her life. It was never graceful. Not even close. "Have you done this before?" she asked, trying to figure out how good Rion might be.

"Mmm, like twice? You?"

"About the same."

After they were laced up, Ava motioned to the ice. "You go first."

Rion began to rotate his neck in circles like an athlete warming up. "You're stalling," Ava said as she blew a hair out of her face and stepped onto the ice. Her ankles felt like noodles as she wobbled, throwing her arms out for balance. Okay, this was way harder than she remembered.

Slowly, carefully, methodically, she scissored a few inches, hoping she didn't eat it. First, she was in a dress. Second, she was in a dress. Ava was so preoccupied staying on her feet, she hadn't noticed Rion enter the rink.

He grabbed hold of her arm.

"I've got it," she said.

"Oh, I was hoping you would hold me up." Rion's muscles tensed under the strain of staying on his feet. He swayed awkwardly, but his jaw was set with determination.

"Maybe this was a bad idea," Ava admitted as they inched across the rink in a series of awkward clomp-glide moves.

His hand slipped into hers, warming the chill that traveled all the way to her fingertips. A wintry silence fell over the moment as he swung her arm gently. "Is this okay?"

Ava nodded and glanced down at their interwoven hands; a small smile crept over her mouth. A smile that made her feel like a traitor. Because the deeper she fell into this, whatever *this* was, the worse she felt for keeping Rion in the dark.

As they neared the far-end handrail, Ava let go of Rion in favor of reliable, stable steel, instantly regretting the loss of his warmth. A biting cold wrapped around her legs as she continued her stomp-glide across the ice while Rion found a sliding sort of rhythm. Soon he was at the center of the rink, where he stopped and watched Ava hold on for dear life.

"You have to just let go," he said.

"Yeah, no. Not going to happen."

"He's right," came Nana's voice.

Startled, Ava lost her balance, barely catching herself as she hugged the banister. "What are you doing here?" she whispered with her head turned so Rion couldn't see. "I didn't call you."

"We haven't found anything yet," Nana said, matching her whisper as if Rion could hear her. "But I do think this is a perfect opportunity, mija."

"For what?"

"To create a collision," Meda said, materializing next to Nana.

"Are you crazy?" she whisper-shouted. "I can barely stand upright!"

"Ava?" Rion said. "Who are you talking to?"

She turned and smiled at Rion, knowing he could probably see how tense and forced it was. "Just myself."

"Are you okay?" He started to come over.

"Wait!" she shouted. "I mean, I can do this. I'll come to you."

"We can hold you up," Nana said, while Meda appeared at Ava's other side.

Ava threw them a glaring *no way* expression.

"Just a bump, a tap," Meda reassured.

"That could land me with a broken leg," Ava whispered.

"We'll guide you," Nana said as she and Meda took hold of her arms.

"I can do it," Ava insisted again.

But as Ava made her way to Rion, she realized that Nana and the saint provided a much-needed safety net that gave her more confidence.

"You learn fast," Rion said. His furry bear cap inched up like his head was too big for it. An unexpected laugh jumped in Ava's chest.

"Are you laughing at my hat?"

Willing her mouth into a straight line, she took a mock-serious stance, frowning. "Never."

Seeing Nana and Meda were still standing there, Ava raised her eyebrows and tilted her head to the right, hoping one of them would get the hint that they could leave now. They didn't.

Gasping, Ava pointed at the other end of the rink. "Did you see that?"

Rion whirled to check it out, long enough for Ava to mouth to Nana, *You can go now.*

Meda blinked. Nana gave a small nod of the head.

"Hang on," Meda groaned. "Why do we always have to leave?" But Nana had already dragged him away with, "We'll stay close by."

A minute later Rion and Ava were skating around the rink. The pace was slow, and at times their steps were awkward, but the conversation was easy. The blue, green, and pink lights sparkled across the ice while a somber song played in the distance.

They talked about Emmanuel's new movie. They talked about sports and books and music and food. About places they had traveled and wanted to travel to. Ava didn't even notice at what point in the conversation she had looped her arm in Rion's.

It was as if time stood still on the ice, as if the ribbons of color floating just above their heads could shut out the world, and for a moment Ava felt safe. Safe enough to ask about the story of Maggie, even if it meant Rion might reject her again on the premise of her not believing in fate.

"All I can tell you," Rion said, gliding in front of Ava, where he took both of her hands and began to skate backward, tugging her along gently, "is that my gramps loved her and, well, things didn't work out."

"They usually don't." Ava stiffened. She hadn't meant to say those words aloud.

Rion stopped. Bringing her to a standstill too. His eyes smiled before he did. "Sometimes they do."

What was Ava supposed to say to that? How could she stab him in the heart with the cold hard truth, that nothing lasts and love is mercurial and only suckers believe otherwise? It would be so easy to argue that all the couples she had ever known were no longer couples, starting with her own parents. And Raul and Loretta didn't exactly count, since they had only been married a few years. Except Ava wasn't so sure she wanted to believe that anymore. Not when Rion—calm, kind, funny, open Rion—was standing in front of her, his gaze asking her a question she *wanted* to say yes to.

She found herself leaning closer, craving nothing more in that instant than to fall into his arms. "But if things didn't work out," she said softly, "why would he name his orchard after her?"

There was a light, almost believable shrug. "You'd have to ask him that."

Flecks of snow began to tumble from the sky. At first, Ava thought it was more of the fake snow Emmanuel had ordered, but when the flakes landed in her open palm, she blinked, astonished.

Rion lifted his gaze. "Do you see a snow machine?"

With a not-so-confident gesture, Ava said, "I'm sure it's somewhere." When her eyes circled back to Rion, he was staring at her, or at the snowflakes tumbling softly onto her head. No, he was definitely staring at *her*. His eyes were sort of glazed over, his mouth parted in a stupefied kind of way. The guy wasn't even blinking. It was as if some supernatural force were pinning him in place. "If I forget to tell you later, you look really pretty tonight."

Ava felt a tight clench in her stomach. Or was it her chest? Her heart fluttered. It dipped. But unlike Elijah's, her heart didn't seize.

It plunged as if the entire world shrank down to this exact breath, this instant of dancing snow and unexpected stares. Her mind tried to control her heart, but every cell in her body was bursting with emotion. And she knew that whatever line her heart had just crossed, there was no turning back.

"Do you like the snow?" Meda said, appearing behind Rion. "See how versatile I am?"

Ignoring him, not wanting to take her eyes off Rion, not wanting to break their connection, Ava realized she was trembling. "You too. I mean, nice . . . not pretty." This was coming out all wrong.

Rion pointed to his hat. "It's the polar bear vibe, right?"

Meda offered, "Now is the perfect time. I can feel the emotion in the air. It drew me back here. Amazing. Look at how bright your blessing is vibrating all around him. I've never seen such changes in intensity. Truly incredible."

Was that what Ava sensed too? Was that what she was responding so strongly to? She didn't want the answer to be yes. She wanted to lose herself in this moment, in Rion, because it was the natural thing to do, because her heart was still plunging.

Nana stood a few feet behind Meda. But even from here, Ava could see the expectation and hope in her grandmother's face as she squared her small shoulders and nodded.

Static hummed in Ava's ears. Meda was right. The stage was set. And she felt like a snake.

Rion said, "Ava?"

"Yeah?"

"Um . . . this is real snow and it's . . ." He tossed his head back again. "It's legit coming from the sky."

"Special effects can be super believable. Hey, you want to race?"

His eyes swung back to her. "Huh?"

Snake!

"Unless you're scared of falling."

Rion hesitated, smiled, then simply said, "Let's do it."

"So, um . . ." Ava was making this up as she went. "You start at that side, and I'll start over here." She snatched his cap and tossed it to the center of the rink before they both skated to opposite rails. "Okay," Ava went on, "you have to skate the half rink to where I'm standing now, and I'll go to where you are. Then we can make a beeline to the cap, and whoever gets it first wins."

He studied her, eyes circling her face. "You really like competition, don't you?"

"Nah—I'm just trying to even things out, since you won the football game."

With a shrug and an easy smile, Rion crouched forward, ready for take off.

"Rion?"

He glanced up. "Yeah?"

She stared, wishing she could see the blessing, the thing she was taking from him. Wishing she could tell him the truth. "Nothing."

"On three," Rion called out. "One, two . . ."

With the help of Nana and Meda, Ava took off.

"Hey!" Rion bolted at surprising speed. Ava didn't risk glancing up or taking her eyes off the bear hat.

The snow came faster, harder. An arctic wind blustered across the scene, nearly knocking Ava back.

"This is wild!" Rion shouted through a laugh.

Coming to the half loop, Ava reduced her pace, thinking she wanted to give him at least one victory before she stripped him of the blessing.

Rion was a second ahead of her. He stooped, reached for the hat. She slowed just enough not to break her head open, still going fast enough to collide with him. Her heart felt so many things in that moment. But more than anything, it felt the sting of her own betrayal.

The instant Rion lifted the cap, he looked up, smiling triumphantly. A smile that turned to fear when he saw Ava was headed straight for him. At the last second, she hollered, "Move!"

But he didn't. He just stood there, threw his arms open, waiting for her to collide with him and all his foolish trust.

She slammed into his chest. An *oomph* of air rushed from his lungs. He windmilled his arms, seeking balance. Ava reached out to grab hold of him, but she slipped as Rion crashed. He slammed his head onto the ice. And then he was still.

"Rion?!" Ava dove to her knees. "Are you okay?"

Nana and Meda squatted beside her.

"Oh my God!" Ava cried. "I think I knocked him out!"

Meda stared intently. He was searching for the blessing, but at that moment Ava didn't give a rat's ass about the bendición, only that Rion was okay, that he hadn't suffered some awful head injury. Or worse.

"Give him a moment," Nana said over Ava's shoulder.

"Rion!" Ava's voice rose to a whole new level of panic as the ice bit into her bare knees. She patted his chest. His icy cheeks. Snow clung to his dark lashes. "Please . . . wake up."

Meda's face was grim and tense. Without words, he placed his hands on Rion's head and closed his eyes.

"What are you doing?" Ava nearly shouted.

Before the saint could answer, Rion's eyes fluttered open.

Looking to Meda, Ava exhaled sharply. "What did you do?"

"I'm a saint. We heal and fix things. Sometimes. Depending on the injury. His is small. He'll be fine. You're welcome."

"Whoareyoutalkingto?" Rion's words came out slurred.

Ava waved two fingers in front of his face. "How many fingers am I holding up?"

Rion smiled dazedly. "You're a fox."

"What?" And then she remembered the hat. "Rion! How many fingers?"

"Beautiful," he murmured.

Ava nearly tipped over, practically shoving her fingers in his face. "How many?"

"Two."

Meda sighed. And before the words "It didn't work" fell from his mouth, Ava already knew: the blessing hadn't transferred. She felt a rush of relief before a terrible guilt pressed against her. Snow continued to tumble from the sky. The cold was inside her now. And all she wanted were Rion's warm arms around her.

"You're trembling," Rion said, sitting up slowly with a wince as the snow came to a halt and Nana and Meda disappeared.

"Rion, you passed out, and you're worried about me being cold?"

"I've passed out before, Nine," he said, like it was the most common thing in the world. "It happens when you play sports. But I had the weirdest dream." He swept his hair to the side.

Ava didn't want to hear about his dreams. She wanted to make sure he was okay. She reached over and placed her hand on the back of his head. There was a small lump.

"You need some ice."

Rion looked around. "Got plenty of that."

"Why did you catch me? I told you to move out of the way!"

In the sincerest voice she had ever heard him use, Rion said, "You might have run into the wall and gotten hurt."

Ava struggled between wanting to punch him and hug him. She had never met anyone so maddening. Or surprising. "Maybe you should go to the ER."

"I'm fine, really," Rion said, getting to his feet woozily. Ava was there, holding him up, making sure he didn't repeat the head slam. "Except that I'm starving."

She helped him to the edge of the rink. "Well, we've got plenty of food too."

"Quesadillas?"

"Pretty sure those are going to be in short supply around here."

Why was he looking at her like that? Like he was halfway between this world and the dream he had mentioned. "Flan?"

Despite Rion's casual lack of concern for his brain, Ava managed a small chuckle. "I've got an idea."

Twenty-Six

A va knew Emmanuel had wanted her to stay for the screening, but surely he would forgive her once he knew her friend had fallen and hit his head and needed to rest. Ava felt a jab of guilt, knowing it was a half-truth. The full truth bloomed in her mind: *I'd rather be alone with Rion.* The thought made her heart skip a beat until she autocorrected: *To work on the blessing.*

A few minutes later, she led Rion out a side gate, away from the crowd and whatever spies were lurking around. The valet pulled up the truck, handing the keys to Rion, but Ava swiped them away first.

"Hey!" he said with a rare pout. "I can drive."

She pointed to his head. "I've got this."

"I've seen the way you drive."

Ava deadpanned, "Rion. You can either get in and let me drive, or we can leave your truck here and call an Uber."

"Yeah, no, the truck is coming with us."

Ava sent a quick text to her sisters, letting them know she was leaving so they didn't send out the National Guard looking for her.

As they cruised down the 101, Rion fiddled with the music on his phone, barely letting three seconds of each song play before he changed it. Finally, he just turned it off.

"Where are we headed? That Mexican restaurant? With the perfect flan?"

"You'll see." Ava didn't know why she didn't just tell him, except that she was in the driver's seat for once, both literally and figuratively, and she wanted to deliver her own surprise.

She could feel Rion's eyes on her, burning a hole in the side of her head.

"That hat is a good look for you."

Ava had totally forgotten she was still wearing the fox hat. She tugged it off.

When they pulled through the gates of her house, Rion said, "Are you taking me home, Nine? To meet the fam?"

She glanced over at him in the shadows, rolling her eyes. "No, Rion. I'm taking you home for some food."

Ava knew she could have driven him to a restaurant, that she didn't need to invite him into the innermost circle of her world, but she found herself wanting to. *I mean, the guy did just suffer a head injury for me. This is the least I can do.*

Rion had an awful habit of touching everything he saw. Pottery, paintings, plants. It was as if his fingers were magnets for any solid matter. As they swept down the wide hall, he slowed his pace, staring at the carefully curated black-and-white photos of the Granados girls from every vacation since Ava was seven. Italy. Switzerland. Mexico. Brazil. Iceland. Greece. And one of Ava's favorites: sunrise at Stonehenge.

"Wow, you've been to some awesome places," Rion said, nearly pressing his nose to the glass. "Is that little kid scowling on the elephant you?"

"It was hot," Ava justified, leading him into the kitchen before she ran to change into a pair of sweats and a T-shirt. Just before she headed back downstairs, her dad called.

"Yes, I went to the party," she answered with a smile.

"Thank you, mijita. How are you? How are your sisters? Why are you home so early?"

Her dad loved to ask questions in threes or fours or fives. "Everyone is good. I had a small headache."

She must have been on speaker, because Loretta said, "Take some belladonna."

"Okay, so how's the trip?" Ava asked, realizing how much she already missed her dad.

"It is beautiful. And relaxing. But I wish you were here with me."

Rion was seated on a barstool, resting his elbows on the counter as he mindlessly flipped through a cookbook.

Ava tied her hair into a messy bun and said, "You said quesadillas?"

Closing the book, he looked up. "You have two refrigerators."

Ava nearly laughed. Rion hadn't been blown away by Emmanuel's house, but now he was impressed by two refrigerators?

"I cook a lot. Here." She handed him a bottle of aspirin and an ice pack. "For your head."

Rion took both.

Ava began to rummage through the fridge. "Okay, any dietary restrictions? Allergies? Nuts? Dairy? Vegan?"

"Uh, I don't eat salmon."

"How come?"

"Got sick on it at a wedding once. Barfed my guts out."

"Okay, no salmon quesadillas then."

Ava whipped up four chicken quesadillas with jalapeños, with extra garlic, and chocolate chip peanut-butter cookies (she always kept dough in the freezer). She was glad to be busy in the kitchen to clear her head, to let go of the confusion she had felt when Meda told her that the blessing hadn't transferred. *Why was I so relieved?*

"Huele delicioso," Rion said. The warm, welcoming scent of sizzling butter mixed with melting chocolate and brown sugar filled the air. But it did nothing to stop the twisting of Ava's guts or the churning of her mind.

I'm a monster.

No, I'm not. This is for Nana. My feelings for Rion can't get in the way. She froze, tripping over this last thought as a thick pressure began in her chest. A pressure that told her there was no more lying to herself, no taking back what happened on the ice rink. Elijah was so right. This feeling wasn't some chemical reaction. It was like wading in a crystal blue sea that's warm and peaceful and utterly perfect, until you realize that a dangerous wave is forming off in the distance, drawing nearer to knock you down. But maybe she could enjoy the sea as long as possible; maybe she could change the nature of the ocean and will the waves in another direction. Maybe.

Rion was already standing on the other side of the island, helping himself to the teary task of onion dicing. "I'm a good onion chopper," he was saying in Spanish as Ava sliced the avocados for guacamole.

Thirty minutes later, they were sitting at a table near the firepit, small flames licking the chilled air. Rion scarfed down the food; Ava merely picked at hers.

"So, you want to hear my wild dream?" Rion said mid–quesadilla bite. He didn't wait for a response. "There was this woman, older. Reddish hair. Purple sweater."

Ava stiffened.

"There was something really familiar about her," he went on. "Like maybe I've seen her before. Except I'm sure I haven't. Anyhow, she kept telling me she needed to go home. That I needed to give her the keys, but I didn't have any keys." Rion popped a chip into his mouth, chewed, then added, "Weird, huh?"

Ava's pulse pounded. Her skin prickled. Her mind was firing in all directions. *No way. Could it be? Is it possible that Nana crept into his dream? But how?*

"So weird," she finally said, pushing her plate away. "Did she say anything else? Or were there any other details that you can remember?" *Like a saint in a silver robe, looking like a stag?*

Rion fidgeted in his chair, cleared his throat. "You were there."

"Me?"

"Your voice."

Ava was almost scared to ask. "What did I say?" *I'm a traitor. Don't trust me.*

Rion rubbed the back of his neck anxiously. "You said, 'I'm the bridge.'"

Ava felt like she might roll out of her chair, but she managed to hide the embarrassment and surprise and confusion with another question. "And this is the first time you've dreamed about her?"

"I've dreamed about you before," Rion blurted, then jumping into autocorrect mode, he added, "I mean it's the first time I've dreamed about the woman in purple. Are you into dream interpretation or something?"

How did he always do that? Turn the tables. Put her in the hot seat. Find a way to melt her into a helpless puddle.

He's dreamed about me?

Rion stood and went over to one of the loungers, where he lay back and pinned his gaze to the sky.

Ava planted herself in the other chair. "You can't see the stars from here with all the skyglow, but if you could . . ."

He jumped up, plopped himself next to her, and took her hand in his. Then, pointing, he said, "The North Star would be about there."

The pool light caught his profile at just the right angle, making him seem younger for a split second before Ava turned back to the unseeable North Star.

"You should come to the farm sometime," he said. "Get a different view. Just make sure to bring Tres a treat. Or she might hold it against you, and she has a *looong* memory."

"Good to know," Ava said, feeling the weight of sudden exhaustion down to her bones. If the moment on the ice rink when Ava admitted to herself how she truly felt about this guy lying next to her didn't transfer the blessing, she wondered if anything ever could.

They relaxed into the moment, with their eyes searching the sky for all the stars they knew were there but that they couldn't see.

They were so close, the skin of his bare arm was touching hers. Electrical currents coursed through her body so fast she thought they might short-circuit her heart.

"This is a very comfortable chair," he said so calmly she was sure his heart was in zero danger of short-circuiting,

"My dad designed it."

"Your dad is good at his job."

A minute later Ava risked a glance, only to find Rion asleep. His face was relaxed, peaceful. Except for his eyebrows. Every two seconds they twitched. He was definitely dreaming, and Ava wished she could crawl into his head to see what the dream was about.

Ava hadn't realized she had fallen asleep too until Rion's phone buzzed on the glass table. She jerked awake to find Rion dozed off, his arm draped over her. She eased herself free and picked up his phone to stop the annoying vibrating. There was no photo. Only a name.

Shelby.

Ava stared. Rion stirred.

Quickly, she set the phone back on the table before he noticed she had it.

The thing kept buzzing. And buzzing.

Don't answer it.

Don't answer it.

Rion drew himself to a seated position, ran a hand over his face, and answered the phone the second he saw her name. "Hey."

With the phone to his ear, he stood and walked away. For privacy. For secrecy. His voice was low, making it impossible for Ava to catch the words. But there was no mistaking the emotion in his voice. "I'm sorry." A few seconds later, Ava caught the last words of the conversation: "I'll be right there."

Ava glanced at her own phone. It was after midnight. She had no missed calls, only a thumbs-up from Carm from her earlier text that Ava was leaving the party.

When Rion returned, his expression was one of . . . what? Guilt? Embarrassment? Panic?

Ava's brows pinched together as she studied him, wishing she knew him well enough to read it.

"Rion. What's wrong?" Ava could feel the tension in the air. She could sense that something had shifted, and it made her feel like she'd been punched in the chest by an oncoming wave.

"I have to go." His voice was coarse, rigid. Not effortless.

"Is everything okay?"

Without another word, Rion turned to leave.

"Rion," Ava said, following. "Maybe I can help."

"I can't do this right now."

This? "Do what? I just . . . you seem upset, and if you'd just tell me . . ." Her voice trailed off and sounded way more desperate than she was aiming for. Not desperate to keep Rion here or even to know about Shelby. But desperate to get back to where they were when they were on the ice rink, when they were laughing in her kitchen and falling asleep under the stars.

He spun. His eyes fixed on hers, searching for a way out . . . or maybe a way in. She sensed the struggle. And then he removed her hand from his arm. "I made a promise," he said, hesitating, "and I can't break it." Then he turned and walked away in a determined rush, like he was trying to create distance between him and Ava as fast as he could.

Twenty-Seven

A va hardly slept the rest of the night.

She replayed the night's events on an endless loop, always landing on Shelby's call. The look on Rion's face. Those words, *I have to go*, as if he had been summoned.

I made a promise.

Ava felt like she was in a haze, or a nightmare. Either way, her insides were twisted with a confusion that ached down to her bones. The one thing she had worked so hard to avoid, these feelings of hope and trust and something deeper, had found her when she wasn't paying attention.

She realized Rion's quick departure was proof that the heart couldn't be trusted. *This is what I get for letting myself fall.*

She felt pitiful for even checking her phone to see if Rion had left her a message, and even more so when she found nothing. How had everything gone from so good to so bad so fast? Quickly, she turned her thoughts to the only thing that mattered: the blessing.

Without warning, her traitorous brain flashed an image of Rion standing in the middle of the rink in that ridiculous bear hat, smiling that *world in my pocket* smile. *You have to just let go.*

Ugh! Squeezing her eyes closed, Ava buried her head under a pillow while simultaneously exploding the image way too violently before she turned to the dream.

He dreamed of Nana. And my voice. "I'm the bridge."

But I'm not. All I have is a guy who is receiving mysterious calls after midnight. UGH. UGH. UGH.

Ava dragged herself downstairs to get some water, but halfway down she heard Viv's voice coming in soft murmurs. She stopped in her tracks. Listened.

There was a breathy laugh. Whispers.

Ava took another step and another, careful not to be heard. This must be the person Viv was hiding from them!

Viv was drawing closer now, close enough for Ava to hear four words loud and clear: "I miss you too."

She didn't know why, but those words, the way they jabbed at her heart, forced her back to her room where she battled between confronting Viv and letting it go. If she didn't confront her sister, then Viv couldn't lie directly to her face, which would be so much worse than this whatever *this* was.

Ava's head filled up with maybes: *Maybe Viv has a good reason for hiding that she's seeing someone. Maybe I misheard. Maybe it's not even a big deal. Maybe Rion has a really good reason for taking off so fast.*

But here's the problem with maybes, Ava thought. *They're filled with hope, and hope is dangerous.*

By the time morning's light filtered into Ava's room, she pitched off the covers with a sigh, threw on a bathing suit, and headed downstairs for some laps.

Long, even, powerful strokes carried her through the water.

Breathe, pulse, dip.

The water was cool, soothing. A place to drown memories. And feelings. To get her head on straight. *It doesn't matter who Rion is, or if he has a girl-friend, or if he's a nice guy or a jerk. Or if Viv is lying. None of it changes the one thing that matters: saving Nana.*

Ava treaded water at the deep end, staring across the full length of the pool, thinking fondly about all the times she and her sisters dove for treasures. They competed to see who could swim the pool's entire length underwater the fastest, and whoever won was crowned reina of the sirenas. But by the time Ava was old enough and strong enough to win the crown, her sisters had moved on to other things.

One deep breath.

Two.

Three.

She slid beneath the surface, swimming to the bottom and then across the pool toward the opposite end. Halfway through the journey, pressure built in her lungs, her ears. The weight of the water pushed in on all sides, extending across her chest and into her heart. Tears pricked her eyes. She let them spill invisibly into the water.

With one last determined kick, she touched the wall and thrust herself upward for air. She sucked it in greedily, triumphantly, wiping away the tears in the chilly morning breeze.

Goose bumps sprouted on her arms just as Nana materialized in a club chair at the edge of the pool.

Ava blinked. "Nana?"

Nana nodded. Her expression was soft, her dark eyes softer. "Mi corazón. ¿Por qué lloras?"

Ava lifted herself out of the pool and wrapped a towel around her waist before she slumped into the chair next to her grandmother. She wanted to lean on the ghost's shoulder, to have her stroke her hair and tell her everything was going to be okay. But everything had changed. The roles had reversed, and Ava had to be the strong one now.

With a quivering smile, Ava said, "I'm glad you're here."

"Why were you crying?"

"I don't know." And it was the truth. Ava could guess—it was the pressure of getting back the blessing, of admitting her feelings for Rion, of losing her grandmother for good—the list went on and on. But it did Ava no good to dwell, to analyze, to pick apart her feelings, because that wouldn't fix the problems in front of her. Instead, Ava told Nana everything that had happened with Rion, including the dream.

Nana's expression was one of contemplation.

"How could you have been in his dream?" Ava sniffed, wiping her nose with the towel. "He's never met you. Unless ghosts can . . ."

"If you're asking if I visited him in his dream, the answer is no." She sighed. "It's hard to explain; it's a knowing that isn't in the mind. ¿Entiendes?" Before Ava could tell her that no, she did not understand, Nana added, "We are all connected at a deep level now, by this blessing, by fate."

Ava fought the insistent urge to roll her eyes at the last word.

"Entonces, it makes sense that he caught a glimpse. And he is right." Nana leaned over and took hold of her hand and squeezed. "You are the bridge; only you can put things back together."

"How am I a bridge?" The frustration grew, spreading across her chest and into her stomach.

Meda materialized at the other side of the pool, pacing, his right hand stroking his beard thoughtfully. "I find it very odd that the blessing was so bright last night."

"Why is that strange?" Ava said.

"Because blessings are constant," the saint said. "They shine at a very specific intensity with no change. Until they dim near death." He gazed off into the distance like a melodramatic poet. "Like a distant star."

Ava didn't press. Her head was still dancing with thoughts of Rion's dream and bridges.

Nana nodded tightly, then said, "Can we have a moment, Meda?"

"Oh," the saint said in a forced gruff voice that led to clearing his throat. "Of course. Yes. Private. Okay. Bye."

Nana turned to Ava. "Why are you so upset? And don't tell me it's the blessing. You've known about that for a while now."

"I just . . . I feel stupid . . . and really bad about . ." Ava hesitated, afraid the emotion in her voice would betray her. "What about Shelby?"

"What about her?"

"I mean, if she's his girlfriend, isn't it bad that he's hanging out with me?"

"¿Por qué? You are his friend." Nana blinked innocently, but Ava knew that ploy, and she for sure wasn't going to bite. "Unless . . ." Nana let the word hang between them.

"It's not like that," Ava said, louder than she meant to. "I just meant that . . . it could complicate things, because of all the rules with real emotion and bridges, and how am I supposed to do that when I don't trust him or even know him?"

Nana pulled Ava closer and planted a beso on the top of her head. "Why don't you ask him?"

Oh. Right. That seemed totally reasonable, except that maybe Ava was afraid of the answer. She'd rather have the Rion she had allowed into her heart than the one with two sides that Achilles had warned her about.

Ava sighed. "What are we going to do? I can't keep knocking into him. I mean, why isn't it working? It's like we're missing something." Ava trusted her gut, that little voice inside that told her to dig more, to not merely accept what was in front of her.

Nana stared across the still water. Maybe it was the morning light, or maybe it was the fact that Nana was now a ghost, but Ava could easily imagine her grandmother as a young woman. Her flawless olive skin, her wide eyes, high cheekbones, and full lips. Raul had told Ava that she favored her grandmother, and until now, Ava had never seen it.

Nana said, "Meda and I are going to continue to search for more answers. So, we'll be gone for a few days."

Ava hadn't meant to say the words, hadn't meant to add stress to an already nerve-racking situation, but they came rushing out. "Nana, we're running out of time. A few days could be eternity."

Nana smiled casually and said, "Which is why I must go now. Do you need to cry any more before I leave?"

"I'm fine," Ava said, not feeling even close to fine.

"Okay. Chin up, amor. We can do this." She paused for a brief moment. Then, speaking softly, she said, "And it's okay that you have feelings for him. That you allowed them in."

No. It's not. Because it hurts worse than I could have imagined.

After she disappeared, Ava was left alone with the question she didn't want to ask: *When will it be our final goodbye?*

Because there was always a final goodbye. Always.

Shivering, Ava climbed onto a lounger and curled up with her towel, snoozing for a couple of hours until her phone rang. Bleary-eyed, she checked the screen, split-second hoping it was Rion.

It was Elijah.

She couldn't answer fast enough. "Hi!"

"Hey, Aves."

She staggered to a seated position. Smiling, Elijah said, "You look like shit."

"Thanks."

"Rough night?"

"The worst." She dragged a hand over her face. "How are you? What are you doing? Tell me about Pierre or whatever his name is. Tell me something good."

"Why the worst?"

"A party," she lied. "Emmanuel. You know how he is."

"Did he serve those little shrimp cocktail things?"

"Elijah. Who cares about food when you're a million miles away and will probably disconnect any second?"

"No worries. I've got primo service." Ava was more awake now and could see he was walking down a bustling city street. His hair had gotten longer. His eyes brighter. God, she missed him.

"Where are you?" she asked.

"Cusco. Now tell me about that cute Rion guy."

"He's not cute, and you need a haircut."

"Oh, okay," he said sarcastically, weaving between people. "Did you really meet him by crashing into his truck?"

"Something like that," Ava managed, before changing the convo. "Tell me about Pierre from London. I'm sure he's much more interesting."

Elijah's eyes flicked to the screen. There was a smile there. "You're going to meet him here in a minute. Be nice, okay?"

"I'm always nice."

"Oh, and I got your texts. No idea what half of them mean, and for the record, I do not think I am God." He smirked and shrugged. "Only sometimes. So, what's the deal with asking me for collision ideas?"

How could Ava begin to tell him about the lost blessing, about her grandmother's ghost, about Meda? About Rion. "I already figured that all out," she lied again. "But I have something else to tell you."

Elijah crossed a busy road and was now in what looked like a shaded park, where he sat on a bench. "Shoot."

"You need to come home."

"I miss you too." Elijah sat forward, placing his face closer to the screen so Ava could practically see his pores. "Aves?"

"Mm?"

"You're into him, aren't you?"

"What?!" Ava nearly choked. "No!" She couldn't admit the truth to Elijah, because if she did it would be out here in the real world, and there would be no putting it back.

"How many times have you hung out?"

"I don't know."

"Was he at the party?"

"Maybe."

"Oh man!"

"What?"

"You're into him. You act like I don't know you."

"Elijah." Ava could feel her anger rising. Elijah knew her almost as well as her sisters did. And she knew him, sometimes better than he knew himself. When Athena Cooper broke his heart last year, Ava made him double-fudge cookies and threw him a Granados sister sleepover bash. That was the night he told Ava he was into guys and girls. She was glad when he told her. But the thing about Elijah was this: He was always giving his heart away. Too soon, too often, to too many of the wrong people.

"Has he met Viv and Carm?" Elijah asked flatly. When Ava hesitated, he said, "Well?"

"It's not what you think."

Elijah rubbed his forehead anxiously. "I cannot believe you let them meet him before me."

"¡Fíjate! I'm hanging out with him because he has something of mine," Ava blurted. But the words rang hollow. "And . . . and . . ." Angry tears pricked her eyes, "I actually hate him."

"Wow, this must be serious. You know there's a thin line between love and hate, right?"

Just then Elijah's gaze slid from the screen. A smile spread across his round face. The screen flipped, and Ava saw a tall guy with brown skin, broad shoulders, and lanky arms waving at her like they were lifelong friends. "This is Aves," Elijah was saying with so much pride, Ava wanted to hug him for eternity.

Pierre's eyebrows raised and his smile got bigger. "He talks about you all the time. Says you were his first love."

Ava laughed. "Sounds about right."

"Hey," Elijah said to Ava. "Sorry, but we've got tickets to this thing. Can I call you after?"

"Go," she said. "Have fun. Nice to meet you, Pierre."

Pierre's and Elijah's beaming faces were scrunched into the screen, and all heartless Ava could think was, *You might be happy now, but eventually you, too, will have a last goodbye.*

Twenty-Eight

The messages began at approximately 3:00 p.m. in the group text:

Viv: Did you get it?

Carm: Yup

Ava: What are you guys talking about?

Viv: From E

Ava: I got nothing.

Carm: At office with Viv. We can watch together.

Ava: WHAT IS IT

Viv: Wait for us. Be there by 6:30. Gree, can you make those cinnamon biscuits?

Carm: And some of that Mexican chocolate with mini marshmallows

Ava: Not unless you tell me what it is!

Viv: Winter of Spies thing. Gotta go

Carm: Same

With Ava's sisters at the office all day, Ava hadn't even had a chance to tell them about Shelby or the dream. She was glad, though, because a part of her didn't feel prepared for the opposing advice and rapid-fire questions that were likely to confuse her more.

No, she had to figure out how she felt about things. Put things in order. Which meant she needed to go see Father Gustavo. The priest had three things going for him:

1. He was a good listener.

2. He wasn't judgy.

And the biggest thing?

He was outside the story looking in, which made him the most objective person in Ava's life.

And right now, she needed loads and loads of objectivity.

With each step, she went from confused to mad: Rion hadn't bothered to call or text. Her pride wouldn't let her reach out to him either, but her promise to Nana was likely to force her hand, which only made her mad all over again.

Settling into the confessional, Ava didn't bother with the usual *Forgive me, Father, for I have sinned.* And really? She didn't see the point. Priests already knew people were there to confess their sins, so why make anyone say it?

Instead Ava began with, "It's me."

"You said six times." There was a smile in his scratchy voice.

"Just to be sure, like, whatever I tell you in here"—she dropped her voice to a near whisper—"you can never repeat, right?"

"It's called the sacred seal of confession."

"'Kay. Good." Ava rubbed her forehead, trying to even out her breathing. Surely Gustavo had heard some off-the-wall stuff in confession, right?

And he can't tell anyone.

She started with the night of Nana's death, stumbled ahead with the blessings that were rooted in her family's history, with the bendición running wild into Rion's life instead of her own, and finally with the consequences if she didn't get the blessing back. After the last word of her story was spoken, she waited.

After all, it was a lot to pick apart, even for a priest.

A couple of beats passed before Gustavo spoke, and when he did, all he said was, "I see."

"Does it sound crazy? Do you believe me?"

He let go of a light chuckle. "I have spent my life investigating mysteries and miracles, so no, it doesn't sound crazy, and yes, I believe you. But why did you tell me all this?"

Ava shrugged. "I guess ... I don't know. I thought maybe you might have some experience with the whole afterlife stuff."

"Ah—well, most of it is anecdotal. This is a first for me *personally*. Although I did hear about a woman in the third or fourth century who had half of her soul stolen while she slept, and she had to get it back."

Ava lunged forward, banging her knee on the wood. "Son of a ..." She gritted her teeth, restraining herself from cussing in church, in front of a priest, during confession.

"Are you okay?" Gustavo asked.

"Yeah, uh, sorry. So how did she get her soul back?"

"With the help of an archangel."

"Oh." Ava rubbed her knee. "Well, I only have a fifth-century saint." Which was way lower than an archangel—not that Meda wasn't cool, but maybe she needed bigger guns.

"May I ask which saint?"

"Medardus."

"Hmmm ... I'm not quite familiar with him."

Ava suddenly felt defensive of him. "Saint of prisoners, teeth, weather, and other stuff? He's really nice and sometimes funny, and stubborn. So, so stubborn. I mean, the guy will not let up."

"Yes, well, I am sure you have been given all the tools you need to succeed," Gustavo said. "It's like a puzzle, and you have to put the pieces in the right place, yes?"

"But I'm running out of time, and I don't know what to do." Ava could feel the panic rising, overwhelming even her steady, logical mind. "I can't just let my nana wander around purgatory with no memory of her life, but how do I get the blessing back when nothing is working? We've tried everything, re-creating the night of the accident, and we even had emotion last night—like, a lot . . . or at least Meda said so, and it still didn't work, so I'm not so sure about having all the tools." Ava took a breath before steaming ahead. "And did I tell you that Rion probably has a girlfriend? I mean, what a jerk, right? Like who hangs out with someone, takes them to a story tree, gets knocked out for them, acts all nice and tells them secrets when . . . Shouldn't he be telling *her*?"

There was silence. The creaking of tired wood outside the confessional. Ava's angry heart thrummed in her ears.

"Father?"

"I'm thinking."

Ava twisted the tips of her fingers. She waited, waited some more. But when Gustavo said nada, she worried she had made a mistake coming here. Or had she just thrown too much at him at once? "So, what do you think I should do?"

"What I think has no bearing on this situation."

What the hell! Ava wanted to shout, but figured that was the wrong thing to say to a priest when she was in church. "Should I call him?"

Gustavo sounded like he was repositioning himself on the other side of the screen. Then with a soft sigh, he said, "What I can tell you is this: You must search the contents of your heart. The answer is there."

"What does that mean?" Ava's blood pressure was rising. She had wanted Gustavo to help her, not throw riddles at her.

"It means you're trying to answer a question with only your mind, but God is closest to your heart."

"You want me to ask God if I should call Rion?" Was this priest for real?

He cleared his throat. "Do you want to get the blessing back?"

"Yes." Ava's response was the answer to her own ridiculous question. Yes, she should call Rion. Yes, she should swallow her pride. Yes, she should . . .

"Are you willing to do whatever it takes?"

"Yes." Ava scooted to the edge of her seat.

"Then, tell me, what are you so afraid of?"

Ava picked at her nails, stared at the dark floor, shook her head. Wasn't it obvious? "I don't want to fail Nana."

"Emotions are feral things."

What does that have to do with anything?

"There is no rhyme or reason, no timelines, no rules, no guidebook," he went on. "They grow when we aren't looking."

"Okay." Ava was doing her best to follow, but her frustration for all this mystery-speak was only expanding.

"Feelings also die when we aren't looking."

A strange yet familiar emotion washed over Ava in that moment. Her stomach dipped, and her heart went silent. There was no answer there, nothing to be heard.

"Tell me again," Gustavo said, "what are you so afraid of?"

Ava was about to repeat, *Failing my family, losing Nana*, when another half thought surfaced. She tried to turn away, pretend it back into nonexistence, but there it was. *That I am way too attached to . . .* She didn't allow herself to finish the sentence. Instead, she buried it in Caroline's fantastical forest. Deep within the poisoned earth.

"Nothing else," Ava said.

"When you find the *nothing else*," Gustavo said, "you'll find your answer."

Ava wandered Montana Ave. Grabbed a latte, bought an overpriced sweatshirt, then stopped at the market for a few items to make the biscuits and cocoa. She was in full pity-party mode with a splash of anger by the time she checked out. *When you find the nothing else*, she repeated to herself haughtily, *you'll find your answer. How useless is that? Is that what they teach in priest school?*

On the walk home, Ava threw a prayer skyward. "Look, God. I kept my last deal with you and even went to confession more than I was supposed to. So, can you please help me help Nana? If you do, I promise to . . ." She hesitated, trying to think of something worthwhile when the words slipped out. "I promise to not kill Rion next time I see him."

Ava glanced around nervously. Had she really just said that? And to God?

"Scratch that," she whispered. "I'm stressed. I'm sure you get it."

The moment she set the grocery bag on the kitchen counter, her phone rang. Ava nearly lunged for it, instantly deflated when she saw it wasn't Rion, but an unknown number that looked familiar. Then she remembered. Reed.

"Hello?"

"Eva?"

"It's Ava. Hi, Reed."

The elderly woman chuckled as if she was used to getting everyone's names wrong. "I remembered something that might help you."

Ava leaned against the island. "Really?"

"My memory isn't what it used to be, and it wasn't until I was tending to my geraniums that it all came rushing back."

"What is it?"

"The man told me his name. Charles."

Ava paused, waited, thinking surely there was more than a common first name. "Did he give you a last name?"

"Something like Lawrence, or maybe it was Lawrence Charles. But that isn't the best part." She giggled like a kid. "He was from here. Imagine running into someone from LA in Mexico City by chance. Well, not chance. Clearly, I was meant to meet him and take his photo, and then you were meant to find the photo and call me, and here we are." She inhaled sharply, then lowered her voice like the two were sharing a well-guarded secret. "What do you think it means?"

Ava didn't have the heart to tell her that it meant nothing. She just happened to be the one to find the photo and she was curious. That was all. End of story.

"I don't know," she told Reed, since she didn't want to hurt her feelings with the truth.

"Please do let me know if you find them. I would love to take their photo. Imagine the story! Maybe that is the reason. Maybe I am meant to share their story, like closing the loop. What do you think?"

So, Reed believed in happy endings. Pobrecita.

"But what if she said no?" Ava asked.

Reed hesitated, then offered, "Oh, my dear. This man oozed charm, a nervous, sweet kind that wasn't at all arrogant. Do you know what I mean? There was something about him that I can't quite name. But I am an excellent judge of character. No girl who knew what was good for her would ever let someone like him go."

A headline flashed across Ava's mind: "The Woman Who Believed in Happy Endings."

After Ava ended the call, she realized with a heavy heart that the whole photo thing had become a distraction, a way to keep herself busy with something other than the blessing.

Feelings grow when you aren't looking.

She pulled out the photo and allowed herself one more glance at the hopeful *Marry Me* guy, carrying his handmade sign through the streets of Mexico City.

Her eyes slid to the clock. The hands were stopped at 8:51.

Twenty-Nine

Ava had read once that whatever you gave your attention to would often show up. For example, if you thought about red cars all day, guess what color of car you were most likely to see?

Except that she hadn't been thinking about 8:51, and yet those numbers kept showing up in her life like irksome little messengers trying to tell her something that probably meant nothing.

But the journalist in her wouldn't let go of the new nugget of information, so she quickly googled Charles Lawrence and Lawrence Charles in Los Angeles and found dozens of listings for each.

"He might not even live here anymore," Ava said as she pulled all the ingredients for the cocoa and snacks together. *And what does it matter? I can't get distracted from the blessing. I have forever to look for Marry Me guy, but only seven days to save Nana.*

Ava scrolled through the music on her phone, selecting a new upbeat indie band, but when she tried to play it through the speakers, the only music that blared was one of her dad's sappy love ballads: "Bésame Mucho."

Seriously? she thought, pounding away at her phone's screen. With a grunt, she finally gave up and let Raul's music into the kitchen, where she spent the next couple of hours baking the cinnamon biscuits, blending the hot cocoa from authentic Mexican chocolate, including freshly whipped cream, and, because she had leftover coconut and rolled oats, she made a dozen Anzac cookies.

Her sisters blew in like two cyclones, racing up the stairs, each calling down their rendition of "What the hell are you listening to?"

In record time they changed into comfy sweats before appearing in the TV room, where Ava had set out the treats on the coffee table. Viv was getting the video set up while Carm plopped onto the cloudlike sofa. "Okay, dude. Spill. What happened last night?"

"Yeah," Viv said, her attention simultaneously on her laptop and the TV.

Ava knew this would be their first question, and she was glad she'd had today to put all the chaos in order. "I thought the screening of this was last night," she said, wondering why Emmanuel would send them the movie.

"These are party outtakes," Carm explained. "He had cameras set up everywhere at the party and filmed people, then replayed them back as part of the screening with music and everything. It was actually kind of cool. Everyone loved it. Anyways, he sent us our outtakes, because he didn't want to put us on display," she said. "It took everything I had not to watch it on my phone."

So that's what he meant by *You never know who's watching*.

"Okay, it's ready," Viv announced. Then, to Ava, "But first tell us how things went with Rion."

Ava collapsed onto the couch. "Did you guys see white light when you got your blessings?"

"Huh? No." Carm pulled a face.

"Negative," Viv added. "Why?"

"Rion said that the night I hit his car, he saw a white light."

Ava's sisters were silent, expressionless.

"Maybe it was the impact?" Viv guessed.

"Or maybe he's just an attention-grabber," Carmen put in with a smirk. "Stop trying to avoid telling us about last night."

Ava chewed her bottom lip, wondering why he saw white light and her sisters didn't. Maybe it had something to do with the fact that the blessing wasn't his? God, she was so tired of all the unanswered questions.

"Earth to Ava." Carm clapped her hands.

Snapping her attention back to the convo, Ava said, "Everything was chill until he got knocked out."

"What?!" Viv's eyebrows shot up.

Ava explained everything because secrets were an impossible feat in their family. By the time she was done, her sisters looked contemplative. They had gotten snagged on Shelby too. Viv sipped at her cocoa, stirring the whipped cream with a tiny spoon. "Shelby might just be a friend."

Carm sighed. "Or not." This earned her a death glare from the oldest. "But, dude, he totally took a hit for you. Like, that says something."

"Look," Viv said in her lawyerly voice. "It doesn't even matter. That has nothing to do with getting the blessing back."

"But it's a complication we can't ignore," Ava said, thinking she sounded like a spy from one of Emmanuel's flicks.

Carm was frowning and picking at a cookie. "If only we could sneak into his house in the middle of the night and just cut it out of him."

That would definitely be easier, Ava thought.

"You have to call him, Gree."

Ava nodded, knowing Viv was right. "I'll call him tonight."

"Call him now," Carm said, way too eagerly.

"Now?" Ava's heart jumped into her throat. It was one thing to say she was going to call, and another thing to actually do it. Pride was such a worthless, useless thing. If Ava was being totally honest with herself, she would have recognized it; she would have seen that it was the only reason she was having such a hard time calling him, because in her mind *he* was the one who should be reaching out.

"Maybe I should just tell him the truth about the blessing," Ava said, worn out by all the pretenses.

Carmen sat up. Crumbs spilled down her T-shirt into the folds of the sofa. "I wasn't going to say anything, but I had this really weird thought."

"What?!" Ava and Viv said simultaneously.

"Now, hear me out and don't shoot me down until I'm done," she began, already pulling her knees into her chest in a defensive stance. "Remember that fairy-fail Mom used to tell us when we were little about the princess?"

The story had been almost the same for all of them, but the biggest difference was what the princess's heart was made of. Viv's story was about a girl with a heart made of wood; Carm's princess had a heart of water. And Ava's princess had a heart of fire.

Carmen went on. "Well, what if this is like that, and . . . and you have to kiss him to get the blessing back?"

Ava narrowed her eyes and wondered for the millionth time if Carm's brain was just wired entirely different from any other human on the planet. "The kiss killed the gardener's son," Ava reminded her.

"In every one of our stories," Viv ground out.

Licking a dollop of whipped cream off her finger, Carm said, "Well, nothing else is working. And didn't Nana say something about emotion? Hello! Kisses always have emotion, even if it's disgust at how bad of a kisser someone is."

"I already asked Meda about that, and he said no kiss. Just a bridge."

"Look," Carm said, "I'm not trying to be mean, but Meda seems to get a lot wrong."

Viv's face was tense, unreadable.

"Viv," Ava pleaded, "tell her. Tell her it's a bad idea—"

"Carm might be onto something here."

Ava cringed, feeling suddenly outmatched and outnumbered. "You can't be serious. Carm herself said it's a total fairy-fail."

"Even *I* would kiss him," Carm nearly shouted, "if it meant saving Nana and the blessings!"

"It's just a kiss," Viv said, her voice gentle and prodding. "And it's worth a shot."

Ava hated that her sisters were right. What was a little kiss when so much was at stake? Then her mind galloped into dangerous territory: *What kind of kiss? Can it be short? What if he doesn't want to kiss me?* "And what if it doesn't work?" Ava argued. "He'll think I'm into him. And then there's that Shelby girl, and I'm not like that."

There was silence. With the exception of Carmen's loud gulping of cocoa.

"First of all, you don't even know who Shelby is. So cálmate. He's never told you he has a girlfriend, right?" Viv said.

Ava could feel her insides tighten. She could feel herself going into shutdown-slash-denial mode. "He hasn't told me that he *doesn't* have a girlfriend. And, I mean, whatever, I don't even know the next time I'm going to see him."

"Gotta see him to kiss him." Viv grabbed Ava's cell from the couch and held it out. "Call him."

Viv's gaze was burning holes in Ava's skull. There was no way she was getting out of here without calling Rion. She snatched her phone and dialed his number.

With each ring, her heart felt jumpier. And then his voice was in her ear: "You know what to do."

No, Rion. I DO NOT KNOW WHAT TO DO!

"Hey," Ava said. "Just wanted to make sure everything is okay, and, um . . . call me back. I have something important to tell you."

She hated the lie but knew she had to dangle a carrot. She'd used the device plenty last school year when people she needed for a story tried to ghost her. Tell someone you have something important to tell them, and nine out of ten times, they call back.

Carm gave her a high five. "Well played, hermana."

"And if he doesn't call back?" Ava said.

"Then we stalk him," Carm suggested half-teasingly, but with a serious enough undertone to make Ava want to crawl out of her own skin.

"No more what-ifs," Viv said. "You keep calling until you reach him. This isn't about you, Gree. Unless . . ." She blinked, and her expression shifted. "You're into him."

"*Oh!*" Carm said, wide-eyed as she turned to Ava slowly. "That would suck. Dude, you weren't supposed to fall for him."

Ava exhaled slowly. "You guys are so wrong. Nobody is falling for anyone." She kept her voice even, controlled. "Now turn on the video."

Viv and Carmen shared a flicker of a glance before the oldest said to Ava, "We're your sisters; you can tell us anything. Safe zone, remember?"

"Like you're telling us why you've been so secretive?" Ava barked at Viv unexpectedly. There. It was out in the open, floating between them. A challenge waiting to be accepted or denied.

Viv blinked. "I'm not being secretive."

Ava could see the stiffness in her sister's posture. She could see the mask fall over her face to protect any emotion that might show. She could sense that the truth was right beneath the surface of the princess with the wooden heart.

Carm's eyes slid to Viv, narrowed and questioning. "Are you seriously keeping a secret from us, vato?"

"Oh my God, guys!" Viv groaned. "I'm not keeping a secret."

"Swear on it," Carm insisted.

"Fine! I swear!" Viv said.

"'Cause I tell you guys everything," Carm added, looking genuinely wounded.

"Can we just get back to the video?" Viv said.

Ava suddenly remembered the part of Viv's fairy tale she hated the most: the girl with the wooden heart knew how to bury the truth.

"I heard you on the phone the other night," Ava blurted. "You told someone you missed them, Viv." *And I snooped through your phone. Who is H, and why are you keeping him a secret?*

Carm sucked in a lungful of air. "You did?"

Viv hesitated a second too long. Then with her usual *I can pluck a lie from nowhere* flair, she said, "Okay. I met someone. And I didn't want to tell you, because it's not a big deal, and I knew you guys would make it a big deal, and as a matter of fact . . . I'm going to end things. There. Satisfied?"

"You lied?" Carm's face fell. "You broke the oath?"

Ava felt a pressure building in her chest, and she wasn't sure if it was because Viv lied or because she had a terrible feeling she was still lying.

"Guys," Viv said, "I'm sorry. Can we just let this go?"

Carm narrowed her eyes to mere slits. "We'll let you off this time, but if you ever lie again . . ." She didn't need to finish the sisterly threat.

"Carm!" Ava cried. "Why are you so chill about this?"

"Because she just came clean, and I really want to watch this video." She turned to Viv. "Is he at least cute?"

"Hang on," Ava said, "I don't care if you break up with *H,* but why did you lie to begin with?"

Viv's face paled. And Ava immediately saw her fatal mistake.

"You snooped through my phone?"

Ava's defensive wall went up faster than a rocket. "Well, I wouldn't have had to if you hadn't been lying."

"You went through her phone?" Carmen said to Ava.

"Seriously? She's the one who lied."

"Can we drop this?" Viv's voice was one inch from being uncharacteristically out of control.

"Stop!" Carmen yelled. "Viv, say you're sorry again. Ava, say you're sorry. Let's all kiss and make up. Now can we just watch the video?"

Two apologies and one pillow throw later, the sisters agreed to let it go.

Viv leapt back to the film way too eagerly. "I forgot that I have to set the stage for you," she said. "Emmanuel did this whole presentation last night about how music is used to create the perfect atmosphere for scenes, like scary music, for example."

Carm said, "Like, last night, he showed a clip of two guys dressed as wolves walking in slo-mo with creepy music, then showed the same scene with light funny music. Totally changed the vibe. Get it?"

The first footage began the moment the Granados girls saw the chandeliers hanging from the trees. A suspenseful, subtle underscore played, making the scene look like something from an edgy spy film, as if they were sneaking up on the house.

"I should go into acting," Carm said.

Viv groaned. "Being a drama queen doesn't make you an actress."

The next scene was of the crowd at the party, panning to Viv while she talked to a group of people. The shot itself was boring, but then music began to play in a slow crescendo: flirty catwalk music that sounded more fashion show than dull party talk. It changed the entire vibe, and the sisters all busted out laughing.

It felt good, the laughing.

Next was a scene with Carmen, Donovan, and Taryn. Carm was leaning close, telling them something she clearly didn't want anyone else to hear. The accompanying music was a slow, somber melody that made it feel like whatever she was saying was the saddest thing in the world.

"Oh my God!" Carm cried. "This looks so depressing, but I swear I was telling them a joke!"

And then the scene vanished. And the only thing on the screen was a still image of the ice rink. There was no sound, only silence. Ava's stomach squeezed tight.

A single piano keystroke. And then another. And then there was Ava clinging to the wall. She remembered the moment when she was talking to Nana and Meda, but of course they were invisible to the camera.

"What's up with the hat?" Viv said.

The camera panned to Rion watching Ava. Zooming in on that ridiculous smile on his face. Next came his voice, rising over the gentle cadence of the piano. "You just have to let go."

Next came the snow. Twisting, tumbling from the sky in giant flakes.

The melody intensified, shifted to heightened panic as the scene cut to the moment Ava made a beeline for Rion. He was thrown off his feet in slow motion. And then she was on her knees, over him, clutching his shirt, begging him to wake up, and the music was growing louder in her ears, and she looked ridiculous in that fox hat.

Slowly, Rion's eyes fluttered open.

Ava's expression softened, and the relief in her eyes said what she couldn't.

The scene faded to black.

Except for a timestamp in the right corner: 8:51.

Ava's whole body went cold. *It's a coincidence; it's the length of the video.*

In the silence, Viv and Carm turned their heads slowly toward her.

"Gree?"

"Did you see the numbers?" Ava pointed in a pathetic attempt to deflect.

"Dude," Carm said, shaking her head slowly at her little sister.

They didn't need to say anything more. Ava knew what they were thinking, because she was thinking it too. She didn't even try to pin it on the music. Even without the crescendos of emotion, she saw the expression on her face when Rion was knocked out. The absolute relief when he woke up. Being on the outside looking in, it was painfully obvious.

Feelings grow when you aren't looking.

Viv's low and careful voice broke the silence. "You've already fallen."

This time, Ava didn't try to deny it. "Yeah, okay. So?"

"Wow," Carm said, "that sucks that you have to steal something from a guy you like."

"You're such a jerk," Ava said, not caring if Carmen blew up at her, but instead her sister came over and pulled her into a hug. It was a rare tender moment that didn't last long. Because when Carm let go, she looked Ava in the face with a smirk and said, "Admit that I was right."

"Here we go," Viv said.

Ava's heart was a ball of scorching heat, threatening to burn out of her chest.

You must search the contents of your heart. The answer is there.

And now everyone could see what she already felt.

Thirty

Ava had barely closed her eyes when she heard footsteps in her bedroom. She opened them to find Carmen sitting on the edge of her bed in a wedge of moonlight. "Carm?" she whispered. "Is something wrong?"

"I lied too," Carm said, pulling the covers back and crawling in with Ava.

"What?"

"Don't be mad—it's just . . . I'm not like Viv or even you. You guys are so good at keeping cool, and I feel like I'm always a bundle of nerves." She propped her head on her elbow, turning to Ava. "You guys always knew what you wanted to do, and me? God, I have no idea. I guess it's fine to work for Dad, but what if there's more? Like, do I even want to go to USC?"

Ava was almost afraid to ask. "Carm, what did you lie about?"

"I mean, I'm glad now that Nana gave me my blessing, because I always felt like you and Viv were so much smarter than me. You guys could memorize everything."

"That doesn't mean we're smarter."

"I know, and I see that now, but I think my poor brain was on overload with this new memory stuff. And I . . . I wanted to do something different, something to flush it all away. Just so I wouldn't have to think, you know?"

"You're not going to work out even more now, are you?" Ava sat up, tense.

"Nothing like that," Carm said. "I . . . I saw this ad for horse therapy . . . like, therapeutic riding, and I went and I really liked it, and when I'm with the horses, I don't think about anything else. I've been going for two weeks, and now I'm not as anxious or worried or doubting myself."

If Ava hadn't been sitting down, she might have fallen over. Carm? On a horse? She was allergic to anything with hair or fur. It was the only reason they didn't have a dog.

"But your allergies."

"They don't bug me anymore." She put her arm around Ava and sighed. "Anyway, I couldn't sleep until I told you. I feel so much better. Night."

Ava stroked Carm's hair, watching her sleep. Carm had always been so in control, so confident, so everything, Ava had never once considered she had a weakness, or an empty spot in her heart too.

"Good night," Ava whispered. She fell into a dream. She was being swallowed by a dark forest.

Antiquated video cameras hung from the branches, swinging in the wind.

The thick black trees closed in, suffocating her, each engraved with names: *Edwin and Ellie. Caroline and Raul. Ava and Rion.*

A pointed branch stabbed at her chest, reached into her heart. She opened her mouth to scream a silent, agonizing scream.

Her mother's voice echoed through the trees. *The heart cannot be trusted.*

Thirty-One

Rion wasn't in the nine-out-of-ten category. Of course he wasn't.

He didn't call back. But he finally answered one of her calls two days later.

"Is everything okay?" were the first words out of her mouth, because she wasn't sure what to say or how to kill the awkwardness growing across the miles between them. "You just took off and—"

"Yeah, um . . ." He went silent, like he was collecting his thoughts or forming his lie. "I've been busy. Hey, I have to go, but I'll call you when I can talk."

Ava was tempted to say, *What does that even mean, and why are you being so distant?* But her anger and her pride wouldn't allow it.

For the next three days, a miserable rain fell on the City of Angels.

Like some kind of omen reminding Ava that the deadline was racing toward them, a mere three days away. She desperately wanted to call Nana, but she restrained herself for no other reason than that she didn't want to interrupt any momentum the ghost and the saint might be having. Except that Ava missed her grandmother; she missed her voice and her smile and her larger-than-life persona.

Ava straightened a stack of papers on her desk and took a deep breath. She had put in double her hours, doing everything she could to pretend her current reality didn't exist. She had copyedited more than a dozen articles, helped Corbin with social media posts, filed anything she could get her hands on, and organized her own desk three times. The mind-numbing work helped for a while, until Corbin or Anmol would ask her what was wrong, and the wounds split open all over again.

This is going to be what it's like living without Nana, except I won't have the choice to call her.

And then a more miserable thought occurred to Ava.

Losing Nana will be painful, but it'll be a million times worse if I know she is wandering aimlessly without a single memory to keep her company.

The rain halted just as a sudden resolve took root inside of Ava. Deeper than her pride or her ego. It no longer mattered why Rion didn't want to talk to her. She wasn't about to sit around waiting another second.

It was easy to find Maggie's Orchard on Google Maps. There was even a website with hours when they were open to the public to harvest oranges: daily, 1:00 p.m. to 5:00 p.m.

It was only 4:10, so if Ava left now, she could easily be there before 5:00 p.m. Quickly, she scanned the site, looking for any evidence that her imagined version of the farm had been accurate, but the only photo to be found was a sunny aerial view of hundreds of orange trees in full bloom.

"What's that?" Anmol asked, peering over her shoulder.

"Research."

"Is this about the *Marry Me* guy?"

"Not exactly. But it's about a guy."

Anmol smiled appreciatively. "Do we like this guy?"

"Depends on the day."

After gathering her things, Ava sent a quick text to her sisters: I'm over waiting. Heading to farm now.

Ava started to head out when Grant stopped her outside his office. "I don't want to see you here tomorrow." His voice was thoughtful, gentle.

Ava nodded.

"I know what you're doing, and I get it, but you need some time off with your family too."

No, you don't know. "Okay."

"And I've been meaning to ask, any luck with that *Marry Me* photo?"

"I found the photographer, but it turned out to be a dead end."

He twisted his mouth into what could have been mistaken for a smile. "Well, I guess it'll just be chalked up to one of life's unsolved mysteries."

Except that Ava hated unsolved *anything.*

As she turned to leave, Grant said, "Hang on." He stood with a white paper sack hanging loosely in his hand. "I brought apple muffins for an editorial meeting. Want one?"

Ava's cartoon self did an exaggerated double take and said, "Huh?" Grant never brought in food, never mind a bag of fresh muffins. And he certainly never offered her anything, except maybe a pencil or a stapler.

"Are they stale or poisoned or something?" Ava joked. But not entirely.

Grant laughed. "They're fresh and really good, from that bakery down the street."

The thought of Grant standing in line at a bakery selecting muffins loosened a laugh in Ava's chest that came out as a snort. "Okay, thanks," she said, accepting the gift and wondering why her boss was being so nice to her.

The drive to the San Fernando Valley was an easy thirty minutes with thankfully little traffic. Enough time to practice what she was going to say to Rion:

Hey, want to see yourself in a hilarious outtake?

Hey, you said I should come see the farm. Surprise!

Hey, I know it sounds crazy, but you've got my blessing, and I'm not leaving without it.

Hey, would you mind if I kissed you?

The MAGGIE'S ORCHARD sign couldn't be missed: It was the size of a billboard, with a big green arrow pointing down a dirt road lined with citrus trees. The tagline read FOLLOW YOUR PATH TO BLISS.

Ava turned onto the road.

Specks of daylight filtered through the canopy of trees, shielding Ava from the blue sky. She rolled down her window to breathe in the clean, crisp scent, and an unexpected calm settled over her.

Soon she reached a dirt lot lined with several cars, most with out-of-state plates. At the edge of the lot was a huge weathered barn, white with flaking paint. It was straight out of a country song. The doors were swung open, and from here Ava could make out that the old structure had been converted to some kind of shop. People milled about, carrying baskets, taking photos, eating orange wedges.

Her phone pinged. Texts from her sisters.

> Viv: we should talk about a plan
>
> Carm: THIS IS a plan. Go for it.

After parking, Ava stepped out of the Jeep, shielding her eyes against the sun now breaking through a bank of cumulus clouds. She scanned the scene for Rion. God, this place was really beautiful, dripping with shade and green and calm.

She hadn't taken ten steps before she halted in her tracks.

There he was.

Walking out of the barn. With a petite blonde girl at his side. She was talking with her hands in exaggerated motions. Rion's head was tipped, his shoulders curled forward like he was hanging on her every word.

Ava froze. Heat rushed her face.

She willed her legs to move, to carry her back to the car, but all she could do was stare.

Rion and maybe-Shelby stopped, exchanged a few more words, and then he reached down and hugged her. Like a real genuine scoop kind of hug, the kind you gave to someone you cared about.

Ava didn't realize she was digging her fingers into her palms, because all she could process was, *I've made a huge mistake.*

She spun to leave before he saw her, before her total humiliation was complete, but instead of making a clean getaway, she tripped over a lanky black dog with floppy ears and three big white spots on her back. Ava landed with a pathetic *oomph* in the dirt.

Tres.

So, she wasn't a golden or a lab like Ava had imagined. The exuberant pup was already sniffing and licking, licking and sniffing, bouncing up and down, making a scene. Ava scrambled to her feet, brushed herself off, and tried to maneuver around the dog, but Tres wasn't having it. She began to bark in playful tones that said, *Wanna play? Where's my treat?*

"Ava?" Rion's voice carried across the lot like a missile while Ava imagined her cartoon self combusting on the spot.

She turned slowly. Rion was already jogging over casually like he hadn't ghosted her for the last week. His hair swooped across his forehead with annoying cuteness, and when he reached her, when he stood two feet in front of her, he gave her a weak smile.

"Hey," he said, "what are you doing here?" There was no judgment in his tone, only surprise. Tres settled at Rion's feet, her furry chin resting on thick paws while she waited for Ava's response.

"Um . . . I . . ." Ava's voice was trapped, and she was going to need a bulldozer to get it out. *No!* She hadn't come here to play small or beat around the bush. *Think about Nana!* "I just wanted to make sure you're okay."

Rion was nodding, his jaw rigid. "Yeah, I'm sorry. I wanted . . ." He rubbed the back of his neck and blew out a long breath. "It's complicated."

A new boldness gripped Ava. "Because you have a girlfriend?"

Rion's dark brows shot up, wrinkling his forehead. "Huh?"

Ava's gaze slid toward the barn where Shelby had just stood. Following Ava's gaze, Rion said, "Shelby?"

Ava hated the sound of her name on Rion's lips. But she hated the uninvited jealousy she was feeling more.

Rion smiled, a genuine smile that reached his eyes. And then he said absolutely nothing.

"Is something funny?" Ava tugged on the hem of her sweater, growing more irritated by the minute.

Tres sat up abruptly, whined, then turned her big chocolate eyes toward Rion as if she wanted to know too.

"Um, she's not my girlfriend," Rion said, still grinning. "Actually, she's twenty-five and like a sister to me."

Ava's heart softened half an inch, but then a stone fortress erected itself, obstructing Rion's words. *What if he's lying to cover his ass?*

If he was, Ava would get to the truth. "I just thought when she called you the other night and you left so quickly—"

Subtext for *Who is she?*

Rion hesitated, glanced through the thicket of trees while he patted

Tres's head mindlessly. "She's actually my grandpa's private nurse and has been for the last three years."

Nurse? Did he just say *nurse*? How many more shades of red could Ava's face turn?

"That night I left your house," Rion explained, "when Shelby called, it was to tell me that my gramps was really sick from his chemo treatment. I was supposed to be here, but I really wanted to go to the party with you, and I felt so guilty and I freaked out."

He has cancer? Ava felt like the world's biggest jerk. "Oh my God, I'm so sorry. Is he okay now?"

"Yeah, but he's been in the hospital for the last few days. He just got home last night."

Ava skirted around *Why didn't you tell me?* with, "I'm glad he's better. I wish I had known; I wouldn't have bothered you."

"I wanted to tell you. It's just that . . ." Rion glanced around furtively. "Can you keep a secret?"

Ava nodded.

"He made us promise not to tell anyone he's sick. He thinks it makes him look weak and . . . that our customers will freak out and take their biz somewhere else. Rumors fly pretty fast around here. Anyways, I couldn't break that promise, and I really was going to call, but then I got busy and . . ." He exhaled sharply, shaking his head stiffly before saying, "That's all bullshit. I didn't call, and kept our one convo short, because I didn't want to lie to you. I'm really bad at it, and I knew you would ask a lot of questions, and also I didn't know what to say."

Ava felt like she had been punched in the chest. She wasn't used to people being so forthcoming, so open. Most of the time they were managing their images and covering their asses and spinning narratives with meaningless words.

"I get it," Ava said. She understood his predicament. She knew the value of a secret, its weight and burden. "And you don't have to worry. I won't say anything to anyone about his cancer."

"So," Rion began with a smirk that told Ava the topic was about to change. "You really thought she was my girlfriend?"

Tres snorted. Cars were filing out of the lot. The barn doors were closing. And Ava's heart was suddenly hammering.

"Something like that." She reached down and rubbed Tres's neck, anything to avoid looking at Rion. Two seconds ago, she had thought his openness was refreshing, and now she wanted to shove it into a coffin and nail the lid shut.

"But why would I hang out with you if I had a girlfriend?"

"How should I know? I mean, it's not like . . ."

He cleared his throat, nearly forcing her eyes back to him. And when she did, he had his arms folded over his chest and he was wearing a mischievous smile. "Are you jealous, Nine?"

"What?! No!"

"Tres, what do you think?"

Tres let out a definitive *woof* in response. Traitor.

Rion nodded. "Yeah, I think so too."

Tres rubbed up against Ava's leg, begging for another neck rub, while Ava's chest prickled with heat. Rion laughed. "She likes you, but I told you, you have to bring a treat."

Relieved to have an excuse to step away from the awkwardness, Ava went over to the Jeep. "Does she like muffins?" she said, turning back.

Before Rion could answer, Tres was already on her hind legs, whining for the treat. Ava stooped down, whispered into Tres's ear, then dropped a muffin into the pup's mouth, who scarfed it down in three chews and a swallow.

"What did you tell her?" Rion said.

Wiping the crumbs off her hand, Ava gave a one-shoulder shrug. "It's a secret between girls."

"Ha! Okay. So, do you want to see the farm?" Rion said as Tres loped ahead of them into the trees.

Ava was nodding, but the words that came out were, "First, I have something to tell you."

My family has this ability to pass blessings and you have mine. Our meeting at the market was no accident. I've been duping you all this time. Can I kiss you?

"Ava?"

His voice pulled her back to the moment.

"Yeah?"

"You said you have something to tell me."

All of a sudden, Ava felt lost, meandering through a forest of doubt and confusion. What were the right words? The right path? Her mind said one thing, but her heart said another.

The heart cannot be trusted.

"Maybe you could show me the farm first." Ava chickened out. "It's so pretty. How big is this place?"

"Just twenty acres. Come on."

As they walked back toward the barn, Ava had the sudden sense that someone was watching her. But the lot was empty. All the patrons had left. A tall figure emerged from the barn. Achilles. His eyes soaked her in.

Then his mouth twisted up into a grin that turned her stomach.

Thirty-Two

Tres bounced way ahead of them, tail wagging as if nothing in the world could ever be wrong.

But Achilles's smile screamed that *everything* was wrong.

"Hey," Ava managed, hoping to keep it chill.

Achilles merely gave her a half nod before turning his attention back to his brother. "What's she doing here?"

Rion's expression was one of solid stone. "Aren't you supposed to be closing up?"

"Bad timing, bro."

It was a tennis match of unanswered questions, as if each brother was waiting to see who might falter first. Their voices were impossibly the same. And seeing them side by side like this, Ava marveled at how striking their resemblance was. But only in the physical sense. Achilles reminded Ava of a knockoff Gucci trying to be the real thing. It looked genuine, but only an expert eye could spot the fakeness in the minutest details.

"He didn't even know I was coming," Ava said with a half-hearted laugh that only made her sound nervous.

"It's all good," Rion said, taking hold of Ava's hand to maneuver around his brother.

Achilles sidestepped, blocking their path. "Just don't take her to the house."

Ava bit back the words *You're such a jerk* as Rion's hand tightened around hers. He opened his mouth like he was going to say something, but in the end, he played it cool and led Ava away without another word to Achilles.

"What the hell was that about?" Ava asked, feeling Achilles's eyes burning a hole into her back.

A voice inside her shouted, *This is not the plan!* She was supposed to take control, test Carm's theory, and kiss Rion. *Ugh!* She was so brave in her imagination, but being here in the flesh with him gripping her hand like this made her woozy.

It's just a stupid kiss, Carmen would say. But to Ava it felt more like it could ruin everything.

"He's just pissed," Rion said, "because he doesn't know anything about you."

"Why would that matter?"

Rion stopped behind the barn where an ATV was parked. "Look, Achilles and I have a rough history. He thinks I get everything and he gets nothing, and he's pissed that I'm happy . . . that you make me happy."

The words *You make me happy too* sat on the edge of Ava's lips. But she held them there as her heart folded in on itself. She felt like a huge, deceptive jerk.

Rion squeezed her hand and threw her a sideways glance. "Want to see something cool?"

"Another story tree?"

"Okay, not that cool." Rion jumped onto the ATV.

Ava stared.

Gazing at her over his shoulder, he said casually, "It's a ways to walk, so you might want to get on."

Ava straddled the seat, letting her hands hang loosely at her sides. At least until Rion laughed, started the engine, and nearly shouted, "You should probably hang on, Nine!"

The ATV pitched forward. Ava instinctively threw her arms around Rion's waist, holding tightly. Rion sped through the orchard, winding through the trees. Ava knew he was doing it just for the fun of it, because there were rows of straight shots he could have easily taken.

"Is this as fast as it goes?" she shouted, daring his boldness.

Rion's body shook with a laugh. Then he turned on the gas. The engine roared, and he sped toward the trees, cutting left and right at the last second to avoid a collision.

Ava laughed, leaned closer into Rion. He smelled of fresh cotton and citrus.

She allowed herself to close her eyes, just for a second. She wanted to pretend everything was normal, that she was merely three-wheeling through a beautiful lush orchard with a boy who was annoyingly cute, way too open, laughed like he meant it, and didn't have a single air of fakeness about him. A boy who still had her blessing.

You weren't supposed to fall for him.

A minute later Rion slowed, jerking Ava back to reality. They had come to the edge of the orchard where a small gray house with a flat roof perched.

Rion cut the engine, and the two jumped off. He was beaming. "Fun, right?"

Smoothing her windblown hair, Ava caught her breath and nodded. "I get to drive back."

"Oh yeah? Is this going to be another competition?"

With a smirk and a telling shrug, she took in the little house. "What is this place?"

Rion led her to the half-rotted front door with a sign that read KEEP OUT. Ava paused, glanced around. "Are we supposed to be here?"

"Oh, the sign?" Rion pointed. "Yeah, I hung that up when I was twelve and this was a superhero den for me and my friends."

A smile played on Ava's lips. "Superhero?"

"Don't tell me you never pretended you were Wonder Woman or Superman or something."

"I was more into mermaids," she said. "So, who did you pretend to be? Let me guess." Ava made a show of thinking, tapping the side of her head. She snapped her fingers. "Spider-Man."

"Psh. Green Lantern! That ring? I got to control everything in the universe."

Inside, the house was made up of a single room with worn plank floors, a dilapidated sofa half-covered with a camo blanket, and a snack refrigerator. Light filtered in through a single dusty window.

"It used to be an old farmworker house," Rion said, standing back so she could look around.

Near the window was a wooden ladder that climbed up to a small platform. "What's up there?" Ava asked, but she already had her hand on the ladder and was climbing to the top. Unlike below, the space was uncluttered. There were only a couple of beanbags. And the walls were filled with messages and signatures. Ava stepped onto the deck, ducking so she wouldn't hit her head on the ceiling.

Matt was here 2009

Tigers rule!

No girls allowed with an *X* drawn through it.

There were drawings of rockets, sports cars, footballs, and lightning bolts, countless signatures, and a battle scene with the Green Lantern, Batman, and Spider-Man going up against hilarious-looking monsters, some with three heads or arms or eyes.

She had been so absorbed in the wall, she hadn't heard Rion's approach until he plopped onto a beanbag. "I painted the place last year, but no way could I cover up this wall. It's like history, you know?"

Ava wasn't one for sentimentality, or for keeping mementos from the past. Why would she, when there was such an enormous future ahead? "It's really cool," she said, just as her gaze landed on a heart with an arrow piercing its center: *Katie and Rion, TLA. 2017.*

"True love always, huh?" she teased.

Rion rubbed his chin, staring at the heart with amusement. "When you're thirteen, two weeks is forever, okay?"

Until now, Ava hadn't noticed the lopsided table to her right. On top was a framed photo.

"Those are my parents," Rion said, following her gaze. "It's my favorite pic of them." Ava could see why. The couple were dressed up as Lucy and Charlie Brown, smiling wide for the camera like they were having the time of their lives. Rion definitely favored his mom with her brown eyes, easy smile, and thick hair.

"You look like her," she said.

"Achilles hates any memories of them, so I keep it here."

Ava eased into the other beanbag. "What is his deal? Why does he seem so . . . mad all the time? I mean, is this about the orchard?"

"It's a long story."

"And you know how much I like stories."

Rion hesitated, studied her face so long she started to feel self-conscious. "What is it about you?"

Was this a trick question?

"What do you mean?"

"I don't know . . . you just make it feel easy. Safe or something."

Ava felt sick. *I'm not safe*, she wanted to scream.

"It was the third thing I liked about you."

"Oh yeah?"

"I mean, your smile was for sure number one."

Ava's heart began to beat uncontrollably, making it hard to breathe like a normal human. "And number two?"

Without hesitation, Rion said, "You're kind of clumsy. It's cute."

"I am *not* clumsy."

"Actually, that wasn't number two. Okay, your turn."

"Huh?" Ava played innocent to buy herself time.

"Yeah, I told you what I first liked about you."

"Oh . . . hmm . . ."

"Don't overthink it, Nine."

"Fine, okay. I liked that you were so confident, like, comfortable in your own skin." Then, racing ahead to maybe get him to stop looking at her that way, she said, "Why do I think you're avoiding the question?"

"What question?"

"About Achilles being so mad?"

Rion caught her gaze, searched her eyes. His shoulders sagged like whatever he had to say was too heavy to carry. "Do you really want to know?"

Despite her curiosity, Ava felt a surge of fear. "Yeah."

"It's my fault my parents are dead."

Thirty-Three

All the air was sucked out of the room.

"Rion . . ." Ava wasn't sure what to say. *That can't be true?* "Why would you say that?"

"The night they died . . . I sneaked out of the house, because my friends and I had this really off-the-wall idea that we were going to go check out some haunted abandoned warehouse—you know, like real superheroes." His hands were trembling. Ava wanted to tell him he didn't have to say another word, but he kept going like he *needed* to. "We caught a ride with my friend's older sister." He let out a nervous laugh. "We were going to set up camp, find the ghosts, do dumb things that I can't even remember now. Achilles told me not to go. But I didn't listen."

Ava was holding her breath. Warm tears pricked her eyes. Rion avoided her gaze, keeping his squarely focused on the floor. "When my parents didn't find me in bed, they made Achilles tell them where I was, and they came looking for me. On the way home . . ." His voice caught. He cleared his throat and said, "A drunk driver."

Ava inhaled slowly, giving his words time to breathe. *God, how did he ever get over something so tragic?* "I'm really sorry," she said quietly. "But that isn't your fault."

"I don't remember any of it." Rion shrugged, keeping his eyes glued to the floor. In that single still moment, all Ava wanted to do was wrap her arms around him. "But Achilles? He's always blamed me. And to be honest, I blamed myself too."

Ava got to her feet and kneeled in front of him. She searched for the right thing to say, but the only thing that came to her was the truth. "I used to blame myself for my mom leaving too. She left when I was seven, and I used to think if I had been better, nicer, *more*, then she would have stayed." Just saying the words brought the tears down her cheeks. "We can't blame ourselves for things we had no control over. You couldn't have known . . ."

Rion's eyes were pools of understanding. "I didn't know that about your mom."

Ava nodded, looking away at a dusty lamp in the corner of the room. "I've never told anyone except for Elijah."

"I'm sorry." Rion's voice was soft, careful. "Have you seen her since?"

Looking back at him now, Ava shook her head and said, "It isn't your fault, Rion. You do know that, right?"

"Do you?"

The question was only made up of two words, five little letters, but it carried the weight of ten years of shame and longing. Ava inhaled slowly. "I do."

"Good." Rion pressed his lips together and nodded. "Me too."

"Maybe Achilles will get there . . . eventually."

Rion stood and paced to the other side of the room. "That isn't the only reason he's pissed."

Oh God, there was more?

"Next month Achilles and I are going to turn eighteen, which, according to my parents' will, is when our gramps can let us go to a storage unit where he's kept our parents' things. He let us go early, a couple of weeks ago, since he's been so sick. Anyhow, it was a shit show, bringing everything up again. Achilles and I fought over every single thing in that unit, from artwork to old books. And then we found this baseball signed by Mickey Mantle. My dad's dad gave it to him, and he loved it. Used to keep it on display in the living room." A warm smile formed at the memory. "One time he let us throw it around. He'd say things like, *You boys feel the magic inside of that ball?* and *Mantle's spirit is still in there, do you hear it?* Anyways, Achilles wanted the ball, and I don't know why, but I told him it belonged to both of us. I mean, I should have just given it to him, right?"

Ava knew he wasn't really asking, so she stayed silent while he continued. "I got pissed and told him he could just have *everything*, and he told me the only thing he wanted was the one thing he couldn't have."

"To have your parents back," Ava said quietly.

Rion inhaled slowly, turning to face Ava now. "So I guess you could say it opened old wounds. And then he had this really bad breakup recently, and when he saw me happy, after I met you . . . I don't know—things got messed up, and I think he took that as me not caring."

As much as Ava thought Achilles was a jerk, she knew now that his actions were born out of pain and suffering. She stood. "Rion, he's your brother. The only one you have."

Rion clapped his hands breezily. "I didn't bring you here for all this heaviness. You said you have something to tell me?"

There was no way Ava could follow *that* with a kiss or the truth. She played it off with a fake smile. "Oh, it's no biggie. It can wait. But if you want to talk . . ."

He stood, pressed his hands against the ceiling. "Thirsty? Hungry?"

"Water?"

They made their way down the ladder, but when Rion found the minifridge empty, he said, "The house is super close. I'll be right back."

After he took off, Ava went outside for some fresh air. She needed to think, to process. Soon she was wandering through the trees near the side of the superhero den. *Twenty acres of heaven*, she thought.

A few yards away, she spied a little table and a wooden folding chair. Curious, she drew closer to find a sketchbook on the table. Just sitting there, begging to be opened.

Let's see how good of an artist you really are, Rion.

She opened the book. The first black-and-white sketch was a still life, a bowl of oranges. It was . . . Ava blinked, taking in the unexpected details. The perfect shading, the shadows, the narrow beam of sunlight that caught the flecks of dust spinning in the gloomy air.

Her first thought filtered through her tightly held denial. *He's the real deal.*

Heart thumping, she turned the page. An old woman sitting on a park bench, her eyes staring beyond the page. The drawing's lines were impeccable, the shading precise. They were all like this: exceptional in technical skill but also in the way they each told a story.

Ava turned to the next page. A card slipped out, falling to the ground. She plucked it from the dirt.

Happy birthday, Gramps.

She turned the card over to find a sketch.

Her heart stopped.

It was *Marry Me* guy.

Thirty-Four

Not possible. Not possible. Not *possible*!

With trembling hands, Ava quickly pulled her phone free from her back pocket, and compared the photo of *Marry Me* guy with the sketch.

The drawing was detailed, skillful, beautiful. The man in the photo and the one in the sketch were a near-exact likeness down to the square jaw, long nose, and big eyes.

Just then Rion appeared. "Hey, I was looking for you. What are you doing out here?"

Ava glanced up, still gripping the card.

Rion's face contorted from breezy to confused. "You look like you've seen a ghost."

"Rion . . ." She was practically breathless. "What's your grandfather's name?"

His eyes darted to the book back on the table. Ava half expected him to be annoyed or even angry, but there wasn't a single trace of either. "Charles."

Ava swallowed hard. "Charles Lawrence?"

"Yeah, well, Charles Lawrence Bennington. Why?"

So Lawrence was a middle name. Speechless, she held up the card, not even trying to hide that she had been snooping. "It fell out of the book."

Rion took the sketch. "That's my gramps when he was young. It's his birthday gift, since the whole eBay thing didn't work out," he said with a laugh. "Hey, are you okay?"

Ava handed him her phone with the black-and-white photo. "Is it just a coincidence?" But the words had barely left her mouth when Rion's face fell.

"Where did you get this photo?" he asked.

Ava explained the whole story, including the night of its discovery.

"Jesus." He exhaled loudly, rubbing his forehead. "That's unbelievable. Like, what are the chances?"

Slim, Ava thought. *Slight. Zero!* But even she was beginning to doubt all the coincidences stacking up.

"I have to know," Ava said quietly. "Is this photo . . . Is it about Maggie?"

Rion was still staring at the photo, wide-eyed, when he nodded.

"So, she said no." Ava spoke in a low tone, remembering what Rion had said about things not working out.

Lifting his gaze to meet Ava's, he offered, "Not exactly."

"But you said—"

"He never got to ask her."

Ava didn't remember when they had started walking through the orchard, or how Rion had begun the story of Maggie and Charles. All she knew was that she was hungry for every word, and Rion couldn't talk fast enough.

"They met in the spring of 1959," he said, "and fell for each other pretty fast, or at least that's the way my gramps tells it.

"Apparently, the two had traveled all over Mexico that summer, but when Charles had to head to Mexico City for business, she couldn't get away, so they agreed to meet the next week at the train station."

"And she just never showed?"

"Yeah, he went back to Oaxaca where they had been, but she wasn't there. Ended up looking for her for a whole year, maybe longer."

"Why didn't he just call her?"

"He lost her number. Well, housekeeping at the hotel threw it out." Rion shook his head. "Talk about the worst luck."

"God, that's so awful," Ava said, feeling a sudden weight in her chest.

"So, then he came back here, and when he started this orchard, he named it after her. I think it was his way of remembering her."

Ava blinked, trying to understand the impossibility of it all. If Nana were here, she would say it was no accident that the photo had found its way to Ava, that she had met Rion and discovered the truth.

But why? So Charles could get his photo back? Seemed pretty far-fetched.

Ava stopped, leaned against a tree. Tried to collect her racing thoughts. "What do you think happened to Maggie?"

"Do you really want to know?"

"You know?!" Her heart took off at breakneck speed. "Tell me!"

"So, he ended up running into her on the street a couple of years later."

"In Mexico?"

Rion nodded. "He said he couldn't leave until he knew what happened to her."

Ava couldn't conceive of that kind of love. Or sacrifice. "And?" She was almost afraid to hear the rest. Did Maggie lower the boom? Tell poor Charles that she never loved him?

Rion said, "She was with another guy."

Why did that feel like a slap in the face when Ava didn't even know these people?

"Maybe it was her brother or cousin or a friend." She didn't know why, but she wanted—no, she *needed*—this story to end happily.

Rion reached up and plucked an orange off a low-hanging branch. "She was wearing a wedding ring, and the guy had his arm around her. "And—"

"And what?"

"She was pregnant," Rion said. "So, my gramps chalked it up to fate and turned around."

Ava's journalistic instincts were screaming that something was off. A piece of the story was still missing. After a quick and somewhat hopeful calculation, she knew that Maggie's baby couldn't have been Charles's.

Rion pressed the orange between his hands before letting it drop to the ground with a tiny *thud*. "It just wasn't meant to be, you know? And then he met my grandma years later, and it all worked out like it was supposed to."

Ava's mind was still reeling. "I mean, there has to be a reason she didn't show up."

"I guess we'll never know," Rion said with a casual shrug that unnerved Ava. "But do you think I could have the original photo, to show him?"

Ava didn't think Grant would mind, but it seemed like a cruel thing to do given the circumstances. "Sure, but maybe he doesn't want to see it."

For a few beats, Rion considered this. Soft shadows played across his earnest face. Then he said, "He's sick, and I think . . . I think he's going to love the whole wild story of how the photo found its way to him." He lifted one corner of his mouth, a poor attempt at a smile. "If you haven't guessed, he's a huge believer in fate."

Of course he is. Then Ava remembered Reed's words—*She's my destiny*—and her heart felt like breaking. Poor Charles had been so wrong. That's what happened when you believed in things like destiny and fate. They kicked you in the teeth when you weren't looking.

Rion stuffed his hands into his jeans pockets. "This is wild. Imagine all the work the universe had to do to make sure everything lined up perfectly. Like, what if you had stayed at work one minute longer that night? You would have never hit my car. We wouldn't have recognized each other at the market, and I wouldn't be able to give my gramps the photo." He sighed with a kind of reverence that Fate didn't deserve. "Must have taken a lot of orchestrating. Right?"

Except for the blessing, Ava thought. What role did *that* have in all this? If Ava were to subscribe to Rion's notion, then he would say that the blessing connecting with him was part of this whole scheme. But over a photo? No way. Ava wasn't having it. If Ava had been on time the night Nana took her last breath, then Ava would have received what belonged to her, and she never would have needed to find Rion.

So how did that work? When fate favored one person's journey over another's?

"Ava?"

She had been chewing her bottom lip, staring at the soft dirt. She looked up.

"I said I want you to meet my grandpa. Today's not a good day, but maybe tomorrow."

"But . . . he's sick, and I thought he didn't want anyone to know."

"He'll say that this is a sign, and I think it might be too."

Rion stepped closer, silent and unblinking. Ava's body froze. Except for her heart. That was hammering away with each step he took. Her stomach muscles tightened.

Ava sensed that push-pull thing again, where Rion seemed to be battling an internal voice. Was it the blessing? Could he be struggling against whatever it was?

"Aren't you going to tell me you don't believe in signs?" Rion said, and then he stopped, turned so he was side by side with Ava now.

He leaned his back against the tree and stared up at the sky.

Ava swallowed over the lump in her throat, both relieved and disappointed his gaze was no longer on her. "I never said I didn't believe in signs. I just don't believe in fate," she corrected. Her mind went to 8:51, the numbers that kept cropping up. Were they a sign? A clue? A coincidence?

Rion reached for her hand casually. He stared down at her palm, tracing the lines with his finger. A tiny shiver climbed up Ava's spine.

"See this?" he said. "This means you're going to have a long life."

"Oh, you're a palm reader now?" She chuckled to hide the tremble in her voice.

"And this one means you're creative and stubborn and funny and definitely pretty and . . . uh-oh."

"What's uh-oh?"

"I mean, I'm no expert, Nine, but it says here you are a terrible ice-skater."

Ava laughed, started to pull her hand free before he said, "And see this one?" He kept his head bent. "This one means you're going to have a really big change of heart about something very soon."

"Like what?" she said, playing along.

Rion shrugged. "Maybe fate."

Ava freed her hand. "Not going to happen."

But as soon as she said the words, she knew they were a lie. Even Ava, as stubborn as she was, could make room for the possibility that maybe she had been wrong. Clinging to an idea about fate that might not be true.

Tres appeared just then, wagging her tail and orbiting Rion like he was the sun itself. Tres lifted the orange into her mouth. Rion laughed, took it from her, and tossed it for her to fetch. He then went after his dog, calling back to Ava.

"Come on, Nine. Let's see those mad driving skills."

Thirty-Five

On the drive home, Ava could only reach Carmen by phone. She unleashed every detail of her trip to the farm, letting the words and memories fill the car. But she didn't tell her about Rion's parents. That felt private, a moment between only Rion and Ava. And she didn't mention the lightness she felt when she admitted, when she understood, that her mom's leaving had nothing to do with her and everything to do with her mom.

"So, no kiss?" Carm said.

Ava rolled her eyes. "We were pretty focused on the whole creepy photo thing. Where's Viv?"

"No idea. Dude, were you so humiliated when you found out Shelby is his grandpa's nurse?"

"Thanks for making me feel it twice, Carm."

"And that whole Maggie thing is the worst. Jesus! How did poor Chuck ever get over it? I feel sick, and I don't even know the guy."

"It's Charles."

"Well, now that I'm good and depressed, come home. I was just going to order Thai from that little place in Brentwood. Can you pick it up on your way?"

"Okay, but get ahold of Viv and tell her to come too."

Ava drove in silence for the next twenty minutes, her mind replaying the day with Rion. Her heart swelled—with relief, with hope, with so many feelings she didn't think she could contain. But how could she feel happiness when Nana's afterlife hung in the balance? And if/when Ava claimed the blessing, what would that mean for Rion? What if the blessing really was his art, and she took that away from him? Which would be made worse by the fact that she had zero interest in being an artist.

Was it awful she was even considering him when Nana was *family*? And then there was the incessant reminder that happiness was always short-lived. That goodbyes were always inevitable.

And that love was always dangerous.

Ava turned off the freeway, thinking a night in with her sisters sounded like exactly what she needed. Although she imagined she would spend much of that time cheering up Carm about "Chuck."

When Ava arrived at the little café, there were no free spaces, so she parked around the corner. Her phone buzzed the second she hopped out of her car.

A smile spread across her face as she answered. "Hi."

"What are you doing?" Rion asked.

"Getting food. Is everything okay?"

"Why wouldn't it be?"

"I just left, and you're already calling me."

Rion chuckled, then, "My gramps said tomorrow works."

Ava halted on the sidewalk. Pedestrians meandered around her.

"What did he say about the photo?" she asked.

"He was pretty surprised. And then he told me Fate has a wicked sense of humor."

"What's that supposed to mean?"

"I asked the same thing, and all he said was, 'When she circles back to you, you have to pay attention, because the story isn't over.'"

The story isn't over?

"She?"

"Fate, that thing you don't believe in." Rion laughed.

Ava had held so long to that belief, she could hardly make room for the possibility that she had been wrong. But maybe, just maybe, fate really did exist.

"Okay, so . . ." Her stomach tied in knots at the thought of meeting THE *Marry Me* guy. "When?"

"Tomorrow night, about eight thirty? Can you come here again? And don't worry, Achilles won't be home." Tres barked in the background. "Tres says to bring her another muffin."

Ava laughed, pressing her phone tightly to her ear. There was that swelling in her chest again. "Yes, I'll be there," she said. "And yes, I'll bring her a treat."

"Did you hear that, girl? She said she'd bring you a treat." Tres panted excitedly on the other end of the phone, and Ava could see the image of her pawing Rion while he laughed. "She's pumped," he said to Ava.

When Ava pressed End, she was still smiling. When she turned the corner, she was still smiling. And when she looked up to make sure she hadn't unintentionally wandered past the restaurant, the smile died on her lips.

There, across the street, standing on the sidewalk, was Viv. In the arms of some guy whose back was to Ava. Viv's smile bubbled into laughter. The pounding in Ava's ears drowned out the world as she stepped off the curb to get a better look. But then she froze when the guy turned enough for Ava to see . . . that it was Grant.

What the hell! Ava's mind couldn't work fast enough to even begin to make sense of the absolute impossibility of it. Of Grant. Of Viv's secret life.

Of the obvious lies that broke their blood oath. Sure, Ava knew Viv was seeing someone, but she had said she was going to end things. Clearly, she hadn't.

As if by sixth sense, Viv's gaze drifted across the street, landing on Ava's shocked face. Viv stood there, stiffened. Through the traffic they stared at each other as if daring the other to make the first move. Or maybe if they stood there long enough the moment would pass, and nothing would have changed. Or maybe Ava knew that the second she moved it would set something in motion that she didn't want to face.

Ava stepped back onto the sidewalk, inching away . . . away.

"Ava!" Viv shouted.

Ava spun, racing in the opposite direction, away from her sister.

With each step, her anger burned hotter. Her sister's betrayal cut deeper. *Grant? Seriously? Why would she keep that a secret?*

And then Viv, having longer legs than Ava, caught up to her little sister. "Ava!" She spun Ava around by the arm. "Hey, talk to me."

"About what?" Ava could barely breathe.

"Stop. I know you saw us."

She glanced across the street. Grant had already vanished.

Ava shook her head, playing it off. Why didn't she just confront Viv? Because if Ava didn't admit it, then it didn't have to be true. She could pretend reality away, create her own world, her own bubble. But there was one problem. It didn't work anymore. Not with Nana, not with Rion, not with Ava's own heart.

"Ava, I'm sorry. I should have told you, but—"

"We swore no secrets. Remember?" Ava's blood was boiling. "And the other night you lied to my face, to Carm's face! You were never going to end things."

Maybe it wouldn't have mattered as much if it hadn't always just been the three of them, if they hadn't shared the same rejection from their mother, the same grief over her abandonment. Maybe the lie wouldn't have felt so gutting if Ava hadn't loved and trusted her sisters more than anyone else on the planet. They were her protection, her safety net, her fortress.

"Please," Viv said, "can we just talk about it?"

"Viv, you don't owe me." Ava knew her words stung, but they empowered her in some strange way. "You don't have to tell me that you've obviously been seeing my boss since . . ."

"Nana's funeral."

A whole month? That's why he'd been so nice recently, the whole big brother act. That's why he brought muffins! Suck-up! Grant was H. Grant Harrison.

"He has two burner phones!" Ava didn't see why that mattered, or what she thought that said about him, but those were the only words that came to her chaotic mind.

"One is for work," Viv defended, "and one is private." She reached for Ava, but Ava moved away.

"I wanted to tell you," Viv cried. "I should have told you. I didn't mean to keep it a secret, or at least not this long. Everything just happened so fast."

"Why?" Ava demanded. "Why couldn't you have just said something?"

"I thought you'd freak and would tell me not to date him, and I would of course do what you wanted, and he was worried it would make him less objective when he wrote your letter of rec, and he didn't want to look like he was playing favorites. And—" She dragged in a long breath. "One day turned into six turned into ten, and . . . I was scared that if I said something it would jinx it. I never expected . . . It's just he's so nice and fun and smart, and we have the same interests, and he loves football, and . . ." In the middle of her babbling, tears sprang to her eyes. "But how unrealistic, right? I mean, no one falls that fast. It has to be a bad sign."

Ava had never known her sister to date casually, and even when she was dating Douchebag Dave in college, she never talked like this, *looked* like this, which could only mean one thing.

The words came slowly, quietly, as if they were living things. "You're . . . in love with him."

Viv looked like she was going to hit her famous recover button, like she was going to throw on her protective mask of *I don't need anyone*, but she took a deep breath, nodded, and said, "Yes."

"And he loves you?"

Love dares the devil.

Those were Caroline's last words to Ava. The very last words her mother ever spoke to her before she turned her back and walked out the door.

Love. Dares. The. Devil.

Viv's cheeks pinked, and Ava had her answer. Grant loved her too.

"But." Ava's mind was spinning. "It's only been a month."

Feelings grow when you aren't looking.

"Gree, please don't hate me."

Ava's heart softened. She wanted her sister to be happy. And she couldn't ignore the fact that she had been keeping her own feelings a secret too. Not only from her sisters, but from herself. Feelings she thought she could control, organize in an orderly, predictable fashion.

Seeing Viv cry only loosened Ava's own tears. "I could never hate you," Ava said, moving out of the way of a couple hurrying down the street like they were late for an appointment. "I want you to be happy, and I think"—

her thoughts and words arrived simultaneously—"that maybe you also didn't tell us in case it didn't work out."

Because it never did, so of course Viv would expect the secret to die before she ever had to tell it.

Viv attempted a small tremulous smile. "When did you decide to start being so understanding?"

"Have you told Carm?"

"Hell no!"

Ava wiped a tear and laughed. "She's going to murder you for not telling her about a boy."

Viv pulled her little sister into a long hug. "I love you, Gree. And I promise to never keep something from you again."

"Does this mean my boss is going to be at Christmas dinners?"

This time they both laughed.

Ava wrapped her arms around her oldest sister, genuinely happy she was happy. When they finally broke apart, Ava said, "So, I think you owe me one."

"Okay?"

"What's up with calling me Gree?"

Viv flashed a knowing smile. "In my fairy tale, the one Mom used to tell me about the girl with the wooden heart, there was a cricket."

"I'm a bug from your dark fairy tale?"

"The cricket was the bravest of them all. And you always reminded me of him."

Ava's face felt all buzzy.

Viv looped her arm in Ava's, and they began to walk. "Sooo, do you have something you want to tell *me*?"

"Like what?"

"Like how you really feel about Rion North?"

Ava pivoted. She had been so hung up on Viv's secret, she had forgotten. "You won't believe what I just found out."

"Well, you can tell me on the way to your car." Viv smiled. "Since my ride has already left."

Ava left Viv alone with Carmen and the very cold Thai dinner. She had offered to stick around, to play defense when Carm inevitably went ballistic, but Viv insisted she could do it on her own.

After a long, hot shower, Ava glanced at her phone and saw two missed calls from Elijah. But there was also a text: I think I'm in love, Aves. Is it too soon? Tell me I'm crazy. Tell me I'm a fool. I wish you were here to tell me to be logical. And why do they say fall in love? Like, why fall? Why not plummet? It is absolutely more of a plummet. Ugh!

Ava replied, You're not crazy. Plummet away.

Caroline plucked a pomegranate from the tree while Ava followed behind her.

"The queen sent word across the land," Caroline said in a silky voice, "that anyone who returned the princess to the kingdom, anyone who possessed her heart, would be crowned king. When the wolf heard the news, he decided that he wanted the crown for himself."

"But he isn't a king," Ava said angrily.

"He could become one. He brought the princess gifts. He told her tales. He

spun lies she took as truths. He made her trust him. And all the while he was patient. Waiting. Waiting. Waiting."

"But he can't be king!" Ava cried. "Maybe we could change the ending."

Caroline didn't respond to that; instead she marched on toward the outcome Ava hated.

"Night and day, the princess grieved for the love she had lost. Night and day, she allowed the wolf in bit by bit. Inch by inch. Until he possessed what was left of her heart. But the fire still burned.

"And the wolf finally understood that the only way to kill the fire was to consume the princess whole."

The first time Ava had heard the story, she said, "But then he wouldn't be king. He wouldn't be able to send her back to her castle."

She no longer asked the question, because she knew it wouldn't change anything. Caroline would only tell her, "Happy endings are for foolish people with foolish hearts."

Now Caroline leaned against the tree, staring down at Ava. "The wolf was smart; he played with words. The queen had been clear: anyone who possessed the princess's heart," Caroline said, allowing Ava to come to the right conclusion.

Ava shuddered. "The wolf didn't just eat her heart. He ate her."

Thirty-Six

A va dreamed of the wolf devouring the princess until there was nothing left of her but her dead heart. He smiled at Ava, teeth glistening with blood. Then he spoke in Caroline's voice:

Love dares the devil.

The entire day Ava ignored the dream and her mother's voice. She ignored them over breakfast with her sisters in which Carmen relived all her suffering over Viv's secret. She ignored them while she made dog biscuits in the shapes of little bones for Tres. She ignored them on her afternoon run to the shore.

Breathless, she collapsed onto the sand. She stared across the hazy horizon, more gray than blue. She thought about tonight. About meeting Charles. She opened his photo on her phone, staring at all his hope. Imagining his utter devastation that Maggie hadn't been his destiny after all.

When she circles back to you, you have to pay attention, because the story isn't over.

Of course the story is over, Ava thought. *Charles didn't spend his life with Maggie. He never even got to ask her the question!*

Just then Nana appeared, sitting on the sand next to Ava.

"Nana!" Ava threw her arms around the ghost, which still felt like hugging a feathery pillow.

"I have missed you too, corazón."

Pulling free, Ava got down to business. "Did you find anything out?"

By the crestfallen look on Nana's face, Ava knew she was no closer to discovering how to transfer the blessing back. "We still have two days," Nana said, but they were just words to fill the moment, to calm the restlessness, to deny the possibility that the blessing might never come to Ava.

Ava's heart sank.

"So cuéntame. How are things with Rion?"

"What do you mean?"

"He has become a good friend."

"Yeah. He's nice." Ava had meant to end it there, but she knew she'd never get this chance again, and she wanted her grandmother to know. "I mean, he told me some things, and I told him about Caroline."

"Ah." Nana traced her ghostly fingertips across the sand without leaving a mark. "I had wanted to tell you something about your mother, something that I never got around to because it just got harder, and I was afraid it would open old wounds."

Ava felt like she was on shaky ground, unsure if she wanted to know anything that could cause more pain. But she trusted her grandmother. "What is it, Nana?"

"She loved someone before your father."

Ava felt like she had been hit by a bus. She hadn't been expecting that. And she was too speechless to say anything as Nana charged ahead. "There was a boy in college; he died in a skydiving accident. Your dad met her a few weeks before the accident, and when he brought her home, I told him it was too soon, that she was still healing, but he wouldn't hear of it. He thought he could change her heart, and so he married her. And in her way, she thought your dad could heal her too."

So that was why the valentine was never delivered. Ava considered what her grandmother was sharing as she watched the waves curl in and out, out and in. She finally understood that her mother's fairy tale had been a warning, a twisted way to protect her daughters from having their hearts broken too. And maybe some people's hearts, like her mom's, never healed; maybe the pain was too great to come back from.

Nana glanced up at a pair of seagulls, winging on the wind. "I think she was always looking for a love that could fill her up again."

"Do you think she ever loved Dad?"

"In her own way, yes. And she loved you too, jita. She was just too damaged to show it."

Ava might never understand her mother's pain, but at least now she could put it away.

She suddenly felt exhausted from all the heavy armor she had been wearing for so long. So, she shared with Nana the details of what she had told Rion about Caroline.

"I am glad that you won't carry that anymore," Nana said. Her eyes softened, and a smile lingered there. She gazed out at the sea, then a moment later back to Ava. "Mija, when did you know?"

"Know?"

"About your feelings for Rion?"

Ava swallowed. "I think . . . they began that first night when we lay on the sidewalk and he told me I wouldn't understand the story of Maggie. But I didn't realize until later."

"Maggie?"

"It's a long story."

Nana smiled softly. "Well, I'd still like to hear about it." Ava knew what her grandmother really meant was, *I want to talk to you about anything but the blessing. I want to hear all the stories that I might not get to take with me.*

So, Ava began at the beginning. And when she was done with the telling, Nana said, "May I see the photo?" Her voice quivered.

Ava held her phone up.

Wide-eyed, Nana stared. Tears sprang to her eyes. Her hand flew to her mouth.

"Nana, what's wrong?"

"Charlie Lawrence," she whispered. "That's Charlie," Nana said, this time with more confidence.

"You know him?"

Nana nodded. And then Ava understood. A slow tremble worked its way up her legs. A prickle, a knowing sensation bloomed in the center of her heart. "Oh my God, you're Maggie." As if that needed to even be said aloud. A nickname for Margarita. A nickname that Nana refused to allow anyone to use, even her grandchildren when they couldn't pronounce her full name. And now Ava saw why. She couldn't even begin to process the magnitude, the chance of it all.

Nana nodded slowly, never taking her eyes off Charles. Ava could see the longing and the love in her grandmother's eyes. "All this time I thought he had given up on me, on us." She lifted her eyes to Ava's. "He never called. I waited, and he never called."

"He lost your number, but why didn't you show up?" Ava asked slowly. Afraid that if she rushed, the memory would somehow evaporate.

Nana took a moment to regain her composure, to consider her words. She began with, "My father was a domineering, controlling man." Nana never talked about her past; she always said that the present moment was the only one that mattered. When Ava was little, she had asked dozens of questions about Nana's life and was always met with clipped responses that didn't offer the details needed to feed a story. So, Ava was only left with a single headline: "Woman Leaves Husband with Son in Tow for Reasons Unknown."

Nana went on, "He found out about Charles, and that he was a white man, an unwealthy white man. So, he forbade me to see him again. But I wouldn't listen, and when it was time to leave for the train, I had packed my life in one suitcase, thinking I would never return."

Ava couldn't begin to process how terrifying it must have been for Nana. "So, did you miss the train?"

"I almost made it," she said with a tremor of anger in her voice. "I arrived with minutes to spare, but then my father's assistant showed up and dragged me back home."

"What?! How could he do that?"

"Like I said, my father was domineering—but he was also powerful. So, that night I sneaked out my window. I went back to the train station, but there were no trains again until the next day. I had no idea how to find Charles, so I began to call every hotel in Mexico City, but there were so many."

Ava's heart was pounding as if the past events were happening in real time. "Then what happened?"

Nana sighed, sitting up straighter. "Time went by, but my heart didn't heal, jita. Still, my father arranged for me to marry your grandfather. A man of wealth and status. He was a good companion, but it wasn't true love."

"Why didn't you say no?"

There was a long pause. Waves rolled to the shore ten times before Nana spoke again. "Grief is a hard thing to explain. I did what my father insisted, because I was too lost in despair to fight him and I knew I couldn't say no forever. And your grandfather was a good man, truly."

"Then why did you leave him?"

"Because I couldn't live a life of pretend. I really thought I could, if I just worked hard enough. But in the end I knew that I was going to drown if I stayed."

Ava's mind began to fit the remaining pieces together. "And you came here because you knew Charles was from here."

"I knew he was from the US. But his father had been in the military, so he moved around a lot. I had no idea that he was so close all this time. Ay! Fate has a twisted sense of humor."

Ava had always admired her grandmother, but hearing the story now, she admired her even more. A woman of color who left comfort and ease to raise her son alone in a time when it was frowned upon. There was nothing humorous about it! Which only made Fate seem all the crueler.

When she circles back to you, you have to pay attention, because the story isn't over.

"He was the only one who ever called me Maggie," Nana whispered.

It was a tragic story, a reminder that Ava's mom was right. Love really did dare the devil.

"I'm so sorry, Nana," Ava said, gripping her hand.

"Corazón. It was meant to be this way."

"How can you say that? Charles thought you were his destiny. You were supposed to be together, and—"

"Don't you see? I *was* his destiny. Maybe not in the way that you or I would imagine, but mira. Our lives have intersected again. Our love brought us here, and now there is you and Rion. You two wouldn't have been possible if I had made that train."

Ava refused to believe this was a happy or even acceptable end to the story. But she also knew Nana was right. Had Nana made that train, had she married Charles, there would have been no Raul, no Granados sisters. How could one decision affect so many lives?

"We have two days left . . ." Nana's voice trailed off, but when it returned there was a fierceness to it. "And I want to see Charlie."

Ava and Nana drove in silence.

Ava took deep breaths, letting them out slowly so they didn't sound like sighs. Every once in a while, she would dare a side glance at her grandmother, who was always gazing out the window.

A sad smile played on Ava's lips. She wanted more time. More walks. More Nana.

Tonight wasn't going to go as she thought. Because she had to tell Rion the truth. That their lives had been inextricably linked a generation before they were even born. That she believed, she finally believed in fate. How else could she possibly explain the impossibility of it all? And that brought her to her last conclusion: Maybe Rion was always meant to receive Nana's blessing. Maybe her memoryless future was a kindness, so she could forget all that she had lost.

"I'm not sure where the house is," Ava said as she pulled up to the barn.

Nana was only half-present, her eyes darting back and forth across the dimly lit road as if she were trying to commit this place to memory. "I know how to find him now."

And then she was gone.

The night sky was thick with darkness when Ava parked in the dirt lot. She walked with purpose. Tonight, she was going to tell Rion everything.

Gripping the sack of Tres's treats, she rounded the old barn. Her heart thundered. *What will he say? Will he understand? Will he hate me? Will he believe me? Just get it out fast,* Ava told herself.

Peering across the darkness, she could make out Rion's form sitting on a blanket, staring up at the stars. The only light, a pale moon.

Ava slowed her pace, swallowed a knot of emotion.

He turned at the sound of her footsteps. "Hey."

She went over and sat next to him.

"Hey," she said, testing the resolve in her voice.

She was glad it was dark. Glad she didn't have to look into his eyes when she told him she had built their relationship on a lie.

"Listen," she said, "I have something to tell you and I don't want you to talk or say anything until I'm done."

"Okay."

For a heartbeat Ava thought she was going to lose her nerve, and then she remembered Nana's story, her bravery for leaving her family, her marriage, for coming to the US, and it gave her the courage to begin. With the night of the storm.

Ava unfolded every detail, even the magic of her family's blessings. She was too afraid to look at Rion, afraid that any flicker of unwanted emotion would steal her voice.

But Rion said nothing. He just kept staring at the sky. Listening. Breathing. Sighing.

Maybe he can forgive me, Ava thought. *Maybe he'll understand the why of it all.* At the end of her story, she bit back the words bubbling up inside of her, afraid they would sound empty. The ones where she tried to parse out her feelings for him.

And when she was done, Rion sat in silence for an agonizing moment.

He released a long exhale. "I think . . . I get it," was all he said.

Ava wasn't sure she'd heard him right. Really? *This* from the guy who believes in fate unapologetically? Just *I get it*? A cool breeze swept through the trees, rustling the leaves.

Rion turned to her. Ava was frozen. He reached his hand out and cupped the back of her neck, drawing her closer.

She relaxed into his touch, allowed herself to be pulled into his orbit.

His lips brushed against hers. She felt a jolt, an alarm that screamed *wrong, wrong, wrong.*

"Ava?"

Rion's voice came from somewhere other than the mouth on hers.

She jerked free, horrified, as she wiped her mouth with the back of her hand. Achilles smiled. "I thought you could tell us apart."

"You jerk!" she cried, jumping to her feet.

Rion launched himself headlong into Achilles, hurling his brother to the ground.

"Stop!" Ava screamed.

The brothers rolled across the dirt, all grunts and curses and years of unspent anger.

"Rion!" Ava shouted, tugging on his arm, until finally Achilles and Rion were on their feet, chests heaving. Achilles spat blood and growled, "You think you're pissed at me? Why don't you ask your girlfriend about all her lies?"

Ava's throat closed up.

"Tell him," Achilles demanded. "Tell him you've been lying to him all this time. Using him."

"What's he talking about?" Rion asked, breathless.

Ava's eyes darted between the two. Never before could she see their stark differences so clearly. How could she have thought Achilles was Rion?

"I . . . I . . ." She looked to Achilles. And then the dam broke. "Is this what you wanted? To make everyone as miserable as you?"

Achilles's smile faded. He brushed his hands together and sighed. "Nah, but have fun telling my brother the truth." He turned and walked into the shadows.

"Ava?"

Unwanted tears burned her eyes. "I . . . I'm sorry. I thought he was you, and . . ."

"What did he mean about lies?" Rion's voice was flat, clipped, terrifying.

Ava spilled it all, a mess of a story, out of order, layers upon layers of deceit that had sounded so much better the first time around. Before she had been all riled up. Before Achilles had ruined everything.

Rion turned, paced a few steps, turned back. "So, it was all a lie?"

"No! I care about you . . . I . . ."

His face went stone cold. "God, I'm so clueless. Blessings? Really? I'm supposed to believe that?"

"You said you saw the white light!" How could someone so open, someone who believed so much in fate, be so closed all of a sudden? "It's true." Ava approached him, arms unfolded. "Rion, please. It came out wrong. Didn't you hear about our grandparents and—"

"So, is that what you need? A kiss?" he said angrily, as if he hadn't heard anything but the deception. "If you had asked, I would have done that a long time ago."

They stood like that in the dark, Rion backlit by the full moon.

Ava hated that things had turned out this way, but she should have known better, should have trusted her instincts. There were no happy endings, only foolish, arrogant people daring the devil.

"Fine," Ava said angrily, realizing that after tonight she was never going to get another chance to get the blessing back. It was a Hail Mary, and she knew it, but she was all out of options. "Kiss me."

Rion's gaze was fixed on her. He didn't flinch or balk. He took two steps closer. His expression vacillated between warm and cold. Soft and hard.

Ava's heart thrashed wildly.

Rion inched closer, Tres's biscuits crunched beneath his feet. He started to say something, but in the end, he just turned and walked away.

Thirty-Seven

The next day's headlines were all the same: "Meteor Shower Tonight."

As if Ava needed reminding. That tonight, her failures meant Nana's memoryless afterlife and the death of future blessings.

Tonight also meant goodbye.

"I think Charlie felt my presence," Nana said, strolling in the shade of her prized pomegranate trees.

"How do you know?" Ava said.

"He looked up, as if he saw me." Her ghostly fingers traced the hanging branches. "And there was something in his face, a knowing."

"Are you glad you went?"

"In my eyes, he looked the same as the last time I saw him." Nana's voice sounded so far away that Ava felt like she wasn't even there with her.

"What do you mean?"

"He was so young and guapo. Maybe ghost eyes just see what they want to see. ¿Quién sabe?"

"I'm really glad you got to see him, to find out the truth." *Even though it changed nothing,* Ava thought sadly.

Nana studied her granddaughter intensely, signaling that whatever Nana said next, Ava didn't want to hear it.

"Corazón, we must move on, and if that means I have no memories and you have no blessing, then I must accept it. *You* must accept it."

No! Ava would never accept it. Any of it. Anger burned inside her. It made her feel sensible, in control; it kept her from seeing all the confusion and hurt buried just beneath the surface. "But you didn't accept living in a loveless marriage!"

"Because I could change that. *This* I cannot change." Nana peered up between the branches. "Can I tell you something?"

Ava nodded, fighting the tears and the tremors in her chest.

"He will forgive you," Nana said. "He just needs time. People aren't rational when they are in pain."

Like Achilles. Like Mom. Like me.

"And if I could go back," Nana went on, "if I could change one more thing, do you know what it would be?"

Ava could only imagine the long list, the choices that would have made a difference, that would have changed Nana's fate: to get on the train, to not get married, to look for Charles longer. But then Ava quickly realized that any of those choices would have altered their lives together, and she knew Nana would never ever change that.

Nana said, "When he left for Mexico City, we thought we were saying goodbye for a week. We were rushed, running about with daily tasks that seem so insignificant now. If I had known the goodbye was forever, I would have told him I loved him." Her eyes glistened with tears. "I never told him. Not once. Can you believe that?"

"But why?"

"I thought I had a lifetime."

Ava had mere hours with Nana.

Past Ava would have used every minute, every second to be with her grandmother. But in that moment, she understood that yes, Fate played a role, but so did Ava's choices. And her choice was to drive like a bat out of hell to Maggie's Orchard. To say the things she hadn't said last night. If she were lucky, she could still get that blessing back. And even if not, she still needed to try to fix things with Rion.

Ava followed the narrow dirt road past the barn and around a deep bend until she came to a two-story home. It wasn't anything like she had imagined. This place was painted a deep brick-red color so reminiscent of the homes in Mexico.

Hurriedly, she climbed up the steps onto the porch, where she knocked on the door using a brass knocker in the shape of a hand.

Please don't let Achilles answer.

A minute later, she heard someone whistling from somewhere behind the house. Ava followed the upbeat tune to the back of the house, which opened onto another piece of the orchard. A thin old man wearing a fedora and suspenders was standing on a ladder, picking oranges and tossing them into a basket below.

"Hello?" Ava called as she made her way over.

The man, who had to be Charles, peered down. "Who might you be?"

"Ava."

Should you be on that ladder?

He smiled. "Oh. So, you're her. We were supposed to meet last night. But now is just as good. I'm pleased to meet you."

How much did he know? Had Rion told him everything?

"Nice to meet you," Ava said. "Is Rion home?"

Charles grunted as he climbed down the ladder and removed his hat before wiping his brow with the back of his sleeve. "Would you like some lemonade?" He gestured to a small table with a glass pitcher atop it.

"Um . . . no thanks. So, is—"

"You look thirsty. Come on."

Ava followed, anxiety digging its claws into her heart.

I don't have time for this.

With a shaky hand, Charles poured her some lemonade. She took a sip of the tart brew to appease him.

"You look like her," he said, before his voice trailed off on, "my Maggie."

"Rion told you."

Charles nodded. "A long view of fate," he said with a chuckle. Ava didn't think any of this was funny, but maybe when you're at the end of your life, your view changes.

"I loved your grandmother very much."

"I know." Then, remembering Nana's last wish, she said, "She told me she loved you too."

"Of course she did," he said with an uptick in his voice. "I never would have planned my proposal if I didn't know that."

"She said she wished she had told you."

He placed his hat back on his head. White wisps of hair poked out. "Words are worthless little things. Not as meaningful as a look or a smile or the brush of a hand." He smiled at Ava. "Do you want to know something? I knew the exact moment I loved her. And the moment she loved me. I could see it in her face. You can always recognize the love when it belongs to you."

A warm breeze drifted through the trees.

Charles said, "You've probably guessed that Rion isn't here."

"Do you know when he'll be back?"

Wiping the back of his neck with a handkerchief, he shook his head. "I imagine in a few hours."

A few hours? Ava suddenly realized that she had never told Rion about the ticking bomb that would explode with the meteor shower.

"I can't wait that long!" And then Ava wondered how much Rion *had* told his grandfather. Had he mentioned the blessing? Nana's ghost? But by his relaxed demeanor, Ava guessed Charles didn't know the details. It was probably better that way.

Should I tell him?

"He's at the family cabin," Charles said.

Cabin? Rion had never mentioned it.

"Can you give me the address?" Ava asked, hoping it wasn't a million miles away.

The old man snickered. "There is no address. It's quite off the beaten path, so I can't tell you how to get there." His gaze floated past Ava. "But Achilles can take you there."

Ava spun to find the evil twin with a fat lip staring at her.

"No way," Ava countered. "I'll just call Rion. Ask for directions."

Charles shook his head sympathetically. "There isn't service. So, it looks like Achilles is your only chance."

Of all the scenarios that had played out in her head, this one wasn't even on the radar.

"He's right," Achilles said, his expression pained. "I'll drive you."

Ava was about to argue again when Charles stepped closer and added, "Ava, I give you my word that Achilles will deliver you there safely."

Ava was torn right down the middle. How could she trust the brother who had pretended to be Rion, who had thrown her under the bus, who had kissed her?

"I'm an ass," Achilles said. "And I know you don't trust me, but if you want to get . . ." He stopped short of saying *the blessing* and instead went with, "What you're looking for, then you'll have to endure me."

Ava turned to Charles with a pleading look, as if to say, *Please tell me there is another way.* Charles gave a half nod. "Fate's in control now, Ava. No sense fighting the current."

Achilles drove a black Mustang. Of course he did. The red leather seats had black racing stripes, and the rest of the interior was meticulous, unlike Rion's truck.

"I know you hate me," he said the minute they were on the highway. "You think I'm an asshole."

Ava said nothing. All she could do was glare out the window and think Fate was pretty cruel for sticking her with this guy.

"Aren't you going to agree or disagree?" he said.

"I'd rather not talk at all."

"I'm really sorry, okay?" he said, more forcefully this time.

"Now you're sorry? It's a little late."

"Because I effed up. Because I never wanted to fight Rion. Because I'm tired and . . ." He glanced in the passenger mirror before changing lanes. "How do you know your grandma will forget her life?"

Ava had never gotten to the part of the story where Nana was a ghost. And now she had nothing to lose. "You won't believe me."

"Try me."

"She's a ghost, and she told me."

Without a beat of surprise, he said, "And you can see her? Talk to her?"

Ava merely nodded. She didn't owe him her story.

Achilles's jaw tightened. He was considering her words. The skies grew darker, an endless stretch of gray. "When I was little . . . after my parents," he said, "I thought I saw my mom in the reflection of a window. Rion laughed and told me I was seeing things, but now I think maybe she was there, maybe for a little while at least."

Ava saw the pain in Achilles masked as self-righteous anger. And as much of a world-class jerk as he had been, a part of her understood that pain made you do and say things that weren't true. Things that hurt other people, so you didn't have to be the only one hurting.

A second later, he reached into his pocket and pulled out a folded piece of paper. He held it out to her.

"What is it?" Ava didn't doubt it could be laced with poison.

"Just take it."

Ava gripped the thick paper. Slowly, she unfolded it. It was a sketch of her. In it, snowflakes fell from the sky. Every detail of her face was precise, a strand of hair blew across her chin, her eyes were shaded with promise, with hope, with . . .

Ava recognized the moment. It was the night at the ice rink. The night Meda said the color of the blessing burned brighter, and he didn't know why. She recalled the way Rion had looked at her.

I knew the exact moment I loved her. You can always recognize the love when it belongs to you.

"Why are you showing me this?"

"When I found it, I guess I knew . . ." He blew out a breath.

"It's just a drawing."

Achilles threw her a side glance. "Then you don't know Rion."

"He told me about the accident," Ava said, glad the words were out in the open. "I think it's eating him up. And I know . . . I know it's been awful for you too, but . . ."

"Things haven't been good between me and Rion since . . . Well, let's just say that they got a lot worse when we went through my parents' things. Did you know the first night I saw you at the restaurant was the same day we had gone through their stuff? God, I was pissed. And worse." He barked out a laugh. "My girlfriend had just cheated on me."

Was that why he was with those two girls, acting like a jerk?

"I guess I wanted Rion to be as miserable as I was. Like, to prove something." Achilles scrubbed a hand through his hair. "I didn't realize how much I had in me, like anger and stuff, until last night, and I thought kissing you would make me feel better, but it made me feel worse, and that's when I got it . . . I can't keep blaming and hating my brother."

Ava watched the world whiz by, thinking how weird it was to think so badly of someone only to find out they were a decent human being underneath it all.

I guess everyone wears a different armor.

"You guys should make up," she said.

He grinned. "Why else would I be driving you?"

A few beats of silence. "How far is this place?" she asked.

"Another hour."

As the landscape changed from valley to forest, it began to rain. A steady pounding.

Achilles turned up the windshield wipers, slowing his pace.

"Maybe an hour and a half now."

"Why is he at the cabin?" Ava asked, still holding the sketch.

With a one-shoulder shrug, Achilles said, "We haven't been here in at least five years. Maybe he just wanted to get away?"

From me.

Was she really talking about Rion with Achilles?

"Do you think you'll be able to get the blessing back?" he asked a minute later.

"I have to try." But it wasn't the only reason she needed to see Rion. She needed to rewrite the ending for the princess with the fire heart. An ending where the wolf didn't consume her. She didn't know if there would be a happy ending, but she knew she wouldn't allow it to be tragic.

The rain pounded the car, slowing their progress even more. Ava had no other choice but to call in the big guns.

"Meda?"

"Who's Meda?" Achilles asked.

The saint appeared in the back seat, vacillating between frown and smile, smile and frown. "Why are you with this clown?"

"It's a long story, but . . ." She pointed to the sky. "Are you doing this?"

"You're really freaking me out," Achilles said.

"Just drive."

Meda rolled his neck back and forth like it had a kink. He pressed his face against the window. "This is all Mother Nature, Ava."

"Can you cut it? So we can get there faster?"

Meda blew out a long breath. "Can I turn it off? Pish. Ye of so little faith."

But when nothing happened, Ava said, "Meda?"

"Um . . . it isn't working."

"You're the saint of weather!"

"Yeah, well, sometimes there are greater forces at work, okay?"

"Hang on," Achilles said, white-knuckling the wheel. "You're talking to a saint that controls weather? In *my car*?"

"Pretty much."

Achilles paled. "This is a lot more than I signed on for, dude. I don't care how much my brother likes you."

After an hour of ghost and saint questions, bad music, and more apologies from Achilles for kissing her, he finally turned onto a muddied road. The car struggled to make the incline. The tires slipped; the engine groaned. "We aren't going to make it," he said, shifting gears, gunning the gas pedal.

"Achilles, we have to!"

Meda sighed. "This is dreadful."

"How far from here?" Ava said.

"About half a mile up the road," Achilles said.

Ava started to open the door when Achilles stopped her. "You're really going out there in this?"

Without another word, Ava jumped out of the car. The rain pelted her, soaking her jeans. She cut into the trees where there would be less mud and some reprieve from the tempest. But even then, the rain found her, followed her all the way up the hill.

With each step, her mind went to work, loosening the questions she hadn't wanted to ask. *How could Rion just take off with my blessing? Without even trying to give it back to me?*

The cabin was a small thing nestled among the tall pines. There was a deep-set porch in desperate need of a new coat of paint.

Soaked and freezing, Ava knocked on the door, peering into the grimy windows. There was no sign of him. She shook the doorknob, but it was locked.

A fit of thunder boomed in the distance, almost shaking the dilapidated porch. Lightning flashed once, twice.

Ava turned to head around back to find another way inside.

There he was.

Standing in the rain about twenty yards away. His eyes fixed on her. His hand wrapped around something Ava couldn't make out before he stuffed it into his coat pocket.

Operating on pure adrenaline, Ava ran toward him. A peal of thunder stopped her in her tracks. Lightning landed, a brilliant flash of white. The violent *crack* forced her gaze up to the tree above Rion, to the branch that was falling . . .

Falling . . .

Falling.

"Watch out!"

Without thinking, Ava ran and shoved him out of the way.

The two tumbled to the ground and rolled across the mud as the branch landed with a terrible crash a few feet away.

Ava was on top of Rion, breathless. Rion's face was streaked with mud and debris. He blinked up at her in astonishment. His heart pounded so hard she could feel it against her own. It took him a few moments before he said, "Are you ever going to stop running into me?"

One heartbeat.

Two.

She tried to think of a clever retort. But all she could think about was the wild thumping in her chest.

Three.

Four.

"Ava . . ."

She felt her body yielding, falling deeper into Rion. And then their mouths met. And Ava was no longer falling. She was dissolving.

The forest and the sky fell silent. The world evaporated. There was only this moment.

Rion's arms wrapped around her, pulling her closer. His kiss deepened, and she followed.

A spark, hot and urgent. Like a jolt of electricity. An explosion of light.

Ava broke their connection first, her voice a small, sleepy whisper. "Did you feel that?"

Thirty-Eight

They were both breathing hard, like they had just run miles up the mountain. The rain was unrelenting.

All of a sudden, Ava didn't care if love dared the devil. She wanted to stay right here in Rion's rain-soaked arms, mere inches from that not-so-mediocre mouth.

"Did you just kiss me, Nine?" Rion asked, breathless.

Ava smiled. "You kissed me."

"Then I guess it's your turn."

Slowly, Ava lowered her mouth to his, swept away by the feel of his lips, the warmth of his tongue, the strength of his arms wrapping around her tighter. "I lied," she whispered. "The first thing I liked about you was your mouth."

Rion laughed. He pushed a strand of wet hair from her face. "Do you think it worked?"

"I . . . I should call Nana and—"

"Or we could stay here . . . just for a minute."

"I should call Nana," she said again, wishing they really could stay here.

Rion groaned, helped her to her feet, and started pulling her back to the cabin. "First, I have something to show you."

The inside of the cabin was thick with dust. Gray sheets covered the furnishings. The air smelled of old memories and cedarwood. Ava was chilled to the bone and so thankful the cabin was warm.

Rion reached into his pocket, then pulled something out and set it in the palm of Ava's hand. A gold hummingbird earring.

Meteors, stars, 8:51. Collision. And the hummingbird.

"It's why I drove up here," Rion said eagerly. "I remembered seeing it in an old box out in the barn when I was a kid. At first, I thought it belonged to my grandma, but then my gramps told me that it was Maggie's.

"When he got to Mexico City, he found it in his luggage. He had never been sure if it fell in there or if Maggie planted it. But he said it was the only thing he had left of her." Rion rubbed the back of his neck, inhaling sharply. "And when you told me the story last night, I had a hunch that this mattered to your getting the blessing back. My plan was to bring it to you tonight, but my stupid truck wouldn't start."

Ava felt like the ground beneath her was crumbling. "I've seen this before," she said, turning the dangling earring over in her hand. "The other one is in my nana's jewelry box."

Ava suddenly realized that Nana's deathbed words were glimpses, moments in time, that added up to the here and now.

Thinking aloud, she said, "So, the meteors represent the deadline."

"Deadline?"

Ava explained, which drew a huge exhale of relief from Rion.

She added, "And the stars represent . . ."

"Me," Rion said with a beaming smile. His voice smoothed the edges of this world, of her mother's words.

Ava felt the pull back to his arms, but there was too much thinking to do. "8:51 was the time of the collision," she continued. "We know what the collision was, and now . . ."

"The hummingbird," Rion said.

What Ava still couldn't figure out was why it mattered.

"Ava!" Meda shouted, startling her so badly she practically screamed.

"Meda, what are you . . ." Nana appeared right next to him.

Rion followed Ava's gaze to the empty space that held her attention. "They're here, aren't they?"

Ava nodded just as Achilles opened the door. Before the brothers could come to blows, Ava quickly told Rion that the only reason she was here was because of Achilles.

"You drove her?" Rion said with narrowed, mistrustful eyes.

"Can we just talk?" Achilles replied.

Ava gave Rion a quick nod as he squeezed her hand and headed outside with his brother. She hugged Nana fiercely. "I'm so glad you're here!"

"Ay!" Nana said nonchalantly. "I just saw you."

Ava showed her the earring. "Look!"

At first, Nana's expression was one of confusion, and then it was as if all the distance back to that memory closed. Nana's eyes lit up. "He kept it all this time?"

With an exasperated tone, Meda argued, "Why are we discussing an earring when—"

"You knew he had your earring?" Ava asked Nana.

"When he left for Mexico, I put it in his suitcase, so he could take a little piece of me with him."

"Ava!' Meda shouted, instantly silencing her and Nana. "It worked! You're wearing the blessing."

"The hummingbird!" Ava squealed. She saw now why the earring mattered. "Rion was carrying the earring in his pocket when the blessing transferred. We had the storm and emotion and a sort of collision," she said, remembering the kiss with a blush she hoped Nana didn't see.

"And you must have had selfless emotion," Meda said.

Nana was already nodding. "That was the final piece of the bridge, Ava. Selfless emotion."

Meda did a tiny leap into the air before dancing Ava around the room. Nana was beaming as if her entire eternity wasn't at stake. Her eyes swept over Ava like she was seeing her for the first time.

And then a memory sparked. Ava halted. She gasped. "Meda, remember when you said it was weird that Rion had received the blessing in the first place?"

"I said it was curious."

"Do you think it's because our fates were intertwined so long ago?" And then it hit her: This was why she felt like she had met Rion before. It wasn't just the blessing; it was this long and strange view of fate that had somehow gotten under her skin and made everything about him feel familiar.

"That is excellent reasoning," the saint declared.

"Of course," Nana said, nodding. "Claro! It is so obvio now." Her expression suddenly widened. There was a beat of silence and then, "I remember now. I remember the blessing."

"What is it?" Ava rushed to her grandmother's side.

Nana took Ava's hands in her own. "I gave you the gift of an open heart."

"An open . . ." Ava could barely speak. No! She didn't want an open heart. That was the exact opposite of anything she could have *ever* wanted. Open meant vulnerable, dangerous.

Nana said, "You have been closed since Caroline; you keep people at arm's length; you don't trust. I didn't want you to go through life closed off from love. I know too well what that feels like."

"But." Ava spoke slowly, quietly. Like she was walking through a mine-field. "My heart opened to Rion."

"Yet you were always looking for a misstep, always leaning into the past, into beliefs that weren't true, isn't that right?"

Ava could only nod, because it was all true. While her feelings for Rion grew, she had been waiting for the other shoe to drop, always hearing her mom's voice ringing in her ears. *Love dares the devil.*

"Oh God," Ava said, suddenly realizing something. "Is that why Rion . . . ?" *Hung out with me? Got close to me? Trusted me? Fell for me? Because he had the gift of an open heart?*

"Of course not," Nana said, as if she knew where Ava was headed. "A blessing can never force or fabricate feelings."

"I still don't get it," Ava said. "Does this mean . . ." She was terrified her heart wouldn't be her own. "That I won't be me?"

"That is absolutely not the case," Meda asserted. "I know what you're thinking. That your heart is going to be some fragile flower, waiting to be stomped on. That it will be weak. But do you know how many humans go through life examining their hearts and minds and souls? Always unsure of who they are? What their passions are?" He smiled. "Consider this a short-cut to a memorable, meaningful life."

So that was why Rion had returned to sketching. It had always been a part of who he was, and the blessing just helped him rediscover it.

"There is more," Nana said. "An open heart will give you the ability to see inside others' hearts, to see people's motivations, their characters."

Had Rion been able to see *her* heart?

"I'm already pretty good at reading people, Nana."

"Perhaps you could see the facade, the side of them they wanted to share, but this is about seeing past all that to the true nature of who they are."

"If that's true, how come Rion didn't know I was lying?"

"Because your intentions were pure," Meda put in. "And the blessing doesn't make you a human lie detector."

"But, Nana," Ava said, "isn't that kind of voyeuristic?"

"I didn't say you could read thoughts."

Meda crossed himself. "Thank heavens. But think of the wonder. You'll be able to tell the . . . how do you call it, goodies from the baddies."

Something stirred inside Ava. Marvel. Excitement. Bewilderment. "And the weakness?" Ava asked.

With the tiniest of grins, Nana said, "You'll have to figure out that part on your own."

Thirty-Nine

Achilles drove like a champ NASCAR driver. He couldn't slow down. Not when they had no idea how long Nana had before she left for good, and that meant Ava had to get home to her sisters pronto.

She had called them on the way, explained everything, had expected them to cheer the good news that the power of passing blessings was now preserved, that Nana would carry her memories to the afterlife. But they were silent, no doubt processing what the end of this quest meant.

Goodbye.

The saddest word in the universe, Ava thought glumly.

Now Ava paced on the rooftop patio, waiting for her sisters to arrive.

Nana stood in a ribbon of faint light from a nearby table lamp. She cast no shadow.

"Are you scared?" Ava asked.

"The unknown is always a little frightening, isn't it?" Nana said lightly.

"But you'll have me." Meda appeared next to Nana. He was wearing his original robes and odd pointy hat. He turned his eyes to Ava. "I didn't want to leave without telling you that I have met and known many humans in my existence, and you are by far one of my favorites."

Ava tried to smile, but she couldn't bring herself to do it. "And you're my favorite saint."

With a nod, Meda leaned closer and whispered, "I never told you this, but we saints get something like points every time something is named after us. So, will you name something after me? Just not a pastry."

Ava promised, hugged the saint, and watched him vanish with his last words, "I'll be waiting, Margarita."

Carm and Viv strolled onto the patio just then, their footsteps light and timid.

Ava knew her job tonight was to be the messenger, to share whatever last words Nana had. To speak the goodbye her sisters would never get to hear.

"This is horrible," Carm said, dragging her feet. "We already said good-bye once, and now . . ." She sniffed, lifted her gaze, and, as if remembering her audience, she stood straighter. "Sorry, Nana."

Ava watched her grandmother watching her older granddaughters. Her dark eyes danced with a joy that didn't feel merited. How could she look so happy, so at peace?

"I have a few words," Nana began.

Carm and Viv gasped simultaneously.

"Nana?!" Viv shouted. Carm threw her arms around the ghost.

"You can see her?" Ava cried.

"I did some afterlife bartering," Nana said with a devilish grin, releasing Carmen. "And there isn't much time, so please listen to me." She drew closer to Viv and Carm. "Viviana, you don't always need to be the brave one, the caretaker. Go have fun."

Viv was already crying.

"Have adventures," Nana continued. "Promise me."

Viv nodded, wiping her nose. "I promise."

Ava's chest ached as Nana's gaze fell on Carmen. "Carmenita, you don't always need to be the whirlwind of magic and energy and entertainment that holds this family together. You can calm the storm inside. Find the quiet and the solitude. An examined life is a good life."

Carm frowned with disapproval. Ava cringed, fearing what might come out of Carm's mouth next.

"This isn't about you trying to make me a nun, is it?" Carm said.

Nana only chuckled. "Ay, Carmenita."

Carm and Viv told Nana they loved her, and after they left, arms wrapped around each other, Ava stood in the shadows, dreading what came next.

"I'm not going to say it," she told Nana.

Her grandmother wrapped her into an easy abrazo. Ava expected Nana to give her some advice, to ask Ava to make a promise too, but she didn't. She merely said, "Will you tend to my trees?"

Ava nodded.

"And harvest the pomegranates. It's so sad when beautiful fruit is left to waste on the ground."

"Okay."

Nana took Ava's hands in her own. Ava could barely get the words out. "I forgot to thank you for my blessing."

Nodding, Nana brushed a hair from Ava's face. Her deep brown eyes smiled. "Don't be afraid to get hurt, to fall and fall again. Find beauty and passion and the things that make your heart sing. It's the only way to make your own stories, corazón."

"I will." Tears fell. "I promise."

"And embrace the surprises." Before Ava could take another breath, her grandmother was gone.

"Nana?" she whispered, but there was no answer. Only the distant sound of traffic. *Wait!* Was that it? Was that all there was? She slumped into a chair, realizing that Nana would never go for a dramatic, drawn-out goodbye. It wasn't her style.

Ava didn't know how long she sat there, searching the darkness, hoping Nana would reappear. Waiting for her heart to start beating again.

"Ava?" Rion came over. "You okay?"

She nodded slowly as she stood, and Rion pulled her into a hug. Her blessing stirred, like a bear waking from hibernation. And in that instant, she could feel Rion's love.

He pulled back, arms still around her waist, and lifted his eyes to the sky.

Ava looked up too. Glowing streaks of light burned across the darkness. Flashes of radiance set on an unknown path.

The meteor shower.

Ava's heart was a quiet, steady pulse.

Rion eyed her, pulling her closer. "So . . ."

"So . . ."

"Do you believe in fate yet?"

Ava was about to answer when Rion kissed her. She melted into him. Her blessing stirred deep within her, radiating warmth as her heart beat with answers to questions she hadn't even asked yet.

Rion wrapped his arms around her and kissed the top of her head. "Your heart is doing that thing again."

"What thing?"

"The thing it did when the blessing transferred," he said. "It's like heat and sort of loud, and . . . It's hard to explain."

Maybe because Rion had once possessed the blessing, he could feel it when it woke up inside her. She could feel new desires blooming, new beliefs, new ways of looking at the world.

Nana said that I would be able to see into others' hearts, but she never mentioned my own.

Sucking in a big breath, Ava broke free. "I just realized something."

"What?"

"I'm never going to be a journalist," she whispered, in awe at the sudden revelation.

Rion pulled back to give her space, encouraging her to go on.

The words weren't for anyone but herself; Ava was thinking out loud, and every single word felt so right. "I think journalism was a way to protect myself, to live in a world of facts. But everything is different now. I want to make my own stories. My own adventures. Filled with surprises and what-ifs and ..."

"You hate surprises."

"That was then."

"Ha!" A wide grin spread across Rion's face. "Okay, Nine. And the first adventure will begin with ..."

Ava's heart beat to the rhythm of a new truth, the realization that there was only one way to finish Rion's sentence.

The two things that every story and adventure begin with. Choice.

And fate.

Epilogue

SIX MONTHS LATER

"**Y**ou look stunning," Viv said as Ava came down the hall toward the staircase where her sisters waited.

"It is truly disgusting," Carmen said, smacking her glossy lips together. Her newly tanned skin glowed from the month she had spent in the Galápagos Islands, away from LA. Away from USC.

Ava looked down at the icy-blue dress she wore—fitted but not tight, short but not mini, elegant but not granny-looking. Even without using her blessing, she knew her sisters were being genuine. She tugged on the gold hummingbirds dangling from her ears, and for the hundredth time she thought about how far they had come to be reunited.

A few weeks after Nana left for good, Ava had sent Reed a photo of a young Charles and Maggie, with Nana wearing the earrings. She also called the woman to tell her that even though they didn't end up together, learning the truth had brought them peace. "Thank you, Ava, dear," Reed had said. "Thank you for helping this old woman remember the power of love."

Viv's gaze fell to Ava's shoes. "Flip-flops? Really?"

Ava wiggled her toes. "And look how good my pedi looks."

"This is an engagement party," Carmen reminded her with a sneer, "not a beach party. Would it kill you to wear heels?"

"It might." Ava squeezed between her sisters, looping her arms in theirs. "Dad's going to have a coronary if we don't get downstairs."

At least fifty people were already gathered in the great room. Servers in white uniforms paraded through the crowd with silver trays. The house smelled of lilacs, eucalyptus, fresh masa, and a pinch of chocolate. There were huge ceramic bowls filled with pomegranates, and the red oranges from Maggie's Orchard newly named *Saint Medardus*. Ava knew Meda would love it.

Viv stopped at the edge of the room. "Guys?"

"What's wrong?" Ava said.

"You're not going to go all *Runaway Bride* on us, are you?" Carm asked.

Viv rolled her eyes. "This is an engagement party, not a wedding. And hello, it's a long engagement, remember?"

"And even two-year engagements lead to weddings," Carm said.

Viv took a deep breath. "I was just remembering last time Dad announced . . ."

"Except you weren't engaged," Ava put in.

"And Doug sucked," Carmen added.

"And Grant is awesome," Viv said, more to herself than to her sisters, as she peeled away and walked toward him. He was at the center of the crowd, beaming in his dark suit. Ava could feel how much he loved Viv, and it made her adore him more.

Carm cast her eyes around the room.

"Your eyes are doing that glowy thing."

Carm smiled softly. "I'm just committing this all to memory." Suddenly, she squeezed Ava's arm. "Alfonso is here."

Ava's gaze followed Carm's. Alfonso was talking with Rion and Achilles. It was so easy for Ava to tell the twins apart now. Her gaze fixed on Rion. He had one hand in his pants pocket, the other was rubbing his chin, and his head was bent to the left, which told Ava he was listening to whatever Achilles was saying. And then his brows lifted and he laughed. Elijah was there too, but his focus was on his phone. Ava knew by the smile on his face that he was texting Pierre, his now long-distance boyfriend.

Carm was tugging on Ava's arm. "So?"

"Huh? Did you ask me something?"

"Does Alfonso like me?" Carm spoke in a low voice, as if there was any risk of him hearing her. "Use your blessing. Tell me."

Carm had asked the same question after she saw him at Charles's funeral a couple months ago. And Ava had the same answer now as she did then.

"I thought you swore off men because you were so busy getting lost in"—Ava paused—"how did you put it? In the world of horses, and all the turtles you studied in the Galápagos Islands?"

"Those turtles needed me. And Alfonso is so—"

"Not your type."

A sly grin spread across Carm's mouth. "My type has changed. Now, be a nice little sister and tell me."

Ava didn't need to use her blessing to determine whether Alfonso was interested in her sister. It was pretty much written all over his beaming face.

"Finalmente," Raul said, coming up from behind Carm and Ava. "It's time. ¿Dónde esta Viv?"

"Next to her betrothed," Carm said.

"Okay, let's go," he said excitedly. "She's going to love this."

Ava had practiced her speech a million times, rewriting the words to get them right, but always coming up empty. But that was because love couldn't be qualified by words; it couldn't be reduced to a phrase or a sentence.

A minute later she and Carm were standing next to Raul as he clinked the side of his glass with a silver spoon.

"Good evening, everyone," he said. "It is a night of celebration, a night to honor amor." His eyes swept across the crowd until he found a smiling Viv, nuzzled closely with Grant. Raul raised a glass to his oldest. "And before I begin, Viviana's sisters have prepared some words."

Carm went first. Her speech was, of course, flawless. She had used her blessing to memorize every word, every beat, every smile. And when she was done, the crowd applauded like she had just given a Broadway performance. Viv laughed, and Ava wanted to crawl under the sofa, because blessing or no blessing, she still hated speaking publicly.

"Hey, everyone," she said, clearing her throat. "I tried to come up with words that would ... express how I feel, how excited I am for my sister, that she met someone who makes her so happy and who I know she will make happy too." She looked at the now teary-eyed Viv. Ava could feel the well of emotion climbing up her throat in the shape of a huge knot. "So, I'm going to keep it simple and tell you something someone once told me," she said, finding her voice. "Words are worthless little things. Not as meaningful as a look or a smile or the brush of a hand." Ava took a breath. "You can always recognize the love when it belongs to you. And Grant and Viv were smart enough to see it when it arrived."

Ava raised her glass. "Make my sister happy."

Everyone toasted, smiled; dozens of congratulations were sent into the air. Ava's eyes met Rion's. He raised his glass and gave a little bow.

In the same instant, a flash of light drew her attention to the foggy garden outside.

Raul was talking, delivering his speech, but Ava heard none of it. She could only stare out the window at the strange pulsing light.

She wanted to investigate, but she couldn't leave in the middle of her dad's speech.

Finally, he finished with words Ava barely caught, but that sounded like a promised threat to Grant. The moment Raul raised his glass, when all eyes weren't on the Granados family, Ava rushed outside into the fog, past the pool and Nana's casita, and into the grove where the light floated like a small orb.

Ava took a slow step. And then another.

The air was cool, crisp. Too foggy to see anything more than a few feet in front of her. And then, as if by magic, the mist parted. Just enough for Ava to see Nana.

Margarita stood beneath her beloved pomegranates. She was young, beautiful. Beaming with joy. And she wasn't alone. Charles was at her side, young and handsome like his photo.

Ava's heart swelled.

The blessing whispered to her, *One last glance.* That's when she knew that if she advanced, the spell would be broken. Nana wasn't here to say goodbye again. She was here to let Ava know that she was okay. She was more than okay.

"So, she was your destiny after all," Ava whispered into the chilly air.

"Ava?" Rion said.

She spun to find him standing right behind her. "What are you doing? It's chilly out here." He shrugged off his suit coat and placed it on her shoulders. From behind, he put his arms around her waist, resting his chin on her shoulder. "That was a really good speech, Nine. Gramps would have liked it."

Ava heard his words, but her eyes were still on Charles and Maggie.

Nana threw Ava the smallest of smiles, and then she took Charles's hand, and the two vanished into the mist.

Ava's heart expanded with joy as she stared into the fog for several beats, unblinking. Slowly, she turned to Rion. She reached up, bringing his lips to hers. Allowing herself to be swept away in his trust, his warmth, his love.

A moment later he buried his face in her hair. She could feel his heart knocking around his chest. "You're trembling," he said. "Is everything all right?"

Ava smiled, holding him closer. "Everything is exactly as it should be."

Acknowledgments

I hadn't planned to write this book. Not yet. Then the stars aligned in such a way that I could no longer say no. So I began the joyful journey of creating the world of *Flirting with Fate*. A story that gave me more light and love than I could ever hope to give in return. A story that fell into the right hands at the exact right time in the most unexpected ways. I have so many people to thank for this book's fate.

First, my tireless agent, Holly Root. From there to here . . . what else can I say but *wow*? You never blink or gasp or shy away from any of my *I want to do this next* ideas. Thank you from the bottom of my heart for ushering this one with such poise and confidence and passion. And to the entire Root Lit family: I appreciate all you do more than you'll ever know.

To my thoughtful, smart editor, Julie Rosenberg. I am so glad you saw the magic in this story and that you loved these sisters from the get-go. More swoony-ness to come! The entire Razorbill team—Casey McIntyre, Simone Roberts-Payne, Esther Reisberg, Krista Ahlberg, Rebecca Blevins, Marinda Valenti, Kristie Radwilowicz, Vanessa DeJesús, and Felicity Vallence—I couldn't have asked for a better home for familia Granados.

And to lovely cover artist Karina Perez—thank you for your talent and creativity as you brought the characters and this magical backdrop to life.

I am so incredibly grateful to have razor-sharp readers to give feedback on my early work. For my dear friend Rosh Chokshi—your generosity is unparalleled. And your mind is a true wonder; thanks for loaning it to me at a moment's notice. Janet Fox, you're always ready and willing no matter what I throw at you! Thank you for your enthusiasm and guidance. I am so incredibly grateful to David Bowles for answering my questions with honesty and remarkable speed. Thanks also to Noah Brooks—your eye-opening feedback is so incredibly appreciated. And to the lovely Cassie Malmo: Thank you for your kindness and friendship. Your brilliant insights are incomparable.

To Kristin Dwyer—it was fate that our paths crossed and I couldn't be happier to take this journey together. Sarah Simpson-Weiss, a million thanks for gracefully handling all the logistics of my book life and being such a good friend in the process.

When I began *Flirting with Fate*, I only had the opening scene, and I had three close-knit sisters. For my daughters, Alex, Bella, and Jules. You inspired these sisters, from their fierce loyalty to their unyielding love for one another. And while they are not you and you are not them, I will always stand in awe of your sisterly bonds, and your out-of-this-world mind-reading abilities.

And speaking of family, I was born into one made up of women with magic in their veins, a magic that has been passed from one generation to the next. You inspire me and the stories I tell every day. Especially my mom—thank you for seeing, for believing, and for keeping me buoyed with your momisms.

This book was the first one I wrote in my writer's studio, a place I had only dreamed of, an inspirational space my husband, Joseph, designed with endless patience. My heart is grateful. Oh, and also, thank you for reminding me the world is round.

For all the teachers and librarians who put books into the hands of young readers: you have my immense respect and gratitude. And to readers everywhere, thank you, thank you, thank you. It's because of you that stories exist.